Arthur Lewis

George Maxwell Gordon

The pilgrim missionary of the Punjab. A history of his life and work, 1839-1880

Arthur Lewis

George Maxwell Gordon
The pilgrim missionary of the Punjab. A history of his life and work, 1839-1880

ISBN/EAN: 9783337289171

Printed in Europe, USA, Canada, Australia, Japan

Cover: Foto ©Raphael Reischuk / pixelio.de

More available books at **www.hansebooks.com**

George Maxwell Gordon

M.A., F.R.G.S.

The Pilgrim Missionary of the Punjab

A HISTORY
OF HIS LIFE AND WORK
1839—1880

BY THE

REV. ARTHUR LEWIS, M.A.

C.M.S. MISSIONARY IN THE PUNJAB

"A staff only, no bread, no scrip, no money in their purse."

S. MARK VI. 8.

With Portrait and Illustrations

LONDON
SEELEY & CO., ESSEX STREET, STRAND
NEW YORK
F. & J. B. YOUNG & CO.
COOPER UNION, FOURTH AVENUE

PREFACE.

I FEEL that some apology is due from me to the Public for venturing to put before them the following Memoir. A few words of explanation may not perhaps be out of place.

When I was in England in 1885-86, the question was put to me more than once, " Is there any biography of Mr. Gordon published?" On my answering in the negative, surprise was expressed that this was the case, as well as the opinion that the facts of such a life as his was, ought not to be lost to the Christian Church. These sentiments were so entirely at one with my own, that I represented the matter to some of the leaders of the Church Missionary Society in Salisbury Square. There I only met with the suggestion, " Why do not you write it ? There is no one else who is likely to undertake it."

Under these circumstances, although keenly alive to my own insufficiency, I resolved to make the attempt, rather than that no one should do so. Accordingly, I made application to Mr. Gordon's brother, Colonel E. S. Gordon, R.A., who was then at Woolwich, to ascertain whether he or any members of his family would object to my compiling a Memoir; and in the event of their approval, whether any material, such as journals, letters, etc., could be placed at my disposal.

I desire here to express my warm thanks to Colonel Gordon for seconding my efforts, and giving me all papers that were in his possession, and supplying information as far as he was able.

I learned from him that, soon after Mr. Gordon's death, one of his cousins had formed the design of publishing a Memoir; but after a short time he abandoned it, in the belief that there was not enough written material to form a foundation. This was discouraging, but, nevertheless, I resolved to see what could be done. Letters of request to the various Church Papers brought in a certain amount of information, and I take this opportunity of thanking all those who sent me answers to them.

But my thanks are especially due to Mrs. Corsbie, and to Mr. James C. Parker, of the London City Mission, without whose aid anything like a consecutive account of Mr. Gordon's life would have been an impossibility.

After all documents had been collected, however, there was not one-fourth of what I had expected. This, added to my own incompetency as a compiler, must be the only apology that I can offer for the omissions of the following pages. Thankful should I have been if a more skilled pen than mine, in the hands of a pioneer of the Gospel, who could boast an earlier and longer connection with the subject of this volume, had sketched with realism the scenes in a life worthy to be an example to Missionaries and Soldiers of the Cross for all ages to come.

ARTHUR LEWIS, M.A., C.M.S.

DERÁ GHÁZÍ KHÁN,
March 21, 1888.

CONTENTS.

ILLUSTRATIONS.

MEMOIR

OF

GEORGE MAXWELL GORDON.

CHAPTER I.

RETROSPECT OF EARLY DAYS.

A MAN's character is brought more vividly before the public by his own words than by those of his friends. George Maxwell Gordon shall therefore, as far as possible, be left to speak for himself. He was the second son of Captain James Edward Gordon, R.N., M.P. for Dundalk, and of Barbara, daughter of Samuel Smith, Esq., of Woodhall, M.P. for Herts, and was born on August 10th, 1839. Elisabeth Brodie, the excellent last Duchess of Gordon, was his god-mother. A beautiful Bible which she gave him interleaved for making notes, accompanied him in after years to India; and, to his great satisfaction, escaped the destruction which befel most of his other treasures from the damp of Madras. His own impressions of his childhood, recorded in a letter to

A

the Rev. H. B. Macartney of Caulfield, Victoria, may be fitly prefaced by a brief notice of his father, Captain James Edward Gordon, from the pen of an attached friend, who thus wrote, in May 1864, in reference to the recent death of that "veteran champion of Christian Protestantism : "

"The early part of Captain Gordon's life was spent in the service of his country in the Royal Navy, where he was distinguished for his enterprise and gallantry. At the close of the war he devoted his energies to the cause of seamen, and to his laborious zeal we are chiefly indebted for the commencement of several naval charities, and particularly of the Hospital in the Thames to which the 'Dreadnought' is appropiated. He was afterwards associated with the celebrated Dr. Chalmers in Glasgow in the institution of those great parochial experiments in what he called 'Civic Economy,' which were the forerunners of our District Visiting Societies and City Missions. Captain Gordon next turned his attention to Ireland, where his efforts were greatly blessed in exposing the superstition of Popery and enforcing the great doctrines of the Reformation.

"The Irish Church Missions were not established till many years later, but Captain Gordon was the first who successfully asserted the true missionary principle of evangelising Ireland by aggressive movements. He travelled through some of the most Popish parts of Ireland with Mr. George Finch of Burleigh-on-the-Hill, and then with Mr Baptist Noel ;

but the weight of the denunciations of O'Connell and the priests rested on Captain Gordon. Such was the effect he produced, and so conspicuous were his information and talents, that he was sent for by Lord Liverpool shortly before his death, and consulted as to the best mode of dealing with the great Irish difficulty.

"In 1830 he was brought into the House of Commons by Lord Roden for the borough of Dundalk; and during the whole of that Parliament he was acknowledged to be the most formidable opponent of O'Connell and the Popish brigade. In fact his labours were so unremitting as to overtax his strong constitution, and ultimately to bring on creeping paralysis.

"For fifteen years and more he was one of the most popular and effective speakers at Freemasons' Tavern and Exeter Hall, and he was the originator of the Reformation Society and Protestant Association.

"In 1836 he married a sister of the late eminent banker, Abel Smith, Esq., long M.P. for Hertfordshire. Shortly afterwards his health became so much impaired that he was seldom able to appear in public. He chiefly lived at Hadlow House, near Tunbridge, till after the death of his devoted wife in the year 1861. Since that period he has lived in Porchester Square, London, unable for any active exertion, but enjoying the society of a few attached friends and relations, and taking a deep interest in all that concerned the progress of the kingdom of his Lord and Master.

"A few years ago (in 1854), in the midst of his growing weakness, he occupied himself in dictating and publishing a little volume, which he called 'Original Reflections and Conversational Remarks, chiefly on Theological Subjects.' The preface to that volume concludes with the following touching and characteristic remarks :—

"'There was a time when the position occupied by the Author would have enabled him to present a more important contribution to the cause of Protestant Chrisianity, but that time, in the mysterious dispensations of an all-wise and gracious Providence, has passed away ; and small and comparatively valueless as his present offering is, it is his all ; and his prayer is that it may be accepted by Him who did not refuse the widow's mite.   It will, at least, serve to revive, in the midst of a very numerous circle of affectionately attached friends, the remembrance of one whose share in the public advocacy of their Master's cause they have not altogether forgotten. It is true, indeed, that the bark once so enthusiastically cheered by them, when she held her onward course to victory, is now a stranded hulk ; but if the ship herself is no longer visible in the open sea, they may feel something like a melancholy pleasure in watching the rockets which indicate the position of the wreck.'"

"The stranded wreck has gone down at last

amongst the breakers, but there are few men of whom it might be more truly said, 'Blessed are the dead which die in the Lord, yea, saith the Spirit, for they rest from their labours, and their works do follow them.'

"Captain Gordon has left two sons, one of them a gallant officer in the Royal Artillery, now serving in Canada, the other serving in the Church of England as one of the curates to the venerable Dr. Marsh, Rector of Beddington."

This second son, George Maxwell Gordon, whose life-story is here to be narrated, thus describes, in the letter already referred to, the scenes and circumstances amidst which it opened. He writes as follows :—

" I will now comply most gladly with your request, that I would give some account of No. 1, although it is such a poor account that I have to give, that I would rather choose any other subject to write upon.

" In recalling my early youth, I do not seem to find indications of a Missionary spirit, such as some Missionaries have shown. I used to think, as a child, that Missionaries had unusual advantages for seeing bright birds and wild beasts, and I believe I sometimes said that I would be a Missionary on this account. Travelling and seeing the world was always my passionate desire, and I earnestly longed to be a soldier and sailor alternately. There must have been much in early training to restrain these strong im-

pulses.   Many men speak of boyish days as the hap-
piest of their life.   I never felt so.   I always yearned
for the strength and independence of manhood.

"To us, as children, there always seemed a cloud
hanging over whatever pleasures we had.   This cloud
was the illness of our father, who, from being one of
the strongest of men, had become a confirmed invalid.
His history was in many respects remarkable.   Entering the navy early, he carried to the discharge of his
duties an ardent spirit and an indomitable will.   It
pleased God to mark him for his own at an early age,
and to make him an example and a help to the few
Christians who then adorned the Service.   At the
end of the American War he was induced to leave the
Navy, and to interest himself actively in the Protestant
movement.   In journeys through Ireland, by holding
meetings, and engaging in open controversy with the
priests, and, finally, by his fearless advocacy of the
truth in the House of Commons, he assumed the aggressive against formidable opponents, such as Daniel
O'Connell, and witnessed the discomfiture of many a
foe by the grace of God, and the prevailing power of
the cause which he pleaded.   Such accounts as he
gave us of these struggles and victories had a strong
attraction for us, and fired many an ambitious thought
with regard to our future career.   But there came
with these lessons, also, one of sorrowful discipline.
It pleased the Lord to lead His servant to his final
rest, not through a life of active labour and honourable
service such as he coveted, but through many years

of sickness, suffering, and retirement. Those labours were suspended in the midst of their keenest activity by a sudden stroke, from which he never revived. A journey to Malta, which the doctors recommended, was a hindrance rather than a help to my father's recovery; and on his return to England, when I was about four years old, he settled at Hadlow, in Kent, where for seventeen years we watched the gradual downward progress of the disease. So acute were the paroxysms of pain which he suffered that it was a constant trial to those nearest to him to witness them, and he was prevented from seeing many of those old friends whose society had brightened his public life. It may well be imagined that children whose home was thus darkened by sickness should have been thrown much upon their own resources. We were three, two brothers and a sister; but after the age of twelve we saw little of our elder brother, whose school life and choice of a profession (the army) kept him much from home. We had no real companions in our retirement at Hadlow, and my sister and I were everything to each other. She was two years my junior, but we were united in tastes and sympathies to a degree which was only intensified by temporary separation. Poetry and classical literature had great charms for us both, and nothing seemed to delight us more than to wander together into a field, and recite passages from our favourite authors.

"At the age of thirteen I went to a private school,

and although I cannot say that I imbibed there any idea of being a missionary, yet there was much interest awakened among us in the mission cause, and two of the sons of my schoolmaster are now missionaries in China."

Such is a brief retrospect taken by Gordon himself of his earliest days. The school which he mentions was the Vicarage of the Rev. Henry Moule, of Fordington, Dorchester, father of the well-known pioneers in China. Another of Mr. Moule's sons, the Principal of Ridley Hall, at Cambridge, gives us his recollections. "I suppose," he says, "it is now nearly or quite, thirty-two years ago that he became one of my dear father's pupils at Fordington Vicarage; and he was with us, I think, some four years. Out of that home (for it was indeed home, pupils and sons together, and the only school myself or any of my brothers ever knew) four missionaries have gone forth—George Gordon, Winter of Delhi, and my two dear brothers in China.

" My recollections of Gordon are full of his exceeding good-nature, his fondness for English literature, his not very active habits, except on occasion, when he could do very well in some athletic exercises, and his constant tendency both to be humorous himself and the cause of humour in others."

In the same sketch of his life sent to Mr. Macartney, Gordon tells us something of his college days,—

" In 1857 (when I was just eighteen), I entered

Trinity College, Cambridge. The last year of my course, when I was reading for classical honours, was interrupted by a serious attack of fever, which made success a hopeless thing; but that disappointment was very slight when compared to another, which has thrown its shadow far beyond any succeeding one. In the beginning of that year, and by the same fever which prostrated me, I was deprived of the one great attraction of my life—the only one I used to think worth living for. My dear sister sunk after a short illness at the age of eighteen, leaving a bright example for me to follow, but a very lonely path to tread. When I look back at that first and great sorrow I seem to be able, by God's infinite mercy, to date from it a starting-point towards the apprehension of pardon and acceptance through Christ. With me conversion was a very gradual thing. I longed for conviction of sin, but it did not come, and although depending solely upon the merits of Christ for salvation, I was disappointed because I could not discover in myself these fruits of repentance of which others seemed to bear decided evidence. A year after my sister's death, my mother followed her to her everlasting rest. A most peaceful departure it was, after a life of most active and ceaseless devotion as a wife and mother. My father, who was prepared for the event only two days before it happened, suffered acutely from a loss which could never be made up to him. . . . After this we sold the house at Hadlow, and took one in London, where my father could be more among his friends and relations."

Once more we turn to the recollections of Gordon's former schoolfellow, the Principal of Ridley Hall. Of the Cambridge days, he says :—

"He was two years above me at Trinity, here. I saw very little of him, accordingly. My own remembrance is again of his quiet, rather 'easiful,' life ; his fondness for music, and for his pet owl—a constant ornament of his rooms in Malcolm Street. Men who were more intimate with him at college would describe him to you as a quiet but quite decided and steady Christian at Cambridge. He was a member of the C. M. Union in its early days.

"I have always understood that his great spiritual lift was experienced when he went to Dr. Marsh at Beddington.

"It is most interesting to me to trace these few lines out of the stores of a far-distant and well-beloved past. It puts dear George Gordon before me just as he was, genial and gentle, full of delightful tastes, gifted with a large share of quiet humour and of common sense, but certainly not suggesting the lofty type of Christian he afterwards by grace became. You will observe, meanwhile, that my recollections are wholly those of a boy. Older observers may have easily seen more of the future in him."

Another, who enjoyed the intimate friendship of Gordon at Cambridge, tells us something of his inner life. He speaks of his extreme humility, and, to some extent, diffidence of character. This displayed itself in a certain lack of fixity of purpose. He was apt to take up a line of action and abandon it quickly, because he did not see results answering his expectations. This friend used to tell him that it was his misfortune not to be a poor man ; that were he compelled to battle with the world and fight for his own living, he must necessarily overcome this tendency to despondency. But it was just this tendency which, checked and controlled by the working of the Holy Spirit, caused his life to be so unique, self-denying, and heroic in his future missionary work.

Such, then, was the quiet and uneventful beginning of a life which was to develop into so marked a pattern. Gordon took his B.A. degree in the ordinary course in 1861.

But we ought not to pass on to the next period without dwelling a little more on the peculiar relations between the brother and sister, to which allusion has already been made. The two, by the circumstances of their lives, and by a sympathy of tastes, were united by the bond of a more than common affection. When the sister was on her death-bed, and her brother was taking leave of her, she said to him,— "If there are such things as guardian angels, I shall be yours."[1] This alone shows the strong attachment that must have existed between them, and the influence Barbara Gordon's wishes would be likely

[1] *Dawn and Sunrise*, p. 102. Seeley & Co.

to have had over her brother.   No wonder, then, that he looked upon her death as in a measure the starting point of his life.   It is to this period that Gordon's decision to take Holy Orders is to be assigned.

Perhaps no better picture of the man, as influenced by bereavement, can be given than by quoting the words of one of his oldest friends, the Bishop of Lahore.   He says:—" In my friend's early youth, the death of a young sister of rich promise, to whom he was deeply attached, and in whose case a very single-hearted piety shed a lovely bloom over what was otherwise a rare attractiveness of character, had cast over his life a softened, mellow sadness—an ' *assom-brisement*,' as our neighbours would call it—and I doubt not her memory survived ever fresh and fragrant in his heart.   If there was any other secret sorrow buried in his heart, that might help to account for the pensive melancholy which was noticeable in him, to myself at least it was never revealed.   This in reality was one of the charms of his character: though he seemed at times to attribute it to his never having been at a public school, of which he would speak regretfully, both because it had narrowed the circle of his friends outside of his own family, and had not fetched out into full development and expansion, germs and capacities of heart and mind, which in the greater isolation of his boyhood he had been tempted to fold too closely within himself."[1]

[1] Bp. of Lahore, *Church Missionary Intelligencer*, Mar. 1881.

CHAPTER II.

CURACIES.

THE final guidance to ordination came to Gordon in
1862. In that year he says :—

"I became acquainted with Dr. and Miss Marsh,
and he offered me a title. As Beddington was only
thirteen miles from London, I accepted the offer,
on the condition that I was to spend two days in
each week with my father. I was accordingly ordained by the Bishop of Winchester in the winter
of 1862. To this step I was led by the guiding hand
of God in a remarkable way. It seemed that door
after door was closed which I would have opened
My desire first to be a sailor, then a soldier (up
to the age of twenty), then a civilian in India, anything, in short, but a clergyman, was overruled by a
wise and watchful Providence. My acquaintance with
Dr. Marsh and his daughter was a great blessing to
me. The heavenly calmness of the one, and the
bright, ardent faith and the comprehensive love of
the other, are pictures which will long live in my
recollection. It was no ordinary privilege to see the
close of such a life as this dear old patriarch had
pursued. Throughout the year and a half which I

served as his curate, my interviews with him, which were often at his bed or sofa side, were a refreshment and blessing.   It was a time of very hard work, and many a Saturday night was spent in sleepless preparation for the Sunday's duty after a toilsome week. It was while I was thus employed that my dear father was at length taken to his rest.   It was my privilege to be with him to the last, and to witness a very peaceful departure, after much buffeting with the waves of suffering and sorrow.   He was carried to the peaceful spot in Hadlow churchyard, where my sister and mother had been laid, and where many a prayer had been offered by the grassy mound that the precious seed thus sown might bear fruit in the lives of the two survivors."

When George Gordon became junior curate at Beddington, he was associated with one who has already been mentioned, and who was destined to have a great influence on his after life.   This was the Rev. Thomas Valpy French, afterwards Bishop of Lahore.   He had but lately returned from the scene of his missionary labours in India, and was acting as one of Dr. Marsh's curates.   The Bishop describes his first impressions of Gordon as follows :—

" We met for the first time in the Rectory of Beddington, of which parish the saintly and patriarchal Dr. Marsh was then Rector.   Gordon was fresh from his admission to Deacon's orders, Mr. O'Rorke and myself being jointly Senior Curates. Gordon became my fast friend from that time for-

ward. Probably he had already felt a secret drawing towards missionary work; and as I had but just
returned in very bad health from my second (too
short) campaign in India, and our brotherly intercourse often took the shape of missionary conversation, it is likely enough that vague, indistinct
yearnings became definite and unalterable resolves.
Yet his quiet, self-possessed manner, his unpretend-
ing humility, his constant devotion of his time to
bible-classes among working men and lads, and his
gentle and dignified refinement prevented my discovering what was working in his mind; and it was
not till after Dr. Marsh's death, some eighteen months
later, when he had become curate of St. Thomas's,
Portman Square, that he opened his heart to me
on the subject of spending the rest of his life as a
missionary."

It was at this period of his life that Gordon first
visited the Continent. A tour in Switzerland and
the north of Italy, which he greatly enjoyed, may
have helped to re-awaken the love of foreign travel
and adventure which mingled with his earliest recollections, and to throw the weight of personal inclination into the scale in favour of a missionary
vocation in his case, as it has done in many more.
Not to thwart the natural bent, but to consecrate it
to high service, is the path of Christian wisdom.

The Rev. Henry O'Rorke thus writes his recollections of George Gordon during his work at
Beddington :—

" It is pleasant to recal the happy intercourse in friendship and work which I had with Mr. Gordon during the privileged season when we were associated with the revered and beloved Dr. Marsh, then Rector of Beddington.

" To have lived in the light of that beautiful life, shining more and more unto the perfect day, we both, young as we were then in the ministry, felt to be an unspeakable blessing.

" The brightness of Dr. Marsh's life, and the ever-sunny tone of his Christian faith and conversation with the cheerful influences of that happy home, were especially helpful and cheering to Mr. Gordon, whose own home had been so sadly overshadowed by loss, and by the protracted sufferings of his father.

" I saw this very markedly when spending a day with him in his home in London, in the sad sight of his father, once so powerful in mind and body, but then utterly prostrated by illness; a helpless sufferer.

" One can understand how this would produce a tendency to depression not natural to youth, nor to one in whose character there was a strong vein of humour, with intense enjoyment of happy companionship.

" Immediately on joining Mr. Southey, now Rector of Woburn, and myself in the work at Beddington, he at once threw himself heartily into the various pastoral duties which we had in hand ; by his gentle and sympathetic manner, and his generous kindness, he soon made many warm friends among the people. He had private means, and he was ever ready to help in any true case of need which came before him.

"During the first winter of his curacy at Beddington, we were especially united in the work of a night-school in a hamlet, about three miles from the church, and many a pleasant talk we had together, over plans for the young men, as we walked to and fro in those dark and often stormy nights.

"There was always manifest in his conversation an eager desire for more of spiritual power and influence in whatever work he might be called to undertake.

"He showed much ability in dealing with the young men in the night-school, one of the most difficult undertakings of any clergyman, who desires to make it not only an educational but also a spiritual help to the young and restless natures gathered before him. Their impatience of discipline, which is so needful, if any real good is to be done ; their proneness to fun ; their inability often to give steady attention, all combine to make the task of night-school teaching no easy one.

"But here George Gordon's character came out most effectively ; his patience, his unfailing good temper, his quiet humour, soon disarmed the restless and mischievous : he first won their attention and then their affection. Afterwards he used to invite them to his rooms, and there, in personal dealing with them, laid the foundation, by God's grace, of a new life in many who, I doubt not, to this day remember with gratitude those well-spent evenings of long ago.

"As a preacher, George Gordon early gave evidence of much promise, by his clear and attractive setting forth of evangelical truth.

"He always faithfully and fully preached Christ and His great salvation ; and his sermons, delivered in a quiet and forcible tone, lived in the memory.

"I still remember one very vividly, after the lapse of nearly a quarter of a century, on the text, 'I will endeavour that ye may be able, after my decease, to have these things always in remembrance,' 1 Pet. i. 15.

"It was on the Sunday after Dr. Marsh's death. He spoke of the abiding influence of the life and ministry of Christ's servant 'being dead, he yet speaketh.' Long after the voice is silent, the presence gone ; the truths taught and the example set live in the new and sanctified lives of those who receive Him, on whom all faithful teaching is ever centered.

"No doubt this has been exemplified in George Gordon's own life and death ; and many among the wild tribes, with whom he lived and to whom he preached as the faithful and loving missionary, 'have these things always in remembrance.' The abiding power of that life will still thus be found.

"He derived much help at that time from the spiritual and thoughtful preaching of Bishop French, who for a time was associated with us in the work

at Beddington before his appointment to the See of
Lahore.

"He used often kindly to lend his sermons to
George Gordon, and we read them together. The
glow of missionary enthusiasm, which ever illumined
those powerful sermons, had a deep influence in
drawing Gordon's thoughts and desires to a missionary's life. Shortly after this, our happy fellowship in the work at Beddington ceased. We parted,
he first to foreign travel, and, after a short interval
of work in London to the mission field, I to charges
in the Lord's service at home.

"Once only did we meet again, when on a brief
visit to England, he came to see me in my home at
Sheriffhales ; a Shropshire parish.

"He arrived unexpectedly, late at night, carrying his bag. He bore the unmistakable impress
of growth in power, independence, and Christian
manliness, with a cheerfulness begotten by his life
of self-denial and true heart-devotion to the service
of his choice.

"He had much of interest to tell us, and my
children were charmed with his stories of scenes in
India and Australia.

"He had to leave the next day, and preferred to
walk to the station. I accompanied him along the
beautiful avenue of lime trees which lead from Sheriffhales Church to Lilleshall Hall, and thence by the
private road towards Newport Station.

"The rich beauty of that fair English landscape—

rich in its verdure and in the marks of culture and order—attracted his admiration, while the far-stretching plain of Shrewsbury and the distant hills of Wales woke up thoughts of the wider plains and far loftier mountains of the land whither he was going.

"We paused by the gate where we were to part, gazed for a few moments on the scene before us, then, bowing our heads in prayer, we commended each other to Him who had blessed us with His salvation, and called us into His service, asking that He would guide us by His Spirit, and guard us by His mighty protection; that He would use us for His glory, and bless our work and words among those to whom He might send us, whether at home or abroad, until, our work being finished, the Master would call us to His presence, to other scenes and higher services, throughout eternity.

"Thus we parted. From time to time, tidings came of Gordon's work among the wild tribes in Northern India and on the frontier; then of his being with our troops at Kandahar; finally, of his noble death in seeking to rescue the wounded soldiers; fitting close to a noble life, which was wholly consecrated to the Lord, and to the spread of the Gospel of His salvation amongst men. 'Thou hast made him most blessed for ever, Thou hast made him exceeding glad with Thy countenance.'"

To resume the thread of the narrative. George Gordon was not very long to remain Dr. Marsh's curate. He left in 1864, owing to the death of the

aged rector. Gordon then took a journey, in company with the present Bishop of Rochester, and the
late Mr Robert Hanbury, M.P., to the lands of the
Bible, which to a great extent coloured the whole of
his after life. The missionary spirit was probably
developed within him, to a greater extent than ever
before, by following in the footsteps of the Divine
Missionary to the human race. He thus speaks of it
himself, and of the London work which succeeded it :—

"In the same year (1864, the year also of Dr.
Marsh's death) I made an excursion to the East, and
refreshed both health and spirit by visiting scenes
consecrated by the ministry and death of our blessed
Saviour and His apostles. It seemed to give a
marvellous reality to sacred history to visit Joppa
and Jerusalem, with the Mount of Olives, and the
mountains of Moab bounding the Dead Sea in the
distance ; and then to explore the neighbourhood of
Bethany, and Bethlehem, and the valley of the Jordan ;
and to go northwards to Bethel, and Samaria and
Nazareth, and Galilee, and Carmel, Damascus, and
the Lebanon. I spent the winter on the Nile ; won-
dering at the remarkable fulfilment of prophecy in
the execution by Cambyses of God's vengeance upon
the 'Idols of Egypt,' and the mighty monuments
of her desolation. In the spring of 1865 I crossed
from Egypt to Palestine by the desert of Sinai and
Petra, following (by conjecture) the path of the children of Israel, for forty days instead of forty years.
The climate of the desert and the primitive associa-

tions of camels and tents I greatly enjoyed, and no
less, the more profoundly meditative reflections which
that district awakened.   The barren, wild grandeur of
Sinai forms a striking contrast to the soft and fertile
aspect of Galilee, and very characteristic is the scenery
of each, of the dispensations which they respectively
witnessed.

"There were many features of my journey home
well calculated to awaken a missionary ardour.   To
stand where St. Paul stood; in the Areopagus at
Athens; where he lived at Corinth; where he landed
in Italy; where he suffered at Rome; to gaze on
Patmos; to visit the land of the Seven Churches
opposite; to mark spots made sacred by the blood
of the martyrs, such as the Coliseum at Rome; and
have sacred recollections so revived might well rebuke
coldness, and kindle a spirit of devotedness.   From
scenes such as these I returned to London, eager for
missionary work among the destitute masses of the
Metropolis.   I   soon found employment with Mr.
Lumsden, in a district which contained 7000 poor
and 3000 rich.   To meet the spiritual, and to relieve
the temporal wants of these, our staff of workers
was miserably small, and for the first three months
I found myself entirely alone, everyone else having
left town for the country.   *Hard* work was what I
desired, but this was *hopeless* work.   Going in and
out of houses (containing sometimes thirteen families
to a single house), often a large family in a small
room, with lodgers at night, one's heart often sunk

at the very small impression which one could hope
to make upon so much wretchedness and sin.

"There were bright features, however, of my work
for a year and a half in London. The schools were
a great interest, and well repaid me. I was much
pleased also to be the means of awakening an interest
in missions at a Needlewoman's Institute, where the
very poorest could get work to do, and earn about
7d. a day. After hearing an address on missions, they
asked for a missionary-box, and it was affecting to
open it at the end of a month or two and find 13s.,
all in farthings."

Such was the life as described by Gordon himself. But while he was here, in the curacy of St.
Thomas's, Portman Square, his friend, Mr. James
C. Parker, of the London City Mission, had an
unusual opportunity for forming a true estimate of
his work. In the next few pages he depicts him
and his work at the time as, perhaps, no one else
could do.

Mr Parker observes :—

"When, in 1865, Mr. Gordon entered upon his
duties as a curate in the parish of St. Thomas's, Portman Square, Marylebone, he was associated with a
warm, long-tried advocate of the Church Missionary
Society, the Rev. H. T. Lumsden, formerly of St.
Peter's, Ipswich. His beloved fellow curate, the Rev.
Henry Seton, a nephew of the Incumbent, died at
the early age of twenty-seven.

"The church was new, the district having been

recently separated from the rectory parish, by the
Hon. and Rev. John Thomas Pelham, afterwards
Bishop of Norwich. It contained a population of
10,000 souls (one-fourth of the rectory parish), 7000
of whom were poor, and of the latter, 3000 were
Irish Roman Catholics.

"This was a many-sided and magnificent field of
labour, but one requiring not only the love of God
in the heart, but a healthy body; a calm, clear,
shrewd mind ; and a firm, fearless, indomitable spirit.
It was a London training ground of the right sort, to
fit young clergymen to be valiant soldiers of the cross
of Christ, in the still more difficult and dangerous
fields of distant foreign lands.

"Very few, I am persuaded, of Mr. Gordon's nearest relations and associates, had at first a true idea
of the high quality of the metal he was made of.
It is not common to expect to see a simple-minded,
humble, gentle, kindly spirit rapidly develop into
a vigorous, sanctified, stalwart Christian ; by the
energy of God's grace, second to none, at home
or abroad, on the long and noble roll of the athletes
who have worked, fought and died, under the life-
giving though blood-stained banner of the Great
Captain of Salvation.

"A change in his sphere of labour did not lessen
Mr. Gordon's thoughtfulness for those with whom
he had previously been associated. One of his first
acts on coming to London, was to invite a score of
working men, from his old district at Beddington, to

spend an afternoon and evening with him, at the South Kensington Museum, free of all expense to themselves. It was my privilege, on this and similar occasions, to assist as a guide and aide-de-camp. The exhibition was entirely new to the intelligent, happy visitors; and when they took the return train home, the parting was like the farewell of brothers, for Mr. Gordon had the natural gift of condescending to men of low estate. One of these men had built himself a small cottage in the country, with the money which Mr. Gordon had lent him, without interest.

"He would often invite to dinner, or lunch, one or two of his more humble fellow labourers. It was very pleasant to be with him at these times, which he made both cheerful and profitable. He would learn from his guest the particular trials and importance of the work in which he might be engaged, and then words of wisdom would be spoken, and personal, practical aid rendered.

"He was well up in the special labours of Mr. Herbrechter, the city-missionary to St. Marylebone Workhouse. There were 1800 men, women, and children in this building; the average death-rate being 550. Mr. Gordon would ask first to see the aged and afflicted who had been previously visited by him in their own rooms, before the final sad day of helpless misfortune compelled them to seek indoor relief. He was quite "at home" in conversation with the unsuccessful old tradesman in cor-

duroy; and the worn-out, rheumatic wife in check
shawl. Many were the urgent invitations of the in-
mates that he would make "the House" his home,
and stay always with them!

"On Saturday nights, Mr. Gordon used sometimes
to accompany another city missionary in visiting
public-houses and low beer-shops. He usually got
on well with the roughs and the depraved, and
always had a faithful, judicious word to speak to the
'drinking congregation.' There was one occasion,
however, on which a brutal, drunken Irish Romanist,
more cruel and savage than an Indian tiger, seized
Mr. Gordon by the throat, and hurled him into the
road. The landlord of the house was hurt and upset;
and the other customers united with him in loud
expressions of regret, and invited Mr. Gordon to
come again soon, and 'receive their friendship.'

"Miss Hovell, the assistant mistress, states, that
the children, boys and girls, at St. Thomas's Schools
loved Mr. Gordon, as the curate who cared for their
happiness, and was well up in all their games. He
saw them in school, half-fed, badly-clothed, pale,
and feeble. The cause was well known to him.
Their parents were industrious, and did their best
in most instances. But small means poorly maintain a large family. In many a 'Court' or 'Buildings,' in Marylebone, father, mother, and four or
six children occupy, day and night, one room only,
at a rental of 4s. 6d. or 7s. 6d. a week. Bread is
often, and meat is always, dear. Pure, fresh air and

sunshine are skilfully and effectively shut out in our narrow, twisted, dark streets. Some of the pining little ones were more like bundles of bleached celery than human beings with skins containing healthy blood, flesh, and bones! What could be done? There were a few generous spirits at St. Thomas's Church ; and Mr. Gordon had 'troops of friends' at Beddington, and its immediate neighbourhood. The Frys, Laurences, Murray-Johnsons, and others were quite uncomfortable because he was not making use of them. And he soon inaugurated a children's treat; and grounds, provisions, games, and every other requisite for the day sprang up, either at Beddington, Carshalton, or Mitcham. On one occasion, a boat or barge was provided, and the boys, none of whom since infancy, if even then, had ever tubbed, enjoyed the salutary experience of a plunge, head and heels, into the water. It was a new idea, afterwards often repeated, in our valuable though makeshift Parochial Baths. Where did all the towels come from? There was no lack, for every bedroom and wardrobe for miles around was laid under contribution.

"Several of the children shed tears when Mr. Gordon wished them, for the last time, 'good-bye,' and said one little dot, 'I can't think why he wants to go away?' Out of their poverty, they gave him 'a Testimonial.'

"His desire 'not to let his left hand know what his right hand doeth,' was ineffectual, as the 'Sun of Righteousness' would not allow His witness and follower to hide his bright, though reflected, light under a bushel.

"There was a 'Mothers' Meeting' held in St. Thomas's Parish. Miss Bontein[1] was the lady superintendent ; and Mrs. Gunn, the quiet, meek, spiritually-minded, ever-ready-to-help 'Bible Woman.' No wonder that Mr. Gordon was always a welcome visitor at the weekly meeting, for he was an admirer of babies ; and mothers are won by this charming and manly endowment.

"The most beautiful trait in his London life, to my knowledge, was his thoughtful consideration and tender regard for the aged poor. His parting gift to all the 'house-confined' men and women, who had reached the age of three-score-and-ten, was a second-hand, comfortable arm-chair. He dragged me to all the furniture and brokers' shops in Marylebone, and would give from 20s. to 25s. for each article. No chair was purchased until both of us had 'proved it' by squatting down, and being unanimous in our opinion, that it was perfectly easy, sightly, and not rickety. This may seem but a very little thing to record, but it has, I thankfully believe, done my own heart more good than some of the most powerful speeches I have ever heard. God's tried saints, not far off from a different world from this, had their faith strengthened and their love rekindled by this gracious manifestation of 'brotherly' affection, and

---

[1] This lady's unremitting life work is now pursued in Bethnal Green, where she is Hon. Superintendent of the Ashley Mission.

the more so as the donor was a single and young man.

"Not many opportunities were given to Mr. Gordon to show forth his powers, as a preacher. His manner was serious, and his matter solid. He would sometimes illustrate his text by an allusion to his much-enjoyed travels in Palestine. He had that pure lightness of spirit, which often led him to smile when speaking of his first sermon. 'I thought,' he would say, 'that I had utterly tired out the congregation by the length of time I had occupied in speaking, and so I suddenly closed my discourse, before I had read half my manuscript. When I descended the pulpit, my friends were disgusted, and demanded to know how it was that I had preached them only a *ten minutes'* sermon?'

"Had I known that Mr. Gordon was some day to have chosen me as his friend; to have used me as his willing servant; or that he was ordained to spend his strength, means, and life in a foreign land, in the Redeemer's cause; most certainly I should have made an entry of most of his words, and works. But I thought only a little of him, and less of myself, when we were both, with a single eye to God's glory, labouring in St. Thomas's Parish as 'ambassadors for Christ.'"

CHAPTER III.

MADRAS.

WE have seen that Gordon, while at Beddington, breathed a missionary atmosphere. He was associated with one who was then a well-known, enthusiastic missionary; one who had himself often hazarded his life in fighting the battles of the Lord on the frontier of His kingdom. That missionary, the Rev. T. V. French, doubtless exercised a great influence upon Gordon, and led him on to his future decision. Moreover, the subject of Foreign Missions was never allowed to be forgotten in Dr. Marsh's parish. Speaking of this, Gordon says:— "Ties which one forms, even in a short experience, especially with the poor, are very strong and lasting. At Beddington I had the pleasure of meeting, every week, about twelve working-men at my tea-table, for a Bible reading—men who had all come to the light under Dr. Marsh's ministry, I may say, in the last year of that ministry. These men used to form a committee and collect among their neighbours for the Church Missionary Society." It is hardly then to be wondered at, that Gordon should himself have been drawn very strongly towards foreign fields of labour.

In his letter already quoted, he indicates that it was at this time that the definite prospect began to open up before him. He writes :—"Perhaps it was at Beddington that my first real desire to become a missionary took shape. I then had the privilege of being associated in parochial work with Mr. French, a missionary whose singular attainments and devoted piety made a deep impression upon my mind."

Accordingly, in the summer of 1866, he offered himself to the Church Missionary Society as an honorary worker. In a letter written to one of the secretaries of the Society, dated August 22, 1866, he says :—"My simple desire is to offer myself and means to the great work of extending the Lord's kingdom to those who are ignorant and out of the way, and be the means of winning souls whom the Saviour died to purchase."

It is almost needless to say, that the Society did not hesitate long in accepting this free-will offer to further the work which the departing Lord committed to His Church ; the preaching of the Gospel to every creature.

Gordon sailed in the autumn of 1866. Writing from Ceylon on December 27, he gives many of his impressions of the voyage ; but as the journey to and from India has become one of most ordinary experience, his description of the landing and visit to Kandy alone is extracted. "Everyone who has experienced the change from Western to Eastern countries knows that there is novelty everywhere, beginning with *Man*. When the steamer anchors off Ceylon, she is immediately boarded by a number of women (?), whose boats of singular build have shot up to the vessel's side like magic. By degrees you learn that these strange figures, with their copper skins, feminine features, and hair turned back with top-knot and comb (*à la Parisienne*) are not Amazons but men. Indeed, I have not yet learnt the difference between the sexes. The drive from Galle to Colombo for seventy miles is an avenue of cocoa-nut palms, by the sea-shore. I accomplished it by a bright moonlight. The fire-flies were glancing all round, and the flying foxes kept flapping from tree to tree, while the moon poured a flood of light over the rich foliage, and the creeks and rivers, which here and there break up the road, and are crossed by bridges."

During this visit to Ceylon he had a fever, which laid him up for some weeks, and was a forecast that he would not eventually be able to continue his work in the climate of Southern India. On January 31, 1867, he writes to Mr. James C. Parker:—"There is nothing like answering a letter at once, but to write askew from an arm-chair is not very easy. How glad I was to get your letter, and to hear about friends at St. Thomas's, among whom you take, and ever will take, a very prominent place. When I arrived here on the 9th, and found a letter from Miss Marsh only, after my three months' voyage, I exclaimed, 'Friends, friends! what has become of your friendship?' I landed very ill, having taken a fever in Ceylon, and

have been since on my back, with the kindest of
friends attending on me. Large doses of quinine
nearly distracted me, depriving me of at least three
senses; but I am most thankful to God that He is
daily making me stronger, and, after change of air, I
hope that my recovery will be complete. It is five
weeks since I first developed the fever, but the doctor
says I must have had it in me longer."

In this same letter, too, we see a touch of that old
distrust, and of that tendency too hastily to abandon
a course that he has made up his mind to adopt, of
which his Cambridge friend speaks. "When I read
your letter," he says, " all my bitter regrets came with
renewed force, that I had not taken my friend Mr. F.'s
advice, and remained in England another year. Not
that there is anything in my present circumstances
that I am not perfectly satisfied with, but Mr Lumsden's absence, and the slender help Mr. Seton has,
is what fills my mind. However, it was always so
with me in every clerical undertaking, to question
whether I have not too much followed my own
judgment, instead of feeling that, having committed
the matter to the Lord, it must be right. *Such* is the
faith that He requires."

Having recovered from the fever of which he
spoke, Gordon was soon fairly launched into missionary work. The first great difficulty which faces
every missionary is that of the language. He finds
himself set down in a strange country, amongst
people walking in darkness on all sides of him ; he

C

is conscious of having light himself, and the most
grievous thing of all to him is, that he is not able to
impart it. He is conscious of being commissioned
with a message to deliver, and yet he cannot find a
single word wherewith to deliver it. No one who
has not experienced this, can imagine how irksome it
is, and how the missionary chafes under it. And yet
it is one of those wise dispensations of God, of which
older and more experienced men see and appreciate
the benefit, while the newly-arrived and ardent recruit
would, if possible, gladly break away from the restraint.
It is of the first importance, that the man who wishes
to influence a class of people should understand them,
their habits of life, their modes of thought, and their
religious belief. All these can only be learned very
gradually by contact with, and residence among, the
people. Hence it is that the learning of the language
puts a wholesome check upon the "*griff*," and pre-
vents him making many a mistake at first which
would perhaps irretrievably damage his future influence. It is just one of those occasions in life which
teach us that in "quietness and confidence," in preparation, "shall be our strength."

In a country like India, even in a single mission,
it is often not sufficient to acquire one language.
Very frequently different nationalities are met with in
one district, and beyond this, different languages, or
at anyrate different dialects, are often used by the
educated and the country people.

It was to this work that Gordon now had to set

himself, and to which he alludes in writing to Mr. Parker. He also gives a peep into his missionary encampment, which cannot fail to be interesting to those whose duty does not call them to spend a portion of their lives in this patriarchal fashion. It must be remembered, in all allusions to camp work, that in India the power of the summer sun is much too great to allow one with safety to live in tents ; canvas of many folds is far too slight a protection, and usually, when the cold season has taken flight, the shelter of a solid roof has to be sought. Writing on April 1867, from Madras, Gordon says :—

"The weather continues mild and cool, and our health through mercy is very good. We are thinking of remaining under canvas all through the hot season in the plain. I do not think that either of us is rashly disposed, least of all, Mr Fenn, who has had fifteen years' experience of India, but our encampment is so cool and pleasant, that we feel there is no excuse for leaving the work and going to the hills or the town. It has taken me long to settle down to work for I have had the greatest difficulty in getting two very necessary things, a teacher of the language, and a horse. It is not that there are not plenty of teachers in Madras (and horses too), but they don't like living in a tent, and nothing will tempt them to do so but a very high salary. However, I think I have got one at last, and am really beginning again with some steadiness. My horse, too, is a great help, a very fine Arab, and quite a companion. He is tied to one tree and my tent pitched under another, an arrangement which dispenses with house and stable-rent altogether. I am now encamped twenty miles south of Madras on the sea, so that I get a sea-bath every morning, and a sea-breeze all day. The little grove is composed of mango trees and palms, and is most quiet and secluded. A village close by supplies me with milk and fowls, but I have to send to Madras for bread, tea, etc. My two colleagues are now en-camped with me, but only for six days. They change their encampment every week, but I find these very frequent changes a great interruption to study, taking often two whole days in the necessary arrangements for moving. Hence I am stationary for the present in a kind of centre, whence their itineration radiates in every direction. The difficulty of getting anything done by these poor natives, without authority, is extreme. When we move our tents we often can-not induce them to hire their carts to us, except at some most unreasonable rate. It is the same when we want a messenger to go into town; although there are plenty of men to go, there is no competition whatever. All they care about is to have just enough money to buy their rice, and then they abandon themselves to laziness. Yesterday I wanted a few nails put into a broken chair. The carpenter came and talked about it for an hour, and then walked off without doing it. Sometimes they will not sell their fowls, and we are in straits. At this moment we have no bread, and have had none for several days. I do not reckon these as hardships, but as things which you must be prepared for and take forethought about. Things are not to be done here in a hurry. Last night my rest was disturbed by the depredations of a wild dog, which had discovered some fish inside my tent; and the night before by a lizard inside my shirt, also a large cockroach on my head."

It will be seen from this, that although Gordon's life was at this time one of whole-hearted zeal in the missionary cause, yet he did not at first launch out into the life almost of poverty for which he was afterwards so well known. We notice his mention of the horse, which, although considered a necessity in India by ordinary Europeans, proved eventually to be unnecessary to him. Here we see him comfortably settled in a tent, and sure of a place to live in. In after years we shall see him almost like his Master before him, not having where to lay his head. In June that same year (1867), we find him again laid up with a severe attack of fever in Madras, which causes him to lay aside his study of the Tamil language.

But it was not merely destined to put a stop for a time to his studies. The fever was so severe and so continuous, that, as time went on, the only chance of restored health appeared to lie in a thorough change. Accordingly a sea voyage to Australia was resolved on. We can perhaps imagine the disappointment Gordon felt after having left most important work in London to devote himself to India, to find,

in a few short months, that he was obliged to turn
his back upon that which he had taken in hand.
He, doubtless, could not understand the trial at the
time, but he must have done so in after life, when he
looked back upon this period. He sailed during the
summer; and from Sydney he writes, on 20th
August, to Mr. James Parker:—"I was refreshed
last evening by receiving twenty-three home letters,
most of them forwarded from India; to say that
they refreshed me with a gush of Spring memories,
would be feeble. They were like the overflow of the
tide, with its music of oars and shining waters, its
sparkling life and glitter of sails. True, it must
recede and leave the blank, flat tide mud exposed,
but still it is a joy while it lasts, and may return
again.

. . . .

"You have drawn a portrait (a very beautiful one)
of *some one* whom you knew formerly, but it cannot
be *me;* it is a great deal too good. My own recollections of myself at St. Thomas's are so mixed up with
selfishness, despondency, and weakness, that I should
recoil from anything like a photographic portrait.
The colours must be laid on by an indulgent hand
like yours, to make it at all sightly. I can but apply
to myself a beautiful passage in one of Tennyson's
Idylls, in which Launcelot disclaims praise. He says
there is nothing great in him, except it be 'Some far-
off touch of greatness, to *know he is not* great.' But
the Christian life is gilded by Another's greatness

which enables him even to 'glory in his infirmity.'
And so, dear friend, it has been a help and a comfort to me, to know that you are spared to take up
the cross, and bear it patiently on in the noble sphere
in which God has placed you, so far more noble, because utterly unmixed with anything like temporal
honour, or preferment, or romance, or gratification.
I think this is the way the Lord has led me of late.
What right have I to aspire to a place in the foremost
rank, to angels' food, to the calling of an apostle?
These are inspired motives, for the disciple cannot
forget the words : 'Ye have not chosen me ; but I
have chosen you,' and he even takes that lofty standard of perfection as his own, but his work is ennobled
more in service and submission than in promotion,
when he has won the victory he does not fly upon the
spoil.

"I thank you for the thought of Philip in the
desert ; and truly grateful do I feel for the opportunities God has given me of preaching and exhortation in these lonely wanderings. A medical officer
on board ship, and a dying man in the infirmary
here, I cannot doubt He sent me to, with a message
of peace. The results of *preaching* I am never permitted to know, but I ever feel it one of my greatest
privileges to exercise."

And so even now Gordon was permitted to see
some of the reasons for which he was compelled to visit
Australia. But the two or three he mentions were not
all. A little later in the year when at Melbourne,

he became acquainted with a clergyman, and what
we might call the accident of their meeting was, as
it were, a seed sown which has borne, and continues
to bear, increasingly precious fruit. This clergyman was the Rev. H. B. Macartney. The latter
writing to a children's magazine, speaks of their
meeting :—

"One day a young clergyman called at my father's
house, and introduced himself as a son of the late
Captain Gordon of the Royal Navy. The mention
of that name was sufficient to ensure him a thousand
welcomes from an Irish heart, for Captain Gordon
loved the Irish people, and for many years went
about doing good from north to south of the island,
and pleaded their cause in the English Parliament.
And so it was that I became acquainted with his son.
He had sailed from England to be a missionary in
India, but he had hardly landed at Madras when he
fell sick, and was ordered to Melbourne for change of
air. Does it not seem strange that God should have
called him to India, and yet, the moment he came,
should have sent him away again ? Well, I think I
know the reason. God wanted him in India, but not
just then. God had work for him to do both in India
and Melbourne, and by sending a 'burning fever,
He taught him that the work in Melbourne was
to be done *first*, and the work in India afterwards.
Now, I must tell you what he did do in Melbourne,
and then you will understand quite clearly that God
was right.

"I was at that time Chaplain to the Industrial Schools at Prince's Bridge and Sunbury. Sunbury was too far from town, so I invited him to come next morning and give a missionary address to the girls at Prince's Bridge. He met me at the gate on Thursday morning, September 19, 1867. We went in together, and, after singing and prayer, we got the map of India, and he described the poor heathen sitting under the shady trees listening to good missionaries, who read and told about the Lord Jesus. He added, that he hoped soon to be doing so himself. The children were delighted; and when the address was done, I asked the children if they would like to help. They all said 'Yes,' so heartily, that I gave notice that when I came again I would bring a little book to begin a missionary society, and to put down the names of subscribers. I have that little book beside me now, and I find that twenty-seven girls had their money ready, and came forward that morning to begin the work—a work which they have never tired of since. The first name I have written down is ' Mary Bromby, 3d.'"

Such was the seed which was sown and which has since become a tree wherein the birds of the air find shelter. It is of this Australian work that Mr Macartney, writing on April 2, 1886, says:—

" He (Mr Gordon) came to Melbourne in September 1867, and we saw him frequently. He was the means of connecting me with Bishop Sargent and other missionaries, so that the Australian Revenue (from £1200 to £1500 a year), which now flows from hence to India, had its source in him."

This, then, was the work in Australia for which he was wanted. A fever, if used aright, may be the means of producing £1200 a year ; precious money for the salvation of still more precious souls. So it is that Christians are permitted in their own sufferings to be partakers of the sufferings of Christ, which are effectual to the salvation of men. They fill up, as St. Paul before them, that which is lacking in the sufferings of Christ. Even here their sorrow is turned into joy.

CHAPTER IV.

ON his return from Australia, Gordon again took up work in the South Indian itinerancy, devoting himself with renewed ardour to the study of Tamil on a fresh plan, which much facilitated his progress, and to which he refers as follows, in a letter to a friend, dated, Sattur, Madras Presidency, January 6, 1868 :—

" My present occupation reminds me of you, because it was you who recommended me to try ' Prendergast on the Mastery of Language.' I sincerely hope you have found the system as helpful to you in Hebrew as I have in Tamil. . . The advantage of such a system *here* is very great, because one cannot get any proper teachers. I began with a professional Munshi. . . . but I was obliged soon to discard him. Prendergast's system offended his pedantry, and gave him (so he said) several fits of indigestion. I am now learning with no other help than a native to repeat sentences, and give the pronunciation ; and I get on famously. I have only been six weeks at work, and I am going to try, very shortly, preaching to the heathen. My plan has

been gradually to master 15 long sentences, with
246 minor combinations. I have also committed to
memory portions of the Prayer Book in Tamil. I
am now beginning to read and write, and it all
seems to come without an effort, although the
language is by no means an easy one. It boasts of
238 letters, and has many parts of speech, which
experienced scholars seem utterly at a loss to
explain."

He writes again from Madras, on May 26, 1868 :—

" I have had several interesting letters from Mr.
Prendergast, whose system seems to be getting very
popular in America, and on the Continent also.
Here, I regret to say, it is too hastily condemned. I
hope he will persevere with his Tamil and Telegu
manuals. He says that I have been at a disadvantage in not having a proper set of sentences to start
with. But the sentences were composed by friends,
who carefully studied his rules. I think there was a
want of clearness in the rules, which will be no doubt
obviated by degrees."

A third reference to the same subject is dated
from his tent, on September 9, 1868.

" I wrote some time ago to Mr. Prendergast (in
reply to a letter from him), sending him a full
account of my experience of his system, and also
showing wherein I have deviated from it."

It is to be regretted that the interesting correspondence between the retired Indian judge and the
young Indian missionary who was profiting from his

labours seems to have been lost. Perhaps a quotation from Mr. Prendergast's handbook may be welcome to those to whom the Mastery of Languages is a subject of practical importance.

His preface observes :—" It is only by the study of nature that we can hope to discover the true method, whether for arranging what the beginner is to learn, or for laying down principles for his guidance, in qualifying himself to speak a foreign language. The simplest and most effective course that can be pursued, is to keep in view the natural process of hourly ringing the changes upon a few sentences, with occasional additions.

" The most successful of all linguists, are children who have already learned to speak their mother-tongue. When taken abroad, and left among foreigners, they acquire two languages at once, without any assistance, and speak them idiomatically, although with a very limited vocabulary. They do not philosophise, but, in pursuance of the dictates of instinct, they imitate and repeat chance combinations of unfamiliar sounds, and afterwards analyse them at leisure.

" The true method underlying their operations, and the causes of their success, have never been detected, nor has their procedure been accurately observed and adopted. . . . Under the classical system, we learn the grammar, and study the language, instead of learning the language, and studying the grammar. Children learn languages without studying them, but we study them for many years, without even approximating to the colloquial attainment." Mr. Prendergast, in short, maintains that the synthetical should precede the analytical method of learning a language, and the experience of those who have tried it, confirms Gordon's testimony, that "all seems to come without an effort," on the Mastery plan.

About this period, Gordon thus writes to his brother :—

"*Tent, March* 11 (1868).

"MY DEAR EDWARD,—I fear that I did not write to you last week, but the fact is, that when I am 'on the move,' as I am at the end of each week, and especially when I am twenty or thirty miles from Madras, letter-writing is a very precarious thing.

"It takes a very long time to know the habits and character of the people. It might be thought that in the course of a year spent in their villages, and in constant communication with them, a large amount of information might be obtained. But such is not the case, owing to their extreme reserve and profound suspicion of our motives with regard to them. They refuse to believe that we are really actuated by any desire for their improvement. Of the various reasons which they assign for our preaching, one is that we are bent upon breaking down caste. A man said in my hearing the other day, 'When the English first came to India, they had some difficulty in holding their ground, so they told us to worship our idols.

Now that they feel more secure, they tell us to worship their God.' Another notion of theirs is, that we
are actuated by mercenary motives, and that besides
being paid handsomely for our work, we should also
gain materially by their conversion. What is the
scale at which they rate our profits, I do not know,
but at a very moderate estimate it would probably
be Rs.50 (£5) for the conversion of a Brahmin ;
Rs.20 (£2) for the conversion of a Sudra ; and
Rs.5 (10s.) for the conversion of a Pariah. I have
heard something very closely corresponding with this
idea in London among the poor, who sometimes tell
the city missionaries that they get 2s. 6d. a head for
conversions from Lord Shaftesbury every Saturday
night!

    " I am often asked by these people how much pay
I get, and when I tell them (as I rarely do) that I
get no pay at all, their perplexity is quite amusing.
They evidently think that none but a fool or a mad-
man would work without recompense.

    " When we tell them not to worship stocks and
stones, they will almost always confess the folly of
doing so, and be ready to join in a laugh against
their idols. But the better-educated classes will
justify themselves by saying, 'It is not a stone we
worship. The idol only *represents* the god.' The
other day a man, of more than ordinary intelligence,
attempted a defence of his religion in the following
way : 'Your Queen,' he said, 'does not live in this
country, but she appoints governors, and deputies,

and judges, and collectors to administer the Government. So we worship one god, but this god has many representatives,—Vishnu, Sivan, Palyai, Subramanigar-Esman, Mariammure, etc., etc., etc., who all receive homage from our different communities.'

"I am now near Coromandel, having conveyed my tent fifteen miles and pitched it since yesterday, distance from Madras about thirty miles. My letters and papers for the past week have not yet arrived, so that my news from home is somewhat stale, but I need not say that I take a keen interest in all matters of political and social interest in the 'old country.' It is about four months since I was in Madras, with the single exception of a day spent there in order to preach one of the 'Lent Lectures,' at the Cathedral, at the request of the Bishop. The course was upon 2 Pet. 1. 5, 6, 7, and my subject was knowledge, so that I had a somewhat comprehensive field for investigation.

"And now, after writing so much about self, I must tell you how glad I am that you like your work at Woolwich so much. Do you find many of your old friends there? I shall be much interested to know whether there is nice Christian Society among the officers, such as there used to be when Colonel and Mrs Travers were there. There can be nothing more helpful than this to one's own spiritual life.

"I have not quite decided how your kind contribution shall be invested, but I rather think of sending half of it in your name to the building of a church in Tinnevelly, to which I shall also subscribe; and the other half to the same objects as last year, namely, the support of a catechist and a school child. A former smaller contribution I am applying to the payment of a schoolmaster near Madras."

Writing from North Tinnevelly, in February 1868, in a circular letter to his former parishioners in England, Mr. Gordon sympathises with them on the loss of their pastor, Mr Lumsden, and, at the same time, gives a very good insight into the state of the Native Church at this time.

" Does that not seem a very solemn question suggested to each of you to whom the voice of your beloved pastor now speaks no more. 'What use have I made of the privilege which is now withheld from me ? What account can I give of all the spiritual instructions, the warnings, and pleadings which I heard from his lips ?'

" To each of us there is a day of grace, which, if neglected, may never return ; and when I think of your opportunities of hearing the Gospel faithfully preached, I cannot help feeling that it will be ' far more tolerable in the day of judgment' for those whom I see around me here, worshipping idols and devils, than for those in London, who ' neglect so great salvation.'

" Yes, if you could only see what every missionary sees on this side of the world, you would thank God for having placed you in Christian England. I have lately been making a very interesting journey through

D

the country, to see what the Lord is doing among the heathen. I travelled for 200 miles in a country cart, drawn by two bullocks, and stopped at the different places where the missionaries live. If you were to make a journey like this, you would think when you passed along and saw the idols by the side of the road, under the trees, and the towns full of heathen temples, that the country was 'wholly given to idolatry ;' and yet, in no part of India is there so much done among the heathen as here. We have to thank God that there are 100,000 professing Christians in this little corner of the country, south of Madras. There are four missionary societies at work here, and there is plenty of room for them all. There is the Church Missionary Society, the Society for the Propagation of the Gospel, the London Missionary Society, and the American Missionary Society." He goes on to speak of the self-help and growth of the church. "One congregation of about 3000 Christians has raised £500 in one year. I tell you this, that you may see that they do not make no return for the instruction given them. While you are subscribing to help them, they also do what they can to help themselves. We are anxiously hoping that one of these days the Tinnevelly Christians will have their own black bishops, and be able to support their own clergy entirely, and then the missionaries will go to some other part of the world.

.   .   .   .

"Is it not a thing to thank the Lord for, that there

are thirty-one ordained native clergymen in Tinnevelly, all preaching the Gospel to those who once were
their fellow-heathen ?   Some of them have lately gone
out as missionaries to their fellow-countrymen, both
in Ceylon and in the distant Island of Mauritius, on
the coast of Africa."

This same year, writing to his brother, Lieutenant E. S. Gordon, R.A. (now Colonel Gordon), he
speaks of that which is a difficulty to every missionary. He says :—

" In *one* respect we work at a great disadvantage.
They say to us, '*Your religion is the religion of the
rich and educated. What are poor people like us to do?*'
I often wish that I could live among them without either a tent or a horse, live, in fact, like one
of themselves, and thus deprive them of this argument. But Jesuit missionaries have tried this plan,
and failed. There are two reasons against it : one
is, that a European cannot live as a native in the
climate of India without shortening his days ; the
other, that there is a certain respect inspired by our
position and elevation above the people, which commands the attention of Hindus. If our position
were to be lowered, in nine cases out of ten we
should not get a hearing, and more often would probably be insulted and even persecuted. Thus much
wisdom is required in one's dealings with them ; but
I often wish that they could have before their eyes
examples such as every Englishman sees in his own
land, of the effects of Christianity in encountering

poverty and suffering, in giving contentment, heroic
endurance, and high-principled integrity. Such as-
pects of our national faith are not to be found in
India."

We see here the longing after that mode of life
which Gordon afterwards adopted when working in
the Punjab. At this time he seems to have been
held back by those reasons which he has expressed.
But whether held back or not, he felt what every
missionary has felt and must feel, viz., his separation from the people. It may be true, as Gordon
says, that the position of a European in India
often ensures his getting a hearing, but it is also
true that it is a terrible cause of separation. A
European, however humble, however poor, is always,
in the eyes of the natives, more or less of a
" bádsháh," or king. This is one of the most ordinary words applied to Europeans by natives, at
least of the N.-W. countries of India. The reason
is, that even if one becomes poor for the sake of
the people, yet the poverty of a European is wealth
to the average native, and on this account it is
probably by no means evident to the latter that
the former is practising self-denial. We can, then,
understand Gordon's wish, which in after years
found practical expression, to give up all comforts, to
make himself one with the people ; to be at a humble
distance, like Him who emptied Himself of His glory
for us.

The month of July was devoted by Gordon to an

inspection of the Telegu Missions, described in the following letter to Mrs Corsbie :—

"MADRAS, _Aug._ 27, 1868.

"I am afraid it is a long time since I received your kind and very interesting letter. Many a time have I intended to write and thank you for it, but, unfortunately, good resolutions are not more productive in a tropical than they are in a northern climate. First there came illness, and then a period of solitary encampment, when I was deserted by my servants, and my leisure hours were varied by such occupations as grooming my horse, etc., etc. Now, I have just returned from a month's tour among the Telegu Mission, with a lame foot, so that I really have no excuse for delaying my letter any longer. As this tour is the most interesting thing that I have to tell you about, I may as well give you a short sketch of it. We started, Fenn and myself, early in August, and took the steamer to Kokonada, a port about 350 miles north of Madras. Our anchorage was some distance from the shore, as all the Madras seaport towns have only an open roadstead for their shipping. Hence landing is always slow work, and sometimes occupies many hours. A more uninviting place than Kokonada you will hardly find anywhere. However, we had only a few hours' detention there, and went again on our journey at dusk by canal to Dauleshwaram. As the travelling in the Telegu country is chiefly by canal, I must say a few words about it, and I fear that your recollections of

the Nile will not assist your conception either of our
boat or scenery. The former is of the barge type,
long and hideous, with first, second, and third class
accommodation. The superiority of the first class
consists only in privacy. The whole boat is roofed
like a railway carriage, and the front part is panelled
off with a few boards and sliding shutters, for the
benefit of 'the quality.' A bare shelf forms a seat
on either side, and if you do not forget to provide
yourself with a pillow, mattress, provisions, etc., you
can make yourself tolerably comfortable for the night.
A kettle and teapot for making tea are most valuable additions, not to say luxuries (for water can be
boiled on board), but of this we were not aware till
too late. Our fellow-passengers were numerous, but
well-behaved, most of them of that clear, chocolate
shade of skin, and superior type of feature, which
betokens 'high caste.' Their gold and silver ornaments seem to be more numerous and tasteful than
those of the Tamil race, and their good-natured and
well-to-do expression often struck us. I walked for
miles along the banks of the canal while the boatmen
were towing the boat. There was little to relieve the
monotony of endless rice fields, save when here and
there a majestic crane or stork would rise lazily at
my approach, and settle again at a little distance.

"The country is thinly populated, and my appearance struck such terror into two poor cattle drivers,
that they ran before me with headlong speed, clearing
the ditches with marvellous agility, and making it

impossible for me to decide whether they ever
stopped or are running still! The cows which they
tended showed a superior order of intelligence, for
they continued to feed without a suspicion of my intentions. It was a night's journey to Dauleshwaram,
a place of no importance except for its engineering
works, the chief of which is a great dam of masonry,
called here an 'anakatt,' across the river Godavery,
two miles in breadth. The Government intends to
make these anakatts at intervals throughout the entire
course of the river, thereby retaining the water in dry
weather, both for purposes of traffic and irrigation.
Five miles of country road brought us to Rajamahendri, a large native town very prettily situate in
a circle of wooded hills. Here the Godavery appears
to great advantage, a majestic sheet of water rushing
along, with the accumulation of mountain torrents,
and from any of the neighbouring heights you may
trace its glittering curves and reaches to where,
sixty miles away, it plunges through a mountain
gorge, the haunt of the tiger and the chetah. At
Rajamahendri we were kindly entertained by the
Resident Judge, Mr. Morris, with whom we spent
three pleasant days. The town has been selected
as the centre of penal operations, and a large gaol
is built in its neighbourhood. I trust it will soon be
also a centre of missionary operations, although the
Telegu Mission has only recently contemplated extending itself so far.

"One thing about the Godavery did remind me

of the Nile. It was curious to watch the natives on little logs of wood careering along in the full rush and whirl of the current, just as you may remember those little black Nubians, who splash about in the full roar of the cataracts astride their miniature canoe. It was a treat to see a real Indian river for the first time. I have so often ridden across river beds without a drop of water (nothing but a parched waste of sand) that this one was a most refreshing sight.

"Another night's journey by canal brought us to the Mission Station of Elur, where we were welcomed by Mr. Alexander, a very active and warmhearted man, who has had very marked success, both in schools and in itinerant preaching. Here first we came into contact with Mr. Noble's work, although still ninety miles from Masulipatam. A young Brahman, one of Mr. Noble's converts, is staying at Elur, preparing for the ministry under Mr. Alexander's superintendence, and one could not help feeling that one such convert was worth the patient toil of a life. His bright, thoughtful, intelligent face and refinement of manners were most attractive, and when you reflect what mountains of pride and debasing idolatry in his own heart, and what fierce opposition and persecution from without, have to be encountered by every Brahman who professes Christianity, then you feel that such a 'vessel meet for the Master's use' is a greater object of triumph through grace than the conversion of such as have little to lose and much to gain in becoming Christians.

"It took us a ride of eighteen miles to reach the centre of Mr. Alexander's Mission work. A slight accident which befel me in dismounting from a restive pony, drew out much sympathy from the simple villagers. It was only a bruise on the leg, but it was sufficient to lame me, and I had several nurses in attendance throughout the day. Their remedy was a decoction of leaves applied. Our quarters for the night were in a thatched barn, which formed their Meeting House for prayer. Here a few Christian families came to welcome Mr. Alexander, and receive words of sympathy and counsel. The wife of the Catechist was a girl from his own boarding-school, and if anyone doubts the refining and elevating influence of Christianity, let him observe that young wife and mother as she stands among heathen women of her own village, caste, and kindred. The contrast in expression of face, neatness of dress, and cleanliness is most striking. I do not say that you could always single out a Christian scholar from heathen relations, but one in whom the principles of her training have at all matured themselves, you certainly could.

"From Palsanpilly we rode on the next day eight miles to another little centre of Christian light, a village where two or three families have embraced the truth. The country we rode through was low jungle, with hills here and there, some of them

crowned with the 'high places' of Brahman superstition. It was the wet season. The rivers were in
flood and the tanks full. In every pond you might
see buffaloes wallowing in the muddy water, their
heads only enabling you to identify their species.
They are kept in large numbers for their milk, as
well as for draught, and as they had no agricultural
employment, time seemed to be 'no object' to
them.

"When I heard the Telegu language spoken, I
wished much that it had been the object of my
studies, for it is far more euphonious than Tamil.
The construction is just the same, and many of
the words are the same, so that having learnt one,
it is not difficult to learn the other.

"The town of Baizwada, although a large and
important one, is a failure as far as Missionary
success is concerned. The blessing and birthright
which it might have enjoyed, has been taken by
the stranger, and it thus affords another illustration of the words, 'Many lepers were in Israel in
the time of Eliseus the prophet; and none of them
was cleansed saving Naaman the Syrian.' At one
of those great annual festivals, when thousands of
pilgrims troop to Baizwada to wash away their sins
in the waters of the 'Krishna,' there was one from
the distant village of Rajhapur, who had heard
of there being 'a prophet in Israel,' and when
urged by a heathen priest to plunge into the river,
declared that such 'muddy water could never

cleanse his sins; the one God was the God of his choice.'

"Hitherto, his faith had had very little to cling to. Some heathens in his native village had brought the report of the true God, which they had heard from a Missionary preaching in a neighbouring town (probably the Missionary Fox). A remarkable dream had united to bring conviction of its truth to the inquirer's mind. From that time his prayer was 'O God, who art Thou? Where art Thou? Show me Thyself.' It was not long before a further manifestation dawned upon his heart in answer to that prayer. He overheard the reading of a tract which had fallen into heathen hands, and he discovered to his joy that this 'Unknown God' was a 'Saviour.' His prayer then became 'O God the Saviour, who art Thou? Where art Thou? Show me Thyself.'

"The next great truth which he was able to embrace was the Resurrection. He heard of a Christian funeral, of its solemnity, quiet, and order. No boisterous lamentation, no heathen rites, no burning of the body. He declared his belief that 'that body would rise again.'

"Three years passed; and not without many a trial of his faith and constancy. Cholera broke out in the village. It was attributed to the wrath of the goddess, and she had to be appeased with a great sacrifice of cattle. A curious part of the ceremonies had to be performed by 'Venkara' (the inquirer after truth). It was the custom to select the largest buffalo's head, and to carry it, with the image of the goddess, to the confines of the district, and there to bury it with the words, 'O goddess, you have got all you want—leave me.' A river had to be crossed. Venkara paused, set down the image, and declared that a goddess ought to be able to cross the river herself. He would go no further. Shortly afterwards, he was seized with cholera, which his heathen neighbours did not fail to attribute to the wrath of the injured goddess. But strength was given him to resist all efforts to drag him back into heathenism. He recovered, made the journey to Baizwada which I have mentioned, and stood before Mr. Darling's door, an inquirer after the true God. The heathen servant, hearing his object, tried to drive him away. He sat down and began to pray, and it was in this attitude that Mr. Darling came out and found him. No time was lost in responding to the appeal from that village 'Come over and help us.' And at Mr. Darling's first visit he had the pleasure of baptising Venkara's wife and children, and four others.

"Such was the beginning of a congregation which now numbers 132 Christians. The work has spread into the surrounding villages, and there are now 400 Christians in the district. It was very pleasant to see them on Sunday, as they filled the little church, with Venkara at their head, the most numerous and genuine congregation in all the Telegu country.

"The story of Venkara seems to suggest some thoughts upon the subject of your inquiry—namely, What is the best method of reaching the heathen mind, while it is very encouraging to the despondent preacher? Venkara was of the lowest and very ignorant class, whose mind is overlaid with the traditional heathenism of centuries. And I suppose that with such men one cannot be too simple in setting forth the truth. The teaching most acceptable to them is by figure and parable; here a little, and there a little. This class are generally very receptive; but the upper class—Brahmans, etc.,—while they show superior pride, do not show, frequently, superior intelligence. Hence, they are less accessible. Their arguments in defence of their worship are mere vain repetitions, and you rarely meet any, in this part of the country, who are capable of controversy. There is no lack of intelligence, however, where money-getting is concerned; and they show just now a very great anxiety for education (even in Missionary Schools) because they see that it leads to promotion and pay. Scholars of Mr Noble's fill Government offices throughout the country, and hence, when I was riding one day through the little town of Condapilly, a number of the chief men of the place (Brahmans) came round me, and besought me to establish a school there. Thinking, perhaps, that they mistook me for a Collector, or a Magistrate, as they often do, I said, 'I am a Missionary. We teach the

Bible in our schools. How would you like that?'

"'Give us a school on any condition,' was the reply.

"I told them I would ask the Missionary of the district, Mr. Darling, and I found that Mr. Darling's great difficulty is in getting Christian teachers for his schools. He would gladly open more schools if he could get the teachers.

"I must now finish this already overgrown letter, and perhaps next week I may send you a supplementary one about the schools in Masulipatam, with a 'sensational' notice of a total eclipse, which I witnessed in that neigbourhood. I have not written to my friends for so many weeks, that I must ask you to have the kindness to give rather a wide circulation to this little account of myself and the missions. If you can make 'missionary capital' out of it, so much the better.'

"Did I tell you about a missionary letter which I wrote to Melbourne? In about two months I received a copy of it printed, 2000 copies having been circulated, and copies of a little photograph of a Tinnevelly school struck off and advertised 'Tinnevelly girls, a shilling a-piece!'

"I am returning to my tent to-day, and to-morrow I hope to begin preaching to the heathen, with my colleague Mr. Fenn, for I can say a little, although I cannot say much. I would earnestly commend myself and the cause to your prayers, for although my trials are but dust in the balance compared with those of others, yet it is a trial to feel oneself doing so little; and as often as the soul feels its solitude in the wilderness, and hears with startling emphasis the inquiry, 'What doest thou here, Elijah?" it is a comfort to think of the seven thousand praying ones in England."

Gordon's next letter draws a picture of the itinerating mission in which he was engaged, and again alludes to the subject of an ascetic life:—

"*September* 9, 1868.

"It is such a pleasure to find myself in a tent again, because it seems 'like business,' and I always feel when I am in a tent, that I am in my right place. With friends in Madras always ready to receive us, and constant invitations to do work, either by contributing to a newspaper or writing a sermon, there are temptations to us itinerates to leave the 'few sheep in the wilderness,' if I might so say, but, alas! 'sheep' I cannot call them yet in a Christian sense. One of our native brethren (I mean one of the native ministers), in a speech the other day, compared us to the trumpeters walking round Jericho, and I thought the idea a very happy one, as far as my two colleagues are concerned. Our work is to itinerate round Madras, preaching only to the heathen, and we long for the day when the walls of her idolatrous and carnal security shall begin to totter and fall. But before that happens, the trumpets

will probably be in other hands. The presence of
a man like Fenn in the neighbourhood of Madras
has a most beneficial effect upon the work that is
going on within the town. He is the president of
the Native Church Council, a Committee which has
lately been formed in order to give the Native Church
a voice and an opportunity for a little internal
administration. His liberal views, genial manner,
and sound judgment win for him the respect and
affection of all the missionaries in Madras, of whatever society, and I think he is of great use to our
secretary. Unfortunately, it often happens that
those men who are best qualified for the secretariat
have the greatest aversion to the office, when their
qualifications are recognised.

"You cannot think what pretty views one gets
framed by the tent doors. I am now in a beautiful
'Mango' tope (or grove), and each of my three doors
encloses a perfect picture of greensward and foliage,
all dotted about with the trunks of trees, fresh with
the rains. The night before last we had a regular
downpour, and I awoke to the consciousness of a
plentiful discharge of the cooling stream over my
feet, which projected beyond the inner tent roof.

"Just now, we were holding what in England
would be a police court, here called a 'kacheri'
in one of our tents. When all three of us are encamped together, we find that we have too many
servants. Hence, a frequent repetition of the pro-
verb about the 'broth' being spoilt. Yesterday,

MISSION TENTS ON THE BANKS OF THE RIVER KISTNA.

they relieved the monotony of existence by a fight
during our absence, and my servant (who is the
only one of high caste), was obliged to yield to
superior numbers, and got the worst of it. The
example of Abraham's and Lot's households pre-
pares us to expect such things, even in the best
regulated communities, and considering that our
servants are all 'Adullamites' (not one of them
having a 'character' to show), I think we are
most fortunate to get on as smoothly as we do, as
far as strife is concerned. In this case, the
evidence given was sufficient for a verdict of
'assault and battery' against the defendants (or
one of them at any rate), and a fine having been
imposed, it was handed over to the plaintiff. One
interesting feature of the trial, which lasted several
hours, was that, while receiving 'depositions,' the
judge perceived a snake outside, and immediately
rushed out to exterminate it, followed by jury
witnesses, plaintiff, and defendant. In passing this
hasty sentence of death, the judge omitted, however,
to put on the black cap, which was clearly informal.
I need hardly add that Mr. Fenn represented the
judge, Mr. Harcourt the counsel for the defendant,
and I the counsel for the plaintiff. The difficulty
in coming at anything like an approximation to
the truth in such a case is such, that one can sympathise with the magistrate or judge. who has the
responsibility of such investigations every day. We
found that the question, 'What do you know about

E

it?' elicited the same answer from all the servants, which showed that they had agreed to concoct the same story, but cross-questioning brought out ridiculously conflicting testimony.

"We have just now two young native medical students with us in our tents. They are trained by Dr. Patterson, a medical missionary of (I believe) the Scotch Missions, and we are expecting Dr. P. also for a few days, if the rain does not frighten him. I most sincerely wish that I could get a medical man (say a 'dresser'), of not too large expectations, to travel about with me and doctor the poor people. I would willingly contribute to his expenses and give him half my tent, or if the expense were too great, I would set about collecting money for it. It is a most useful thing to have a knowledge of medicine oneself, but it takes up a great deal too much of a missionary's time, because he is sure to be beset with patients wherever he goes, and the preaching or study must necessarily be neglected. But healing and preaching ought not to be separated, and it is almost the only way in which one can benefit these poor people physically, as they do not want money or food, being so exceedingly simple in their habits.

"I have been reading an interesting speech of Sir Bartle Frere at the S.P.G. Meeting. Referring to the great strides which education is taking in India, he asks how we are to cope with a nation thus suddenly elevated by us to the knowledge of that which we have taken centuries to learn, unless we bind them to us by religion as well as science. I do not suppose that he would consider that the Hindu race is rising in the scale of nations at all *in proportion* to the advancement which we offer, but there are many out here in both Services, who think that we are going on a great deal too fast in our promotion of natives to high office under Government, and placing them in positions of independence. The real mistake is, that *religious* advancement is not aimed at first and last.

"I am writing a very rambling letter, instead of doing what I proposed, which was to give you an account of the Telegu Mission Schools, at Masulipatam. There are three of them—Mr. Noble's 'Anglo-Vernacular' Boys' School (as it is called), now carried on by Mr. Sharp; a Vernacular Boys' School, under Mr. Thornton; and a Girls' Boarding School, which Mr. Sharkey started, and his widow now carries on.

The name of Masulipatam is familiar to all who take an interest in South Indian Missions, from its connection with Mr. Fox and Mr. Noble, whose lives have been written. The former laboured there but a short time, giving promise of much usefulness, but being early called to his rest. Mr. Noble's work, however, was the work of a life, and a life of active labour in such employment cannot fail to leave behind it a lasting benefit. Those who are best acquainted with him say that his memoir gives but a feeble picture of the man and his labours. However, it does give some idea of the difficulties

with which he had to contend in carrying out
his schemes of education. Whatever differences
of opinion there may be about the expediency of
educating the higher castes separately from the
lower, there can be no doubt about the success of
Mr. Noble's experiment. There are now about 280
boys in the school, and seven boarders in the Missionary's house, who are being trained for the ministry.
Three of the boys have become converts to Christianity since Mr. Noble's death, and while there we
had the satisfaction of seeing a fourth offer himself
in the same manner. If a Brahman convert re-
nounces heathenism there is usually a great demonstration made by the Brahman relatives, and once
or twice Mr. Noble was regularly mobbed by them,
and had to bar his doors, and appeal to the police.
In fact, usually the relatives take the initiative, and
go to the law court themselves, in hopes of proving
that the boy is under age, etc., and not a free agent.
This time there was no attempt of the kind, partly
no doubt because the boy in question was a Sudra,
and not a Brahman. But it was affecting to see
the poor heathen mother using every persuasion
and entreaty to induce her son not to leave her
and become a Christian. I think the sight of her
grief, as she cried and wrung her hands and appealed
to every sentiment of her affection in her son's heart,
made me feel more sympathy with the poor heathen
relatives than I had ever felt before. It is really
a tremendous trial to them, because when the con-

vert places himself under the Missionary's protection
and 'breaks caste' by eating his food, he cuts
himself off from all intercourse with his family.　It
is not that they renounce him spontaneously, having
a choice to do so or not as they please, but it is
that they are bound to do so by certain social laws,
inevitably connected with their religion and their
recognised position in society.　In the case of Pariahs
there is no such disagreeable difficulty, and therefore I think that one of these Telegu converts is
worth a dozen of the Tinnevelly converts.　There are
instances in which Brahman families have relented
after many years, towards their Christian relatives,
and received them to a certain measure of former
intercourse; but this may be either because after
a sufficient display of austerity, natural affection
demands its rights, or else because in these instances
education may have loosened the hold of superstition.　No Pariahs are admitted in the school of
which I am now speaking; if they were, it would
be broken up, for the Brahmans and Sudras would
leave at once.　And one cannot wonder at this,
when one reflects that our English system also has
its distinctions of caste, and if you were to introduce English Pariahs into Eton or Harrow, probably the same results would ensue.　The only difference is that the *sons* of wealthy Pariahs (English)
do find their way into Eton and Harrow, whereas
among the Hindoos such intercourse would not be
tolerated.　The schoolmaster is one of Mr. Noble's

converts, a very able man, and a fine specimen of a Brahman Christian. He receives £120 a year, which, for a native who lives on rice, and does not keep an equipage, is a very large salary, probably equal to a fat living of £800 or £900 in England. In Tinnevelly, it would be considered extravagant, but the competition of various societies has greatly raised the scale of salaries to native agents in Madras. Besides him and Mr. Sharp there are sixteen native teachers in the school. Many of the scholars go in for the Government competitive examinations, and get good appointments in the Civil Service. The highest tribute which I heard paid to this school was that of the 'Collector' or Chief Magistrate in the station. He said that during the short time in which he had been in charge of the district, he had seen much of Mr. Noble's pupils, for they held appointments in his own 'kacheri' as well as others throughout the country, and he always found them honourable as well as intelligent—'above taking a bribe.' This testimony can only be appreciated by those who know the insatiable craving in the native mind after the idol 'Rupee,' and the lamentable absence of anything like 'principle,' where *interest* is concerned. And coming as it did not from a friend to Missions, but from a man of the world (a 'Gallio,' at best), it was very impartial testimony. I may add that the man in highest office in his court, and the one whom he praised most, is a Christian in every sense of the word.

"Second only to the deep interest with which I visited the scene of Ragland's labours and death, was that which I felt in staying in the very house at Masulipatam where Noble lived, and where he daily gathered his little band of converts round his own table. And although it was not my privilege to know him personally, yet I saw his life reproduced in his converts, some of whom seem to reflect his gifts and graces.

"But I must now say a little about Mr. Sharkey, whom I did meet at Madras, at the time of my illness, soon after arriving from home. He was an East Indian, and therefore a very good Tamil scholar, a man endowed with great sweetness of disposition, and a peculiar aptness for his work, which was a girls' school. That school has a very melancholy history. At the time when it was most flourishing there came that sudden and awful visitation of which you have doubtless heard, which brought desolation and death into so many houses in Masulipatam. Although it is now two years since that night of the 'cyclone,' yet many of its effects are still most unmistakably visible. In fact, they say the place will never be the same again that it was before. Here and there you may see trees twisted into fantastic shapes, or torn up by the roots, and on many houses the water line which the sea wave left when it receded, is quite ineffaceable. The number of deaths on that night is estimated at 40,000, and as many more are said to have died in the following days in the town and its neighbour-

hood, from famine. The sea wave which rose with
the hurricane extended along eighty miles of coast,
and advanced ten miles inland. Numbers were
drowned, numbers killed by falling houses. The
wells, with one exception, were rendered unfit for use
by the salt water, and provisions could not be obtained from Madras for five days. The missionaries
escaped in marvellous ways, some of them by climbing into the roof or upon the roof of their houses.
Thirty-three of Mr. Sharkey's girls were drowned in
the house where they slept, and this terrible trial appears to have been the cause, more or less direct, of
his subsequent death. There are now sixty-four girls
in the school, and Mrs. Sharkey carries it on with con-
summate ability, but she says that it is not what it
was, and this may well be imagined. She has taken
for them a larger house, and one which stands on
higher ground. It is more like a *home* than a school,
and the girls are all her daughters. One little
Brahman girl whom she has adopted from infancy
fully believes that Mrs. S. is her mother. We saw
them first as they stood round the harmonium for
morning prayers at 6.30. Every eye was fixed
upon the hymn books, and every voice seemed to
join in the hymn. Some of the voices were very
sweet, and they have a much prettier language to
sing than the little Tamil girls. Then we saw them in
class under teachers trained themselves in the school.
Some of these teachers have very interesting histories,
but you should hear Mrs. Sharkey tell them—I should

be afraid of spoiling the story. One of them is a
Brahman widow, who offered herself for instruction to
Mr. Noble, one of her brothers being in his school.
I believe that the immediate cause of her doing so
was the reading a little Christian book which took
hold of her mind. Such a case is really a 'brand
plucked from the burning,' for heathen widows, not
being allowed to marry again, are exposed to great
temptation, and generally lead a life most servile
and degraded. I saw one poor little widow of high
station in Tinnevelly, whose husband had died soon
after marriage, and left her a mere child. At the
husband's funeral she was loaded with jewels and
ornaments, and carried with all the pomp of a bride.
At the grave all the ornaments were taken off, and
she returned to a life of retirement and perpetual
widowhood.

"In the evening we went to see the girls at
their croquet and other amusements. I like to see
children play as heartily as they work. In this
respect Hindu children are generally a contrast to
English, for they are exceedingly good at their lessons,
but show a want of spirit in their games. On the
whole, this girls' school appeared to me superior in
some respects to any that I had seen in India,
superior, in fact, to any in England, when you take
into account the class educated. Most of the girls
are paid for by private individuals in England.
One lady, Miss Batty, sends, I believe, thirty different contributions which support that number of girls."

"*Sep.* 11. I am very sorry that this letter is too late for the mail, owing to a freak in the postal arrangements which sent the mail before its time. These freaks are not unusual, and when you inquire the cause, it is always 'the monsoon' which is to blame. There is evidently a misunderstanding between the post office clerk and the clerk of the weather. However, I will take care that it is posted in time next week.

"A little incident in connection with the cyclone at Masulipatam struck me as a subject worthy of a poem. I saw an old and well-used Bible of Mr. Noble's which had been washed out of the school by the sea and carried into a heathen temple at some distance, where it was discovered. I am sure the idol must have fallen before it, like Dagon before the Ark of the Lord."

In a closely succeeding letter, dated Tent, October 4, 1868, we have a very graphic description of the total eclipse of the sun, which had recently taken place. As it contains touches which illustrate Indian life and native character, it is given here almost *in extenso.*

" I fear that you are tired by this time of my Telegu journal, but having given you the bright side of the picture, it would not be complete without the dark side also. I must tell you how the practical lesson was enforced upon us that happiness, however bright, must have its ' eclipse.'

"It were well if such eclipses could always be re-

garded with the same satisfaction as the one which
we witnessed from the heights of Kondapilli, August
17, 1868. You have probably seen some account of
this event in the papers, although in England you
could not see the thing itself.

"Mr. Fenn and I were just in the right line of
country to see the total eclipse. We happened at
the time to be with Mr. Darling at Baizwada, and
wishing to visit Kondapilli for its scenery, we made
an excursion thither on horseback. It was dark
before we arrived there, and the road was covered
by the overflow of the Kistna, which was in flood
after the rains. However, by means of a lantern, we
were guided to our quarters for the night in the
verandah of a deserted barrack, where we spread our
mattresses and were soon asleep. In the morning
we foraged for fowls and milk, and then began to
ascend the hills.

"I was glad they were not of Alpine height, on
account of my lame foot, but, such as they were,
they well rewarded the effort, and showed some very
interesting scenery. Anything that takes you out
of the plains is pleasant, and as these were the first
Indian hills that I had ascended, by so much were
their attractions enhanced. Many of these hills are
crowned with the 'high places' of heathen idolatry,
which are approached by flights of steps well polished
by pilgrims' feet. Arriving on the first plateau we
found, however, not a heathen temple but the ruins
of an old palace with a tomb and mosque attached,

all bearing traces of the Muhamadan rule. Close by
was one of those magnificent banyan trees which
seem far more venerable than the ruins they shadow.
The saplings which their branches throw out take
root in the ground and grow till they rival the
parent trunk in stature, forming great natural but-
tresses, and often assuming the regularity of arched
colonnades. Here too was a tank formed by art
in the basin of the surrounding hills. However,
we did not stop, as the sun was up and our climbing was not done. A little path, which sometimes
almost lost itself in the thicket, brought us in another
hour to the summit, where we awaited the 'perform-
ance' of the day. About 9 a.m. it began to be
manifest that the moon was edging upon the sun,
and as she advanced it seemed to me that her edge
was rather ' frayed ' with continual wear and tear.
However, she came very well out of the contest,
having managed very effectually to blot out the
sun for the space of five minutes. 'Shorn of his
beams,' he still presented some singular phenomena.
A nebulous 'corona' of light seemed to play around
the darkened disc of the eclipsing moon, and with
a telescope we distinctly saw radiant spikes which
issued from the sun behind.

" As the shadows deepened on mountain and river
the landscape began to take a strange and unnatural
colour, as though nature refused to be deceived into
the belief that night was approaching. The darkness was never total, but there was a kind of lurid

light round the horizon which shifted according to the advance and retreat of the moon. The prevailing colour was that kind of deep purple which you see in mezzo-tinted paper. The stars came out (a few of them), the wind fell, and the birds, which had been in anxious consultation about the departing light, hushed their notes and probably went to roost. At Masulipatam the event was also marked by the cows rushing into the girls' school. But it was not till the reappearance of the sun that the most striking effect was produced. When the darkness had lasted about five minutes there was an almost instantaneous effulgence, which resembled nothing so much as the bursting of a rocket, although far surpassing a rocket in brilliancy. Instantaneous also was the response from mountain, wood, and valley, and the arrows of light quickly sped over the plains of Golconda and the broad reaches of the Kistna. In another half-hour the sun had resumed his sovereignty, as a giant coming out of his chamber and rejoicing as a strong man to run a race.

"In Baizwada hundreds of people took occasion to bathe and recite their incantations, but either the suddenness or the darkness frightened them so much, that they rushed from the river into the streets in the most headlong terror.

"The Brahmans had a most curious solution of the difficulty. They gave out (it is said) that a large snake would shortly swallow the sun, but that, in obedience to their magic spells and incantations, the

snake would disgorge the sun and disappear. Among
the ignorant people, the spectacle thus predicted gave
the Brahmans a wonderful ascendancy.

"Descending the hill, we took up our quarters in
the ruined castle during the heat of the day, and
in the afternoon walked round the tank which I
have mentioned, to a spot whence a most charming
prospect opens out. The scenery is so well described
in Fox's life, which you have probably read, that
any words of mine would contrast feebly with his.
It was certainly the finest, and, in fact, the only fine
scenery which I have yet seen in India; and for
richness and variety of vegetation surpassed even
that of Ceylon, if it can be surpassed. Our first
glimpse was framed by an old stone doorway, and
a most complete picture it was. Passing through
the picture frame the sphere of vision was at once
enlarged. The hills to right and left formed a valley
such as the 'Lotus-eaters' might have envied for its
shady nooks and luxurious foliage. At the end of
this valley rises a remarkable and well-wooded hill,
and through distant gaps the eye rested upon broad
lagoons, made by the overflowing Kistna, enclosed
by more remote mountains beyond. Not the least
interesting feature of scenery was a troop of majestic
monkeys scaling the rocks. Their black faces, grey
bodies, and unusually long and leonine tails har-
monised most perfectly with their rural habitation.

"The town of Kondapilli, at the foot of the
mountains, is remarkable only for a trade carried on

there, and nowhere else, as far as I know. This art consists in the manufacture of little miniature models, illustrative of native dress and customs. They are made of wood with ordinary instruments, and so well formed and painted, that they are very greatly in request (as you may suppose), chiefly for exportation to England. Some were sent to the last Paris Exhibition. This neighbourhood used once to be rich in precious stones. When riding with Mr. Darling late one evening, and coming to a very ordinary village, I was told that its name was Golconda; it sounded like a page out of the Arabian Nights. 'Can this be the Golconda of the diamond mines?' I exclaimed, and was assured that it was no imagination. The diamond mines of Golconda have long ago been exhausted, and the poor villagers who still turn the soil in search of a stray ruby or other stone, have not yet found that 'pearl of great price' which has never disappointed the seeker. Among the surest methods of securing eternal happiness is supposed to be the life of the 'Sanniâsee' or religious recluse. One of them I visited at Baizwada. His life was spent in a little cave in the side of the hill. Having attained the spot with no great difficulty, I found that the old man was not at home. His cave was very well chosen, sheltered from sun and rain, and altogether 'eligible,' if not 'well furnished.' Two Brahmans were there at the time. They looked very cross at my intrusion, mumbled something not very courteous, and then took themselves and all their pots and pans to a neighbouring tank, where copious aspersions of water were supposed to wash away the defilement which my presence entailed. As they were very dirty, I viewed their bath with extreme satisfaction. These Sanniâsis will sometimes build a little altar by the roadside, and place upon it a small box for subscriptions, and they will continue their austerities till they collect enough money to build a tank or a temple, according to their vow. I saw at Madras an iron cage which a Sanniâsee had worn for many years upon his head, having vowed to wear it till he should collect money enough to build a tank. Having worn it for many years, he was brought under the influence of the American missionaries, laid aside his cage, and embraced Christianity. There is another sect of religious beggars called Fakirs, who travel about, begging by the way, and are not (I fancy) so stationary as the Sanniâsis, or so sacred. I do not know that we missionaries have much to learn from these religious devotees, for there is much 'shamming' in their austerities, I imagine. Certainly we have much to teach them, both in example and precept. We are sometimes accused of 'boiling our peas,'—softening the asperities of missionary life, instead of 'enduring hardness as good soldiers.' You have doubtless heard of the old story of the two pilgrims who went to walk with peas in their shoes, and of the one who found that by 'boiling

his peas' he could more easily accomplish his pilgrimage. I confess that I hope, personally, that I
shall constantly hear these objections made, in order
that I may be stirred up to greater self-denial by a
rebuke to the selfishness which so continually besets
me. Still, upon the whole, I think there are as many
' peas boiled' in England as there are in India, and
that too in every profession. The 'cross' has come
greatly into fashion as an ornament and a play-
thing, but how little there is of 'taking up the cross'
in a Christlike spirit. How little there is of enduring the shame."

It is the common experience of Europeans in
India, that natives of the country give them credit
for being doctors, and every one, probably, from time
to time does something in the way of medicine.
Speaking of this amateur kind of work, and looking
at the humorous side, Gordon says, if medical men
were more often sent out to accompany the itinerating evangelists, the latter "would not have to enter
in their journals, 'morning devoted to extracting
teeth,' nor would they discover, after an operation,
that they had amputated the wrong leg."

On the prospects of the work he writes :—"One
village has given us special cause for thankfulness,
I came into it one Sunday morning, more by accident (as we should say) than design, for I was alone,
and intending only to take a quiet, early walk. The
people met me with evident delight, took me to the
house of their chief man, and insisted upon hearing

F

my say! There were about thirty men and boys
(the women rarely come forward), and after I had
preached, I invited them to our tents, where I told
them Mr. Fenn would explain the way of God more
perfectly. They came over to our tents day after
day, and listened with remarkable intelligence and
interest, and two of the more earnest ones declared
that they would like to become Christians. We were
obliged to leave that encampment, and at the next
one we had a native brother minister with us; so I
rode over one morning at five o'clock to this village
with him. It was about five miles, and when we got
there, there seemed to be no one in the street; but by
degrees one and another saw us, and soon the whole
village came and gave us a very hearty greeting,
and for one hour and a quarter the native minister
stood opposite one of their houses and preached
and answered their questions."

After an interval of several months, on May 26,
1869, Mr. Gordon writes from Madras:—

"I must not forget your question about a missionary's 'credentials' in appealing to the heathen
mind, now that we have not the signs and wonders
to show which the apostles and evangelists had.
There is no demand which we have so frequently to
meet as this:—'Give us some proof' (outward sign)
'that your religion is the right one.' 'Your religion
is the religion of rich people with fine houses, and
horses, and carriages, and servants, but it is not the
religion for poor people like us.' Unfortunately we

cannot point them to instances of poverty and suffering borne with resignation and thankfulness, such as
the Christian experience at home so often furnishes.
Nor can we hold up our civil and military servants
in India as examples of holy living and consistent
conduct.   When we have pointed them to the rapid
spread of Christianity in Tinnevelly, and the moral
and social benefits resulting therefrom, both in communities and individuals, then we can but appeal to
reason and argument, and challenge them to show
proofs of the elevating power of their own systems.
Conversion among the Hindus is never, I believe,
a rapid work, as is so often the case in our experience.   It generally follows a long period of instruction, during which the truth is gradually leavening
their character and conversation.   I mean, of course,
real conversion· in distinction from that nominal conversion which is so far more frequent.   I am anxious
to get hold of some of the journals of the native
candidates for ordination, such as they are always
required to present in Tinnevelly.   I believe they
are sometimes very interesting, and would be especially so in the case of a Brahman, such as the one
to whom you refer as mentioned in my last letter.
There is another very interesting man in the country
whom I have since heard of, and whose history I
must get written down.   I cannot trust to memory
to relate it now.

   "Since I wrote, we have been establishing four
schools in our district, by way of a little commence-

ment of organised work. The schoolmasters are
not Christians but heathens, the former being most
difficult to get. However, they teach the Bible, and
we go and examine the boys every now and then.
My last encampment was at a village where one of
these schools was, and the boys (to the number of
forty) were intelligent little fellows, and fond of their
books. When we were there, there was an annual
procession of the village god to the 'tope' or grove
which we occupied. The people said we must move
our tents, for the idol must have the ground to himself. Mr. Fenn had gone to Madras at the time,
and I refused to move for any idol in their catalogue.
Eventually they gave in, and had their idol and procession in another part of the tope. Hundreds came
from Madras and different parts, and they made a
great noise at night with their rockets, and drums,
and cymbals, but they did not molest me. I told
them they might come to my tent, and hear a good
sermon, but they were too intent upon their feast
that day. However, they came on other days. One
day there was a wedding among the Pariahs, and
part of the ceremony consists in the bride riding
round the village on a horse, to which, of course, she
is *held* by her friends. As they could not get a
horse, Mr. Fenn very kindly lent them his, mine being
voted 'too spirited.' The ceremony was at night,
and the bride was very glad when it was over, as
she had a great aversion to riding. She appeared
about twelve years old, and was dressed like a boy

for the occasion. The women of this country go about bareheaded even in the heat of the day. When they do wear turbans like the men, it is very becoming ; in fact, I know nothing more becoming than a turban for man or woman. The next day we heard a similar procession outside our tents, with drums and fifes, and apparent rejoicing. We thought it was part of the marriage festivities, and found to our astonishment that it was a funeral! So little distinction is there between the one and the other! The body of the old man was being carried off to the burning ground with the most hasty and unseemly levity."

For those who are not acquainted with India, some interesting notes about the hot weather are given. Gordon takes occasion to deprecate missionaries following the example of other Europeans in India, who flock as far off as ever they can to the various hill stations.

When there is not merely heat, but a heavy and damp atmosphere as well, " then it is that you wish," he writes, " you could put off your flesh and sit in your bones," as Sydney Smith suggested. " Then it is that *prickly heat* scourges you all over with its hundred little knotted cords, and you are told that the only remedy is neither to eat, drink, nor bathe— sleep being already out of the question.

" People are rushing off to the hills on every side, and I might easily move off also, with the very plausible excuse of *studying Tamil under more favourable circumstances*, and superintending the missions on the hills, etc.; but I do not like the idea of even seeming to be an *amateur missionary;* and although I quite agree that 'prevention is better than cure,' yet I had rather preach than practise the maxim. It appears that nothing *cools* in this climate so quickly as *missionary ardour*, and it is a great deal more than I can do to keep mine warm. However, I try to commit it to safer keeping than my own."

Under such circumstances as these, it is hardly surprising that missionaries find one of their greatest trials, the difficulty of showing consistent and Christlike examples in "the trivial round, the common task." The author of the *Christian Year* discovered what every European in India who attempts to follow Christ, must discover, that the small trials are the great trials. It is of these that Gordon writes, in July 1869, to Mr. J. C. Parker, of the London City Mission. Here, as in most things, he always sees a humorous side as well as the other. It was this vein of quiet humour which struck those who were associated with him in work as one of his chief characteristics. The very letter in which this humour is evident was written while he was suffering from a severe attack of fever :—

"The same wind will blow hot and cold the same day, besides shifting to at least *three* opposite quarters. At one moment a gust will fly through the tent, fill it with dust, and send all your writing materials sailing amongst the neighbouring trees, giving you the recreation of a 'paper chase' under a tropical sun. At another moment there will be such a lull as to make you gasp for breath, and disbelieve the thermometer if it is below 110 degrees. And it is much the same with bodily sensations. Sometimes I am the better for a meal, or a night's rest, sometimes the worse. Sometimes happy and contented with men and things, sometimes discontented and censorious; sometimes quite sure I am wrong in ever hoping to be a missionary; sometimes equally certain that the fault is not with the gifts which God has given me, but with the measure of faith and patience exercised in their use. And all this has a great deal to do with variations of pulse and discolouration of tongue. When I hear myself or others giving utterance to narrow-minded or uncharitable sentiments, I often think that a dose of quinine or a breath of mountain air would reverse such opinions altogether. And I sometimes wish that homœopathists who analyse 'symptoms' in their books with such wonderful accuracy, would publish a little manual to be carried with a case of globules in the waistcoat pocket, and adapted to such symptoms as doctors do not sufficiently take into account. I would have, for instance, a 'Missionary's Manual,' with prescriptions for crises like the following :—

"*Sympt.* 1.—General discontent, commonly called 'home sickness.' Dose, 5 to 20 pils Bryonia, to be repeated every half-hour.

"*Sympt.* 2.—On arriving at a camping-ground,

and finding that one of your bandies has upset and broken your crockery—anger rises. Dose, 15 pils belladona, to be taken on the spot.

"*Sympt.* 3.—On preaching to the heathen and finding them derisive and insolent—vexation and disappointment. Dose, 12 pils aconite, to be taken on the spot.

"*Sympt.* 5.—On receiving no letters by the English mail—sensation. Dose, 13 pils nux, to be repeated daily till next mail.

"*Sympt.* 7.—On searching through your 'things,' and finding that you have only 3 buttons to 6 shirts; needlecase nowhere—desperate resolve to marry and 'be done for.' Dose, 14 pils opium and prudentium duly mixed.

"*Sympt.* 8.—On finding that some people who promised to become Christians have gone back to heathenism—emotion, and resolve to go home and take a country parish in England. Dose, the whole contents of your case (*i.e.* medicine case) to be swallowed at once, and another case sent for as soon as possible. I have got a little homœopathic manual by my side, and I only regret that it does not prescribe for sensations like those which I have stated, although it appears to include almost every other bodily or mental indisposition."

Gordon goes on in the same letter to speak of one cause for little fruit in missions in India. All missionaries might do well to think over what he says.

"I think we missionaries are too apt to point to

the heathen and say, 'Their leanness, their leanness!'
instead of hanging our heads in shame and saying,
'My leanness, my leanness!' How little we know or
think how much *we* have been shortening the Lord's
arm by our unbelief, or how much more blessing we
might have drawn down had our prayers been more
earnest and our love more fervent. Such reflections
have been awakened lately by the preparation of a
report which Mr. Fenn and I have been required to
furnish for the last year. When it is published, I will
send you a copy. The very name of a report is so
suggestive of dryness, and therefore so odious to
many, that we have endeavoured to bring out as
much of *interest* as was consistent with the exact
truth, and with the object which has ever been before
us. Very different views of 'interesting and valuable
information' are taken by various missionary peri-
odicals. One well-known writer in the *Intelligencer*
seems to think it necessary to preface his articles with
illustrations of more or less domestic familiarity to the
public. As for instance: 'Behold the palm! With
what steady and gradual but stately growth it rears
its head to the blue firmament! Just so the progress
of missions.' Or, 'Behold the banyan tree! With
what extraordinary productiveness and firm tenacity
it sends forth pendants from its branches to take root
and form support to the parent tree, etc. Just so
the rapid and far-spreading growth of our mission
stations, etc., etc.' Then another periodical, issued
more directly from the mission field, will furnish a

different model for composition. One writer, relying upon the 'logic of facts,' and rejoicing in mathematical terms, will fill his journal with decimal notation, and record his progress in the style of 'Colenso's Arithmetic.' As, for instance: 'Another year past, during which the following deeply interesting facts suggest matters for encouragement and satisfaction. I have this year preached 780 sermons, had 10,950 listeners, visited 1240 villages, examined $878\frac{1}{2}$ children, superintended 15 catechists and $22\frac{1}{2}$ schoolmasters, been abused by 49 heathens, lost 32 tempers (since recovered), and eaten 713 fowls. When these notes are compared with the following table of statistics, etc., it will readily be seen,' etc. I will not quote the 'table' referred to, nor will I vouch for the above as facts, but only *specimens*. Some will say, perhaps, that these are not things to joke about. For myself, I believe that grave matters are often made ludicrous by the way in which they are treated . . . and that a lively and truthful style of writing . . . may be productive both of interest and profit."

The following extract is from a letter dated November 9th :—

"My brother Edward's marriage is indeed a matter of deep interest and thankfulness to me. That *he* is so happy in the prospect of it, is a sufficient cause for me to be so, and I feel quite sure that to be married is the very best thing for him. It is also a great satisfaction if I have been in any way helpful in the matter. I introduced him before

I left England to Miss Knyvett's family. . . .
I had little opportunity of seeing the younger sisters,
so that I can form little idea of Edward's bride.
All I can do is to wish him well with all my heart,
and pray earnestly that she may also be happy and
a blessing to him. It will be a great pleasure to
me to have a new sister, and a correspondent who
can tell me all about him. All that you kindly say
about my circular letters is very encouraging. I
feel very grateful for your sympathy. It is such a
great help to hear of the views taken of missionary
work at home by friends who are really interested
in it."

The latter portion of the year 1869 was occupied
in making a tour of the Travancore Missions. Gordon's
companion on this occasion was his colleague the Rev.
D. Fenn. His letters, giving an account of this tour,
are of the deepest interest, but being more particularly about other people's work, they will be given
separately as a whole in the next chapter.

During the winter of 1869-70, Gordon's health
seriously gave way, insomuch that he considered
work in South India no longer a possibility for him.
At this crisis, came an offer which must have been
most gratifying. It was from the Bishop of Sydney,
asking him to become the first Bishop of the new
diocese of Rockhampton. He speaks of its being
an unremunerative office, but it must be borne in
mind that this was no drawback in the eyes of one
who received no stipend as a missionary, but gave all

his private means to the service of the Lord. The
refusal to accept the offer, therefore, exhibited the
utter humility of the man. It is clear that it was
not position or power, as the world judges, which
he sought.

His own feelings are evident in a letter to Mr.
James Parker. It is written in June 1870, from the
Hill Station of Utakamand, where he had gone to
recruit his health.

"My plans for the future have lately given me a
great deal of thought, and led me to continual prayer,
in consequence of a proposal which came from the
Bishop of Sydney, that I should make Australia my
future sphere instead of India. He offers me a position of much responsibility and labour, not less than
the Bishopric of a new diocese, which is to be formed
north of Queensland. If you look on the map you
will see a large promontory to the N.-E. of Australia,
with the Gulf of Carpentaria on the one side and the
ocean on the other. It appears that settlers have
occupied the whole of this, and their spiritual wants
have to be provided for. The Bishop of Brisbane's
diocese is the furthest at present, but he finds himself unable to extend his limits. The new diocese
is to be Rockhampton, from the name of its largest
town on the coast.

"It will be apparently a very unremunerative work,
since a man could not live by it, but must have independent means. Also, it is in some respects a
missionary work, as the state of things at present is

very elementary ; and, moreover, an opening exists for
a mission to the aborgines.   This last is an attrac
tion to me, and as I work in India at the disadvantage of feeble health, I felt at first that the call was
from the Lord.   All my friends in Madras urged it
upon me to accept the Bishop's offer, but my friend
Mr. French, in N.-W. India, does not view it in the
same light, and as I had previously made an offer to
him to join him if the Committee approved, we have
mutually agreed to leave it to the Home Committee
to decide whether they can accept my offer to go to
N.-W. India.   If they do not, then I shall turn to
Australia, as I feel that my work in South India is
accomplished, there being a man ready to take my
place when called for.   I have now told you at some
length my position, in order that you may unite with
me in prayer upon this important subject.

"I should mention that, stimulated by the advice
of my friends in Madras, and after three weeks' de-
liberation and prayer, I wrote the Bishop of Sydney
to accept his offer, but I have since written again
to ask him to allow me a little more time for consideration.   I feel very evenly divided upon the subject, being most willing and anxious to prosecute
my Missionary work on the one hand, on the other
being ready to undertake the great work, of laying
the foundation of the Church of Christ in a remote
colony of our own countrymen."

It will be sufficient to conclude this episode by
quoting the words of Mr. Baker, of Cottayam, who,

when writing to the children of Melbourne, with
whom Gordon had a special link, says,—" Nor must
I forget to tell you that dear Mr. Gordon has determined, after long consideration, *not* to accept the
Bishopric of Rockhampton.   He feels himself called
to be a missionary *to the heathen* still."

The autumn of the year saw him on the voyage
home *via* Hong Kong and San Francisco.   He chose
this long route for the benefit of his health as well as
the pleasure of travel.

CHAPTER V.

TRAVANCORE.

"*Madras, Nov.* 5, 1869.—It seems quite a long time since I wrote a circular letter home, and the interval has been one of more than usual interest to me, but it is difficult to write when one is travelling about from place to place. My itinerating work was suspended early in August, and I had no sooner reached Madras than I had an attack of fever, which took the same 'intermittent' form which it has taken in previous years, but happily was slight. After about ten days the doctor gave me leave to travel, and Mr. Fenn and I started together on a tour through the Missions of Travancore. It is marvellous what a change there is between this country and that. We crossed India by rail without a single tunnel, and found ourselves in the midst of a mountainous district, fertilised by fine rivers; luxuriant in vegetation. The contrast is as great as though a continent lay between the two countries, instead of a single range of ghâts. Whatever respect I may formerly have had for the flat, arid plains of Madras was dissipated at once. We got out at a

small railway station, put our things in two bullock-
carts, and commenced our march for the first mission
station to be visited.   It took us about eight hours,
the journey being twenty miles, and this was very
rapid for bullocks!   In springless carts the jolting
is severe, especially on a road which is seldom mended,
and where the ' laterite' crops up abundantly through
the very superficial covering of gravel which is meant
to conceal it.   However, the prospect on every side
was charming, and reminded one in many respects
of Ceylon.   The paddy fields on either side were of
that very bright, almost dazzling, green, which you
never see in English cornfields; and the forests, which
enclosed them, were adorned with many species of
palms, and thick clusters of feathery bamboos.   The
road was one continual avenue, with sufficient un-
dulation to make a variety.   Overhead, troops of long-
tailed monkeys would here and there make our appearance the subject of general conversation, and birds
of brilliant feather would insist upon being admired.
We reached the mission station of Trichur by the
help of a brilliant moon, and the missionary himself,
one recently arrived from England, gave us a hospit-
able reception.   We did not see much of the place,
because we had to start early the next morning on
our journey; but it is not a very hopeful mission
station, I regret to say.   Trichur is the stronghold
of Papists on the one hand, and of Brahmans on the
other, and the Protestant native congregation is in
an unsatisfactory state.   However, there is a very

good native minister, who does much to lighten the burden of the newly-appointed missionary. Our next stage was by boat to Cochin, a native town of some importance on the sea. I must describe the mode of travelling, as most of our journeys through Travancore were taken in boats.

"There are large inland lagoons, called 'backwaters,' running parallel with the sea, and here and there uniting with it, all along the coast. They are very convenient for traffic, as the forests are dense, and there are no roads. Boats of various kinds ply along these lagoons, from the full-sailed barge down to the little canoe, just big enough for one or two men. As our journey was long, and it was an object to get through it quickly, we engaged a cabin-boat with eight or ten rowers, reminding one much of the Nile 'dahabieh' on a small scale.

"It is a characteristic of sailors of every clime to be tuneful, and these of Travancore form no exception to the rule. They row the better for their song, so you are obliged to let them have their way, save when nightly rest is invaded by some strain of surpassing dissonance, and endurance can no longer brook the outrage. They are a good-natured set. These boatmen much astonished me by their power of rowing. They seem to think very little of going on for twelve hours at a stretch, with a single, very short interval for food. The scenery in places was very pretty, and softened by moonlight, seemed to answer to those lines in *Locksley Hall*,—

G

' On from island unto island at the gateways of the day,
　Larger constellations burning, mellow moons and happy
　　skies,
　Breadths of tropic shade, and palms in cluster—knots of
　　Paradise.
　Never comes the trader, never floats an European flag,
　Slides the bird o'er lustrous woodland, swings the trailer
　　from the crag,
　Droops the heavy-blossomed bower, hangs the heavy-
　　fruited tree,
　Summer isles of Eden, lying in dark purple spheres of
　　sea.'

"At one point we passed a large Roman Catholic church and convent, and it was curious to see our sailors (who were Roman Catholics) stop their rowing, steer up to the landing-place, and pay their *toll* to a fat native priest, who was waiting to receive it I There were many villages along the shore, inhabited apparently by a fishing population ; and I was much struck with a novel and easy method of catching fish which they practise. At intervals on the margin of the water were planted lofty posts in the form of ' cranes,' over the top of which a rope, working by a pulley, suspended a net which was let down into the water. The net was kept stretched by cross pieces of bamboo, which looked at a distance exactly like a huge spider holding his web, reticule-shaped, with each of its eight legs. As soon as there was a reasonable hope that the fish had made themselves at home inside the net, the rope was pulled, and the spider ascended with his prey. So plentiful are the fish, that I was told by a

resident at Cochin, that he has seen two boats filled
by one draught. We reached Cochin late at night,
and put up at the house of Mr Sealy, the principal
of a large Government school, who, though not of our
mission, was true to the character, so widely established
in India, of hospitality to strangers.

"Cochin is a curious, old-fashioned place, with such
a liberal rainfall, that 'grass upon the house-tops,' in
plentiful crops, is a common sight. Our host's little
'compound,' although no larger than the 'area' of a
good-sized London house, was stocked with a very
great variety of beautiful ferns (such as are never seen
in England) and tropical plants. We had the pleasure of preaching on Sunday to an English and East
Indian congregation, in the oldest church on the west
coast—one which was built by Roman Catholics, and
afterwards handed over to Protestants.

"Cochin is so prolific of palm trees, that from a
height above it, such as the top of the lighthouse,
you see hardly anything of the houses and streets,
and find it difficult to believe that a population of
40,000 is somewhere hidden away below.

"In the bazaars we saw all shades of complexion
and dress, including merchants from Guzerat, Bombay, etc. The most interesting part of the population are the black and white Jews, who live together
and occupy separate streets. We went into one of
the synagogues. The latter, who are almost as fair as
Europeans, and the women, whom we did not see, said
to be very handsome. The least interesting and most

sinister-looking community of the inhabitants are a sect of Muhamadans, who hate all our countrymen most religiously, and are occasionally addicted to deeds of violence and bloodshed.

"Not many years ago an English collector at Calicut was murdered in his own house by a gang of them who had made their escape from prison, and when troops were sent to apprehend them, they fought so desperately, that an officer and several men fell before the murderers could be destroyed.

"Capture was impossible. They were all shot down to a man.

"In Mr. Sealy's school we saw some 260 boys of high caste, who are receiving a very good English education. As the school is supported by the native Rajah of the country, there is no encouragement given to proselytism, and the Bible is not allowed except as a book of reference.

"Still, Mr. Sealy is able to give them a good deal of Scriptural instruction indirectly, and Cowper's *Task*, which is one of the Government text-books, often furnishes an opportunity for Scripture reference. In describing to you another much larger Native Government School at Trevandrum, I shall have occasion to say more upon this point another time. One of the principal articles of trade at Cochin is timber, and it was very curious to see the way in which the logs of wood are piled on the shore for exportation by means of elephants. Each log has a short rope attached to it, and the elephant, according to the directions of his rider, takes the rope between his teeth by means of his trunk, and draws the log which ever way is desired. It is a very slow process, but the elephant's ingenuity is often displayed in the most amusing way, and his knowledge of the centre of gravity and the principles in mechanics, makes him a first-rate engineer. There is a small Native Protestant congregation at Cochin, under a catechist ; but I shall have more to tell you of missionary interest in my next letter, which I shall hope to write next week. I must be content to leave this one very deficient in this respect, as the mail is about to start."

"*Nov.* 15.—I must begin this letter by saying that I am not at all in a *mood* for letter-writing, being subject to one of those many forms of indisposition which are constantly 'in attendance' in this climate. I shall not, therefore, be much surprised if I am unable to finish it for this mail, which goes in a few hours. However, I must not omit to mention that I am under homœopathy, and homœopathy ought surely to assist in writing letters. I gave you some account last time of our visit to Cochin, and now I have to tell you about Cottayam, and thus introduce you to the centre of the Travancore Missions.

"We reached the place in one night by boat, having been somewhat delayed by the amount of water which spread over the country, and made it difficult to find the right channel, and more difficult, when found, to make way against the rushing

current of the stream. At last, by great efforts, our
boatmen brought us to a little gap in the thick forest
on the bank, and we saw a bullock-carriage, which we
felt quite sure was the only bullock-carriage in all
that country, and could belong to no other than the
senior missionary, Mr. Baker. In a few minutes more
we had wound our way by a narrow and steep road
between high fern-covered banks and tall trees, up
to the mission station. Cottayam is, to my mind,
by far the prettiest mission station in South India.
There are many mission buildings, which I shall
proceed to describe, and each of them stands on an
eminence commanding a view of the surrounding
country and the other buildings. The view from Mr.
Baker's house is, when clear, both distant and grand,
and takes in a very fine range of mountain. Other
views, which are more circumscribed, have delightful little peeps of river, rice-field, and jungle ; but in
going from one house to another you have first to
descend, and then to ascend, by a narrow road, which
has no view at all.

" Mr. Baker, who has been from twenty to thirty
years in the mission, has inherited the missionary
spirit by 'apostolic succession' from his father, who
was there before him. Mrs. Baker has many talents
and accomplishments which eminently qualify her as
a missionary's wife—not the *least* of them being a
very bright and cheerful disposition. In a life of
constant seclusion this happy feature of character is
seldom found, and may truly be called a great gift.

The old missionaries of the Travancore Mission seem to have passed away, and now Mr. Baker stands alone of his generation (although he cannot be said to be old, except by contrast with the others, who are all young and recent).

"There are two educational institutions at Cottayam, one called the College, the other called the Nicholson Institution, which was built by the 'Nicholson Memorial Fund,' raised, I believe, at Cambridge.* They are both designed for training native youths for missionary employment as schoolmasters, catechists, and ministers. Attached to the College is a beautiful chapel, which was built by a special fund, and reminded me forcibly of the college chapels in Cambridge. The College is now presided over by a young missionary named Bishop, and the Nicholson Institution by a younger missionary named Smith. They both seemed very hearty and earnest about their work. Close to the College is the mission church, a large and handsome edifice, which was filled on Sunday by a very good congregation.

"There are two girls' boarding schools in Cottayam, the one under the watchful and motherly superin-

---

* This is a mistake. The C.M.S. College, Cottayam, imparts a *general* education on Scriptural principles, to about 300 Syrian, Protestant, and Hindu youths, up to the matriculation standard of the Madras University, with which it is affiliated. Between fifty and sixty Syrian and Protestant Christians are boarders. The College is mainly supported by an endowment in lands originally granted by the native Government for the education of youths of Syrian parentage. A considerable sum is now collected in fees. The stipend of the Principal is paid by the C.M.S.

tendence of Mrs. Baker, senior ; the other under Mrs.
Baker, junior.   They are designed to supply female
native agents, in other words, wives for the youths of
the two above-mentioned institutions.   Mrs. Baker,
junior's, school, includes many little girls from the
hill tribes (of which I must give an account in my
next letter), and they come from a long distance.
Mrs. Baker, senior, has been at the work of education
so long, that she is now teaching some of the grand-
children of her former pupils.   One of the sights of
Cottayam is the printing press, where copies of the
Scriptures are daily printed and bound, together with
other works and tracts.

" One of the presses, which is on a recent American
principle, does the work with astonishing rapidity, and
it is not safe to go too near it, lest one should suddenly
be caught by it and printed, bound, and published
at 2½-pence a copy.

" What interested me most was to see the original
press and types made with indefatigable labour by
Mr. Bailey, the former missionary of the station.   The
language of Travancore is called 'Malayalam,' and the
character is difficult even to write.   Some idea may
therefore be formed of the ingenuity and patience required in making those little minute Malayalam types
without proper tools, proper workmen, or proper
materials.   My friend and fellow-traveller, Mr. D.
Fenn was specially 'at home' in Cottayam, because it
was his birthplace and the residence of his father, who
was one of the first missionaries there.   There is as

great a contrast between the Malayalam and Tamil people, as between the climate and scenery of their respective countries. The former are of a fairer skin, and, to my mind, they are a handsomer race.

"They dress in a different way, and wear their hair differently, both men and women. The women invariably wear white, which looks nice when clean, but has not the pleasing variety of bright colours which we see on this side of the country. They tie their hair in a simple knot behind instead of doing it in the form of a chignon, as the Tamil women do. The men in Travancore are peculiar for wearing no turban and no cloth over the shoulders, however wealthy or high caste they may be. Their only article of clothing, as a rule, is the cloth round the waist. Their hair is shaven all round the head, but allowed to grow longer on the crown, and then tied in the form of a pigtail or kudumi, in the direction of the forehead. In this country they tie the kudumi behind, and it is considered as a mark of heathenism by the C.M.S., who do not allow their agents to wear it. The Syrian Christians also shave their heads entirely.

"This reminds me that I must define the expression 'Syrian Christian.' There are two main divisions of the people at Cottayam, namely, Nair and Syrian. The Nairs are heathens of high caste, the Syrians are members of a church which traces its origin to the Apostle St. Thomas, who is traditionally believed to have visited South India and evangelized the people. At

any rate, there has been in Travancore for centuries a
body of native Christians, who have their own churches
and their own ritual, and look upon Antioch as their
parent city. They have their bishop, who is called a
'Metran,' and comes from Antioch, and they have
an extensive priesthood, embracing seven orders from
'Acolytes' up to 'Cattanars.' The old Syrian Church
is a very corrupt church, resembling in many things
the Roman Catholic, and having their service in Syrian,
an unknown tongue to the natives. A reformation has,
however, commenced among themselves, and is strongly
advocated by the present Metran, Mar Athanasius,
who conducts the service in the vernacular. I did not
see this man in person, but I read an interesting
letter, in which he warmly thanked the Bible Society
for a present of Bibles which they had sent him.
There is much ignorance among the Cattanars, but
one of the better sort ingenuously told us, that though
he could not preach to the people himself, he always
got an intelligent layman, a member of his congregation to do so. The Cattanars use the tonsure,
and have pictures over the altar and crucifixes, or,
what is as bad, namely, a painted representation of
the Saviour on a wooden cross. Their churches
are very solid, but have little architectural merit.
One of them is interesting for its antiquity; but there
seems to be very little pains bestowed in keeping
it clean and making necessary repairs. It was from
the altar of that church that Menezes (a former
Metran) cursed one of the Cattanars who had dis-

pleased him, and in a short time the poor man and all his family died, probably by poison. The congregations are not always very subordinate, and I saw a small room outside the church where a section of them had set up an opposition 'Mass,' because they declined to pay some impost which the Cattanar had made, and consequently were excommunicated. Another sign of this insubordination is, that there are churches belonging to a sect who are neither Syrians nor Roman Catholics, but Adullamites, who embrace all dissenters of either faith. I believe that the best book for information about the Syrian Church is Hough's *Christianity in India.* The first efforts of the C.M.S. were directed towards the reformation of this Syrian Church, and they have been very successful in bringing numbers of them to the Protestant faith. One difficulty which they have to contend with is, that although the Syrians do not professedly recognise 'caste,' yet they are a very exclusive body, regarding themselves quite as high born as the Nairs, and objecting strongly to 'communicate' with lower native Christians. However, we were very happy to hear that this feeling is diminishing; and that as regards intermarriage, which is the severest test of Christian principle among the natives, the people of Travancore are showing more enlightenment than the people of Tinnevelly. I think we have to show the greatest judgment and forbearance in this respect to them, when we recollect how strong the 'caste' feeling is among ourselves at home. Still,

the native Christians in India have much to learn,
when the feeling of caste remains so strong, that
sometimes two divisions of the same caste (and that
a low one) will refuse to intermarry.

"But I must not go on longer about the Syrians,
or I shall weary you. We spent three days very
pleasantly in Cottayam, seeing the institutions, ex-
amining the schools, and, on Sunday, attending
the services; and then we made an excursion to
some of Mr. Baker's hill stations, an account of
which will, I hope, make my next letter more
interesting than this."

"*Madras, Nov.* 20.—It will be a pleasant task for
this letter to try and recall my visit to the hill stations
in Mr. Baker's districts, and if I can make it half as
interesting to you as it was to me, then I shall feel
highly gratified.

"We started from Cottayam, in three bullock
bandies, one fine evening, and as the scenery would
have been lost altogether to me under the windowless
roof of the bandy, I walked half the distance of our
first night's stage, which was fourteen miles. Every
now and then we met parties of men with guns, belonging to the 'hunter caste,' whose trade is in wild beasts
and game. We came across tracks of various creatures,—elephants, leopards, deer, etc.,—but did not see
any, as they are chiefly about at night. There is a
certain thrill of pleasurable excitement (in me, I must
confess strongly developed) in being really among

the tigers and elephants. Not that there is any danger at all on those roads, for if one wants to encounter these animals, one must go after them in a systematic way, and make the cultivation of their acquaintance a regular science; but still there is a satisfaction in only seeing their tracks, and feeling for the first time in the ancestral domain of such a primitive and ancient race. It is in countries like Travancore that missionary anecdote depends for much of its sensational element.

" It is there that you hear of crocodiles swallowing little children, and a tiger in attendance to take vengeance on the crocodile. It is there that you hear of missionaries exchanging amenities with tigers and cobras, and living in a tree, because the elephant has taken possession of their houses below 'for the season.'

" Mr. Baker has been in the country long enough to have plenty of these stories to tell; and as he is a genuine naturalist, they lose none of their interest by his description. In walking along I observed several wild flowers of great beauty, which I had not previously met with even in India, but, after all, nothing to come near the violet for scent.

" I was glad to read, in a review of a book of travels in Java, and other islands, that the writer of the book, after many years of travel, gives the palm to old England for wild flowers, even over the tropics. I had a narrow escape in going over a bridge which had recently broken down, for the man with the lantern

was behind the bandy instead of in front, and there
was no other light except the flashing of fire-flies.

"The wild elephants are very mischievous on those
roads, both in breaking the wooden bridges and re-
moving mile-stones, to which they show a special
aversion. As the making of these bridges is often the
work of trained elephants, who have to bring the
materials and pile the stones, there is evidently a
lamentable misunderstanding between the wild and
the tame. We halted for the night at a little native
house which Mr. Baker has purchased, and enjoyed a
cup of tea, which was extemporised with astonishing
rapidity by an excellent travelling servant.

"Next day we reached Mundakayam, a village
which has a very interesting history. It was here
first that Mr. Baker came at the invitation of some
Arrians who wished to be taught Christianity. It is a
very lovely spot among the hills, as pretty a combina-
tion of mountain, forest, and river as I have seen south
of Madras. When Mr. Baker arrived, he found the
people delighted to see him, but there were not many
of them, and it appeared that the wild elephants were,
for the most part, the masters of the soil. I saw the
tree in which Mr. Baker used to sleep at night when
the elephants were about, and I saw other trees with
snug little houses in them (like great nests), which are
still used by the natives as 'sentry-boxes' to guard
against the depredators. They are generally in the
middle of a corn-field, and are occupied at night by
a man with a gun, who shoots at whatever he sees.

Mundakayam is situated in the bend of a river, at some height above it, so Mr. Baker set the people to work at making a barrier against the elephants on the side unprotected by the river, and then a colony was speedily established and security prevailed. Now the jungle is cleared in different directions, and large tracts are under cultivation. There is a nice little church, and within eight miles of the church 1000 native Christians, who have all come over to Christianity since that first visit of Mr. Baker. We walked over to see another congregation, three miles off. Our road was an 'elephant path.' The elephants are capital hands at making roads, and they are always very straight. The thickness of the jungle makes their help in this way doubly valuable. There is a large undergrowth of very thick grass, reeds and shrubs, corresponding to the hazel nut, and when ground is cleared for cultivation, it can only be done by setting fire to the forest, and then cutting down the hard charred trunks which refuse to consume. The worst of these jungle paths is the leeches which abound in the little water-courses in the woods, and fix eagerly upon the ankles and legs. I have found six or seven of them on me at a time, and had to stop and search half a dozen times in a walk before going on. The effects of their bite generally last a long time. They sometimes drop from the trees upon the passer by, and I was once invaded by them at night when sleeping out in a tent.

" On reaching Assapian, the little congregation

were soon called together, and we had a talk with
them, through Mr. Baker as interpreter. At prayers
an elephant outside rudely interrupted us by a tremendous 'trumpet.' When they see anything that
frightens them they make a noise as loud and shrill
as seven or eight trumpets and a violoncello together.

"Next day we walked to another village, whose
name I will not spell lest I make a mistake. We
passed through some very rich corn-fields, and Mr.
Baker pointed to a place which used to be the lair of
a tiger of great notoriety. That single tiger is said
to have killed no less than one hundred and seventy
of the unfortunate natives. At last he met one day
with a party armed with guns. He sprang upon
their leader and killed him, but the rest all fired
their guns, and then ran away as hard as they could.
Such was the terror inspired by this tiger, that it was
not till two days after that they returned to the spot
and found the tiger lying dead by his victim. A
little off the path we were shown some 'elephant pits.'
They are eighteen feet deep, and sufficiently wide for
the purpose. The top is concealed by boughs and
grass, and the elephant or tiger who falls into them
becomes an easy prey to the hunter. It is recorded
that once an incautious young missionary got trapped
in an elephant pit, but fortunately a brother missionary was at hand to pull him out, and he was hauled
up, a sadder and a wiser man. We had to cross
a river in a very shaky canoe (merely a hollowed
trunk), and then we came to the Arrian village we

sought. Like the other, it had a look of great prosperity, and the native house which we put up in for
the night was quite a study. It reminded me, in its
elaborate carving and finish, of a Maori house in
New Zealand. The Arrians make their houses like
cabinets, so that they can take them to pieces and
carry them away if they wish to move. They are all
made on the same plan, and are entirely of wood,
except the tiles, and I saw one which had been sold
by its owner for £150. He was a rich man, possessing
two elephants, and much timber, but he was just like
all the rest to look at, wearing no kind of turban, and
no cloth whatever over his shoulders. The history
of this village also is interesting.

" The natives, who formerly lived in another part,
being much persecuted by the petty Rajah of the district, emigrated by Mr. Baker's advice, and built their
village beyond the Rajah's territory. They found an
old heathen temple, and built a Christian church on
its site with its stones. In this village I observed a
curious relic of antiquity, an ancient Scythian vault,
consisting of a large flat stone, propped up by other
smaller ones, between which the bodies were placed.
These Arrians are a fine race, and differ from other
natives of India in being simple and truthful, which
is a virtue very rarely found.

" Our next day's walk was up the mountains to
a coffee-planter's bungalow. It was not *high* in
comparison with those hill stations in the Nilgíris,
where people go in search of health from Madras

every year, but it was high enough to feel cool, and
give an excuse for a fire in the evening ; the first fire
which I had seen since I left Australia two years
before. Here I spent five days walking all day among
the mountains, and laying in a stock of health for the
plains. I felt for the first time a sensation of English
vigour, and a freedom from those restrictions which
keep us indoors during the day, down in those miserable plains, and I wished that I could always live on
the hills, or rather that my *work* lay in higher lati-
tudes. The coffee-plant which is so extensively cultivated on the hills in South India, is very much like a
low holly bush, and the berries when ripe are red like
holly berries. It is difficult to say how many crops
it yields, because the picking of the berries is continually going on as they ripen, and on the same
bush half the berries will be ripe, and half unripe.
Coffee planters lead at least as isolated a life as missionaries do ; but they have the advantage of mountain air, and excellent sport with the rifle among
various kinds of deer and buffalo, which enlivens their
existence, and supplies them with excellent food.

"There is another class of people beside the
Arrians, among whom there has been rapid progress
lately in the spread of Christianity. They are called
'slaves,' and are the very lowest order of natives,
corresponding very closely to Pariahs. They were
formerly in a state of rigorous servitude to the richer
portion of the native community, but they have been
emancipated by Government, and their condition

very much improved in consequence.   However,
the laws of the caste seem stronger in Travancore
than even in Tinnevelly, and so wide is the gulf
between the slaves and the Nairs, that if a Nair
comes along the road he raises a cry to warn off
all his inferiors from his sacred presence, and the
'slave' has to run away into the jungle for fear of
a beating.   As I was coming down the ghât, I had
one of these slaves to carry my bag.   Happening
once to look round, I saw that the bag was in the
road and the slave nowhere.   As a man of high
caste passed at the same moment, I guessed the
reason, and called the slave out of his hiding-place.
The next time I met a high-caste man, seeing the
same thing likely to happen again, I told the slave
that he was on no account to run away, as he was
my servant for the time, and under my protection.
The high-caste man finding I was determined upon
the point, and not choosing to risk contamination
with the slave, quietly climbed up the rocks by the
side of the path, until I had passed, and descended
and resumed his journey.   Further on I met several
large companies of these poor people with their
wives and families on their way up to the hills for
the harvesting season, when they make large profits
as free labourers.   They all displayed a large array
of teeth at seeing Mr. Baker, and some told him that
they had been waiting two days in the hope of meeting him and getting his blessing before the harvest.
Most of them were Christians, and their Catechist ac-

companied them.   It is a very severe test of the reality
of Christian principle, when these degraded and
despised slaves are brought side by side with the exclusive and proud Syrians in the same congregation,
and invited to partake of the Lord's Supper together.   We can little understand or make allowance
for the keenness of their feeling in the matter.

"I will not extend this letter further, but shall
hope in my next to give some account of Trevandrum,
the capital of Travancore, where we had an interesting audience with a native prince, the ruler of the
country.   In taking leave of Cottayam, I felt much
refreshed by intercourse with Mr. and Mrs. Baker,
and the introduction to a new and most promising
mission-field.   One who has his lot cast entirely
among the heathen (as mine is), needs much the
stimulating influence of occasional contact with
Christians, both European and native, lest in per-
petually seeing the *worst* side of the native character,
he should forget that there is also a brighter aspect
to be looked for; and lest, in the absence of these
means of grace, which make our English Sunday so
dear to us, his own soul should grow parched, and
his faith and love fail.   There is, however, something
better than Christian intercourse, and that is the
prayers of Christian friends; and I would, therefore, earnestly request of you, and of other kind
friends who may read this letter, that while praying
for the extension of Christianity in Travancore, and
for the missionaries who labour there, you would

also remember those who are entirely engaged in preaching to the heathen, as yet with no apparent results."

"*Madras, Nov.* 29.—I must try and finish my 'say' about Travancore in this letter, or I shall weary you It has been a fertile subject of correspondence, and last week alone I dispatched twenty sheets of this size by post in various directions by way of awakening public interest.

"A letter of ten sheets in length started on its journey to Melbourne, where the Industrial Schools are continuing to take a most true interest in missions. They have collected among themselves and despatched to Tinnevelly not less than £60 in a single year for the education of native children. I really think this ought to be reported in the little green book, as a proof of what children may do. It is not one school, but several, which have raised this amount, still it is highly commendable.

"I am sorry to say that the interest shown by the English community who live in the centre of heathenism, is miserably small in comparison with this. I only wish that candidates for the Indian Civil Service were compelled to spend a term at the Islington College, or some other institution, where they might learn something of the necessity and advantage of promoting Christian Missions.

"But to go on with my story.

"On leaving Cottayam I had two other mission

stations to visit (by boat as usual), namely, Tiru-
wella and Mávelikara.

"The first is now occupied by a missionary named
Johnson, a nephew of Mr. Baker, who has lately
married a sister of one of our Madras missionaries.
I could only spend two nights with them, but I had
time to visit a Syrian priest, who lives about two
miles off in a very picturesque village. He showed
me his church, of which he may well be proud, for
it is a very fine and solid structure. The original
church was burnt down by the heathen, but the
Syrians were rather the gainers than otherwise, for
Government compelled the aggressors to refund a
large sum of money, which defrayed the expense of a
much finer church than the former. The priest is a
very intelligent man, and belongs to the Reforming
party. He is moreover, much more cultivated than
they usually are, and studies the Bible with a commentary, in Syriac, Malayalam and Tamil. He was
educated by a former missionary, and will, it is to be
hoped, in course of time bring his congregation over
to Protestantism. He has a little prophet's chamber,
with a bed and chair and table, adjoining the church,
in a kind of gallery. I forget whether I mentioned
in my former letters that we heard of a Syrian priest,
who, though not learned enough to preach to his
people himself, was sufficiently enlightened to employ
one of the lay members of his congregation, who
'had the gift' to do so! I observed that the Archbishop of Canterbury has been recently discussing the

question of lay help with some of his clergy, but I fear that this fact would not have helped him much in determining what is the proper sphere of laymen in church work.

"I must not linger upon Mávelikara, which was my next stage, because I was there only for one night. Mr. Maddox is the missionary there, and I was much pleased with his schools, in which he takes a great interest. The former missionary, Mr. Peet, who founded the station and built the church, is buried with his wife in the very prettily-situated churchyard close to the river. A missionary's tomb in the place of his labour is always an object of great interest to me, and I very much admired the simple inscription which he had written on his wife's tombstone, 'She lived for Christ. She died in Christ. She reigns with Christ.'

"It was a lovely moonlight night when we left Mávelikara, and as we shot along a rapid stream to the music of the oars between palm forests, whose feathery crests were kindled with the silvery light, I could not but linger long on the roof of the cabin beneath which my companion slumbered. Next morning at sunrise we reached Quilon, which is a military station, where the London Missionary Society has a settlement. The missionary, Mr. Wilkinson, was away, but his wife kindly received us for a few hours, and in the evening we got into our boat again. The rain came and dispelled all the charm of moonlight, and at twelve o'clock we were awakened to the conviction that the canal had come to an end. The reason of its refusing to proceed, we found to be a barrier of high ground which forms the spur of a very inconsiderate range of hills, which upset all the calculations of the engineer who made the canal. Leaving it for legislation to decide whether hills have any right to have spurs (especially on a rainy night), there was nothing for it but to turn out of our warm cabin into the mud and wet, and put our things on a bandy and cross the barrier with as good a grace as possible. It was about five miles broad, and then the canal resumed its course. I have since heard that Government is intending to make a tunnel through the barrier for the canal, and thus remove the interruption which now exists in the water communication.*

"We resumed our journey in a very different sort of boat. It looked, as it lay on the water, like a huge, long chrysalis, and we could see no boatman belonging to it. But after shouting awhile, a hole began to appear in the back of the chrysalis, and a man's head protruded. The hole was then sufficiently enlarged to receive our two selves and luggage, and then closed again to exclude rain, and we started. There was not room to sit up inside, but there was just room to arrange one's mattress (a never absent accompaniment to travel in South India), and lie upon it.

* The barrier has since been pierced, and a tunnel constructed. It is called the Wurkalay Tunnel, and is one of the finest engineering works in South India.

In the morning the chrysalis had expanded into a butterfly, with oars for legs and sails for wings.

"The canal broadened out into an occasional lake, and as I found that I knew much more about navigation than the boatman, I took the direction of sail and paddle, and we reached Trevandrum about ten A.M. Trevandrum is the capital of Travancore, and the seat of Government. Although ruled by a native Rajah, there is nothing in Trevandrum or Travancore to distinguish it from a province administered by a most enlightened European Government. Indeed, it is said, and said I believe with truth (according to my experience), that the respect shown to the English by natives in Travancore is greater than in the Queen's Indian dominions. There are fine roads in and around Trevandrum, and fine engineering and architectural works. These, of course, are all of British construction and design, for the Rajah is wise enough to employ English hands and brains in every department of his administration.

"He does not appear to spare expense, but does everything on a most liberal scale. The English community at Trevandrum is as large as in any other military station, and consists entirely of officers, schoolmasters, engineers, etc., in the Rajah's employ. We stayed three days with Mr. Bensley, who is the original master of a very large Government school. It started with a score or two of boys, and increased very rapidly, till it numbered upwards of 800. Then two Scotch 'Professors' were sent for, to take the upper divisions and Mr. Bensley retains about 500 boys of the lower. A large proportion of the lads are Brahmans and Nairs, and these are always the most apt for study, and the most covetous of *English* education. It is among these that the future rulers of the land are to be sought, and the Brahman will eagerly embrace every opportunity of getting power and pay, although he never contemplates the idea of wearing an English hat, or being anything else than a Brahman to the end of his days. It is remarkable that in this school the Bible is *allowed* to be taught by a heathen ruler, although forbidden in all our schools by a Christian Government. I am speaking, of course, of Government schools, where it is allowed only as a book of reference, and forms no part of the regular Government curriculum. The reason is because our Government are very much afraid of seeming in any way to make the knowledge of our religion *compulsory* with the people. There are no Christian boys in the Trevandrum school. Perhaps it would be too much to hope that any lad would have the courage to embrace Christianity in a Rajah's school, but still they are taught what Christianity is, and perhaps the knowledge may some day, by God's blessing, bear fruit.

"Mr. Fenn and I sought at once for the opportunity of an interview with the Rajah. A letter was sent to his Highness to request the favour, and a very courteous reply was returned, written in English, to say that he was in mourning for a relative, and therefore unable to see us for a few days. The following week, however, the interview was granted. The term of mourning had not quite expired, but as we were visitors to the place, an exception was made in our favour. We heard, incidentally, that this arrangement would be quite as convenient to his Highness, as it would save him an extra _bath_. He was ceremonially defiled by his period of mourning, which demanded certain ablutions at its expiration, and as these ablutions would also be entailed by the defilement of intercourse with Europeans, it would naturally be an economy of soap and water to see us at a time when the two baths could be combined.

"The interview was fixed for seven o'clock in the morning, and was punctually observed by us. The Rajah did not receive us in his own palace, but in a house called the Observatory, where he has state apartments for such receptions. We were introduced by Captain D., who holds a command in the Nair Brigade.

"His Highness came out from his room, and met us with great courtesy at the top of the staircase which formed the approach from without. He shook hands with us heartily, and then made us sit down in a very free and English way.

"The apartment was furnished in a thoroughly English fashion, with pier glasses and rosewood furniture and beautiful water-colour paintings, and everything showed the greatest taste. The Rajah is small and fat in person, with a quick, bright eye, but by no means a dignified mien. The dress in which he receives Europeans by no means does justice to himself, although intended as a compliment to them. It is a great pity that he should lay aside his handsome native robes and jewelled turban for a shabby-looking alpaca coat and white trousers, such as probably cost about 3s. 6d. at some marine store shop. And yet such is his pleasure. On his head was a little tinsel cap, such as is worn in India by little Muhamadan boys, and on his feet neither shoe nor stocking! He stammers a good deal in speaking English, and is very nervous, but evidently made a great effort to be agreeable, and to natives this art is always much easier than to Englishmen. After a few common-place remarks, he directed our attention to the beautiful views in every direction from his verandah, and pointed out the objects of interest. We should have been very glad of an opportunity of speaking to him upon the subject of religion, in which he shows his liberality by allowing the Bible to be taught in his school; but our interview was very short, and the nervousness which he showed made one very nervous in talking to him. It would have been much easier to introduce such a subject at a second interview than a first. Although a very enlightened man as to the interests of his country, and the advantages of European intercourse, he is in close subjection to the customs of his religion and the authority of the Brahmans. Being himself not a Brahman but a Nair (of inferior caste), he is ecclesiastically (so to speak) inferior to his Brahman subjects. He cannot even eat with them, and a curious illustration of this bondage is shown in the fact, that he is about to go through certain austerities and *fines*, from which Rajahs of his caste and position are never exempt. Part of these ceremonies consist in his being weighed first in gold and then in silver, then in copper, and the equivalent in cash being distributed among the Brahmans. Then he has to pass through a golden bull, sit on a golden lotus, etc., and after this he will be eligible to the dignity, not of *eating with* his Brahman subjects, but of *seeing them eat!*

"These ceremonies are supposed to take place at the end of seven years of rule, and as there is a tradition that Rajahs do not long survive the ordeal, the present Rajah is naturally anxious to defer the evil day as long as possible. I believe it is fixed for January next, and meanwhile the Brahmans are trying to get the Rajah made as *fat* as possible, that he may weigh the heavier!

"I have a good deal more to say about Trevandrum, as we stayed there about ten days; but the messenger is waiting to take my letter to the post, so that I fear I must inflict another letter upon you next week."

"*Tent, Dec.* 13.—I intended to finish my account of my late journey in Travancore last week, but I failed to do so for several reasons.

"I was requested by our good Bishop to examine

in Scripture, etc., the first five classes of the Military
Female Orphan Asylum, including about one hundred
girls and ten teachers. It took me two days to examine them all, and another day (nearly) to write my
report. Besides, I had also to examine in mathema-
tics the first class of a mission school for Muhamadan
boys, and between these two examinations my week
was almost entirely taken up. Then when Monday
came, which is the day of the departure of the mail,
I found employment enough for three brains such as
mine, and the same number of sets of limbs in the
necessary preparations for moving out of Madras to
my tent. Yesterday another labour was completed,
namely, my annual letter to the Home Committee,
being a summary of the year's proceedings, which
they always require. And now all the old pleasurable
sensations are returning with a recommencement of
the work which I consider my calling for the present,
—preaching the gospel to the heathen.

" It is with more than usual thankfulness and hope
that I now return to my tent, for the one great object
for which I have been striving and praying the last
two years has been attained, and we have a staff of
six young native catechists to help us in the work.
To my friend and brother Mr. David Fenn, this
addition is not very welcome, and I consider it a kind
concession to my weakness. His views of itinerating
missions are, I think, peculiar to himself, and can
only be carried out by himself. In a word, he thinks
that *preaching* is the object of the itinerator, not *con-*

version, and to this end he would endeavour to cover a very large tract of country, preaching from village to village only *once* at a time, and not returning to the same place more than once in the year.

" He would have no catechists, no centre of operations, and no converts to take charge of. My own views on the subject, so far as my short experience goes, have not the advantage of novelty or originality, but are much the same as those of the majority of South Indian missionaries.

" I think when a tract of country is to be evangelised, the first thing is to get some thoroughly efficient native agents to assist the missionary in his preachings, and then to look about at once for a centre where schools may be commenced, a congregation found, and a church and bungalow built. Then I think every effort should be directed towards the conversion of individual heathens, and until this is done I think the missionary should remain if possible entirely in his tent. Even when the centre has grown into a flourishing mission station, I think that every missionary ought to be in his tent among the heathen for several months in the year, and this, I think, the Tinnevelly missionaries are apt rather to neglect, although the American missionaries at Vellore and Arcot carry out this principle very thoroughly. They have a large body of native Christians who have been gathered in, but they spend five months of the year in their tents among the heathen.

" However, I must not go on theorising, or I shall

be tempted into a long digression. I have only said thus much to prove how widely different two views of the same department of mission work may be, and how little these differences of opinion may interfere with the peace and fellowship of two missionaries living together in tents. I shall have another opportunity of telling you more about our new acquisitions, as well about several other new features of our itineration. Now, to return to Trevandrum.

"There is a small congregation of the London Missionary Society which we visited, but the most interesting feature of mission work there comes under the head of Zenana missions, and is carried on by a lady, Miss Blandford.

"Miss Blandford belongs, I think, to a society with a very long name,* but she considers herself connected with the C.M.S. Her school numbers under thirty pupils, who are not boarders, but they are the children of very respectable parents, all high caste, so they are very well dressed ; and the arrangements are all so good that it looks very like a boarding school. They are taught English, and worsted work of every variety of pattern, and music, beside the ordinary branches of education. Some of them are very nice-looking, and the richer ones wear a great many jewels. Of these the earrings peculiar to natives of Travancore astonished me most. They are not rings at all, but large gilded ornaments of the shape and

* The Indian Female Normal School and Instruction Society. She now belongs to the Church of England Zenana Missionary Society.

size of a small door handle.   In order to insert them,
the ear has to be distended into an aperture corresponding to that of the handle of an ordinary milk
jug, and this is effected by the cruel process of sus-
pending four or five heavy leaden rings in the ear of
the child when almost an infant.   It quite moves one
with compassion to see the little girls of Travancore
going about with their heavy rings, which drag down
the lobe of the ear and make them look as though
they were undergoing a penal sentence.   Perhaps,
however, *they* would be equally astonished at some
of our English fashions, such as that of high-heeled
boots, said to be in vogue just now among English
ladies.

"Miss Blandford's work is by no means confined to
her school.   She visits all the principal native ladies
of Trevandrum, from the Rajah's wife downwards—
or rather from the Ranee downwards, for according to
the native law the Rajah's wife is a mere private lady,
and the mother of the future Rajah happens to be an
adopted member of a collateral line.   The law of succession in Travancore is very difficult to understand,
and I should be sorry to attempt to pass an examination in it, although I have often had it explained to
me after a fashion.   Suffice it to say that the *Rajah's*
sons are not his successors, but his *sister's* sons, and
if there are none, then another lady has to be adopted
as the Rani, or mother of the future Rajah.   This is
only, however, one part of it, for the Rani must have
a *daughter* to make the succession legitimate.   There

are now two Ranis. One of them had a daughter not long ago, which caused immense rejoicing in the court, but the latest news was that the infant died, so there was corresponding tribulation and woe. The *next* heir is called the first prince; an agreeable youth, whom we met at an evening party, but it is to secure the succession *after* him that all this anxiety is manifested. At the Rajah's death, his sons are turned out of the palace like so many obscure individuals, and have to live as they can.

"Miss Blandford is received by those ladies with the greatest affection, and several of them have been taught by her reading and writing, and ornamental work. Some of their prejudices have been broken down. They drive about in carriages, which they never used to do; and though they still refuse to see European gentlemen, yet exceptions have been made in several instances, and one of our missionaries has been favoured with an interview with the two Ranees, who converse fluently in English. This same missionary had a portrait of the Rajah presented to him by one of the family, who executed it himself. It is a miniature on ivory, and is so accurate and so finished, that it looks like a coloured photograph of the highest class. It is so very rare to find cultivation of the fine arts among the natives, that one is the more astonished at this portrait. In Miss Blandford's school there are no girls as yet who have embraced Christianity, but there seems to be a growing desire among them to learn our religion; and their Bible lessons interest them much. The school is mainly supported, I believe, by Government grant, and this is of course a hindrance.

"The open profession of Christianity by any girl, would be a matter of great anxiety, as it might lead to the withdrawal of all the other scholars, but of course the conversion of a single child would be worth any sacrifice, and it often happens (as in the case of Mr. Noble's school) that although the scholars may be withdrawn for a time, they return again, and the Lord does not suffer the enemy to prevail.

"Miss Blandford has just welcomed an assistant in her work, a Miss Dalton, the daughter of an English clergyman, who has lately arrived from home.

"One of the duties of a visitor to Trevandrum is to call on the Diwán, the Rajah's prime minister, and this duty Mr. Fenn and I did not neglect. This gentleman is a Brahman of considerable polish and prepossessing exterior, and our Government has not failed to recognise his ability and prominence, by making him a K.C.S.I., with the title of Sir Madava Rao.

"We were received by the Diwán in a bungalow, furnished according to every rule of English luxury and taste. He is a very agreeable man to talk to, and exceedingly popular among the English residents, especially the ladies. He showed us a book, which he told us that the ladies of his family 'devoured' with the greatest interest. It was a description by a native, in Mahrati, of English scenes, manners, and customs, properly illustrated and beautifully printed, and bound. The author was evidently an eye-witness of the things he described, but his illustrations were often borrowed from other books; especially from a book which I have seen, descriptive of the various ways of obtaining a livelihood in London. It was amusing to see accurate pictures of an English dinner party, Rotten Row, the English costermonger, and even the blind man of Portman Square, who begs with the help of a little dog, with basket in its mouth. With these were interspersed other subjects, such as the Mansion House, the Trosachs, and the best specimens of statuary, such as the 'Reading Girl,' by Magni, etc., etc. It is quite a new thing for a native of India to write a book of this kind. I heard lately of a novel, with a very good moral, being written by a native of Bengal, and it is to be hoped that educated natives will soon begin translating English standard works into their own language. In theology, this is being done by some of our native Christians. One of our native ministers is translating Trench's books on the parables and miracles into Tamil, and another is engaged on a commentary of the New Testament, based on Alford, Wordsworth, etc.

We were invited by the Diwán to a 'soiree' at his house one evening, but we were unable to go, as our departure prevented it. The invitation came in the most approved form, printed in English on a large card, with the Diwán's monogram above, and we heard afterwards that the soiree was attended by all the English residents of Trevandrum, and was highly successful in every respect. A good many specimens of native manufacture of the best kind in gold and silver and ivory were shown by the Diwán to his guests, and in all these the natives of Travancore are very skilful.

"I will now add only a little account of my visit to the southernmost mission station in India. It belongs to the London Missionary Society, and is called Nagercoil. We addressed a very interesting congregation in the native church, on the subject of 'Sinai and Palestine,' and paid a visit to one of the first Roman Catholic mission churches in India, built by no less a person than Xavier. Over the altar there is a glittering effigy of the builder, which does him but scant justice, for it is more like a Spanish hidalgo than a great missionary. About twelve miles from Nagercoil is Cape Comorin. We drove halfway in a bullock cart, and then ascended the last of a range of rocky hills, which commands a most striking view of the Cape and the whole south country. The day was very clear to seawards, and as the nearest land to the south was Australia, the sea-line was unbroken. To the east and west the shore trended away in a northerly direction, with the slightest fringe of foam, and in the foreground the eye rested on large forests of palmyra and cocoa-nut palm, with here and there a patch of bright red sand. It was pleasant to realise a gospel beacon on India's southernmost shore, and a chain of such beacons right away to the extreme

north at Peshawur, 2500 miles. We crossed another
range of hills, and then found ourselves in the familiar
scenes of Tinnevelly.

"Such a change it was,—from green, moist mountainous Travancore to dry, flat, thirsty Tinnevelly,—
and from a point where one can see both countries
at once, the contrast is most striking. We greeted
familiar faces, and revisited places dear to Mr. Fenn,
from many old associations, and then returned to
Madras, much refreshed in body and mind, not *least*
by the promise of as many catechists as we needed
for our work. We have been waiting in Madras till
the monsoon should be over, but at last we got tired
of waiting, and the result is, that we are getting rather
a 'ducking' in our tents. However, it is delightful
to be out again under any circumstances, and you
will, I am sure, congratulate us upon it."

CHAPTER VI.

THE PERSIAN FAMINE—ISPAHÁN, 1871-72.

FROM the digression of the last chapter, we now return to Gordon's own more immediate work and history. By the end of the year 1870 he was at home once more, only, however, to remain a short time. The Committee of the Church Missionary Society had accepted his offer, to join the Rev. T. V. French in his work at Lahore in the Punjab, and he was anxious to fulfil his promise without delay.

Believing, however, that the Persian language would be most useful to him in his new work, he resolved on travelling to India through Persia, and to spend some time in the latter country for the sake of learning the language. Accordingly, the autumn of 1871 again saw him setting his face eastwards. It so happened that this brought him into Persia just as the terrible famine, which occurred that year, was at its height. This naturally gives his letters and journals an unusual interest, as he was not merely a spectator of passing events, but an actor in them. He spent his time in company with the Church Missionary Society's Missionary, the Rev. Robert Bruce (now Dr. Bruce), in relieving, as far as the

means placed at their disposal would allow, the appalling distress which faced them on every side.   In
a circular letter, written to the children of Melbourne, Gordon gives an account of the first part
of his journey into Persia:—

"I have not time to tell you all about my journey,
and if I did it would tire you to read it, so I will pass
on at once to Persia.   I soon found that all that I
had heard about the difficulties of travelling in Persia
was quite true; there are no carriage roads in the
country, so when I left the Russian conveyance in
which I had travelled several hundred miles from
Tiflis, I had to mount a horse and begin my ride of
1200 miles through Persia; it was not at all like
riding through the Australian bush, for there was not
a tree to be seen, or any sign of life for days together,
except when a little village here and there came in
sight.   The horses were poor, half-starved animals,
sometimes almost ready to drop.   I hired three to
start with, one for myself, one for my luggage, and
one for the postilion; then when I got to a station
where others were to be had, I changed horses
and continued the journey.   In this way I reached
Tabreez, a large town on the way to Teheran; but
as there is nothing that would interest you about
Tabreez I will not stop there.   The ride to Teheran
is 400 miles, and by changing horses every fifteen or
twenty miles, and riding day and night, I got to Teheran in five days.   It was very tiring, as the horses
were bad. and could not go quickly, and sometimes the

mountain track was very slippery with ice and snow,
and my hair was stiff with icicles. Wherever you go
in Persia, the country always looks the same—wide,
barren plains, surrounded by high, barren mountains.
You ride across the plain, then over the mountain,
then down to another plain, and so on. As these
plains are 4000 feet above the sea, they are often
covered with snow in winter, and travellers lose their
way. It is necessary to start with a good supply of
food for the whole journey, as the post stations where
the horses are kept are often nothing more than
stables, with nothing to eat ; and if a traveller wishes
to be comfortable, he must take his bed with him,
as he will find nothing to lie upon—not a bed, chair,
table, or carpet. My bed is a bag, which I roll up
and carry on my horse, and when I get to the stable
I fill it with chopped straw, such as they feed the
horses with (for straw in this country is too valuable to give horses to lie upon; it is all chopped for
food!), and then I do not mind lying upon the
ground. I was very glad to reach Teheran in
safety, and there I found English people who made
me very comfortable."

After a very short stay in Teheran, he continued
his journey to Ispahan, in company with Mr. Bruce.
His letters and journals are quoted, as giving the
best possible description of the state of affairs.

"I am now," he says, in another circular letter
written on January 28, 1872, from Korood, " on my
journey from Teheran to Ispahan, and if there is any

travelling in the world which is more calculated than another to call up by contrast the comforts and associations of home and friends, I think it must be Persian travel in the depth of winter. . . . .

"I have been spending two days in one of the Persian *hotels*. The reason of my detention is, that I am weatherbound by a heavy fall of snow, which has closed a lofty mountain pass just in front. The greater part of the ride (270 miles) has been accomplished in three and a half days, but the worst part still remains, and reports are daily spreading in this little village of the danger of advancing. Two of the villagers have been lost in the snow, and several caravans have had to leave their burdens on the mountains and escape as best they could. My '*hotel*' is the best the village can afford. It consists of a single chamber or cell open-ing into a stable. Chair, table, carpet, or bedstead there is none. When I first came in certain *repairs* had to be made. The mud floor was scraped with a handful of twigs, which raised the dust in clouds. The orifice in the wall admitting light had to be stopped with stones and rags to keep out the cold, and a similar operation had to be performed in the roof, which gave an easy access to a heap of snow. Then a hole was dug in the centre of the floor as a stove, a few sticks were lighted, and for want of a chimney the door had to serve as a passage for volumes of smoke. To keep out the cold and let in the light is hopeless, so I sit over the fire on my travelling-rug, wrapped in my fur coat, with the door open to enable

me to read a book and see through the smoke, while
some water has frozen in a vessel at my side.   But I
am better off than my companion Mr. Bruce, for his
mind is filled with anxiety about his wife, who is
very ill at Ispahán, without a doctor to attend to
her, or a friend to advise her; and so he is most
keenly impatient of this delay, which keeps him
from her.   Hence we are resolved to press on at all
hazards, as soon as ever we can persuade any guides
to accompany us.

"Our day has not been uninterrupted by visitors
of a certain class—not the local aristocracy (for there
are none), but a throng of pale, shadowy forms, in
every stage of emaciation and rags, whose wail for
relief is a sound as familiar to the ear in every Persian village or city, as the cries of the hawker, the
dustman, and milkwoman, are to a resident in London.
And yet, a few years ago, if report be true, begging was almost unknown in Persia.   To meet the
wants of this starving crowd, I have happily a fund of
about £50, the greater part of which was given me by
Mr. Alison, at Teheran ; but the hopeless part of it
is, that this famine is of such gigantic and appalling
dimensions, that such sums of money are swallowed
up like a cup of water poured upon a burning desert,
without leaving a trace behind, and nothing but the
working of a daily miracle, such as the 'loaves and
fishes,' could at all alleviate the universal distress.

"Another difficulty is, that when you have given
a few pence to a starving man, you cannot be sure

that it will not be extracted from him by·some creditor, or the collector who has got information that charity has been dispensed. Even at our wretched halting-places on the road, I never could be sure that the poor wretches had not paid highly to the stable-keeper for the right of admittance to beg. And in a country where every office is sold, from the highest to the lowest, and every salary extorted by oppression, deceit, and fraud, it is probably beyond the mark to suppose that one-half of the funds raised for the support of the sufferers ever reaches the hands of the destitute. In the light of this great national corruption, which poisons the sources of prosperity, and gives a retrograde impulse to all social and moral improvement, one is not surprised to find Persia a wilderness, and half her towns and villages in ruins. And the lesson is one which was enforced of old by prophetic lips, 'Behold the Lord of Hosts doth take away the stay and the staff, the whole stay of bread and the whole staff of water ; and the people shall be oppressed every one by another, and every one by his neighbour.' 'The earth is defiled under the inhabitants thereof, because they have transgressed the laws, changed the ordinances, broken the everlasting covenant. Therefore hath the curse devoured the earth, and they that dwell therein are desolate. There is a crying in the streets ; all joy is darkened, the mirth of the land is gone. In the city is left desolation, and the gate is smitten with destruction.—Is. iii., xxiv."

The letter is continued by extracts from Gordon's Diary :—

"*Korood, January* 29.—Clear morning and all fair for a start. Invasion by a crowd of famishing people —one child of eight or ten, with limbs as lean as a crow's leg, and a horrible expression of suffering. Bruce did his best to make a selection of some of the worst in the throng for relief, but found it very difficult, and we could hardly force our way through the crowd without violence. Agreed with seven sturdy guides to escort us for high pay, but we had hardly started before they 'struck' for higher wages. Heard bells behind us, and saw a cafila (caravan) of mules on the same journey. Stopped to let the cafila advance, and they made a capital track for us through the snow, which was up to our stirrups on either side. Had a stiff pull up to the top of the Korood Pass, reminding me of Switzerland ; then a valley on the other side, dreary and deep, in which travellers are often lost, and where my horse fell twice, and could not recover his footing till I dismounted. Found walking no easy task. Took six hours to accomplish eight miles, and as snow began to fall, and it would be hopeless to reach the next station (twelve miles more) before night, resolved to put up at a 'house of refuge' on the way. Saw bales of goods lying in the snow, which the Cafila had abandoned and were come to retrieve. Arrived at the 'hospice,' and found nothing but bare walls for a night's shelter, in forty degrees of frost—a mere cow-house, at which an English cow would be indignant. On entering by a doorway without a door, Bruce stumbled into a pit in the floor, and nearly sprained his ankle. Took our four horses into the inner chamber, and kept the outer one for ourselves. Found a most providential supply of firewood in some old telegraph poles, without which we must have been frozen. . . . Had more trouble with the guides, who were led by a desperate ruffian, and extorted most of their pay by threats of violence. Apprehensive of a possible attack during the night, I took shots with my revolver at a mark in the corner of the chamber, to show we were prepared, and slept with it under my head."

"*Jan.* 30.—Rose at five, in much thankfulness for rest and quiet, and prepared to start. Fresh demands made by our guides and their ringleader, who seized our horses, barred the gate of the caravanserai, and refused to let us go unless they were satisfied. Bruce tried conciliation and firmness in vain. We forced open the gate and ordered the courier to bring up the horses; but, finding ourselves in a minority of two to nine, were obliged to compromise by paying all but the ringleader, on condition they would fulfil their contract, and escort us to the next station. Three only, however, remained with us. On reaching the next station, where an Englishman in charge of the telegraph resides, we lodged our complaint against the defaulters, who, if arrested, will be sent for punishment to Ispahán."

.   .   .   .

"*Jan.* 31.—Another weary day's march of forty or fifty miles through the snow, unbroken by incident, unrelieved by the sight of a single tenanted habitation, except the post station ; consisting only of stable and caravanserai. Some of these caravanserais have a most imposing appearance, and can be seen in the clear sky eight miles off. When you come up you find only the remnants of former grandeur, ruined walls, roofless chambers without a door or an occupant. Some of them are resorts of highway robbers, but at this cold season even robbers will have nothing to say to them.

" At 2 P.M., halted to rest our horses, and met some of Bruce's native friends, who had come out to escort him. At 5 P.M., the city of Ispahán came in sight, beautifully set off by snow mountains and the rosy touch of the setting sun. Two hours more, through streets and bazaars, brought us to the Armenian suburb of Julfa, where B. resides. Found Mrs. Bruce in a low and weak state, but happily free from fever."

"*Feb.* 3.—. . . To a mind not wholly callous to the claims of suffering humanity, it is a terrible thing to witness daily evidence of distress which it cannot relieve ; to see men, women, and children lying down to die in the snow and frost, with hardly a gar-

ment to cover them; or to see a mother mourning
over her dead child, which she is unable to bury;
or a son over his father; while the haggard expression and bony limbs show that it is only a question of
days or hours how soon that mother or son will lay
down the burden of life, and become themselves the
prey of the raven and the jackal, and yet this is no
fiction but a fact, which I have daily witnessed.

"In the streets and bazaars of Teheran, within
sight of the baker's shop and the merchants' stores,
at the doors of the wealthy, and in the pathway of
the proud rulers of the land, the helpless victims of
starvation, and, in many instances, of oppression,
extortion, and misgovernment, are perishing like dogs,
and being flung into a nameless grave. It was stated
officially by the governor's secretary, that in one
night alone in that city, which is but four miles round,
there were 300 deaths from cold and want. Had the
evil been a little less palpable and glaring, it is certain that it would have been concealed altogether by
the Persian Government, as it was disowned at first
by their minister in London. But now that the eyes
of all Europe are opened to the fact, through the
medium of the English telegraph and press, now
that subscriptions have flowed in from London, and
a local relief committee is being organised, the king
and his government are forced to take action. The
stern will, which no amount of human misery could
have moved, has been bent by the force of English
public opinion, and some of the coffers of Persian

THE SHAH'S PALACE AT TEHERAN.

avarice have been unlocked. . . . Poorhouses have
been opened, into which some of the starving crowd
are forced by the police, who occasionally parade the
streets with sticks and cords to compel the refractory.
Once incarcerated in these penitentiaries, they are
not allowed either to escape or to die, but the reluct-
ance with which they are conducted there shows that
they would prefer the latter alternative. They evidently consider Persian relief as a species of penal
servitude, and it is well known that the money entrusted to subordinates for their support diminishes
rapidly by misappropriation.

.   .   .   .

" The severity of this season (which is said to be
an exceptional one) proves fatal to thousands of the
homeless and destitute, who might otherwise struggle
through to the spring. The morning of the day I
arrived in Julfa the thermometer (Fahrenheit) had
stood at eleven degrees below zero, *i.e.*, forty-three
degrees of frost, and it was probably much colder in
the open country.

" In the earlier part of our journey between Teheran and Kashan, we counted no less than seven corpses
by the roadside, who had sunk in the way from ex-
haustion and cold. Some were partially destroyed
by birds and beasts of prey. Others, more recently
dead, had been stripped by passers-by, and then partially covered by falling snow. Some were ghastly in
death, with pinched faces and skeleton limbs.

.   .   .   .

"We were constantly coming upon bones of one sort or another,—the camel, the mule, or the horse; while here and there you might see by day the group of vultures or ravens, or by night a wolf, a jackal, or fox feasting upon a recently fallen carcase.

"But the most painful sight was to see poor travellers struggling along on foot, having left some famine-stricken village, buoyed up with the hope of improving their condition at another, which they were destined never to reach.

". . . We had hardly proceeded a mile further through the snow, which was lying deep beneath and falling thickly above, when we saw something in the way, which looked like a bundle that someone had dropped. At first it showed no sign of life, but upon our calling it moved, and we found under a piece of sacking a poor, emaciated boy at the point of death, lying down to sleep his last sleep. We gave him a little brandy and a piece of bread, but he could neither masticate nor articulate, nor stand for feebleness. He staggered a step, and then fell to rise no more. The consciousness of pain seemed to be past with the consciousness of things around him, and the vital spark just flickered for a moment, to drop into the socket and expire. A little further and we met another youth in a hardly less pitiable condition, trying almost hopelessly to reach the post-station before nightfall. Upon our giving him a little assistance, he said that the only food he had tasted was part of the carcase of a donkey. There is something affecting in the resigned way in which these people meet their fate. It may be called fatalism, and is doubtless a part of the Muhamadan creed ; still it is all done in the name of God. There is no more frequent expression upon their lips than ' Insh 'allah,' ' if God will.' When they bid you enter their house, even when they hand you a cup of tea, they say ' Bism 'illah,' ' In the name of God.'

" Upon one occasion, when thousands of starving people assembled at Ispahán under the impression that Mr. Bruce was possessed of unlimited powers to help them, a few words of explanation were sufficient to disperse the crowd. They merely said, ' Be it so ; you are better to us than our own people' (governors), and quietly went home to starve.

" It is no doubt the case that this spirit of resignation is mixed up with a great deal of laziness and apathy, which is one of the national characteristics of the Persians. As a Persian captain in the Black Sea remarked to me, of the cause of the failure of the crops and the famine, ' Vous savez, Monsieur, que les Persans sont bons pour dormir, pour mentir, pour voler, mais pas bons pour travailler.' Still it is the power of the mullahs (or priesthood) and misgovernment that are the real curses of Persia. Many in straitened circumstances adopt the language of the steward in the parable, ' I cannot dig, to beg I am ashamed,' and then pursue the same unscrupulous course.

" Others take to the trade of highway robbery, and

reports are rife almost daily of this kind of violence
in roads which were formerly so secure that people
could travel unarmed. One night, as Mr. Bruce and
I were quietly riding along, we suddenly came upon
twelve or fifteen men sitting together in a hollow of
the road, evidently for no good purpose. We felt for
our revolvers, and asked them what they were doing?
'Watching the crops,' was their reply, but the postilion
who was with us affirmed that they were robbers.
They evidently did not think us worth attacking; but
we heard on our arrival at the next post-station, that
a cafila of mules had been attacked and two loads
of rice were carried off, thus proving that our friends
were at anyrate 'watching for crops' to some purpose.

"*Feb.* 25.—I am now engaged in a work which is
new to me, although past experience of parochial
work in London proves very useful in its discharge.
My duties are those of relieving officer, doctor, pur-
veyor, poorhouse guardian and inspector, outfitter,
and undertaker to a community of eight hundred
poor Armenians from the district of Feridun. As I
go my rounds among them, morning and evening, I
often long to be their pastor also, but, unfortunately,
I do not know a word of Armenian; and at present
my knowledge of Persian, which is the only medium
of communication with the servants employed to take
care of them, is very defective. They are a very illi-
terate set of mountaineers, and therefore the distribution of Bibles and tracts is useless. It is painful to

see them dying, as many have died, and to be able
only to relieve the body without a word of comfort to
the soul.   I am daily trying to devise some means
for their instruction.   My first effort was to establish
a hospital for the sick, and improve their general condition.   But even physical relief is very difficult, for
there is no European doctor here, and those of the
natives who profess to be doctors are all utterly
ignorant.   The one whom I employ cannot even tell
me what their complaints are, and if I give him
medicine for them he does not use it, so I am obliged
just to make him a medium of inquiry, asking questions in Persian, which he translates into Armenian,
and administering with my own hand such simple
remedies as I have access to.   There is a very small
stock of medicines in the place, and the only useful
ones which I can obtain are rhubarb and opium ; but
I use largely a decoction of cinnamon and ginger,
which, with sugar, makes an excellent tea, and the
natives are very fond of it.   This I serve out, with
bread, to my seventy patients morning and evening,
and soup in the middle of the day.   Yesterday I had
the greatest difficulty in making them take the doses
of rhubarb which were necessary, and a few were so
refractory that force had to be used.   Fortunately I
had no surgical operations to perform, for I doubt
whether I could muster any better instruments than
a carving-knife for amputation, and a pair of tongs
for the extraction of teeth.   However, I do my best
to relieve Mr. Bruce of a department of work which

he could not possibly manage in addition to his already overcharged list of duties.

"It is difficult to believe that in Julfa, which is the Armenian quarter of Ispahán, with a population of 2700 Christians, there is a bishop, twenty-two priests, and sixteen nuns, for they seem to take no interest whatever in the people, whose spiritual charge they have, and unless I go and call upon them, I see nothing of them. It is true they are poor and without funds, but they might be very useful in the case of the sick if they chose.

"The snow has greatly abated under a genial sun and those of the Feridunis who have left families in their native villages are now able to return to them. I have been paying off about a hundred, and making an allowance for their domestic claims when on a reasonable scale. As personal security, however, is not possible, I am obliged to take them at their word, except in a few cases; as, for instance, when one man claimed twenty-four 'hopefuls' of his own in a distant village, others eighteen, seventeen, etc. In such cases the 'family' generally means uncle, brothers, nephews, and cousins twice and three times removed! Altogether, they got a sum amounting to £81, 10s., which includes expenses for a journey of four days, and the balance to start with till they get work, such as the spring generally brings.

"In the course of a few weeks I hope to start off the rest on their journey home, and very thankful I shall be when they go, for they now occupy my whole time. They are scattered about in seventy-five different houses, which is a parish of itself, and I have not the advantage of district visitors to manage clothing clubs, soup kitchens, etc.; nor can I trust one single Armenian or Persian servant to do anything except under my own eye. I have discovered gross frauds in the banking department, and when I know that fraud and oppression enter largely into every department of the social and religious system in Persia, I cannot help regarding this famine as a national chastisement. It is against the very same sins that the Prophet Amos was sent to denounce judgment, and his language (chap. viii. 4-11) is strikingly applicable to Persia, 'Hear this, O ye that swallow up the needy, even to make the poor of the land to fail, saying, "When will the new moon be gone, that we may sell corn, and the Sabbath, that we may set forth wheat, making the ephah small, and the shekel great, and falsifying the balances by deceit, that we may buy the poor for silver, and the needy for a pair of shoes, yea, and sell the refuse of the wheat?" 'Shall not the land tremble for this, and everyone mourn that dwelleth therein?'

"From many of the towns and villages of Persia there is a cry like the cry of Egypt, on the night of the Exodus, not a house where there is not one dead. What a bright prospect might open for Persia, if her repentance were like the repentance of Nineveh, at the preaching of Jonah!"

.   .   .   .

"*Feb.* 27.— I have to-day been giving a feast to about seven hundred Feridunis. It was not much, being only bread, rice and salt, boiled with a little meat, but it rejoiced many, whose only diet is three cakes of bread a day. The daily allowance of bread costs only 2d. a head, even in this famine season. The rice was ½d. a head more, and the meat, etc., was the relics of soup boiled for the sick, so that it was altogether a very economical feast. It was some difficulty to get them to sit down in rows, as they do not at all understand arrangement, but we had fortunately some long walls to make them sit against, and a fair staff of helpers to keep order. It reminded me much of an English school treat, such as might be assembled in some of the raggedest districts of London, but they were much more quiet than a set of hungry London lads would be. It was touching to see them contented and grateful for so frugal a repast. As I stood at the door by which they went out, taking a list of them, many kissed my hand as they passed, and made a profound and not ungraceful bow. The women wear a peculiar and very quaint head-dress, not unlike a lancer's helmet, over which they have a cloth which serves as a veil, and is tied over the mouth, in token perhaps of their control over the 'unruly member,' in which they differ from some of their sex. I seldom hear them speak above a whisper, and this rule holds especially in the presence of their husbands. The Armenian women generally wear a long white cloth which covers them from head to foot, and distinguishes them from the Persian women, whose cloth is dark blue."

"*Feb.* 28.—I have this morning been engaged in distributing clothes to about sixty applicants. It is no easy thing to keep a list of female articles of attire here, as they are remarkable for their variety, and yet do not come under the ordinary names of bonnets, shawls, aprons and gowns. In regulating the accounts, whether for food or clothing, I take pains to impress upon my agents the responsibility of stewardship in the expenditure of public money. They seem to think that minuteness and accuracy in the accounting for large sums is quite unnecessary, and that wholesale prices should be on the same scale as retail. We have been well supplied with funds at Ispahán, in proportion to what has been subscribed for other parts of Persia, in consequence of Mr. Bruce's urgent appeals to England and India, and his diligence in affording information as to how the money is spent; but the difficulty of preventing imposition would sadly perplex the cleverest relief officer in London. My chief objection to the plan hitherto pursued is, that the vast majority of Persian applicants for relief are women, who all wear exactly the same dress, and are so completely muffled up in their veils that recognition is impossible. In the case of the *men*, you can always see their faces, and can generally judge by the expression and features whether they are really starving. The expression and appearance

are the only index, for it is quite hopeless to attempt
to find out about a man's circumstances in a large
Muhamadan city where no one speaks the truth.
One rule, therefore, which I should make is to give
relief to none but the male members of a family
whom I could recognise again, unless the ladies chose
to unveil, which they often do when in great straits of
poverty.

"Mr. Bruce takes care to give no relief except by
ticket, and always to give it with his own hand ; for
nothing is easier than for the same woman to come
(closely veiled) several times in the week, each time
with a different name, and the claims (of course) of a
large family, and then on the day of relief to make a
series of calls, and obtain a large sum of money, to
the exclusion of more deserving cases. I have no
doubt that imposition in this way has been practised
on a large scale, although detection has followed in
comparatively few instances. Another plan which I
hope we shall be able to carry out by degrees is, to
give no relief at the door of the house, but to assemble
all the poorest of the people once a month for the ap-
portionment of their claims in the districts where they
reside. It is much easier to make inquiry into their
circumstances on the spot, and to do them justice.

"When they are allowed to come in crowds to
the house at odd times, as they do at present, much
time is lost, and much indiscriminate charity bestowed.
We found the benefit of this plan in dealing with the
Jews, of whom there are about nine hundred on Mr.

Bruce's list, most of them in a very destitute condition. When we went to Ispahán on their last monthly pay-day, we found that sixty had died of their small community in two months, in spite of relief. They were all arranged according to their families in a large court or walled garden, so that when we came, we had nothing to do but call over their names and give them the money, which was ready tied up in bags, according to the number of their households. In this way we paid off the nine hundred in three hours. It was a heart-stirring sight to see their poverty. They sat in rows on the ground, which was cleared for the occasion by the snow being heaped up in great banks, but the mud was so sticky that I was nearly rooted where I stood to give the money. By the time we had done, a crowd of Persian beggars had collected, who seized our clothes and our horses' bridles, and even threw themselves under our horses' feet, and it was all we could do to get away. This scene is always repeated whenever relief is given. Yesterday, on going to a neighbouring village for the purpose, a crowd collected outside the court where we had assembled the beggars, and as we had not our horses, we were obliged to steal out by a side door, run down several back streets, and emerge from the opposite end of the place.

 "It is often most difficult to get in and out of Mr. Bruce's house here even on ordinary days, and whenever I go about, I take a servant with me to clear the way. On two occasions, when a scramble took place

for food and money given from a rich man's door in
Ispahán, several people were killed by being trodden
to death.

"Our Committee of Relief in Julfa consists of four
persons, representing the entire 'Society' of the place.
They are Mr. Bruce, Mr. Preece, — a younger man
than ourselves, who is in charge of the telegraph,—
Mr. Aganon, the head of the Armenians, and agent
for our Government, and myself. We meet every
Saturday for the transaction of business, and accounts
are made up once a fortnight.

"These accounts do not enable me yet to give an
accurate statement of the number relieved and the
sums expended, but I hope we shall get them into
order, and publish a little report. As far as I can
ascertain, about £5120 has been spent altogether, and
there is a good balance in hand. At present there
are between three thousand and four thousand Persians on the relief list, about one thousand or one
thousand five hundred Armenians, and nine hundred
Jews. A large sum of money has been raised in Calcutta by the energetic efforts of Colonel Haig, of the
C.M.S. Corresponding Committee, and about £1000
has come from Germany. The Persians themselves
have done nothing as yet for Ispahán, but at Teheran
and Shiraz they have of late awakened to the necessity of action."

CHAPTER VII.

IT was impossible for Gordon, employed as we have seen him in the last chapter, to carry out his original intention of reaching the Punjab early in the year. He therefore resolved to stay in Persia for the summer, and to proceed to India in the fall of the year, since it is unadvisable, if it can possibly be avoided, for a new arrival to land in that country just as the very great heat of summer has set in.

It has been stated that Gordon's primary object in visiting Persia at all was the acquisition of the Persian language. While, staying at Julfa, however, he found it impossible not to give up the whole of his time to the relief of distress. Accordingly he determined upon leaving his quarters there, and going for a time to Shiraz, in order to have more leisure for the prosecution of his object. He accordingly writes :—

"I therefore wound up my accounts for the Feridunis, a large number of whom I was able to discharge with a sufficient sum of money for their families. Just before I started, I heard that these unfortunate men had been attacked by some Persians on their way back to their villages, and robbed of all their money, to the amount of some £78. I fear that small redress will be obtained from the Persian authorities.

"The road from Ispahán to Shiraz was not very safe at the time when I started, and it was necessary to take an armed escort part of the way, and to be well armed myself. It was reported that a body of one hundred and fifty Baktiaris (a marauding tribe of nomads) was in possession of a mountain pass which had to be crossed, and that they were plundering every cafila and caravan that passed. Sufficient evidence of the truth of these reports met me as I advanced. Very few cafilas were bold enough to undertake the journey, and those which were to be seen were always attended by men with long guns and pistols."

However, the journey was accomplished in safety, partly owing to the fact that he fell in with Captain Pierson, the chief of the telegraph, who was travelling from Shiraz to Teheran. The guard of one hundred horsemen that had accompanied him was now returning to Shiraz in advance of Gordon, and so the road was clear. The description of the approach to Shiraz will be interesting to many readers. It proves what Gordon says, and what every one who knows anything of the East will always maintain, viz., that the outside of a town is far superior to the inside, and that a little "distance lends enchantment to the scene."

" The first view of Shiraz through a gap in the
mountains is very striking. It looks like a beautiful
mosaic framed in the rocks. There is a line of tall
dark cypresses in the foreground, over which rise the
walls of the fortress, surmounted by two pear-shaped
cupolas encased in a bright green and blue enamel,
which shines in the sun like turquoise. The Persians
are very fond of colour, and they paint all over the
gateways of their cities, the front of their houses, and
the walls of their rooms, with designs of more or less
taste. They are fond of decorating their buildings
with portraits of their kings and courtiers, as well as
with roses, birds, etc.; and though these drawings
often verge on the ludicrous, yet when they take
pains they show considerable skill in the art. Their
architecture is monotonous and generally flimsy and
gingerbread ; and when (as a natural consequence) it
crumbles into decay, they take no trouble to restore
it. Their streets are narrow and filthy.

"The chief attractions of Shiraz are its gardens.
These gardens are sometimes attached to private
houses in the city, but more frequently they are outside the walls. They are enclosed and entered by
doors, but open to the public at all hours. In this
respect the Persians are very good-natured. There
are no notices to visitors posted up (as in our public
gardens at home) 'not to pluck the flowers,' partly,
I suppose, because the Persians (although great
thieves) recognise an obligation to 'behave themselves ' in a garden, partly because, from the nature

of the gardens, even if they did trespass a little, they
would do no great harm. The fact is, our ideas of
gardening, as of most other things, are very considerably in advance of theirs. The Persian garden is
monotonous and formal in the extreme. It is utterly
neglected as far as weeds are concerned, and they
have little taste and no knowledge in the arrangement or cultivation of flowers. Their chief object is
to keep it well supplied with water, and for this purpose a gardener is employed. The best that can be
said is, that nature is allowed to have her own way
when once the trees and flowers have been planted.
You enter the door and proceed by a straight path
between an avenue of cypresses, or other trees, till
you reach a square tank of water, whence channels
are conducted to all parts of the garden. In the
middle of the tank there is a design for a fountain,
but I have not yet seen it play, and have some
doubts whether it can. Beyond the tank you ascend
steps to a large tea-house, profusely adorned with
mural paintings, and much frequented by loungers.
From the balconies and roof of the house there is
generally a pleasant view of Shiraz to be had. Their
houses were built by former benefactors of their race,
but are now fast falling to decay. The middle walk
is generally intersected by cross walks, which lead
again to parallel ends. The favourite flower of the
Persians is evidently the rose, but the season for
roses has not yet come. There are now wallflowers,
stocks, violets, narcissus, and hyacinths in bloom.

besides a beautiful variety of blossom on the fruit-bearing trees—peach, almond, apricot, etc., and the lilac is just coming out.   Between the walks there is a thicket of small trees in which the nightingales sing from morn till night.   Hence there is a great charm in these natural gardens, especially when contrasted with the stony desert, where it is uncultivated."

"*April* 11.—I found, when I arrived at Shiraz, that there was a great deal of distress from famine, and that great numbers had died during the winter for want of support.   Moreover, the Governor of Shiraz, who had levied a tax upon the rich people, and fed about 1200 beggars, had just died, and the acting governor was not inclined to trouble himself in the matter.   So these poor beggars were all cast off, and in my daily walks I am repeatedly solicited by them for bread.   I therefore lost no time in organising a committee for relief among the members of the tele-graph staff, and we telegraphed in every direction for funds.   I am happy to say that we have just got £1000 by telegraph from England, and £200 from India, so that we shall be able to do *something.*   The Jewish portion of the community have been well sup-plied by Sir M. Montefiore all through the winter ; but I fear they have been plundered (in proportion) by the Persians, whose tyranny over them is outrageous. They exact taxes, which no Persian is required to pay, from the Jews, and these taxes are enforced at compound interest by the subordinates who are em-

L

ployed to collect them.   Thus a tax which the king
imposes at, say £40, becomes £80 at the demand of
the governor, £160 to his deputy, and perhaps £1000
to the man who has the actual collecting of it.   In
addition to these grievances, the poor Jews suffer in
many ways in which they have no redress.   Any
Persian thinks himself at liberty to ill-treat a Jew ;
and I have seen even a boy strike a woman passing
by in the bazaar for no other reason than because she
was a Jewess.

" There are two orphanages which have been established in Shiraz for boys who have lost their parents
by the famine, and this is about all that has been
done in Shiraz by the English residents.   They support at present about 200 orphans ; and when I saw
these boys, who could neither read nor write, I felt
a natural desire that they should be taught these
elements of education ; but when I proposed it to the
committee, my 'motion' was 'lost,' on the plea that
the Persians would resent any interference in the way
of education !

" I called the other day on the Governor of Shiraz,
in the hope of getting him to do something for the
relief of his fellow-countrymen.   He received me very
civilly, but his face showed what he was, one of the
richest and most miserly of the inhabitants of Shiraz.
He said he had received a telegram from the Prime
Minister to raise funds for the poor (and this was
in consequence of a telegram we sent to the British
Legation at Teheran), but he had telegraphed back

for 'further instructions.' These 'further instructions' are never likely to come, and it is certain that nothing will be done by him.

"I have taken up my quarters in a Persian's house, and have a large garden all to myself. My little room serves as bedroom, sitting and dining-room, but I do not feel pressed for space, as my wants are small; and I might have other rooms, only I could not furnish them, as they are all empty. I believe I am in the very same house which Henry Martyn was in, as I heard to-day that my host is the grandson of his host Jaffier Ali Khan, and that the house has come down from father to son. This gives me quite an additional interest in the place."

Gordon remained through the whole of May in Shiraz, and afterwards returned once more to Ispahán. Writing to Mr. J. C. Parker in June, he is able to give a much better account of the condition of the people now that the summer had set in.

"We are breathing more freely now, for there has been a palpable abatement of distress the last week, owing to the fruit and harvest season having begun. The poor are no longer obliged to eat grass—they can get mulberries, apricots, and, in many instances, bread.

"The price of the latter has fallen to a quarter what it was three weeks ago, and is still going down."

Again, on July 15, he says:—

"We are now, thank God, out of the famine, which is a great relief. The harvest is abundant, bread

cheap, and work to be had, so that begging has most
sensibly diminished, and yesterday Mr. Bruce had
his final distribution of money to the Persians 'for
the season.' He has just made a 'return' of sums
received and distributed among Persians, Jews, and
Armenians during the past year, from which it appears that £14,500 is the sum total which has reached
and been expended by him from all sources, England,
India, and Germany. From the latter £1500 has
been sent, which is a most creditable thing, considering that it was raised by a German pastor. I
do not know how much money has been received at
Teheran and Bushire, but I know that Shiraz got
£1700 while I was there, and the whole Relief Fund
cannot have been less than £25,000, or perhaps
£30,000. When one considers that almost all of this
large amount has come from our own countrymen
who have no interest connected with Persia, one
cannot but thank God for so noble and disinterested
a spirit of generosity."

The famine had been such an all-engrossing subject, and so prominently brought before the English
public, that not much else was spoken of in Gordon's
letters. However, in the February of this same year,
one letter written from Ispahán had contained a
very interesting account of the difficulties with which
Mr. Bruce had to contend.

. . . .

"The law which makes it death to a Muhamadan to change his religion, holds here in full force,

and the Moollahs have such power, that the king and
all the rulers of Persia are afraid of them.

"It is for this reason, and because our North
Indian Missions are feeble for want of men, that our
Home Committee have decided that the time has not
yet come for the commencement of a Persian mission,
and they look upon Mr. Bruce's residence in Julfa as
temporary only.   .   ·.   •   •   •   •   •   •

. . . .

"To Mr. Bruce himself it seems otherwise, and he
not only feels a strong call to labour in Persia, but
thinks that is the duty of the Society to commence
at once a Persian mission.   He has had much encouragement, from the fact that a remarkable spirit
of inquiry into the truths of Christianity has been
awakened among some Persians in Ispahán of the
Bâbi sect, dissenters from the doctrines of Islam.
The first convert was before Mr. Bruce's time.   He
fled from Ispahán because he was condemned for
drinking a glass of wine in a European house, to
have his ears cut off and to pay a heavy fine.   He
was for some time under Roman Catholic teaching,
but came at last under the instruction of Dr. Koelle
at Constantinople, who baptized him by the name
Ibrahim.   I met him at Dr. Koelle's, and he gave me
a remittance to his family, who are here, and have
been baptized recently by Mr. Bruce.   The next inquirer, a friend of Ibrahim, was a man in mercantile
business, also a pupil of the Roman Catholic priest
in Julfa.   His name is Syad Hashem, and Mr. Bruce

being satisfied of his sincerity, baptized him privately. This man was the means of bringing others to Mr. Bruce, who has baptized privately about twelve Persians, including a Mujhtahid, or chief priest, who is now in Teheran. Most of these converts I have seen, but unfortunately I cannot yet converse in Persian, so I can form no idea of their views of Christianity from personal communication. They have none of them made an open confession of Christ, as they would endanger themselves thereby, and their visits to Mr. Bruce are generally Nicodemus like, as well as their meetings for discussion and prayer, in their own homes. On Sunday there are generally two or three of them at the service in this house, but they do not come in a body. I naturally feel a deep interest in these converts, and long to know more about them. It is a very difficult question to decide how far the objections, which our Home Committee, and all others whom I have discussed the subject with, entertain on Scriptural grounds to the practice of secret baptism, and a concealment of the confession of Christ before men, are removed or affected by the circumstances of the case. As far as my present observations go, I am not convinced that they are removed. Mr. Bruce thinks that the Ethiopian nobleman and the Philippian jailer are examples to prove that the Apostles baptized privately ; and he has been told that Judson's first converts in Burmah were also baptized in this way. Beyond these, there are no precedents that I have heard of in the history of Christian missions of the Protestant faith.   It is true that some of Robert Noble's Brahman converts were baptized in his own house ; but it was known all over Masulipatan, and violence immediately followed.   In the case of these Persian converts, the questions occur : 1*st.* What intention have they of declaring themselves the followers of Christ? if asked point blank whether they are or not by their neighbours.   2*nd.* In the meantime, what conformity do they practise to the customs of Muhamadan law and religious observance?"

Once more, in June, the same subject is referred to.

"The other day Mr. Bruce was visited by a 'Syad,' that is one of a class who wear turbans, and call themselves descendants of the 'Prophet,' and claim privileges denied to others.   This man had been reading the Gospel in Persian, and said he wished to become a Christian.   When asked if he believed in Christ, he said, 'Yes, the glory of Christ (as opposed to Muhamad) is that He bore our sins, and gives us His righteousness instead.' There are many like him, who would gladly put off the yoke of Muhamad, but dare not openly confess Christ for fear of their lives."

The account of Gordon's residence at Ispahán may be brought to an end with his description of a visit paid to royalty.

"We have lately had royalty in Ispahán.   One of the king's sons, called the 'Zillah Sultan,' was passing through on his way to Shiraz, where he is governor.   He occupied a large house or palace, nicely situated near the river, and Mr. Bruce and I called to pay our respects.   Eastern princes are not scrupulous about appearances, and nothing could be more dirty or neglected than the garden, or 'compound,' of the house, where he stayed for ten days.   A few hours' sweeping would have made it neat, but though he had no lack of servants, it did not seem to occur to him to give the order.   We called about 6.30 A.M. by appointment, and were kept waiting some time, during which tea and the never-failing Persian pipe or 'Calean' was offered us.   At last the prince emerged from an opposite room, and we followed him to his reception-room.   He is very young and boyish-looking—apparently not twenty,—but has a family of (I believe) six children, was Governor of Ispahán five years ago, and is now for the second time made Governor of Shiraz.   Our interview was formal and brief.   He amused me by saying that he supposed I should make an entry of my visit to him in my journal. When asked about the dangers of the road, he said that he had sent a large troop of cavalry in front to catch the thieves.   'But,' he added, ' Persia is not the only country where there are thieves.   I believe that in London you have your pockets picked sometimes, and your watch stolen."

CHAPTER VIII.

JOURNEY TO THE PUNJAB—FROM ISPAHÁN TO
BAGHDAD—BABYLONIA—THE PERSIAN GULF,
1872.

THE extract of the letter with which the last chapter
concluded was written from Ispahán in the middle
of July.   On August 12, 1872, Gordon again left
the latter city, and set his face towards Baghdad,
a journey of about 600 miles.   His progress was
slow, as he accompanied a *cafila* of two hundred
mules laden with tobacco, salt, and other produce of
the country.   He himself rode a horse, and put
his luggage on another.

Describing the march, he says :—" We started
after sunset, or at midnight, according to the length of
the march ; and when the morning came, and we
reached the village at which we were to stop, the
animals were unloaded and fed, and the day was
spent in rest.   Sometimes the march was very long
—twelve hours in the saddle at a stretch—and then
it was very difficult to keep awake.   The monotonous tread of the mules, and the chime of bells
which they carry round their necks, and the silence
and darkness, all tended to make one drowsy.   I

used to watch the constellations as they rose and
set, and wish that it was time for me to 'set' too.
Sometimes I drove away sleep by singing 'Pilgrims
of the Night,' or some other tune ; and sometimes,
when I felt myself nodding and falling off my horse,
I dismounted and walked."

In nine days Hamadan, the ancient Ecbatana,
was reached. It was at this time in a most desolate condition, no less than 20,000 persons it is said,
having perished in the neighbourhood during the
famine.

Here Gordon not only distributed some money,
which had been sent to him from England, but he
was also asked to undertake the disbursement of a
large sum which had been sent by Sir Moses Montefiore for the Jews in Hamadan.

The chief object of interest in this place seems to
be a building which the Jews point out as containing
the tombs of Mordecai and Esther.

Six days from Hamadan brought the party to
Karind, which is on the frontier of Novidistan.
"Here," he says, " I was delayed by the report that the
road was beset with robbers, and that soldiers must
be collected to disperse them. While this was being
done, I had a slight attack of fever, and thus I was
detained a fortnight at Karind. My medicine soon
failed me, and there was no doctor nor any European
in the place, but a young Koordish chief, with whom
I stayed, showed me the greatest attention and hospitality. He not only entertained me for a whole

fortnight, but supplied me with some medicine also, and I quite recovered through the goodness of God. I found the natives very civil and kind all along the road from Ispahán, during which I never saw a single European, and was quite alone, but I was able to talk to them in their own language. In several places I met those who were familiar with our Bible, having 'read the translation into Persian by Henry Martyn.'

"From Karind I had four days' journey to the Turkish frontier at Khanakin. The last night's march was an anxious one.

"The neighbourhood was said to be highly dangerous. A caravan had been attacked the night before, and fourteen mules, with their burdens, carried off by the Arabs. I therefore took an escort from the previous station, consisting of five Khoordish soldiers. It was about midnight when our journey was half over, and my escort came to a halt. I asked the reason. They said, 'It is dangerous here; we can't go on.' I said, 'If there were no danger I should not have taken you. Go on.' They said, 'You must give us twelve kraus (francs) if we do.' I said, 'I will give you nothing till we get to Khanakin' (the question of payment being entirely optional and conditional on the good behaviour of the escort). They then tried intimidation; but, finding that device fail, they left me and returned. I told my servant and the muleteer to go on, but the latter was so frightened, that he lay on the ground and refused. At last I coaxed him to proceed, but he was in the greatest terror till daylight, pointing to the spot where the previous night attack had occurred, and saying, 'There the two men were killed last night. What shall we do if the Arabs come?' Seeing a man alone in a dark valley, he sprang upon him with his gun, and I thought would have shot him ; but fortunately he did not, for the poor man turned out to be a solitary wayfarer, as much frightened as himself.

"At Khanakin I asked for the caravanserai, and was shown an ominous building with tents round it. 'What's that?' 'The quarantine: you must go there for *ten days !*' I said, 'Oh, but I am not infected, nor do I come from an infected city, and I am in a hurry to get to Baghdad.' 'No matter, it's the law for every one who comes across the frontier.' I found myself in a wretched stable, with no kind of accommodation except for horses. The place had not been cleaned since it was built. It consisted of a large court, with stalls all round. Not a room nor door did it possess. A few miserable people, who looked diseased and sickly, and a horse-dealer with fifty horses, were the occupants. Amongst these, swarms of flies and mosquitos revelled, and gusts of wind, blowing across heaps of refuse and filth, covered every hole and corner with dust, so that a seat could nowhere be found. I sent a letter of introduction to the governor of the town, and a telegram to the English Resident at Baghdad, to ask his help. The former despatched his secretary with proper assurances of 'attention and consideration,' and I was bidden to make myself com-

fortable, and ask for whatever I wanted!' I at once
demanded my release, but this was politely refused,
and I learnt what Turkish courtesy meant, for I saw
nothing more of the secretary, and received no more
assurances. A day passed in suspense and discom-
fort: it was Sunday, and although I had my usual
'service,' yet it was never under circumstances more
uncongenial. On Monday a telegram came from
Baghdad. To my great delight the quarantine was
suspended, and I was free once more. I quickly
ordered horses and started that night. As I passed
through the suburbs of Khanakin, I found that it was
not without its attractions, gardens of date-palms,
laden with such gorgeous clusters of gold and crimson
fruit as I had never seen before. It was just the
season for the fresh dates, and they were delicious.

"We encamped (or rather halted) at a place outside the walls, and waited for the coming morn. A
very large company of pilgrims to the holy shrine of
Kerbela, beyond Baghdad, rendezvoused in the open
plain, and made the air vocal with their noise. Many
of them came from the distant mountains and forests
of Lenkoran, on the south border of the Caspian ;
others from the highlands of Kurdistan and the plains
of Persia. The former were sturdy men, with the high
sheepskin cap, which I had become familiar with in
the Caucasus. They formed a troop about 150 strong,
and a better mounted troop of cavalry I never saw.
From the uniformity of their dress, arms, and accoutrements, I thought at first that they were soldiers,

but was told that they were *bonâ fide* pilgrims, and travelling at their own expense. I rode in their ranks for several nights, and amused myself with the study of them. They were no less curious about me. They spoke to me in some unknown tongue. I answered them in Persian, but they could not understand. At last they got an interpreter, and I found that they set me down for a Russian (the only species of European with whom they were acquainted), and believed that I must be a pilgrim, like themselves, to Kerbela, and therefore of course, an orthodox Muhamadan. England they had never heard of; India puzzled them as much; so I fear they did not carry away very distinct ideas of any nationality. I found that many of them were women, the wives of the party. They bestrode their horses with an erect and martial air, and seemed to think nothing of a nine hours' ride through the night; some of them even carried a child or an infant, and one had a musket slung across her back. Every night on mounting, and at intervals on the march, these cavaliers joined in a hymn, the refrain of which was very effective, breathed forth from a hundred deep bass chests.

.   .   .   .

"I reached a place called Sharaban one morning, and was congratulating myself that in two days more I should be in Baghdad. I waited for my servant, who was on a mule with my bedding and clothes, and wondered why he did not come up, as I had given him strict orders to keep up with me during the

night's march.   After two hours he arrived but empty
handed!   'Where are my things?' I inquired.   Then
came a long story of how he had fallen into the hands
of the robbers, who had attacked him with spears
and carried off everything that was in his charge."

On discovering this loss Gordon pressed on to
Baghdad to try and rouse the authorities to get back
his stolen property.   Colonel Herbert, the English
Resident at Baghdad, did what he could, but unfortunately he was just on the point of going away for
some weeks.   The result was that the Turks in his
absence would do nothing.   "Telegrams passed between the Pasha and the local authorities, and the latter
had the assurance to say that there was not a thief in
their neighbourhood!"

"Baghdad is a disappointing place, for two reasons,"
Gordon's narrative proceeds, "1_st_, You naturally hope
to see an ancient city, such as you read of at the time of
the Caliphs, or such as you imagine from the 'Arabian
Nights.'   But you find hardly any remains of the
ancient Baghdad, so completely has it been destroyed
by successive invaders.   The city was formerly built on
the west side of the Tigris, but as one now sees it, it is
all on the east side.   A small piece of the old river-wall,
an inscription on a gateway, and a venerable _khan_ are
almost all relics of ancient splendour.   The only thing
to remind you of the 'Arabian Nights' is the tomb
of their authoress, the Lady Zubeidah.   This tomb is
covered by a handsome old monument, which is fast
crumbling to decay.   If you reproach the gallant

Muhamadans with this shameful neglect, they say,
' What would you have ? It's a *woman's* tomb.' They
are careful enough of the tombs of their old sheikhs,
which present a marked contrast to that of the queen
of the great Haroun Al Raschid. An enthusiastic
American was going to repair Zubeidah's tomb at his
own expense, but was dissuaded by the intimation,
that if he did the Muhamadans would certainly pull
it down ! The second source of disappointment in a
visit to Baghdad is, that there never was a time when
the city was at so low an ebb as the present. It is
suffering from an irremediable disease, the blight of
Turkish government, and will only sink lower and
lower. The history of its decline is melancholy, but
instructive. Founded in A.D. 762, it flourished for 500
years under the Caliphs, till 1257, when it was stormed
and sacked by Halaku and his Tartar hordes, and its
streets deluged with the blood of 160,000 inhabitants.
In A.D. 1400, it was again taken by Tamerlane, who
raised a trophy of 90,000 human heads of its principal
men outside the gate. In 1508, it was invaded by
Shah Ismael Sufi, and fell into the hands of the
Persians. In 1534 Suleiman wrested it from the
Persians, and made it a Turkish province. Subsequently Shah Abbas recovered it for the Persians, but
they finally lost it in 1638, since which time the
Turks have held it against two Persian invaders.
Its revenue, under Caliph Al Mamun, was £56,000,000
a year. Its revenue in 1854 was only £350,000. I
do not know what it is now, but probably much

less ; and in the same proportion has its population diminished.

"The author from whom I have borrowed these few statistics adds, that it is probable that Baghdad, like Seleucia, will eventually be no more than a name, swept away by the waters of the Tigris, and plundered by the wandering Arabs. In 1832 it was devastated by a flood and by a terrible plague, which carried off one-third of its inhabitants. Every year the river is becoming more unmanageable, through a neglect of proper precautions to direct and utilise its impetuous current. The cultivation of its banks is checked by oppressive taxation, its channel is continually shifting, and the Arab chiefs, who offer to build dams and dykes, are unable to do so because no remission of their burden is made, and no encouragement given.

"Still, for all this, the streets and bazaars, and even the government of Baghdad, contrast favourably with those of any city in Persia, while the view from one of the minarets, as your eye ranges over 737 acres of flat housetops, varied by Oriental figures and costumes, and graceful date palms, and blue glazed mosques and battlemented walls, and shining river, or to the wide sandy plain of Arabia, is interesting and effective. Here also are the evidences of toleration secured by the British Government after the Crimean war. Four large synagogues are attended by contented and prosperous-looking Jews (unlike their care-worn brethren in Persia), while 1200 of their children are saying their lessons in school. Christian churches rear

their heads on all sides, French, Latin, Armenian
and Chaldee, while the public baths are frequented
by Mussulmans and Christians alike, irrespective of
caste, creed, or religion.

"One evening I hired two horses and started for
Babylon. The road lay over the flat plain of Meso-
potamia, with nothing to diversify the scene except a
a solitary khan (corresponding to the Persian 'caravanserai') every eight or ten miles. As I travelled
at night, I had a mounted escort of Arabs by way of
precaution, but on the second night they lost their
way, and we were wandering about for several hours,
as there was no moon to help us. At last we judged
it better to lie down and sleep till daylight. Then
we easily found the road, and I saw in the distance
the huge mound where all that remains of Babylon
is entombed. It is called by the Arabs 'Mujehbo,'
that is 'overturned.' No name could better express
the desolation of the oldest and proudest city of the
world. I crossed a dry canal, and marked how the
ground was strewed with ancient bricks. Then I
came to a large quarry where men were digging out
bricks by thousands, and carrying them away on
donkeys. The modern town of Hillah has been built
with the bricks of Babylon, as was also the ancient
town of Seleucia. I climbed the huge mound (in
size like a small hill), and walked from end to
end of it. It is composed entirely of bricks and
rubbish. Here and there an excavation has been
made, and a wall or chamber or well laid bare.

Why has this mine of interest been left so long
unexplored ? "

. . . .

"People go to Babylon and come away saying,
'There is nothing to see.' I confess I went there *prepared* to see nothing—nothing, at least, like Thebes
or Baalbec, or Persepolis. But what one does see is
the exact fulfilment of Scripture—'Babylon shall become heaps, a dwelling-place for dragons, an astonishment, and an hissing without an inhabitant. Her
cities are a desolation, a dry land and a wilderness,
a land wherein no man dwelleth, neither does any son
of man pass thereby.'—(Jer. xvi. 37-43). . . .

"It is difficult to sit on that ground and try to
reconstruct in imagination, the stupendous temple of
Belus (the 'Bel' of Scripture), or the hanging gardens,
or the miles of streets, or the lofty walls. So complete was the destruction of the temple by Cyrus, that
history tells us, even Alexander the Great, when he
wished to rear it again from the heaps of rubbish,
failed in the attempt. It is difficult to realise that
Daniel here witnessed a good confession, and rose to
be the first minister at a court before which the world
trembled.

. . . .

"It is curious to observe how the modern Arabs
pursue the customs of their ancestors. You see the
same primitive dress, and the manner of life which
fancy pictures in the days of Nimrod. They navigate
the Euphrates and Tigris in the same wicker boats,

lined with bitumen, which are seen depicted in As-
syrian sculptures.   These boats, called 'Guffa' (literally, a basket), are perfectly circular, and warranted
not to upset.

"After a refreshing bathe in the river, and a
caution from the Arabs against sharks, which make
up in these rivers for the absence of alligators, I
reached the town of Hillah, and crossed the Euphrates
on a bridge of boats.   Before sunset, we were again
in the saddle with our faces towards Birs Nimroud
(the town of Nimrod).   I had scarcely left Hillah,
when I saw it, at the distance of seven or eight miles,
rising from the plain, corresponding strikingly with
one's conceptions of the Tower of Babel.   Soon the
shades of evening hid it from our view.   We came to
an Arab encampment, and my escort proposed a halt.
I knew there was another Arab camp further on, and
refused to yield till we got nearer to the tower.   An
hour more brought to us the sound of voices, and the
barking of dogs, and the tents and fires of a camp.
The chief received me with oriental politeness, and
bade me welcome to all that he possessed.   I asked
for a little milk and firewood, spreading my plaid on
the ground, and soon enjoyed my cup of tea over a
Book which carried me back to the days when men
journeyed from the East, and found a plain in the
land of Shinar, and said, 'Let us build us a city and
a tower, whose top may reach unto heaven.'   Meanwhile the fire-light flickered upon the fine bronzed
features of a ring of Arabs who sat mutely watching

me, and upon picketed horses, and ruminating camels, and low tents, and tall spears stuck before them in the ground ; and inside Arab women chatted and sat grinding at the mill, the one turning the upper stone round and round, the other pouring in the grain. I found that the Arab dogs showed the same hospitality as their master. No sooner was I an acknowledged guest, than they ceased barking, and commenced wagging their tails. The largest and most powerful of them took charge of me for the night, and walked round and round me as I lay, with all the grave dignity of a sentinel at Buckingham Palace. If any intruders, dog or man, came near, one growl was enough (he knew that a *bark* might disturb me, and refrained). Of course he got his 'bakshish' in the shape of some chicken bones, and our mutual friendship was firmly cemented.

"I rose at earliest dawn, and soon reached the foot of Birs Nimroud. A high mound is surmounted by a ruined and unfinished tower of brick, the summit of which is 235 feet above the plain. An examination of the mound shows that it is composed of the same elements as the mound of Babylon—masses of brick and rubbish, interspersed with broken pottery. These bricks are all of them inscribed on *one side* with cuneiform characters. I was searching for specimens of cuneiform among the chaos of bricks that strewed the mound, when my Arab guide came up to me, and insisted that I was looking for inscriptions in the wrong place ; he would show me some really good ones. I followed him with some little incredulity, when he led me to the tower itself, knowing that there were none there. 'Look here!' he exclaimed triumphantly, and pointed with the utmost gravity to a series of recent scratches, which spelt, 'TIMOTHY SNOOKS, 1856,' 'JOHN THOMAS, 1862,' etc., etc. My laughter quite astonished him.

"There is something truly mysterious about this remarkable ruin. On one side, where excavations have been made, you may see walls of brick ascending tier above tier with masterly ambition. On another, all is convulsion and disturbance—huge masses of brick-work, rent and overturned, yet so solid in their ruin, that it is easier to pulverize the brick than to separate it from the mortar. One of these blocks has rolled bodily to the foot of the mound. Others are vitrified or fused by a process which can be none other than electricity or fire. Curiously enough the Arabs have a tradition that it has been destroyed by 'fire from heaven.' The sides of the mound are pierced with holes and strewed with bones, which plainly indicate the lairs of wild beasts. The view from the summit at sunrise is distant and varied. The broad sheet of the Euphrates winds for many a mile, till lost in the distance in a 'sea-like plain.' Looking along its bank to the south you see the white minaret which marks Ezekiel's tomb. Modern cities appear like miniatures of the ancient Hillah, Tamasia, Mohawil. In the foreground are the 'tents of Kedar,' and the flocks, with patches of tall green corn, which the Arabs call ' idtleva.'

" It is difficult to resist the conviction that Birs Nimroud is the tower of Babel, the oldest ruin in the world. There are those who (like Mr. Rich) believe it to be the tower of Belus, and regard it as a part of the ruin of Babylon, but I prefer to hold the older tradition. And surely it is when standing on ground like this, that the language of Scripture acquires a vividness and reality which rewards the toil of patient investigation, and makes the privations of travel forgotten ; and a voice seems to breathe from the resting-places of the prophets beside these mighty rivers, which is daily more heard and felt, rebuking the sneer of the scoffer and the sceptic. ' I have cut off the nations : their towers are desolate. I made their streets waste that none passeth by ; their cities are destroyed, so that there is no man, that there is none inhabitant. Therefore wait ye upon me, saith the Lord, until the day that I rise up to the prey. . . . For then will I turn to the people a pure language, that they may all call upon the name of the Lord, to serve Him with one consent.'—(Zephaniah iii. 6, 8, 9)."

Taking a review of his stay at Baghdad and its neighbourhood, Gordon thinks that the history of certain Christian churches—such as the Nestorian, Chaldean, Armenian, and Sabean—which have taken root there, would well repay study. " Of the last-named," he says, " very little is known, owing to the reticence and reserve of its professors. I happened to meet the Sabean chief priest, and having heard a report of the peculiar tenets of his followers, was anxious to obtain further information. It was at the 'Garden of Eden' that I first saw him. His village is within a short distance of the place, and as I was cutting a stick from the 'tree of life,' I was accosted in English by a venerable old man in Arab dress. I did not know who he was at the time, and my steamer was just starting, so that there was no opportunity for conversation; but two days ago he turned up at Bussorah, and called at the house where I was staying. I found that he had learned English at the Residency, Baghdad, and has had much intercourse with travellers who have visited him in his village; but my experience only confirms the testimony of the rest, that he is a most uncommunicative old man, and, for some reason or other, will not indulge the curiosity of inquirers. We tried him in English, Persian, and Arabic, but failed to gain any intelligible information from him. The Sabeans (or 'Soobies' as they call themselves) are believed to be followers of John the Baptist, and baptize by immersion. The old man insisted that his religion 'is as old as Adam,' and that he has books written by God. He has been offered very large sums for these books by travellers, but he will not part with them. He told me that they have infant baptism and adult baptism, but declined to say anything about the form. They have no church, and I could make out nothing about their religious observances, except that they have a feast

once a year, which lasts five days, and at which they
partake of bread and wine.   They number about 500,
scattered in different villages, and it would seem that
they have no land of their own, but gain a livelihood
by working in iron, gold, and silver.

"They were formerly molested by the Arabs, but
are now free from annoyance.   He wished me to
write a letter for him to the Queen.   I told him that
I would willingly be his amanuensis, but he must
dictate what I was to say.   The letter was very brief,
the gist of it being that he was very poor, and wanted
assistance, and that he always prayed for her Majesty.
I suggested that he should inform her Majesty about
his history and religion, but he declined to do so.
They have a distinct language of their own, and he
wrote me some sentences as a specimen.   They are
said to allow a plurality of wives, and will not eat till
sundry purifying ceremonies have been performed."

Being anxious to press on to Lahore as soon as
possible, Gordon availed himself of the first steamer
going down the Tigris to Bussorah, instead of visiting Nineveh and other places as inclination and
pleasure would have led him to do.

He writes, during the journey, on October 20,
1872 :—

"*On the Tigris, Oct.* 20, 1872.—I am now steam-
ing down the Tigris, and hope to reach Bussorah
to-morrow night.

"As I look out of my cabin window, the scene is
monotonous and flat.   I see low sandy banks and an

Arab encampment in the foreground. Some of the Arabs are mounted, others with their flocks of buffalo, sheep, and camels, which have come down to the water to drink. I am the only 'first-class' passenger on board, but the deck is covered with Arabs, Chaldees, Indians, etc., some smoking, some eating, and some chatting with their families around them—150 altogether. The captain and purser are English. The latter is amusing himself by knocking over poor pelicans on the bank with his rifle, a sport against which I have protested. The captain has just called me out to look at a fragment of an ancient bridge, by which Alexander the Great is said to have crossed the river on one of his expeditions.

" The most interesting (and, indeed, the only) vestige of these ancient cities which once studded the banks of this noble river, is a ruin called Tâk i kest, which I visited some days ago. It consists of an immense vaulted chamber 100 feet high, with two flanking walls, and other signs of what was once either a palace or a temple. It is believed on good authority that here stood the city of Ctesiphon. On the opposite side of the river the site of Seleucia may be traced, founded 291 B.C. by Seleucus Nicator, one of Alexander's generals, and destroyed by the Romans in the reign of Marcus Aurelius, A.D. 165.

"Ctesiphon shared the same fate, but recovered itself, and successfully resisted the Emperor Julian in 363. It was at last destroyed by the Saracens in 636. *Now* the wandering Arab feeds his flock on the

mounds which cover royal palaces and silent cities.
The Arch of Ctesiphon (as it is commonly called) is
most impressive and sublime, certainly the finest arch
I have ever seen.

"It is devoid of ornament, inscription, or sculp-
ture, and stands alone in the plain with a defiant
aspect, that looks as though it intended to hold its
own till the end of time.

"We are now (Oct. 22) passing 'the Garden of
Eden.' . . .

"I have been on shore and surveyed the spot which
is supposed to be the site of Paradise.   It is at the
junction of the Euphrates and Tigris.   A long line
of date palms fringes both rivers on either side.   A
few boats are lying at anchor.   Some Arab houses
appear between the trees, and a Turkish flag-staff
and guard-house stand stiffly and formally in front.
Otherwise all is natural and primitive, even to the
children, who run about in the costume of their first
parents.   I cut a stick from the 'Tree of Life,' as it is
called by western visitors.   It has, of course, no claim
to this name, except that it stands alone among the
surrounding palms, a species of mimosa.   . . .

"It is mere speculation which places Eden in this
locality.   The fact that we find here *two* rivers
only, instead of four mentioned (Gen. ii. 11-15), leads
us to inquire, 'May not the flood have altered the
courses of these rivers?' and if so, then the conflu-
ence of the Euphrates and Tigris may have been
elsewhere.   We know that the courses of these two

rivers has materially changed (higher up) in the last few centuries.

"This morning we passed the tomb of Ezra. A handsome building in the Eastern style, surmounted by a blue-glazed cupola, marks his resting-place, close to the river's bank. Every year the Jews of Baghdad and other places visit the spot in pilgrimage. A little Jewish boy from among the passengers came up to the captain as we approached the spot, and begged (on behalf of his mother) to be allowed to go ashore and visit the tomb. I felt strongly inclined to support the little fellow's petition, but I knew that the captain was in a hurry to land his 150 passengers at Bussorah before dark, and that he would not stop the ship at the request of two. The answer was, 'Tell your mother to pay £20, and I will stop.' So the mother's wish, alas! was ungratified."

Arrived at Bussorah, Gordon embarked on board the "Kashmir," one of the British India Steam Navigation Company's boats. She was bound for Bombay, calling at various ports *en route*, such as Bunder Abbas in Persia, Muskat in Arabia, Guada in Bilochistan, Karachi in India. One object of interest at least is described on the way :—

"Opposite Lingeh, on the Arab coast, is an island called El Bârein, a great place for pearl fishing. Here there are very remarkable springs, which force their way up through the bed of the sea, half a mile from shore, and rise to within a few feet of the surface. I am told that ships sometimes fill their casks from these

springs by means of skins, which are made into a bag
and closed.   A diver goes down with the skins into
the fresh water, opens, fills, fastens them, and they rise
naturally to the surface, fresh water being lighter than
salt.   What a striking type this is of those 'living
waters' of God's Holy Spirit, which have so often
refreshed the believer in his bitterest experience of
adversity, and supported him in his conflicts with the
cares of this troublesome world ! "

About November 17, Bombay was reached, and
here we may pause, while Gordon pursues his way
to the Punjab, his new field of labour.

CHAPTER IX.

LAHORE.

NOT far from one of the gates of the city of Lahore is a garden known by the name of Mahá Singh, a Sikh chief, who was its original owner. Though the change which has come over the place is very great, it is still known by its former name.

In 1869, having been purchased by the Rev. T. V. French, new buildings were put up, and St. John's Divinity School sprang into existence. The garden being thoroughly native in character, was laid out in rectangular forms, thus readily adapting itself to the college quad plan, which is one of the first features which strikes the newcomer.

The first quad has on one side the principal's house, faced on the other side by the college chapel ; these are flanked by the library and lecture room.

The next quad contains various students' quarters and a swimming bath, which was built, I believe, by Gordon. One quad is set apart for married students.

This last is a feature at least which one is not familiar with in the English collegiate system. It is necessary, however, in India, for two reasons, the first being that young men, Christians as well as non-

Christians, marry at an early age ; the second, that in the present state of Christianity, converts of all ages are joined to the Church of Christ, and therefore students of all ages are being prepared for the ministry.

This was the place in which Gordon now found himself stationed.   It might have been expected that a man in his position would have had to live the life of a mere teacher and student, passing his time in learning himself and imparting knowledge to others. But no one who knew Gordon could for a moment imagine his spending all his time in this way.   He was a man who loved and believed in books, but not in books alone.   His letters in this memoir will hardly have been read aright, if they have not disclosed to the reader, that he believed in practical life and action preaching more eloquently, than many a ser-mon echoing through vaulted cathedrals.

Accordingly, although in a place of study where young men are trained for the sacred ministry of Christ's Church, Gordon, with the Principal, the Rev. T. V. French, was continually to be found during the vacations giving practical expression to the lessons they had inculcated, by going forth into the 'high-ways and hedges of the Punjab jungles, accompanied by a native band, themselves enduring, and teaching to endure, hardness as good soldiers of Jesus Christ.

Thus, very soon after reaching the Punjab, on New Year's Day, 1873, we find Gordon writing from his tent :—" I am now encamped in an Indian jungle, engaged in my former work, for the time being, of

preaching to the heathen, or rather of accompanying
my friend, Mr. French, in preaching, for I am not yet
sufficiently familiar with Hindustani to preach myself.
I find that in the Punjab quite a mixture of languages
is spoken, of which the principal are Hindi, Punjabi,
and Hindustani.   At present I confine myself to the
latter, and my Persian is a great help to me, although
I do not often meet Persian-speaking people, Mr.
French's wonderful gift for languages has enabled
him to master them and several others, and it is a
great treat to be with him, and to see what a commanding influence he often has over his audience,
who appear here to be much more highly educated
than the same classes in the South of India.   We are
spending in this way three weeks, which form the
vacation of the Lahore Training College, and we hope
to start a new mission in a part of the country which
has hitherto been unoccupied by missionary labourers.
Our tour commenced at Jhilam, which is 100 miles
north of Lahore, and we are making a circuit of 130
miles, travelling ten miles every day, and carrying our
little tents with us on mules.

.   .   .   .

"I find many points of contrast between the
Punjab and the South of India.   Climate, language,
scenery, and people are all different—as different as
Italy from England.   My Tamil is unfortunately useless here.   .   .   .   The winter climate is cold and
bracing, and we wear English clothes, and are glad
of fires when we get them.   It has been hard work to

GARDENS OF THE DIVINITY SCHOOL AT LAHORE.

get warm some of these frosty nights in a tent, where
fires are out of the question. We usually make a
march before daylight, in order to reach the next
camping ground in time for the servants to pitch the
tent, and get breakfast by eleven or twelve. Then
we go into the village, or town, and take up a position
in some vacant space ; while the people collect to
gaze at us, and this gives the opportunity for preaching. They have never seen missionaries, and they
generally take us for Government officials, until we
tell them that we are not 'great Sahibs,'—as they call
officers and civilians,—but poor men like themselves,
who are come to show them the way of salvation.
Mr. French holds strongly the necessity of our laying aside, as much as possible, the externals of the
' English gentleman,' and approaching them like their
own teachers and ' fakírs,' who live on charity, and
whose self-denial commends itself to the native mind.
I quite think that this method seems to inspire them
with confidence, and open their hearts in the north
of India, although I am not certain that it does so
always in the south.

   " Some very intelligent inquirers have visited our
tents from time to time, and one or two appear to be
drinking in the words of eternal life.

   " We have been conversing to-day on the vast importance which some of these days of preaching will
assume in the light of eternity, as perhaps the birthday of some inquiring soul, and the dawn of immor-
tality to some disciple whom Jesus loves. I am more

N

and more convinced of the great need which there is in North India of a body of faithful, earnest, and self-denying native ministers, such as Mr. French is training at Lahore, who shall be not merely pastors, but evangelists, thoroughly instructed in the doctrines of the Bible, and inflamed with a true desire for the salvation of souls. I believe that the regeneration of India can only be effected under God by such an instrumentality, when we consider all the disadvantages at which European missionaries are placed, and the great difficulty we seem to have in winning the confidence of a race so naturally suspicious and alien, as the Hindus and Mussulmans. There are at present thirteen students in the college, and more than this number have been rejected as disqualified. They are a very thoughtful and intelligent set of youths, drawn together from various districts to a common centre for a common object, and their histories would be very interesting, were they ever to be thrown together into a little sketch of the college and its objects. But more than this can be said of them, for Mr. French has the well-grounded confidence that they are all truly converted to God, taught of His Spirit, and animated with the love of their Saviour."

The object of the college as being a place designed to train men for practical life, as well as intellectually and spiritually, is pointed out in a letter of Gordon's to the Rev. H. B. Macartney, of Melbourne. He has been describing the students individually, and he concludes :—

"Mr. French's design for these men is not that they should settle down in ease and dignity upon a pastorate, but that they should be simple and self-denying evangelists, preaching the gospel from village to village, gathering out here and there those whom the Lord shall choose, and forming little congregations for others to minister to, while their own work is to be continually carrying the word to the 'regions beyond.'"

One thing which Gordon seemed to delight in, and to think of the first importance, was that of interesting children in missionary work. We have seen, when recording his visit to Australia, how great an influence was exercised, and how, under the guidance of the Rev. H. B. Macartney, it was sustained. It may have been a seed sown in weakness, but God raised it in strength, so that to this day Indian missions receive a vast amount of support from the Children's Association in Melbourne. And it is easy for each one of us to see the wisdom and expediency of exciting this interest. For the lessons we learn in childhood, and the attachments to persons and pursuits which we form, are, in the experience of us all, those which are most secure throughout life. Childhood, too, is the period when impressions of good or evil are most easily given. Why, then, should not all who long for the spread of Christ's kingdom and the salvation of souls, seek to enlist the sympathy of children in the great work, and from them raise a noble army of missionaries, who shall make the world

ring with the glad tidings of salvation, and send forth
"hosannas" to the praise of the King that cometh
to Zion. But were all questions of wisdom and expediency put aside, can we forget that the Lord himself always delighted in bringing forward the little
ones, in admitting them to a share in His kingdom
and its work, and that one of His last instructions to
His great Apostle was, "Feed my lambs," as well as
"Feed my sheep."

Accordingly, one of the most pleasant sights in
turning over Gordon's letters, is the finding that the
lambs were never forgotten, but that letter after letter
is addressed to children.

There is one written in April of this year (1873)
to his little cousins, the children of Alexander Leslie
Melville, Esq., of Lincoln, in which he gives descriptions which may be interesting to older heads as well.
It is written in Katnap (a vacation of the Lahore
College being occupied as usual in itineration), from
the neighbourhood of Sháhpur, a town which is situated near the Salt Range of Mountains. In this
range, at a little place called Khewra, are the Government salt mines, which produce a large annual revenue, and to them allusions are made.

"About four weeks ago I left Lahore and took a
native preacher with me, and went a long journey
into the jungle, to preach to people who perhaps had
never heard the beautiful story of the Gospel before.
When there was a large town, I stopped there and
went into the street, where the people were buying

and selling, and I offered them that salvation through Christ, which is 'without money and without price.' Some of them listened very attentively, and wished to hear more, and others made light of it and went away, 'one to his farm, another to his merchandise.' Then I got into a boat and went 100 miles down the great river Jhílam, and I preached at three great towns upon its banks. Once I made friends with a Hindu 'fakír,' that is, a man whom they consider very holy, because he lives all alone, and spends his time in reading and thinking upon religion. He spoke a language which I know very little at present, but my native companion knows it, and I left a message with him to think about the true God, and pray to Him and that I too would pray for him, that the eyes of his understanding might be opened, and that he might find peace in believing.

"And I saw a number of little boys just out of school, and some spoke in English and asked for some of my books; but the little girls and their mothers were very shy, more shy than they used to be in South India, and so I saw nothing of them. Then I got into my boat and went to another town. There were no pretty trees and meadows on the banks, such as there are at Wilford, but a few hills on one side, and a flat plain on the other, and here and there an alligator or some wild fowl basking in the sun. And the hills were made of salt, and I saw thousands of men working away at the salt mines, and making a great tunnel through the hill, and putting the salt on the backs of camels in great sacks, and the camels walked away with it in a line three or four miles long.

"Then I came to Shâhpur, and there was a fair going on. Hundreds of people had come from a distance to visit the tomb of a 'holy man' who is buried there, and they think that by this pilgrimage they are doing something very acceptable to God. So I told them about Nicodemus, and what Jesus said to him, and especially the words, 'God so loved the world,' etc. And there was one man there, a Muhamadan, who was very angry, and did all he could to prevent the people from listening, because he was their priest, and what I said was just the contrary to his teaching, and he was afraid that they would believe me rather than him. So he made a great noise, and said that what I said was false, and that my religion was Satan's religion. I could only pray that God would change his heart, as He has changed the heart of many a hardened sinner before.

"I was very much pleased to find that there were two hearts whom the Lord had touched among the many thousands whom I saw in my journey living 'without hope and without God.' These were two servants, a man and his wife, at Shâhpur. They are very poor, but they are Christians, and that makes all the difference, and to believe on Christ with the whole heart is to have great riches. I was so glad to be able to cheer and encourage them in their lonely life. Just think of a journey of 350 miles, from one end

of England to the other, and only _two_ Christians! I
hope that one day I may write and tell you that
these two have become a hundred !

"On my journey from Sháhpur to Lahore, I have
seen very few _people_, because it is all wilderness ; but
there are plenty of inhabitants in it, great and small,
under ground and above ground.   There are large
herds of cattle, which roam about and get what they
can from the herbs and bushes ; and there are beautiful wild deer, which stop and look at me with their
bright eyes, and wonder what I am come for to their
desert home ; and there are numbers of ring-doves,
which make such a pretty cooing at sunrise, and seem
to enjoy themselves and everything about them.   And
there are partridges and quail, and plovers and ' pee-
wits,' who don't seem to understand a white face at
all, and when they see me they began to cackle and
say, ' Tut, tut, what can it mean ?   Let us be off and
tell all the rest, tut, tut, tut !'   And there are green
parrots, who are not at all afraid, and they scream
out, ' Fie, fie !   Why, you are not afraid of a white
face, are you ?   _I_ live in towns and often see white
faces, but you are simple jungle folk.'   And there is
the pretty ' mongoose,' like a large ferret, with a furry
skin and long tail ; and the jungle rat, which makes
numbers of holes in the ground, and is very fond of
company, but a little suspicious of my designs, so
when I come near, he runs to the mouth of his
hole and sits on his tail and _stares_, and then, if I
come too near, he pops in like a shot.   And I have

a great many more admirers than these—namely, squirrels and jungle cats and jackals, and many pretty little birds, such as the woodpecker and the kurata, with its shining green feathers, and the kingfisher and jay—many of these you have at home ; but I have no thrushes or nightingales to remind me of the Longhills."

The summer vacation of this year was spent in Lahore, as it is not possible, without some degree of risk, to say nothing of inconvenience, to be in camp in the plains of the Punjab after the month of April.

Preaching to the heathen in the bazars was carried on regularly, and as Gordon was the only one of the Church Missionary Society's Missionaries left in Lahore at this season, he was accustomed to join the members of the American Presbyterian Mission, in order to show as great a force as possible to the enemy. Writing on August 3, he says :—

"One of the most curious features of the bazar preaching in Lahore is, that it has aroused opposition preaching on the part of the Hindus, Brahmans and Mussulmans alike. It was commenced by the latter, and for weeks Mr. French was annoyed by a Waháb, who took his stand at a particular place in the bazar, close to a little chapel, which we have built conjointly with the Americans. In front of this little chapel it is the custom of the missionaries to arrange benches for those who like to listen, and generally there has been a good attendance. Of course the preaching is not *confined* to this place, but as it was one much frequented, the Waháb[í] chose it as his point of attack, and often succeeded in drawing away all Mr. French's audience. By-and-by, a Hindu, ambitious of hearing his own voice, started a preaching on the opposite side, and attracted a large congregation. Then a Brahman followed, and the missionary of the Gospel was between three fires. Now (strangest of all) the Mussulman, Hindu and Brahman have made a joint-stock company, and they all preach from the same platform to the same audience.

"This goes on night after night, and so the three missionaries who are left in Lahore feel it a point of honour to coalesce in the daily duty of repelling this systematic attack upon the true faith, and maintaining a garrison in the citadel.

"In this warfare one has constantly to remind oneself that the weapons of our Master's ordnance are not carnal, and that we do indeed wrestle not with flesh and blood, but with principalities and powers, with the rulers of the darkness of this world, with spiritual wickedness in high places. As I walk through the bazars, I mourn over the wideness of the breach which separates us from this people, or rather which separates them from the Gospel, for one would be quite content to be hated by them, if only the Gospel were loved. I can never convince myself that the people, as a people, have the smallest affection for us, or ever will have, but I believe that they are fully capable of being animated, not by self-interest, but by the love of Christ."

Under date of Divinity College, Lahore, December 4, 1873, addressing the Honourable Mrs. Leslie Melville, Gordon dwells on the encouragement suggested by the Day of Intercession for Foreign Missions, then newly established.   He writes :—

"Yesterday was a day of great thankfulness to me, because I felt that so many kind friends at home would be remembering us in prayer ; and it was a delightful thing to feel that God's people, throughout the (English) world, would be 'lifting up holy hands' on behalf of Missions.   Coming from the Archbishop of Canterbury, such an appeal for prayer would have great weight, and who can tell what blessings would attend such united intercessions.   Here in Lahore we had various services and prayer meetings for Europeans, as well as natives, two in our college chapel at 8 A.M. and 5 P.M. for our students and their families, and one at noon which they had among themselves, one at the native church in the town at 6 P.M., and those for Europeans in the two English churches at 8 A.M., 5 P.M., and 8.30 P.M.   Besides these, the American (Presbyterian) missionaries had also two or three prayer meetings for natives and Europeans, which we should have liked to have taken part in, but could not do so, as they were at the same time as ours.   So that, altogether, there were no less than ten assemblies in our little community of Christians at Lahore to observe the day."

One subject which was forced upon Gordon's attention at this time, was that which probably every missionary has to take into consideration at some

time or another—church architecture. When missionaries, foreigners to the country in which they are
working, have the management of almost all matters
in their own hands, a great danger arises of their
endeavouring to implant their own ideas of the fitness
of things into the native mind, as though they were
essential parts of the Christian religion. The European, and especially the Englishman, with his insular
prejudice, is very apt to think that nothing can be
good which differs from what he has been accustomed to. Thus we find him despising the language
of the people amongst whom he lives, considering
himself above conforming to niceties of pronunciation.
If he finds a people who, for hundreds of years before
England was ever heard of, were accustomed to sit on
the ground instead of on chairs, or to eat with fingers
instead of with knives and forks, he pronounces them
uncivilised and barbarous. Similarly, in the missionary world, at least in earlier years, to make a
man a Christian was too often to denationalise him.
It was to cut him off from his own people by calling
him John Smith instead of Ghulam Rasúl; it was to
give him a hat, coat, and a pair of trousers, and, in
short, to make him well-nigh a laughing stock to his
fellow countrymen. Too often, it is thought, if the
missionary belongs to the Church of England, that
our liturgies, and even minutiæ of arrangements in
service, should be transferred bodily from one country
to another. Happily this state of things is rapidly
becoming one of a past generation. Every year sees

more liberal views, while that which is essential and fundamental is retained with honest tenacity.

One of the minor matters in which the missionary may well modify his inherited views, is that of the style of church in which he will summon his converts to worship. The older buildings are more

THE CHAPEL OF THE DIVINITY COLLEGE, LAHORE.

or less reproductions of inferior places of worship, such as are to be seen under the dull sky, and in the damp atmosphere of an English parish. The elegant dome, the scolloped arch, the lofty minaret, which must appeal to the feelings of the people, have been in years gone by sadly overlooked. But in this, as in other matters, better days are coming, if not come. The most notable instances of improvement in this direction in the Punjab are, perhaps, the Peshawar Mission Church, which might almost be taken as a fine masjid, and the chapel of the Divinity College at Lahore, with its adaptation of the Moorish(?) arch.

But it is to such men as Gordon was that these improvements are due. He was one who endeavoured to make himself one of the people, living as far as possible in their way. It was by thus putting himself in their position and looking at things from their point of view, that he was enabled to adopt and adapt for Christian purposes what was either good, or in itself harmless, in their systems.

The consciousness that errors had been committed caused him to write to the Rev. C. G. Curtis, whom he had met at Constantinople when on his way to Persia, asking for assistance. " I am about to build," he writes on Feb. 12, 1874, "a college chapel for our native divinity students, and I am anxious that it should be of an eastern and not a western type. I should like much to get a plan of such a building as the early Christians used, and the Byzantine style has always seemed far more suitable for eastern countries than the Gothic. Knowing your interest in, and familiarity with, eastern antiquities, I should feel very much obliged to you if you would kindly assist me, either in recommending me some book for my guidance, or in obtaining for me a few drawings of these churches at Constantinople, and I would gladly be responsible for the expense of the drawings.

"There are of course many details to be taken into account, such as size, materials, climate, etc., etc. We should want accommodation for 150 or 200. To admit the air and exclude the sun would be desirable, but the Punjab has a very cold winter, so that this has also to be taken into account.

.   .   .   .

"We could not contemplate anything very ornate,—in fact, simplicity would be necessary, as well as desirable, on account of our limited funds.

"We might raise £800 without much difficulty. My idea would be a small dome with nave and transept in the form of cross. I think that if some good eastern style were to be adopted, the example would be followed in other parts of India."

This chapel was not destined to be built by Gordon. He gave the money for it, but it was not until after his death that the present building, to which reference has been made above, was erected by the Rev. H. U. Weitbrecht, who was then stationed in Lahore.

From the time Gordon arrived in Lahore, it has been seen that his vacations were generally spent away from the College, in itinerating, and in the country districts. Mr. French, the Principal of the College, was now about to go on two years' furlough to England. Gordon, being thus deprived of his European companion, formed a plan for the good of

the native church. Of this he speaks in a letter to
Mr. Parker, dated March 2, 1874 :—

"We want _Evangelists_, and seeing, as I do, that
one great difficulty we have to contend with in Lahore
is, the proximity of a large city and high salaries
(which are apt to dazzle and turn the heads of all but
the most highly-principled of native Christians), I
propose, while Mr. French is at home, to take some
of our students with me into the Jhílam district, 100
miles away, and itinerate with them, and preach in
the villages, as I used to do in South India, thus
innuring them to a little hardship, and carrying on
their training at the same time. Perhaps you will
hear more of this plan hereafter."

This plan developed to such an extent, that we find
him practically from this time adopting an itinerating
life only, and becoming that which he is best known
as, both to Europeans and natives in the Punjab—an
Anglo-Indian fakír.

CHAPTER X.

JHÍLAM ITINERANCY—PIND DÁDAN KHÁN—1874-75.

IT is in March 1874 that we may consider Gordon's life took that decided form of fakírism for which he was ever afterwards conspicuous. We saw his tendency towards this mode of living in his early days in the Madras itinerancy. We heard him then lamenting the necessity of keeping a horse, the trouble that is caused by servants, the separation between the missionary and the natives of India, caused by the comparative luxuries of even the humblest Englishman. We heard him say how he would rather preach than practise the necessity of finding a summer retreat among the waving pines of the Indian hills.

At the same time, however, he thus regarded all these things as more or less necessary. Now, however, in the third year of his residence in the Punjab, he begins to find that he can dispense with one thing after another. His heart's desire is fulfilled. He wanders on foot, often not a single servant accompanies him, and, like His Master, he often does not know where at night he will lay his head.

On one occasion, writing to the Rev. H. B. Macartney, of Melbourne, describing his life, he says :—" I
am generally able to walk ten miles a day, and thus
am independent of a horse. This method seems to
bring one nearer to our blessed Lord's example. Besides, I think that it would spoil that verse, ' How
beautiful upon the mountains are the feet of him
that bringeth good tidings,' etc., if _feet_ were exchanged
for _hoofs._"

The new work which Gordon now found himself
engaged in, was named by him the " Jhílam Itinerancy." The Jhílam is one of the five great rivers of
the Punjab, and it is from this, and not from the town
of the same name upon its banks, that the new
mission was called. The river wanders through the
country at the foot of the Salt Range of Mountains,
until it joins, and is lost in, the Indus, which swallows
up all the five rivers of the country.

There are five important towns upon its banks.
Jhílam, Pind Dádan Khán, Bhera, Sháhpur and Jhang.
Gordon's plan was to place native agents in each
one of these, making Pind Dádan Khán the central
mission station from which all the work would be
supervised.

In each of these towns at the time of the commencement of the Mission, at least one native Christian family was resident, which formed the nucleus of
a church.

Leaving the line of the Jhílam, and ascending on
to the higher plateau of the Salt Range, other centres

O

are to be found, such as Chakrawàl and Talagang, valuable from a missionary point of view.

It is a great matter of regret that this district has not been taken up and worked more vigorously by the Church Missionary Society. Since the death of Gordon the Pind Dádan Khán Mission has, it is true, been kept alive. But this is all that can be said.

There has been no attempt to carry out the scheme proposed by Gordon in its entirety.

To know when to extend work, and when to expend one's means and force in strengthening old positions, is one of the perplexities which is continually facing a great society like the Church Missionary Society. The missionaries in the field often complain that they are left single-handed, and are not supported as they should be by the Home Society. On the other hand, perhaps at home the offer is made of a large sum of money to commence work in hitherto unbroken ground, and the Society cannot but look upon such an offer as a call from God. But it cannot be denied, that too often the tendency seems to be evident of pushing on to regions beyond, before there is a strong base from which outgoing posts can be supported.

It may be that in India the missionaries themselves are to blame. Possibly they have not yet discovered the method of training native churches to stand alone. Could they do so, the European workers would be able to push forward, and avoid settling down as pastors.

Writing at the commencement of the Jhílam Itinerancy, Gordon puts this view forward. He says, " It is of the essence of this undertaking that it should have as little external aid as possible, that the European element should gradually sink to a vanishing point, while the native agency develops and expands."

But from whatever cause, the Jhílam Itinerancy for which Gordon spent so much of his time and money, and which seemed to be a field so full of fair promise of a future harvest, has never, humanly speaking, had a chance of success given it.

To return from this digression. It was said at the beginning of this chapter that Gordon now settled down into that work for which he is chiefly known, and for which nature had to a great extent marked him out.

And yet it was not without an inward struggle that he definitely severed his connection with the Lahore College. Indeed, at the time, only a temporary severance seems to have been intended. After two years' work in the jungles, he apparently thought of rejoining Mr. French in Lahore on his return from England. Gordon was, however, being led by a path he knew not. That plan was destined to be frustrated by Mr. French's appointment to be the first Bishop of Lahore.

In a circular letter, on April 21, 1874, Gordon writes :—' It has been rather a serious uprooting, as I began to think that Lahore was my settled post of duty, and it certainly was more congenial to me than any other.   But the circumstances which combined to point me to the Jhílam Mission seemed to amount to a call from the Lord of the harvest, and so, after some hard wrestlings in prayer, I yielded my judgment and inclination and obeyed the call.

"After a few short years it will seem of very little account whether we have been working in a city or a jungle, so that the Master's call, 'Follow Me,' has been heard and responded to.

"It is hoped that this wide field, from the Jhílam to the Indus, may be occupied in time by some of the students of the Lahore Divinity College.   One of them, named Andreas, has been already out here since September, at a place called Sháhpur, holding his ground manfully and prayerfully in solitude and petty persecution.

"Mr. French thinks also that after two years' itineration in this district, I shall be better fitted for work at the Lahore College.

.   .   .   .

"So now I am at Pind Dádan Khán, 150 miles from Lahore.   It has a large population of natives, with one resident English magistrate.   Within five miles is the 'Salt Range.'

"The Salt Range has a history; but no archives or inscriptions, and few traditions to assist in compiling it.   One longs to penetrate the secrets of its ancient Hindu temples; its ruined hill-forts and crumbling cemeteries.   Some of these cemeteries are far from any town or signs of habitation, as though indicating the scene of a battle-field. They seem to betoken times of change, insecurity, and warfare, which have now given place to peace and prosperity.

"The villagers are a great mixture : Hindus, Sikhs, and Muhamadans, bound together by sympathy of race amid much diversity of creed. The Muhamadan (whose ancestors were Hindus) mingles freely in Hindu festivals, and salutes Hindu fakírs ; while the Hindu shows no less respect for Muhamadan observances, and the boundary line between Sikhism and Brahmanism is gradually diminishing. The outward harmony may be partly due to mutual dependence for the necessaries of life, the cultivators being all Muhamadans, while the shopkeepers are mostly Hindus. Here, where the Muhamadans are in the majority, Hinduism appears under a very different garb from what one is accustomed to see in the South of India. There is none of that marked ascendency of Brahman over Sudra ; none of that shameless exhibition of wayside idols ; no colossal temples like those of Madura and Kánchiveram. The Hindu in these parts seems ashamed to confess to idolatry in the presence of a Muhamadan. His religious belief takes a more speculative turn, and he is generally a Vedantist or Pantheist. Amongst this class, and amongst the Muhamadan zemindars, there is generally a willingness to listen to the preacher ; and I have often felt enlargement of heart and speech in delivering to them the Gospel message.

"In addition to the advantage of a patient hearing

(which one embraces most thankfully of all), there are also other facilities for itineration, such as the comparative ease with which our two temporal necessities, fowls and milk, are supplied ; and the civility of the headmen of the village, through whom a camel or a mule may often be hired for the journey.

"We have not, like our itinerating brethren in Madras, fine slopes of tamarind or mango to encamp under, for the rains are scanty and the soil impregnated with salpetre; but I have been able hitherto to dispense with a tent altogether, as there is in almost every village the ' dárá,' or guest-house, to which every traveller is welcome. As this hospitality is extended to cattle as well as men, the dárá is not always clean ; but it generally has four walls and a roof, and its central position in the village has often given me the opportunity for long conversations, which are always sustained with more freedom when natives are visitors, and not visited. Considerations of caste do not, as in the South, exclude Christians from lodging in a native house, or walking through a Brahman street ; and more than once (in the absence of a dárá) the use of a villager's house has been offered me, which the occupants have vacated for my accommodation. This act of hospitality, however, is much more rare in India than in Persia.

"The other nucleus for an audience, especially in the evening, is the village masjid, where the zemindar, having arrayed himself after his day's work in his most respectable clothes, comes and washes his feet and head preparatory to the evening prayer. He does not wait for the bell-like summons of the Imám who proclaims the hour of prayer. He is generally in his place at the appointed time—a pattern to Western church-goers both in punctuality and de-voutness of demeanour. No less instructive is it to meet him in the early morning, going out to his work with the dust of prostration on his forehead. His first act has been the acknowledgment of the One God, before whom he has bowed, not only his knees, but his face, to the ground, in the house of prayer; and if you ask any Muhamadan, however unlettered, what is his duty, he will always acknowledge the duty of prayer as his foremost obligation. How far more suc-cessfully would our day's difficulties be encountered, if we could thus always arise to them from the dust of humiliation, or the act of self-dedication to God!"

It was Gordon's custom, when permitted, to find a lodging in those village masjids. On one occasion he writes:—"I am spending the day in a village mosque, which is always the cleanest place of enter-tainment which the simple villagers have to offer to a traveller.

"They are very strict about my putting off my shoes and leaving them outside the mosque; but they do not object to my eating my meal or sleeping in-side, and they have given me all the entertainment that their village can afford, namely, a fowl and some milk. The mosque has three or four divisions. There

is the outer court for ordinary worshippers, who are
called to prayer five times a day, but only a few
respond.   There is the inner sanctuary, consisting of
four walls and a roof, opening by three Saracenic
arches to the outer court, and adorned all over with
paintings, illustrating trees, fruit, etc., but no *human*
representation whatever.   There is an inner chamber
again, used in winter to sleep in, and shut off from the
rest by a door, but wholly devoid of all furniture.   In
fact (with the exception of the very large mosques
of Cairo, Delhi, etc.,) you never see such a thing as
a pulpit, still less pews, chairs, table, altar, or font.
Then there is another little room at the side, with a
place to wash, and vessels of water all set in order,
that those who come to pray may first wash their
head, feet, and arms to the elbows.

"It is but natural to expect from among the Maulvis, whom one finds in the village mosques, the keenest
opposition to the preaching of the Gospel.   Still there
are among this class men of devout minds, and true
seekers after God.   With one of these, who lives in
Bhera, I have had some very interesting discussions,
and have found him to be a man not only of learning,
but of a liberal and inquiring mind.   He has been
supplied at his request with the Old Testament in
Arabic and the New Testament in Urdu, and he is
very anxious to purchase a commentary. . . . This
Maulvi has undergone considerable persecution from
his co-religionists, who, after a very stormy debate,
which nearly reached the point of actual violence,

excommunicated him, 'for holding doctrines at variance with their interpretation of the Muhamadan creed.'"

Not many miles from Pind Dádan Khán, about 2000 feet above the plains, in the Salt Range, is one of the most celebrated places of Hindu worship. It is called Katáksh. Here annually pilgrims flock in large crowds. Winding up the road from Choga Saidan Sháh, along the course of a sparkling mountain stream, overshadowed by rich foliage which is most grateful to the eye of one who has long been in the plains, suddenly at a bend in the road one comes upon the _holy_ place nestling down in a gorge. A large pool of water surrounded by picturesque temples reveals the source of the stream by which we have wandered. Speaking of this, and of the great annual assemblage of pilgrims, Gordon says :—"The story is that the pool was formed by the tears of the god Vishnu, on the death of one of his wives. So the Hindus consider that the water has cleansing virtues, and that to bathe in it is to be purged from sin. There were vast crowds of people there from distant parts, and I tried to draw their attention to that 'fountain filled with blood, drawn from Immanuel's veins,' which has been opened for sin and for uncleanness. They listened very attentively, but when I began to offer them books, I found that few of them could read.

"One man in the crowd recognised me and followed me a long way in conversation. He was a

Muhamadan whom I had conversed with in this place more than a year ago.

. . . .

"It was curious to sit on a height as I did the next morning, and watch the long file of pilgrims winding in and out of the hills on their return to their distant homes. Some were on foot, some on camels, some on horses and donkeys, all in their best holiday attire, and many decked most profusely with gold and silver ornaments, and gems on head, neck, arms and ankles. Most of them seemed to regard it as a fair, and it had much of the ordinary accompaniments of a fair, in exhibitions of juggling, dancing, wrestling, etc.

. . . .

"When I was at Jhílam on my way here, I met a very interesting Muhamadan Maulvi, who has recently embraced Christianity, with all his family. He had been for years a seeker after the truth, going about to establish a righteousness which was after the law and therefore fruitless of peace. He is now rejoicing in the treasure he has found, and it is his daily prayer that his old father may find the same peace and joy in believing. Such a man may prove a pillar of strength to the native church, if he is allowed to retain his simplicity and humility. There is such a temptation to make an 'interesting case' of each new convert, for the benefit of our English friends, and our native brethren, who find out how much is made of them, get their heads turned, and gradually lose their 'first love'

" At Jhílam I baptized a native soldier of the 22d
Regiment, at his earnest request ; he said that he
'loved Jesus with all his heart,' and had endured
much opposition for the step he was taking, as he
was the son of a Muhamadan Seyyid. He certainly
could gain nothing, as far as I know, by becoming
a Christian (in a worldly point of view), and would
lose the support which he had hitherto had, for all
Muhamadans think it a duty, and a meritorious one,
too, to maintain the son of a Seyyid (or descendant
of their Prophet). Not having much time at Jhílam
to instruct this young man, and knowing the difficulty
of being a Christian in a native regiment, it was in
sore fear and trembling that I baptized him ; but I
trust and hope that he may prove a good soldier of
the cross, and not a traitor."

Somewhat later Gordon puts on record an un-
solicited native testimony to English good government:—"Just now, as I was walking along the
road, I met a long string of camels laden with
sugar. The owner, after making his salaam to me,
involuntarily exclaimed, 'I can carry my goods in
safety now !'"

He was thinking of the time when (in his own
recollection) these roads were so infested with robbers
that neither person nor property were safe.

On another occasion he writes :—"After preaching
in a distant village one evening, I was followed by a
man who earnestly asked for instruction, saying that
he had purchased some religious books in Pind Dádan

Khán, and wished to have them explained. It was getting dark, and I had a long walk before me, so I invited him to my lodging next day. He described himself as a stranger from Ráwal Pindí, whither he was then bound, and I have not seen him since, but I hope that he may find a Philip at Ráwal Pindí."

The case of this man was similar to many that are met with in India. One missionary labours, another enters into his labours. We hear of this inquirer, that he ultimately came to Multan and there was baptized by the resident missionary on March 14, 1875.

Again we read,—" On a recent walk I met another man who accosted me, saying, I had spoken to him once after preaching in the bazar. He described himself as a fakír, and disciple of a certain Maulvi of repute (now dead). He had paid several visits to the bookshop, and had purchased the New Testament in Urdu, and several portions of the Old Testament. He then produced the New Testament, which was reverently wrapped up with one or two Arabic books in a cloth, and invited me to explain one or two passages, which were obscure to him, such as Gal. iii. 13, 'Christ being made a curse for us,' and the words of the angel in Acts i., which seemed to him to imply that Christ must necessarily return during the lifetime of those who saw Him ascend. So we sat in a ploughed field under a tree, and had an hour's conversation, which was listened to by other passers by. He has since attended my preaching with Andreas in the bazar; and, although he still has difficulties, yet I feel hopeful as well as interested in him."

Instances like this might be multiplied, clearly justifying both the opinion of Gordon, that the people of this district are open to instruction, and the regret already expressed that his plans have not been more warmly taken up by the Church Missionary Society· One of the best methods of showing appreciation of such a man as Gordon, would be to support the solitary missionary at Pind Dádan Khán by efficient helpers.

> " PIND DÁDAN KHÁN,
> _September_ 13, 1874.

"I am convinced that in India we might see like results if we were all on 'fire for Christ.' Too often, alas, the fire pent up is sadly stifled in a long and tedious (but necessary) contest, not with 'the rulers of the darkness of this world,' but with verbs, and tenses, and conjugations — often also with physical and mental prostration. And while one hopes to lift up one's voice like a trumpet against some heathen or Muhamadan Jericho, one staggers home under the conviction of having been barely understood. But while there is some ground for heartache, I feel there is more ground for shame and confusion of face.

"I have been mercifully preserved from anything but slight illness this trying season, and enabled to do a good deal of work.

" To walk ninety miles in seven days and preach twice a day, is what I could not have believed that I could have accomplished in the hottest season of the year in India. But I have done even more than this through mercy. I can make myself perfectly well understood in Hindustani, but not yet in Punjabi. However, there are some in every village who know Hindustani."

Gordon's letters during this period are full of little sketches of individuals, which perhaps bring before the reader the hopes and fears, the success and failure of a missionary's life more than anything else.

Besides, these little incidents help us, perhaps, more than hundreds of descriptions in general terms, to realise the people with their different habits and thoughts.

For this reason, perhaps, this chapter cannot be concluded in a better manner than by giving a few of these in the original.

In one letter, Gordon has been lamenting the·difference between Persian and Indian Muhamadans. According to strict Muhamadan teaching, whether in the Kuran or not, the true Muslim ought to have no caste prejudices. As long as he abstains from what are laid down as unclean meats and alcoholic drinks, he may mix freely in social intercourse with Christians. Thus we find in Turkey, in Arabia, in Persia, Muhamadans eat and drink with Christians without any restraint. But when we come on to India all this is changed. The main population of the

country is Hindu, and it is well known that caste restrictions form the most evident and prominent part
of their system in the eyes of a casual observer. Not
only will the Hindu decline to eat and drink with a
person of another religion, but he will not, if he be of
a high caste, even touch meat with the tip of his finger.
And among those who are of the same religion, the
higher caste will have nothing to do with the lower.

Now, Muhamadans in India are very similar in
their habits. This is partly a consequence of their
Hindu origin. The original customs were not
thoroughly effaced by Muhamadan conquests, and
the conversion of the people to Islam. It also partly
arises from mere contact with the Hindus. I have
seen this myself in the case of border people. Those
who some few years ago had no notion of what
caste meant, now, as our Empire gradually extends
itself and our officials bring up with them Hindus
and Muhamadans of India, so they bring caste too.
It takes root and spreads, and those who once were
quite free and independent in their social intercourse
with Europeans, gradually become shy, and eventually refuse to partake of the same dish.

Speaking of this Gordon says :—" Here in India
the miserable system of caste prevails . . . and if a
Muhamadan eats with a Christian, his neighbours
reproach him as though he had thereby become a
Christian. I have lately had a sad instance of how
far Muhamadan bigotry can go. A young convert
has been going about with me preaching. I took him

to his own village, fifty miles away, in order that I might help him to bear testimony to Christ before his relatives, but I found them as hard as a flint, and as cold as ice towards their son, who had (as they considered) disgraced them by becoming a Christian. In fact, I was told that the father, who is head of his village, has been excommunicated by his friends and relatives on account of his son's defection from the Muhamadan faith!

"It was in vain that I asked them to give up their son's wife, whom they withheld from her husband. So I was obliged to pass on with a heavy heart. But this was not my only cause of uneasiness. For by means of threats and promises, the young convert's faith and constancy were quite shaken. He began to talk of a compromise, a serving of two masters, the world and Christ, and although the day before he had been earnestly cautioned by me for using over-confident language, like that of St. Peter, yet, like St. Peter, he fell, and denied his Master. I could only commend him in prayer to that gracious Master for repentance and forgiveness ; and although he has for the time 'forsaken me, having loved this present world,' yet I hope that he will be preserved from the fearful consequences of his backsliding, and be brought again to the foot of the Cross.

"When lately preaching in a village, some fanatical Muhamadans, finding that noise and ridicule did not silence me, threatened me with violence, but their conduct only disgusted the more sober class of my hearers, and secured for me an attentive audience, while they were obliged to walk away ashamed."

It is, I believe, of this same place that Gordon writes at a later date :—" It happened that a villager of Kariála, going to B—— on business, heard sounds as of mourning for the dead. Upon inquiry, he found that the lamentation was for one considered morally dead—that is, dead to Muhamad; alive to Christ. It then appeared that one of those Mullah's sons who had opposed me had become himself a convert to the true faith. Beirig thus separated from his home, he had gone to Jhílam, where he found an American missionary, by whom he was further instructed and baptized.   As a general rule, there is hardly any part of the Bible which I find more attentively listened to than Matt. v., etc. The remark of Dean Stanley is a true one, that however much controversy there may be about the authenticity of the Gospels, 'the whole world bows down before the beauty of the eight Beatitudes, and the parable of the Prodigal Son, and the story of the Sufferings and Death of Christ.' I remember hearing of a Hindu in the South of India, who, although he never became a Christian, yet was so struck by the 5th of St Matthew, that he wrote a commentary upon it in Tamil.

" A dervish, whom I lately met, was so arrested by the Gospel story, that he walked with me six miles in order to hear it, and then walked back again, promising to come and visit me at Pind Dádan Khán.

"'Why,' he exclaimed, 'are there no preachers

P

of these glad tidings in our parts?' And he added, with fervour, 'When we inquire into the nature of God and salvation, the pleasures of earth seem like broken potsherds in comparison!'

"Two years later it was evident that the seed thus sown had germinated, for the man presented himself as a candidate for baptism.

"Another said, 'Your Government ought to place the Gospel in the hands of every Maulvi in the neighbourhood.'

"Two days ago, I was conversing with a very intelligent Maulvi, who keeps a large school, and whom I had furnished with a Bible only a few weeks previously.

"He had read the New Testament before, but had certain doubts in his mind, and after reading a number of passages with him, I asked him whether his doubts were removed. 'Yes,' he said, 'I am satisfied that Jesus Christ is the Son of God, and that His Word is true. I believe that there is no contradiction between the Law and the Gospel. I believe that the Kuran is not the Word of God, for it is contradictory to itself and the Gospel. The Maulvis know this, and that is why they forbid Muhamadans to read the Gospel.

'I have great hopes of this Maulvi, as being near the Kingdom of Heaven, but he will have a hard struggle when it comes to the point, for he has two wives and a large family, and a number of relations, who will all be against him. What I am so anxious to impress upon inquirers is, 'It is not Christianity that can help you, but Christ.'"

In the following summer we find Gordon still giving this Maulvi instruction. In the heat of July he writes :—"I ride over now and then to Kariála, but as there is no shelter there from the fierce noon-day heat, my only opportunity for conversation with the Maulvi is in the hours of the night, between a double journey of fifteen miles each way."

We find subsequent allusion to this man in various letters and journals. For instance, Yakub, at Gordon's request, took up his abode in Kariála. This Maulvi gave him quarters and showed him hospitality. This "so stirred up the enmity of the head man of the village—a bigoted Muhamadan—that he incited the people to deny the Maulvi access to the village well and the village bakery, and withdraw their children from school (which it will be remembered the Maulvi kept). Yakub then wrote to me that he had left the Maulvi's house, and as no one else would give him quarters, for fear of the lambardar (headman), he was living with his wife and child under a tree."

This persecution, with the assistance of a district officer, was put down, and a lodging for the Christian provided.

Again, writing to Mr. Macartney, of Melbourne, Gordon says, doubtless in allusion to the same man : —" A poor persecuted villager is now waiting to see me. His avowal of his belief has cost him the loss of one wife, the estrangement of another, the reproach of all his friends, and the destruction by his enemies of his three crops of corn. He speaks most resignedly of all his losses."

One more, an extract from a journal, shall conclude this chapter.

"I sat talking in a blacksmith's shop, when a boy who was there went out and brought a vicious-looking Mullah, who rudely insisted on my going to the masjid and holding a controversy there. I represented to him that I came not to controvert but to instruct such as were willing to listen. He then turned to the people and told them not to listen, for that we were unbelievers, who observed neither fasting, prayers, nor anything else. Finding himself in a minority, he went and got several other Mullahs worse than himself, one of whom, named Ali, was, *facile princeps*, in ill-condition and churlishness.

"As he refused to let me be heard as a teacher, I offered to become the taught. My first question, How can man be just with God ? elicited so very shifting and evasive a reply, that I was obliged to repeat it several times. As each time my interlocutor got more noisy and vehement, I shut the sacred Book and asked a question out of the Kuran, which he did not find it convenient to answer. After begging him again to hear the message of peace, with the same fruitless result, I was obliged to leave the people to judge between the true and the false religion from the example of their own teachers, with a prayer that God would lead them to the right choice."

CHAPTER XI.

JHÍLAM ITINERANCY—1875-76.

IT has been already said that, in the life which Gordon was leading in this Mission, he followed more nearly the example and practice of our Lord and Saviour than he had previously done, and than missionaries in India in general find themselves able to do.

When the Jhílam Itinerancy was first commenced, with Pind Dádan Khán as headquarters, there was no comfortable home to greet the missionary when he returned travel-worn from his marches. Nothing more than a hired native house, which we might almost call a hut, protected him from the "smiting of the sun by day." Some time later, Gordon was able to procure a better shelter. Just outside the town of Pind Dádan Khán is the site of an old fort. It is marked by one solitary tower and sundry mounds, where buildings were once. This tower, the property of Government, was rented to Gordon for the modest sum of about £4, 10s. per annum. He subsequently purchased it, and to the present time it remains the property of the Pind Dádan Khán Mission.

Perhaps when we read the words of General Maclagan, R.E., in the "C. M. Intelligencer" for October 1880, we may almost seem to get a glimpse of the missionary in this *sumptuous* abode, enjoying a little well-earned rest.   After speaking of the privations which Gordon endures, the account continues :—

"Yet his little *tower* at Pind Dádan Khán (it was the corner bastion of an old fort, of which little else remained) was not without comforts for its occupant when he paid it occasional visits.   A few well-chosen books on the shelves, and some good engravings on the walls, sufficed to give it such a home-like aspect as befitted the abode of a man of literary culture and refined taste, and was suitable to the simple character of the building.   The roof of this tower commanded a general view of the three villages which, united, form the town of Pind Dádan Khán, and beyond, the prospect extended up to the salt hills in one direction, and over the river in another."

At the time, however, of which we are speaking now, there was no such luxury as is here indicated.

In July 1875, he writes a circular letter, which seems to bring us face to face with the apostolic life.   It is headed by the address, "Banyan Tree at Bishárat."   He says :—

"I have taken a house for two days, which is beautifully furnished (with leaves), and has a noble column in the centre, with other smaller columns forming arches and cloisters round it.

"The lower storey only is mine, the upper storey being occupied by a number of small tenants, who are

GORDON'S TOWER AT PIND DÁDAN KHÁN.

for the most part night lodgers, and who waken me
in the morning by their song of praise long before
sunrise. I often envy the simplicity of their arrangements for food, clothing, and service. I envy also the
lightness of their hearts, and the sociability of their
habits. For the work in which I am engaged—a work
that demands much retirement in prayer, and much
accessibility to the natives—I find that solitude (in a
certain sense) is very desirable. I mean, that a solitary evangelist gets nearer to the people than if he
were accompanied by companions. As I sit writing,
I am by no means alone (except in spirit). There
are at least thirty men (to say nothing of boys) lying
and sitting around me under the same tree, at their
noonday rest from the plough. And yet they are so
well-behaved, that I am often quite unconscious of
their presence. I am quite certain that thirty plough-
men from an English district would not compare with
them for politeness and good manners, or for intelligence either.

"One of them is an old pensioner, who has seen
sixteen years' service in the Indian army, and has
medals for the Mutiny and the Bhootán campaign.

"He has just brought me his little boy, who is
learning to read (from a book), and if I let him, he
would entertain me (in native style), at his own expense, for a week. Two others of my companions are
young soldiers from a cantonment about fifty miles
off, on leave amongst their friends and relations. Another is a Hindu merchant, who invited me just now

to expound from the Gospel, and gave a deferential assent to every word I said. The rest are Muhamadan zemindars (or cultivators), and one or two fakírs.

"Yesterday I had a most intelligent visitor, who explained with great composure that he was a convict just returned from ten years' transportation in the Andaman Islands. He had nothing of the gaol-bird expression of our convicts at home, and seemed to be much respected in his village. I was curious to hear his history. He said, 'I was a boy just out of school when it happened. My family had a feud, and killed their enemy. I was identified as being on the spot. Some of us were hanged, and some transported. He had had a very pleasant time in the Andamans. One clergyman was very kind to him; he was taught English, and Persian, ... he passed an examination with credit, and was appointed schoolmaster to the children of the convicts. He had purchased an English and Hindustani New Testament in Calcutta, which he showed me, and when I expounded passages, he gave an intelligent response, and promised to come to see me in Pind Dádan Khán.

"This man's history is not an uncommon one. In this district feuds are sadly frequent, in which blood is shed. It is exceedingly difficult for the magistrate to decide who is in fault, in consequence of the prevailing tendency to untruthfulness, but it generally happens that both sides are at fault.

"This morning I climbed a hill on which there is a very ancient shrine, frequented by Hindu as well as

Muhamadan pilgrims. There is no idol, not even a
tomb or a fakír, only a tradition that fakírs used to
sit there hundreds of years ago. So anyone who is
in trouble, or pain, or childless, goes and pays his
vows, and sacrifices his kid or goat, and believes he
gets relief. No doubt, for certain disorders, a stiff
walk up a steep, rocky path would (by quickening the
action of the liver) produce a desirable reaction, and
be regarded by the credulous as a miraculous cure."

About this same time Gordon writes :—

"I can so thoroughly endorse your valuable
remarks about the 'empty pitcher' being the vessel
most honoured of God. Self takes a deal of empty-
ing, even under favourable circumstances. Solitude
and retirement, watchings and fastings, 'living on
sixpence a day and earning it,' habituation to fatigue
and self-denial—these I have found to be very favourable when rightly directed to the work of Evangelisation, and yet it often astonishes me to feel what a
sturdy grip old self has got, and how much there is
for grace to do.

"And one is driven more and more to the acknowledgment of that greater miracle of the Christian Dispensation (as Leander truly states it), viz. :
—the communication of the Life of God to the
Soul of Man.

"Having a young civilian friend with me lately,
vigorously preaching, and sharing my tent for a
week, set me thinking upon the great advance that
Mission work might make if all civilians and military

men were brought under the influence of a revival. At home, if one were to start a mission, there would be no lack of missionaries, lay and clerical, to assist. Here one stands 'without the camp,' and calls, but no one comes. Chaplains are asleep. Civilians (such as my nearest neighbour) are sceptics or sensualists, and those few who are of the right sort are too far away to come.

"Meantime one has no leisure to be despondent— the work is so vast, and the night cometh."

Again, on another occasion, the following is extracted from Gordon's diary :—

"*2nd.*—Started by moonlight, and walked 10½ miles to Núrpúr. The road ascends at once to a higher plateau, with very fertile land and villages dotted about. Passed some very ancient tombs, one of which seemed like a mosque with four doors but no roof. On entering found it to be a family burial-place, with twelve tombstones hoary with age. No inscriptions whatever. The village of Núrpúr has no accommodation (as most villages have) for travellers, so I spent the day under a tree. The people soon collected, the village barber sitting at my feet, and beginning to manipulate the muscles of my leg. This shampooing custom is evidently an attention shown to wayfarers, and reminds one of the similar courtesy of washing the feet of a priest in Bible lands. It is by no means an unwelcome, and certainly a wholesome, method of treatment after the fatigues of a

long walk. Our meal was cooked and eaten before
a large audience, who afterwards listened attentively
while Andreas and I sung a hymn and prayed the
Litany. They were afterwards addressed by both
of us on the Gospel rules of devotion. Had many
visitors during the day, as my tree stood in a public
place in the middle of a street. Their questions show
how difficult it is for them to realise our object.
'What is your salary?' 'Where is your home?'
'Have you no tent?' etc. The other day a Sikh
hit upon a happy solution, 'I see you are what we
call *Sádu*, the Muhamadans say *fakír.*' In the
evening some little schoolboys came and requested
to know what I could possibly mean by saying, as
I did in the morning, that Muhamad Sáhib could
never make atonement for our sins. Had they not
read that even the world could not have been created
without him? A shopkeeper sat conversing till late,
when the street began to be paraded by two wedding
processions with music. This was kept up through
the entire night with relentless severity. All my
experiments at sleep proved fruitless. It is only a
native who can sleep through the wild discords of
a hymenæal chorus.

During this period a great grief befell Gordon.
He had, as his journals have implied, a most faithful
native helper named Andreas, one on whom he
seemed to rely with the fullest confidence. In the
Christmas of 1874-75, Andreas took cold in Amritsar,
consumption set in, and in spite of the summer spent

in Kashmir with Dr. Maxwell, he rapidly became worse on his return to work.

"In Nov. 1875," Gordon writes, "he is now holding on to life by a very frail tenure. I miss him much, because although his good qualities are those of a pastor rather than an evangelist, yet, in faithfulness and readiness to remain at his post, he has been a true pattern and a valuable helper. Although feeble in body, he is strong in spirit, and most patient in suffering. 'Tell Mr. French,' he says, 'that I have no fear of death, but joy and confidence.' Among his visitors in sickness are an old Hindu pundit, and a young Muhamadan school teacher, who show a kindly sympathy and appreciation of his former counsels. A recently-converted Muhamadan Maulvi, of Jhilam, has spoken to me of him in terms of true brotherly affection. To another Muhamadan Maulvi, who is an inquirer, he has written a letter of Christian exhortation as a dying message. His loss is a heavy blow to a young mission like this, and the more so that I have no one to supply his place. For this kind of work offers a searching test to the sincerity of applicants for employment as preachers; and sometimes with only depressing results. Of three native candidates who have withdrawn their applications, one stipulated for a salary which exceeded the limits fixed by a very liberal estimate, and which would certainly have excited the envy of his worthy acquaintances. Another estimates his services for Christ at their possible commercial value in the

Government market. He 'cannot afford' to evangelise his countrymen for less than £120 a year, a salary equal relatively to £480 to a European. A third, who entered into an engagement with me, and came with his family at my expense more than 200 miles, although trained in one of our orphanages, is far too respectable to share my native house, walk with me from village to village, and make his chupatties as I do mine.

" He confesses that he never expected this kind of work, and it does not suit him at all. He must seek employment elsewhere. And thus he leaves me, and embitters by his conduct the last days of poor Andreas, who mourns over such unfaithfulness to One who ' had not where to lay His head.'

"These men have all been trained in mission schools, and although unfitted for spiritual work, might succeed well in some other department. They are not strictly natives of the Punjab, and one is led to the conclusion that as for countries so also for provinces, the right teachers are those who are country-born. When the Gospel takes hold of the hearts of the hardy and simple Zemindars of the Punjab (as it is beginning to do), they will doubtless be the true leaders of a spontaneous movement towards Christianity. None the less searching and anxious, however, should be our inquiries as to whether our methods of training the Native mind are the most judicious.

" *Feb.* 12*th*, 1876.—Since I began this letter, which

I've been obliged to lay aside for two months, Andreas
has been taken to his rest, and our little cemetery has
received the first mission seed 'sown in corruption,'
to be 'raised in incorruption.' During his last few
months he seemed to be ripening for his promotion.
He had failed to pass at the last Catechist's examination at Amritsar for a higher grade ; but within a year
he obtained the highest place which a faithful disciple
can aspire to. I do not repine at the issue so plainly
appointed by the Master. We did all that we could
to prolong his life, but the disease was one which
often proves incontrollable by human skill.

"What I most desire is that his example in thus
dying at his post should not be lost upon his native
Christian brethren who survive him. And yet I fear,
not without reason, lest it should have an intimidat-
ing rather than a stimulating effect upon them.

"Andreas was a man of few words, and one who
took a sober rather than a sanguine view of things.
When, after preaching in a village one Sunday, I
tried to animate him by an account of revival work in
Scotland to hope for a corresponding revival here, he
remarked very justly, 'You cannot compare the two
cases. In my country the bones are *very dry*, in
yours there is *some* flesh upon them.'

"On St. Andrew's Day he received the Holy Communion in his bed for the last time. I remarked to
him that St. Andrew's example was one which he
had well followed. He replied, 'Ah! our work is
poor enough, and we deserve nothing for it ; but

what a beautiful text that is in Revelation, " Be thou faithful unto death, and I will give unto thee a crown of life." Oh that I may obtain that crown !' He added, ' Christ left everything for us ; it is only right that we should give up a _little_ for Him. Mr. French was always saying this to us. Alas, how few there are who are willing to do this ! I should greatly like to finish my work at Pind Dádan Khán. I have a great desire to preach. The people are bad, yet we must tell them of the Lord's mercy.'

"The Rev. J. Lapsley, who saw him about this time, wrote to me afterwards :—' One might envy the tranquillity and resignation with which he can contemplate his fast approaching end.' Many kind inquiries were made after him by English friends, and especially by Capt. Hutchison, the Assistant Commissioner, who, by reading and praying beside his dying bed, performed that office of true Christian brotherhood which ' availeth much.'

"We were a very little band as we stood round his grave on the 9th December—only Yakub, the native Christian chowkeydar, and the native Christian schoolmaster of Bhawa, and the Collector of Customs at Khewra, who kindly came five miles to show his sympathy—a very small company, in view of a very large town of heathens and Muhamadans. I earnestly desired that all my native Christian brethren in Lahore and Amritsar could have been there too, to gather some instruction from that open grave, if perchance there might be one heart touched by a generous impulse to stand in the breach and to say, in response to that silent appeal, 'Lord, here am I, send me.'"

In 1876, Gordon writes from Pind Dádan Khán :—

"Our chief interest at the beginning of 1876 was a promised visit from the Bishop, a visit to which subsequent events have given a melancholy prominence. It is hardly likely that so remote a place as Pind Dádan Khán will ever be visited by a Bishop of Calcutta again. Bishop Milman came on February 18, looking remarkably well, after a very cold and wet night-journey from Gujarat in a dooly, followed by another down the Jhílam in an open boat. Our little church was filled by a congregation of twenty, most of whom had come from distances of from five to fifty miles. Mr. Jacob and Mr. Lapsley took part in the service, at which the Bishop confirmed seven candidates—four European and three native,—and gave a very solemn and fatherly exhortation, the singing being led by a harmonium, which was his own kind gift to the church.

"The native Christians who were confirmed were Yakub and his wife, and Goolab Khan. A few weeks later the scattered members of that little congregation heard, one by one, through various channels, that their chief pastor was removed, and we sadly realised that Pind Dádan Khán, Rawál Pindi, and Peshawur had been the Gilgal, Bethel and Jericho of our honoured leader's departing steps. God grant that some true 'sons of the prophets' may be raised up at each.

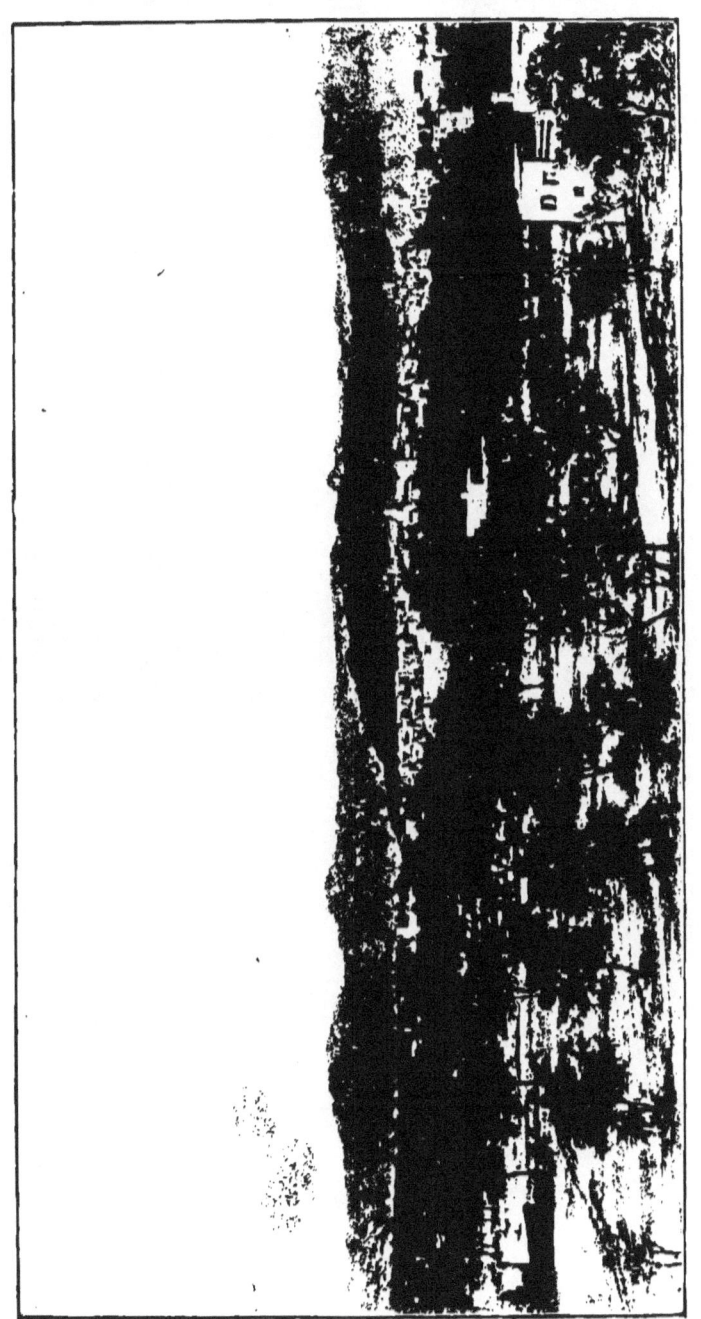

PIND DADAN KHÁN, FROM GORDON'S TOWER.

"One great cause of thankfulness during the past year has been the immunity which this district has enjoyed from the epidemic which has visited so severely other localities. While we heard of hundreds a day swept off by fever at Amritsar, Jalandhar Marí and other places, our death rate was comparatively low, proving that our district contrasts very favourably with others. Occasional outbreaks of cholera we had, but they were confined to small villages, not to be attributed to local causes so much as to individual carelessness. Still, during the sickly months of August and September, one had plenty of applicants for medicine among the villagers. With the Bible in one hand, and quinine in the other, there was abundant access to houses which would otherwise have been closed, and some very valuable experience was gained. The conviction was greatly strengthened that the medical element, when combined with missionary work, is a powerful auxiliary for good, and I earnestly trust that this district may not be long without a medical missionary. The helplessness of the people and their prejudices against hospitals, even when available, is a reason for some special effort to visit patients in their own homes.

"Sometimes they tell you that their mullahs and pundits forbid them the hospital and the dispensary, on the plea that the medicines are mixed by heretical hands. Sometimes there is a famous 'peer' or quack in their neighbourhood, whose amulets are potent to confer anything, from a son-and-heir to a good appetite,

the amulet being probably a scrap of paper with a
text of the Kuran to be taken in water. Sometimes
there is a shrine to be visited with votive offerings.
If the defunct saint be a renowned one, he must be
propitiated by the sacrifice of a goat ; if an ordinary
individual, it will suffice to tie a piece of rag over his
tomb, or strike a peg in front of it. A man has
been bitten by a snake. He is a Hindu, so he sends
for two Brahmans to pronounce mantras or incantations, and, in case they fail, he employs also a
Muhamadan, that he may be saved by the Kuran
if not by the Shastras. At the same time, there is a
general impression that the white man's incantations
are the most powerful, and that we have instantaneous
(albeit illicit) cures for everything. One poor old man,
who has cried himself blind over the death of his son,
wants his sight restored ; another, who is bedridden,
wants the use of his limbs ; a third asks a remedy
for chronic chest or liver complaint. The solicitations
become increasingly urgent if one's remedies have
given relief; and a case of cholera, which I treated
successfully from a book, brought me many patients,
and was, I believe, gratefully remembered.

" The months of August and September brought
me into contact with no less than eighty different
villages, chiefly those of the Salt Range (a larger
number than I had access to in any other two months
of the year), and I thankfully record the fact, because
it shows that such precautions as a daily dose of
quinine, a Spartan diet, teetotalism, and constant

exercise on foot, with change of air, may, by God's
blessing, enable even a feverish subject like myself
to pursue the work without interruption. And any
suspension of such duties for a month, or even for a
week, would be a most serious hindrance ; for when
one has traversed 3500 miles of one's district in the
year (as far as to Cape Comorin and back), and
preached in 213 different towns and villages, more or
less frequently, then there is the painful consciousness
of twice that number left unvisited. For the administration of law, we think it necessary that each district,
like Jhílam, Sháhpur and Jhang, should have a full
staff of European officers, with scores of native subordinates. In the name of religion, it is considered
enough for three such districts to have one missionary.
What if in our slowness to discern God's purpose of
mercy towards these great cities, the work be committed to other hands, or some drying up of the
'gourd' of our national prosperity, be the lesson employed to arouse us to a more earnest effort ?

"The year has been intersected by three journeys
to Sháhpur and Jhang, which were extended to
Multán and Derá Ghazi Khán, and this is equivalent to a London clergyman having Lincoln, York
and Newcastle in his charge, to be visited periodic-
ally without the assistance of railways or coaches.

"I have not been able yet to replace the loss
of my native brother Andreas, but I believe that
Yakub does his best as the 'Luke' of the Pind
Dádan Khán Mission. He readily consented to

my proposal that he should take up his quarters at Kariála, a village thirty miles from Pind Dádan Khán, where there is an inquiring Maulvi named Shirreff Deen who gave him quarters in his own house. This hospitality to a disciple of Christ so stirred up the enmity of the headman of the village, a bigoted Muhamadan, that he incited the people to deny the Maulvi access to the village well and the village bakery, and withdraw their children from school. Yakub then wrote to me that he had left the Maulvi's house, and as no one else would give him quarters for fear of the 'lambardar,' he was living with his wife and child under a tree. By the assistance of the officer of the district I was able to obtain shelter for Yakub, and afterwards the headman deemed it better to conciliate his superior by helping him to a lodging. From the same friendly source I obtained an adjoining site, where I raised a little Christian mosque for my own habitation, at the moderate cost of £3, including the compound wall. By visiting the place from time to time I found that (the opposition of the headman withdrawn) the people were peaceable enough, and only once had I to arbitrate in a case where some personal violence in the heat of controversy had been shown to Yakub. An entry in my journal at a subsequent date says, 'I have been spending several days at Kariála where we were trying to fan into brightness a spark of spiritual life which

Satan is doing all he can to quench.   The Maulvi
is working with both hands at his school and his
glebe, and doing all I believe in the name of
Christ, although shrinking as yet from the ordeal
of baptism.   At first he seemed to succumb to
the opposition which his Christian principle aroused,
and withdrew himself awhile from instruction.   Now
he is creeping out again, comes to Yakub after
his day's work, for prayer and reading, and joins
the service in my little mosque.   When urged to
make a bolder stand for Christ, he tearfully pleads
his difficulties, but does not attempt to justify his
faintheartedness.   He has gained over one of his
two wives to the true faith, but the other is still a
thorn in his side.'

"Near Kariála is the village of B——, where at
my first preaching the fanaticism of the Mullahs
carried them past the bounds of insult, even to
personal violence.   Their excesses as usual over-
reached themselves and procured for me an attentive hearing from the respectable class.   After this
my duties took me hundreds of miles away, and
it was not for more than a year that I revisited
that village, and heard that the seed had not been
sown in vain.   It came to me first through another
source.   It happened that a villager of Kariála
going to B—— on business heard sounds as of mourning for the dead.   Upon inquiry he found that the
lamentation was for one considered morally dead,
that is dead to Muhamad, alive to Christ.   It

then appeared that the son of one of those Mullahs
who had opposed me had become himself a convert to the true faith.   Being thus separated from
his home he had gone to Jhílam, where he found
an American missionary, by whom he was further
instructed and baptized.

"Two other candidates for baptism came to Yakub
in my absence and pressed to see me.   One was a
dervish whom I had had an interesting morning walk
with two years before, the other a steward on a tea
plantation in Cachar who had heard us in his own
village.   They were both on their travels, and have
not since been traced.   I mention them as instances
of a class of inquirers who seek instruction from the
European missionary, and whom it is difficult to
reach while the cardinal points of one's itinerancy are
300 miles apart.   It seldom happens that one finds a
disciple so free from worldly ties as the Sádu mentioned in my last report.   Trained in the rigid school
of asceticism, this simple unlettered fakír is ready to
'endure hardness as a soldier of Christ,' and though
he has not been yet enrolled under His banner, yet
his apprenticeship for more than a year as a follower
and learner gives me a good hope that his baptism
will be no mere form, but an intelligent and faithful
oath of allegiance to Christ.

"One of the most valuable (as well as difficult)
lessons taught by this kind of work is the quiet abiding God's time.   'It is good that a man should both
hope and quietly wait for the salvation of the Lord.'

"Pind Dádan Khán lies low, but the hills are never out of sight. There is the Salt Range in front, and there are glimpses on clear days of the snowy barriers Kashmir behind, reminding one of that ridge of Moab mountains which was in David's view when he said, 'I will lift up mine eyes unto the hills from whence cometh my help.' 'We see not yet all things put under Him, but we see Jesus crowned with glory and honour;' and He is not without His witnesses everywhere. The expectation of His coming and kingdom is alive amongst Hindus as well as Muhamadans. They find nothing unfamiliar in the thought of the absorption of all creeds, castes, and languages into one at His reign. The former often reconcile this doctrine with their popular belief in one whom they call Né Kalank, the 10th, or 'Sinless' Incarnation; while the latter speak of Imám Mahdi as the coming deliverer. But the Mussalman holds among his traditions, 'Mal Mahdiyo illa Isabni Mariyama,' *i.e.*, there is no Mahdi save Jesus, Son of Mary. An old Sikh one day stopped me on the road with the question, 'When is Christ coming?' as though it lay much on his mind. A Muhamadan officer, who made me his guest, hoped that His coming might be near, 'for when He comes, I will lay my turban at His feet,'— and he gracefully suited the action to the word."

A few extracts from my daily journal which I append will illustrate in an unvarnished way some of the various phases of mind which present themselves.

One naturally avoids dwelling upon the gloomy

side. It is not pleasant to descend one of the mummy caves of Egypt, and tread among the bones of former generations, or to meet the caravan which carries the Persian dead for interment in the cemetary at Kerbela. And there is much that weighs heavily on the spirit in our pleadings with the deadness and dulness of heathen bondslaves, but we believe in the Holy Ghost as the Lord and giver of Life, we acknowledge the power of Christ over the darkness of the tomb, and we look to see his name inscribed over these mosques and temples.

"It is a matter of great thankfulness that succours are coming from Cambridge to assist our brother Winter at Delhi, and that Australia is beginning to give her sons and her daughters to the Southern Missions.

"May many more be led to obey the call as Myconius did, who, seeing in dream the solitary reaper on the harvest plain, and being led by the Guide to the fountain of life, hesitated no longer to leave the cloister and to grasp the sickle so nobly wielded by a Luther. What an impulse would such a crusade give to our holy warfare, and how different an account would our reports present of the work of the Lord as prospered in our hands."

"*January* 31.—Walked fourteen miles to S—— stopping at the fakír's temple near Myani on the way. He showed me, preserved with great care, the Bible and other books which Mr. French had given him

three years ago. He cannot read himself, but his
disciple has 'read them to him.' His personal testimony to Mr. French reminds me of Justin Martyr's
record of the 'meek and venerable old man' whom
he met on the sea shore. 'I saw him no more, but
forthwith a fire was kindled in my soul, and I was
filled with a love for those people and friends of
Christ of whom he had spoken. And when I pon-
dered all his words I began to see this was the only
philosophy that was safe and suited my needs.'

"*March* 11.—Walked to Jhang and called on G.
M., the native Christian schoolmaster. Maulvi Ali
Muhamad, another teacher in the school, and a great
reader of religious books, came to see me—also
Chiragh Shah, a fakír of the Sufi or philosophical class
of Muhamadans. He is not a reader, but a thinker,
and has a numerous following, to whom he expounds
his doctrines. In the course of conversation he remarked, 'We are all travellers, this is not our home,
why should we set our affections on things of this
world? What is it that guides us? yes, the Spirit of
God. The heart of man is impure: it must be
swept; and God's Word is the broom to sweep it
with (the illustration of the Dark Chamber in the Interpreter's House pleased him). A man wandered by
the sea and picked up a casket of jewels. Not knowing their value he sat down and began pelting the
birds with them as they settled near him. He kept
one and brought it home. Some one saw it and
advised him to take it to the jeweller, who pronounced

it to be a pearl, and gave him a large sum of money
for it. "Oh that I had not thrown away the rest!"
he exclaimed. So do we trifle with our lives and
faculties, and don't know their value till they are
taken away. The mind of man is like iron, over
which rust has crept, and defaced the image of God
in it. Yes, I am a great sinner, greater than Satan,
for Satan served God faithfully for 150,000 years, and
was condemned for one act of disobedience, whereas
I have sinned all my life.'

"*March* 14.—Had an interesting conversation with
Chiragh Shah who appreciates the parables and
teaching of Christ, but shrinks from the doctrine of
the atonement as unnecessary. He condemns the
sectarianism of Muhamadanism and says, 'You
Christians are much better than our Sunnis and
Shiahs. Sectarians abound, but believers are scarce.
The wave retires from the beach and leaves little
pools which grow stagnant, but when the tide rises
and refills them they are fresh. So must we all be
brought into contact with God.

"*March* 15.—Had a call from B. P., the Assistant
Engineer of the district, a very enlightened native
gentleman, who inclines to Brahmoism. He says he
cannot find any speciality in the Christian doctrine
which the purified Hindu doctrine does not possess.
'If you have martyrs, so have we—if you have a
Mediator, so have we.' On being asked whether
Christ's life did not contrast favourably with Krishna's
he admitted it at once as loftier and purer, but said,

' I don't see among you Christians evidences of His teaching and inspiration being better than our's.   We have our Sádus and Sants, the Sádu who aims at, the Sant who attains perfection.   Sádus are many, Sants few, so in every religion.'

" _March_ 16.—B. P. called again and opened his heart more.   Said he had tried everything, Hinduism, Brahmoism—had been to Calcutta to see Keshub Chunder Sen, but was not satisfied, felt that it would be a great gain to him to be a Christian in a religious, although not in a worldly point of view.   Had, however, difficulties about Inspiration, and the Divinity of Christ.   ' I can believe that He raised himself by His virtues and austerities to the level of a god, but not that He was God from everlasting.'

" We then read together passages of Scripture such as John xx., I Cor. xv., Phil. ii.   He said, after much thought, and evidently with a struggle, ' Well, my mind takes hold of this, it is all possible.   But this is my difficulty, when I read other books of other religions, my mind also consents to them and I don't know which to choose.'   Afterwards he came to me again, and again expressed a great desire to learn more.   We read and prayed together daily.   He expressed a willingness to be baptized if he could be received on the merits of his present attainments in religious belief.   But he has a lingering desire to consult the Hindu fakírs of Lahore, Delhi and Agra, as well as the Brahmoists, and he would fain, if it were possible, get into the kingdom of heaven 'direct,' instead of 'through a Mediator.'

"*May* 20.—Walked to S——, about twenty-four miles from Jhang. Was called upon by the Tahsildar and by N. M., a Muhamadan gentleman in Government employ, who is very friendly, and evinces a very enlightened perception of the moral benefits of Christianity. 'I regard,' he said, 'your preaching as a very excellent thing. You go and invite people to turn to God. This is quite right; you are much better than we. We are not manly enough; we are afraid of your ways; just as when education began, the Government had to seize the boys and send them to school, and even then they ran away—now they all come willingly.' After commending our institutions, and especially certain devout and Christian officers of his acquaintance, he inquired, 'Is there not a new sect among you who say they believe nothing but what they see, and regard prayer as unnecessary? He named certain leaders of the sect among the civilians in the Punjab, and added, 'We do not admire them at all. I look upon it as arising from intoxication of the mind—pride of intellect and power.' He then asked several questions, such as, 'Are not English theologians engaged in revising the New Testament?' (He thought that the original Greek was being altered.) 'What do you hold with regard to Muhamad and his mission? Did not Christ say in the parable of the vineyard that He would give the vineyard to another Overseer (meaning Muhamad)? Has not the curse

of Ham been fulfilled in the present idolatry of the Hindus?'

"*May* 21.—N. M. called again, and brought a Maulvi of some celebrity, whose ancestral shrine is visited from far and near for the potency of its reputed cures. The Maulvi was exceeding affable, and anxious to agree to the teaching of the Bible, which he had read and studied. After a question or two about Seth, whom the Muhamadans regard as a prophet, and about Daniel (as to whether he lived before or after Christ), he quoted a saying of Muhamad enjoining that the Christians should be respected, and intimated that they should have great power. He wished to prove that there was nothing in Christ's teaching to alter the Mosaic law as to clean and unclean animals, and on the passage in the Kuran being quoted where it is said that Christ 'allowed some of the things which were forbidden in the Law,' he replied, that this is interpreted as referring to a habit of Jonah (or Job) of eating fat, which was forbidden in the old dispensation but permitted in the new. Upon the *precepts* of the New Testament, the Maulvi and N. M. were both agreed that they were holy and good, but, as regards observances, they thought that change might prevail. N. M. inquired whether any prophet were alive at the time of the authorship of the Hindu Vedas. Upon my suggesting that probably according to received dates, the prophet Samuel was alive, he exclaimed with some harshness, ' then the idolators have no excuse.'

" The Maulvi then asked me whether there was any

record concerning the dress and food adopted by our Lord. The Muhamadan mind is apt to regard these details in close connection with religious observance.

" In the evening, on going to preach in the bazar, I passed a garden, where my friend N. M. was sitting with the clerks and officers of his Kacherí round him. He invited me to sit down and converse.

" The Maulvi was with him, and also the Police Officer, and I had an unusually attentive audience— took for my subject Nebuchadnezzar's vision of the kingdom of Christ, Dan. ii., which led to discussion on prophecy and its fulfilment. I was particularly struck with the Maulvi's recital from memory of some of our Lord's miracles, and of His death and resurrection, before so many Muhamadans, who would naturally in- quire the law at his mouth, and who are accustomed to be told by their Maulvis that the Old and New Testa- ments are abolished, and that Christ never died at all but was translated to heaven, to die hereafter. N. M. remarked, ' In this country there are many Governors, but none, next to the Queen, so honoured as the Prince of Wales. So are there are many prophets, but none so honourable as Christ.'

" *Aug.* 12.—Morning preaching at N——, evening at A——, with a walk of six miles. The general cal- lousness of the people was redeemed by one man who walked back some way with me saying, ' You have shown us the way to God, I must show you the way home.'

" *Aug.* 17.—A nice walk to J—— where I put up

for the day under some trees, dodging the sun as best I could. The leading people of the village are Seyyids (reputed descendants of the Prophet), a class who live upon others, do not work, and are distinguished for ignorance, conceit and intolerance. They reminded me of a mineral spring in their neighbourhood which has petrifying properties. Whatever you put into it is turned into stone in the course of a few weeks or months. The classical legend of Medusa's head, which petrified you at a glance, may have had some such origin as this.

"A walk of six miles brought me to the spring, which is approached by a steep descent down a gorge in which the stream has been known to rise 100 feet in the rains. The genius of the place is a hermit, who unhappily owes a grudge to another hermit, who lives on a rock overhead. So he declares that a stone which fell upon his disciple from the cliff and killed him was directed by the rival above. The official investigation acquitted the rival, but did not satisfy the plaintiff. This happened three weeks ago. The spot is a very picturesque one. Several old banyan trees cling to the precipitous rocks and shade the hermit's cell, form-ing also a dripping well. Spent a sleepless night be-tween closeness, prickly heat, boils and mosquitos, who almost pull one out of bed, or rather off the ground, for charpoys are unknown here. Had a refreshing bath in the spring before daylight. I was glad to climb the rocks and get on higher ground again.

"Walked to Salowi in the Salt Range, a little village

where there is an ancient tomb, and a garden watered
by a stream, a Muslim paradise, all but the Houris
My retreat was shaded by a leafy screen of vines and
plantains, with a noble banyan for a roof. Went to
the Masjid and found an old Hindu fakír, who poured
out his grievance, which was that he had lost his jaghir
(Government grant of land) many years ago in a disturbance at Jhílam, in which he got imprisoned.
After explaining something of the way of peace, of
which he seemed completely ignorant, told him that
fakírs such as I, who had obtained mercy, felt con-
strained to tell every one the good news. He confessed that he had never considered it a part of a
fakír's duty to preach. ' If I tell people to repent they
will not listen to me.' I said that our book taught
that it was incumbent upon every good fakír to call
others to repentance. At last, when others had
assembled, he rose and explained to them that I was
a fakír who regarded not this world, and that I told
them the way of truth ; 'a way which none of you
know.' This comment (from a Hindu) fell like vitriol
upon the moral sores of a crusty old Maulvi behind,
who resented it bitterly. ' I'll hear the Sahib,' he said,
' but I won't hear you,' and some very hard words
passed between Muhamadans and Hindus, proving the
accuracy of the old fakír's prediction, and giving me
an opportunity for appealing to all alike as brethren,
brethren in sin and brethren in the title to forgiveness.

"Had an interesting audience of rustics at C——.
One of them plumed himself on having ' seen London.'

He explained that he had been to Lahore and seen
in the Museum a Model of London, which he described as 'a city with a big church in the middle,
and a river running through it.'   This gave me a text
for a discourse on Christian Ordinances as a source
of National Life and Prosperity.

"*Oct.* 22.—At S—— met a native of Multan
who goes about the country exhibiting juggling tricks,
among which is a human head that is supposed to
answer questions and converse. He seemed a thoughtful man, and said he had read the Gospel, which he
had obtained for himself. He begged me to instruct
him further, and suggested that we should make a
joint concern, he exhibiting and I preaching.

"*Nov.* 2.—A pleasant day with Mr. T., a Christian Magistrate, who reads the Bible daily with his
heathen and Muhamadan servants, and has their children instructed. Was much interested by Allah Dad
Khan, the native Deputy, a very enlightened man
with no Muhamadan caste prejudices, who holds with
us the universal reign of the Messiah. Our conversation did not commend itself to some of his
brethren, who scowled on me as a heretic.

"*Nov.* 3.—Rode twelve miles on a camel along
a shady road, with fine Sheesham and Peepul trees,
crossed the Indus by a ferry. It has not so gorged
an appearance as one would expect, but seems to have
swallowed up the five great rivers of the Punjab as
easily as Moses' rod swallowed those of the magicians.

And yet its capacities are great, for its minimum volume is stated at 18,000 cubic feet per second, that of the Nile being only 12,000. The fact that its value is estimated from £40 to £60 per cubic foot, proves what a source of wealth it is to the country, and yet, till you actually reach the river, the land on either side is for the most part sandy waste.

"*Nov.* 6.—Preached in the morning at a mosque in Derá Ghází Khán; was rejected inside, but a venerable looking man got me a good hearing outside. In the evening had a large but noisy audience in the bazar. A hostile stall-keeper created confusion by upsetting a number of listeners whose foothold was precarious. Vendors of singing birds were also in the conspiracy, which reminded me of Whitfield's similar experiences at the English fairs.

"*Nov.* 8.—At Choti, the headquarters of Jamal Khan, a Biloch chief. Visited the school of sixty boys, one of whom was put forward to recite certain geographical rhymes in Hindustani, illustrative of the principal towns of England and their manufactures. Some of the parents of the children came, and also the Khan and his son, which gave me the opportunity for religious discussion. The schoolmaster, who has a reputation as a Maulvi, inquired concerning the origin of our race, and whether we had any mention in the Bible. I gave him the prophecy about Japheth (Gen. ix. 27). He then asked how we should prove the authenticity of our Scriptures as against Hindus, Jews and Muhamadans. He afterwards accepted the

Gospel of St. John.   The Khan listened attentively
all the time without making remarks, as we had previously discussed the matter together.

" Numbers of villagers came for medicine, many of
them with chronic complaints.   The woman covered
their faces as usual, and it was difficult to get at their
tongues.   The Bilochis seem so fond of medicine,
that a dose never comes amiss to them, well or ill.
The interior of a Biloch house is a scene of admir-
able disorder, in which cocks and hens, sheep and
goats, are all equally self-assertive.

"*Nov.* 9.—Walked twelve miles with Shirreff to
Zeradan, which is across the British frontier, at the
foot of hills, which here are broken into cliffs of loose
pebbly composition.   A little rill of water makes good
pasturage, and long grass, which made a very good
extempore bed at night, in the absence of a charpoy.

The Khan provided us with twelve men " in
buckram," sworded and shielded as an escort, and
safeguard against any possible marauders, but deer
and wolves were the only strangers that came in sight.
In the evening some shepherds came round us armed
with their very long guns, all mounted with silver and
brass.

" One of their number was a woman, and Shirreff
remarked that the men had a monopoly of the good
looks.   One of them gallantly replied, ' It's because
the women do all the work and the men none.'

" *Nov.* 11.—Started before daylight, and walked
eighteen miles along a mountain track to a village

called Sakhi Sarwar which is a place of pilgrimage to
Hindus and Muhamadans. The path took me along
the border of a stream, which might be a source of
great wealth, but is allowed to waste itself unheeded,
except for cattle. Saw only one little strip of cultivation. Passed an ancient cemetery, which my guide
said was a relic of the occupation of the Pathans.

"*Nov.* 12.—At Sakhi Sarwar is a large tomb with
shrine of pilgrimage, and accommodation for hundreds
of pilgrims. Not a charpoy is to be found in the
village ; every one must lie level with the saint. To be
elevated above him would imply disparagement. Went
and preached to some of the guardians of the shrine.
Their principal relic is a copper cooking vessel of great
antiquity, and large enough to roast a bullock whole.

"*Nov.* 18.—Arrived at Jànpur after a fifteen-mile
walk, and put up in the town, which gave me access to
a number of visitors. A Hakim (physician) named
Mohkam Din, a man of great repute, was one of the
first to call.

" He told me he had formerly known Mr. Bruce, and
as his manner was very polite, we soon became good
friends. His first questions were somewhat frivolous,
such as whether we English had the alchemist's art
of manufacturing gold, whether in my travels in the
Caucasus I had seen Gog and Magog, whether the
account in the paper was true that a man in America
who was shot out of a cannon had reached the moon
and come back safely, whether it was not probable
that the mountains of the moon were reflections of the

Himalayas, etc. Having at last got him upon religious subjects, he showed a great deal of interest, and brought two Maulvis to see me, with whom I had much discussion. I afterwards saw the local native doctor, who knew, and spoke very highly of, our friend John Williams, of Tank."

We saw that Gordon had to leave South India on account of his health, and that the Punjab so far suited him that he was able to work permanently there. To the casual eye he appeared to be always in robust health and a tower of strength. Nature had undoubtedly endowed him with a splendid constitution, but few, except his most intimate friends, knew to what extent his privations told upon him. What he says in the foregoing extracts is interesting, because, instead of attributing the ailments which he had to bear to the mode of life adopted, he professes to find in it a source of health. He truly did not "fast before men." His right hand never knew what his left was doing. His complaint about the fewness of those who go into the highways and hedges, to compel the people to come in, ought to strike a responsive note in the hearts of those who read it, and at the same time love the Lord Jesus Christ.

Persecution has been frequently mentioned in the accounts given by Gordon, and probably with most persons the persecution in store for the new convert, is the prominent thought in connection with missionary work in India. Perhaps, then, it will be a matter of surprise to some to hear that even in a province like the Punjab, where missionary work is comparatively young, there is a large section of the people who sympathise with Christian effort, and who believe that Christ and this teaching are finally to embrace all nations. But these, alas, in most cases, act on the policy of "peace at any price," with or without honour. They do not face the open disgrace which baptism must entail.

At the end of this year Gordon's journeys were extended beyond their usual limits. From Multan he was induced to go westward, and visit the Bilochi country. This visit was fruitful in the foundation of another mission, which must form the subject of another chapter.

CHAPTER XII.

As it has been stated, in the end of 1876 Gordon, in company with the Rev. F. A. P. Shirreff, of Lahore, was induced to extend his journey from Multan in a westward direction. From that place, on a clear day, the sun can be seen setting in all its glory behind the distant range of the Sulaiman Hills, which form the boundary between the Punjab and Bilochistan. It may have been that the sight of these re-awakened in the heart of Gordon a desire felt years before, when, on his way from Persia to India, the steamer touched at the Port of Guadur. The people of that then almost unknown country had claimed his sympathy, but from that time to the present there had been no opportunity of giving it practical expression. It may be, that he now thought an entrance from the Punjab side might be effected, and the country taken possession of in the name of the King.

Accordingly, in the beginning of November 1876, Gordon set out from Multan. Twelve miles would bring him to the Chenab, one of the five rivers of the Punjab. Crossing the ferry here, which at this

season of the year would present no difficulty, he
would find himself for the next six miles walking
through some of the most beautiful avenues of trees
that can be found in the Punjab. These extend from
the river to the town of Mazaffargarh, where there is
a civil station. Here also is a native agent of the
Church Missionary Society, who was for a number of
years supported by the generosity of a civil officer,
formerly Deputy Commissioner of the district.

From this point, setting his face again westward, he
traversed ground at that time unbroken by the Christian ploughman. The shady avenues of trees lining
the roads are now gradually left behind, and the
traveller sees before him tracts of country, here rich
in cultivation, there undulating with barren sand hills.
About twenty-two miles more, and the greatest river
of the country is reached,—the Indus, into which,
about fifty miles to the south, at Mithankot, all the
five rivers of the Punjab flow.

At this season of the year the giant river can
hardly be called interesting. After May, when the
snows begin to melt in the heights of the Himalaya,
the river rises, and frequently a sheet of water five
miles broad may be seen. But in the cold weather
the melting of the snow and the rains are over, and
the water diminishes to an insignificant amount compared with the extent of sandy river bed. The traveller goes on mile after mile, and might imagine
himself to be in the middle of a huge desert, until at
last, coming upon the river itself, he realises that at

another time the miles over which he has toiled are flooded by a river-sea.

Once more crossing the river, the impression is given that one is approaching a second Jericho, a city of palm trees, so many date-palms are to be seen on all sides. Perhaps it was with some such thought as this—"Another Jordan crossed, another Jericho in front, here is a land which is to be the inheritance of the Lord! But where is Joshua leading the host of the Lord?"

This Jericho is Derá Ghází Khán, and, as we have seen by his journal, Gordon himself preached there on Nov. 6th. It is the southernmost town of the trans-Indus country, known as the Derajat, so-called because it contains three towns the name of each of which begins with _Derá_ or _Camp_—Derá Ismail Khán, Derá Fath Khán, and Derá Ghází Khán.

In 1861, Colonel Reynell Taylor, then Commissioner of the Derajat, proposed to the Church Missionary Society to found a mission in the country. He himself backed up his proposal with a gift of £1000 towards carrying it out. The result was the commencement of work at Derá Ismail Khán. Colonel Taylor had wished to establish mission stations at the northern and southern towns, the former as a base for evangelistic work among the Wazírís and other Pathan mountain tribes, and the latter as a similar base for the Bilochis; while at both places efforts were to be made to preach the Gospel to the travelling merchants from · Central

Asia, who yearly descend the passes into the plains of India. But at the time, it was only found practicable to carry out the former part of the scheme. The Rev. T. V. French (afterwards Bishop of Lahore) was placed in charge of the new work.

To carry out the latter portion was left to the energy and means of Gordon. Writing of his first visit he says:—

"Derá Ghází Khán is a large city with no missionary traditions, about the same size as Pind Dádan Khán, but with much finer mosques and bazars. We took up our quarters for a week or ten days in the Serai (native inn), where our lodging reminded us of the cell where St. Jerome spent the last thirty years of his life, except that his was in the cave at Bethlehem, hallowed by the memory of our blessed Lord's nativity, and ours in the midst of a thronged and busy Indian bazar. Thence, morning and evening, we visited the mosques and temples, where we found more apathy in religious matters than actual opposition. One exception may be mentioned as characteristic: We were sitting shoeless in a mosque, conversing with an old Muslim, when some ill-disposed person went and got other kindred spirits, who came with a tumult that reminded one of the tuning of orchestral instruments previous to a concert. But just as the harsh discords are followed by the harmonies of the oratorio, so, by a few calm words of expostulation, the furious disputants became quiet listeners. In dealing with these people one often

finds that, if the right note is struck, there will be a
right response.

"This town of Derá Ghází Khán is not itself in a
Bilochi country. Many of the chiefs, or tumandars,
of the border tribes, have houses in this place, which
they visit from time to time with numbers of followers.
But it is not until one has gone about twenty-four
miles still further west, that one finds oneself in the
real home of a chief, and among a Bilochi-speaking
people." Gordon further writes :—

"In our preparations for visiting the country of the
Bilochis, we were very kindly assisted by the Commanding Officer of the cantonment, and the Deputy
Commissioner, who both take a warm interest in the
welfare of these people. Provided with a letter of introduction, and with medicine for the sick, we started
on Nov. 1st (1876), and jogged along for twenty miles
on a camel to the headquarters of one of the many
clans of Bilochis. The chief and his son were fine
specimens of a noble race—men of great stature,
striking features, and long curling hair down to their
shoulders. Among some of the tribes, the Jewish
type could be distinctly traced. They take a great
pride in their horses, the breed of which is famous,
and this chief has carried off the first prize at the
Government horse fairs. We had a long conversation
together, for they are remarkably open to discussion
on religious subjects.

"They admit the purity of the Christian faith, but
the old objection, so painfully frequent, recurred :—

' We perceive that you English are very much divided
in religious belief. Some of your Sahibs tell us that
they have no need of padres; they can interpret God's
Word for themselves.' This was a polite way of saying,—' You clergy are not always accredited by your
own people, who regard God's Word and ordinances
as open to criticism, and matters of opinion, whether
they are to be respected or not. How, then, can you
commend to us that which you are not unanimous
about yourselves ? '

" This is a charge which is constantly coming up in
one form or another. We do not find it objected by
the natives of these parts that some of us hold the
Episcopal and some the Presbyterian form of church
government. But what they do say, sometimes in a
cavilling, sometimes in an inquiring, spirit, is, that we
are very loose as to religious ordinances,—to daily
prayer, reverence for God's Word, etc.

" It was easy to converse with the chiefs of the clans,
because they are familiar with Urdi and Punjabi; but
the more ignorant of the people did not understand so
well. They knew, however, how to appreciate quinine
and other medicines, as they had many who were
sick of fever, and we soon became very good friends.

" A journey of thirty miles further brought us to
the foot of a range of mountains that we had been
wistfully gazing at for days, in the hope that we might
have the opportunity of planting the cross upon ground
beyond the British frontier, where no missionary foot
had ever trod."

The range of mountains here mentioned was the Sulaiman, and perhaps a few words may be said about the inhabitants of these hills, while we leave Gordon and his friend resting at Zaradan, and probably speaking words of life to an assembled group of Bilochis, who have never before heard of the gospel of salvation.

If we could imagine ourselves in the Highlands of Scotland a century or two ago, amongst a people split up into different clans, and these clans often fighting one against the other, we might have, *mutatis mutandis*, the scenes of many parts of Bilochistán before our eyes. The phrase *mutatis mutandis*, perhaps, would have to include a good deal. For the wild beauty of the Scottish hills, for their waving trees and rippling streams, we should have to place bare hills, and often waterless plains, not without their beauty and grandeur, but forming a far sterner page in nature's book than anything in our more favoured western land.

A swarthy complexion, white flowing garments, a shaggy beard, and aquiline features, set off by the full array of arms, the sword, the shield, and the gun, make up a figure which one would rather meet as a friend than a foe.

Clanship is one of the most striking features in the social system of the Bilochis. The headmen of tribal sections are obediently loyal to their chief, or tumandar ; the people, in their turn, are equally obedient to their headmen.

Tribal warfare is extremely common, and the law

of an "Eye for an eye, and a tooth for a tooth," or in other words, "blood for blood," is one of the most fruitful causes of it. What would be only accounted as an injury to a private person, where the clan system does not exist, is often taken up by the whole clan where it does, and thus the tribes become embroiled.

These people claim for themselves Arab descent, but as to the justice of the claim, one may well be permitted to have doubts. In their nomad habits and their pastoral employments, without any fixed abodes, they do, however, resemble their supposed ancestors.

In many respects, they form a most happy contrast to the people of India. There is more of the western element in their constitution. They do not take their pleasure sadly like the Hindu, but almost in the spirit of an Englishman. A Biloch can enjoy a joke and laugh at a good story. He is truthful, except when it very much suits his end to tell a lie, and com· paring him with his neighbours of Afghanistan, to quote from the Census Report of 1881, "He has less of God in his creed, and less of the devil in his heart."

The Bilochis are supposed to be Muhamadans of the Sunni sect in religion. But even the most in-telligent among them know next to nothing of what they profess. Carelessness is perhaps their greatest characteristic in this respect. This may be imagined when one day a headman naïvely remarked, "We

HEADMAN OF THE BILOCHIS IN THE SULAIMÁN HILLS.

are called Mussulmans because we are followers of *Hazrat Músa* (Moses), just as you are."

A strict Biloch custom is, that one man should invariably ask another on meeting him, " What is the news?" And perhaps it was this question which greeted Gordon and his companion on their meeting that group at Zaradan, and perhaps, too, they had an unexpected answer to give in the first message of salvation and pardon for sin in Christ.

The two companions turned their footsteps northward, skirting the range of the Sulaimans. About twelve miles over a remarkably rough country, huge boulders under foot, stretching away as far as the eye could reach on the right, the bare hills reflecting the sun's rays down on the left, brought them to Sakhi Sarwar, a very famous place.

The journal says of this place :—" Here is a large tomb with shrine of pilgrimage, and accommodation for hundreds of pilgrims. Not a charpoy is to be found in the village. Every one must lie level with the saint. To be elevated above him would imply disparagement. Went and preached to some of the guardians of the shrine. Their principal relic is a copper cooking-vessel of great antiquity, and large enough to roast a bullock whole."

The remark about a *charpoy* or *native bedstead* is not strictly correct. For when I visited the place during the fair in 1880, I was told that there was one in the place which I might have if I wished, but when they added, in explanation, that it was kept for the purpose of carrying the dead to burial, the offer was declined with thanks.

The history of the founder of this place, as given in the Settlement Report of Derá Ghází Khán is interesting. It is therefore quoted as follows :—

"Sakhi Sarwar was the son of Hazrat Zenabuldin, who migrated from Baghdad and settled at Sialkot, twelve miles east of Multan, 650 A.H. (1220 A.D.). Hazrat Zenabuldin had two sons, one Saidi Ahmad, afterwards known as Sakhi Sarwar ; the other, Khan Doda, who died at Baghdad, and was not famous.

"Saidi Ahmad studied at Lahore, and from there went to Dhokal, near Wazirabad, in the Gujrat district. Whilst here he saw a mare, the property of a carpenter, and asked the carpenter for it. The carpenter denied having a mare, whereupon Saidi Ahmad called to the mare and it came up to him of its own accord. Saidi Ahmad then told the carpenter to sink a well, which he did, and the descendants of the carpenter are the guardians of the well, at which a fair is held every year, in June, to Sakhi Sarwar's honour. After this Saidi Ahmad went, by his father's order, to reside at the foot of the Sulaiman range and settled at the place now called after him. Shortly after, retiring into the desert, Saidi Ahmad performed another miracle. A camel, belonging to a caravan which was going from Khorasan to Delhi, broke its leg. The leader of the caravan applied to Saidi Ahmad, who told him to return to where he had left the camel and he would find it sound. The merchant did as he was directed, and was rewarded by finding his camel recovered. On arriving at Delhi, the merchant published the miracle and the emperor heard of it. The emperor, anxious to inquire into the miracle, sent for the camel and had it killed. The leg was examined and found to have been mended with rivets. The emperor, convinced of the miracle, sent four mule loads of money to Saidi Ahmad and told him to build himself a house. Sakhi Sarwar Shrine was built with this money. One Gannú of Multan now gave his daughter in marriage to Saidi Ahmad, who had miraculously caused two sons to be born to him. Gannú endowed his daughter with all his property; and it was for his generosity in distributing this property to the poor that Saidi Ahmad obtained the name of Sakhi Sarwar, or the bountiful lord or chief. Sakhi Sarwar now visited Baghdad; on his return he was accompanied by three disciples, whose tombs are shown on a low hill near Sakhi Sarwar.

Still, the scheme of a mission was destined to be for some time postponed. Gordon himself believed that the best manner of commending the Gospel to this rough but genial people would be to couple it, as our Lord Himself did, with temporal blessings as well. That which they stood most in need of was medical aid. Their wild life and tribal warfare often caused much suffering from wounds, which surgical skill would have alleviated. Hence he proposed to establish a medical mission amongst the Bilochis, and to give the Church Missionary Society a sum of Rs. 10,000 wherewith to commence it. It was not, however, until 1878 that Dr. Andrew Jukes offered himself for work. In the autumn of that year, he and the editor of these pages came to the Punjab to join Gordon.

After this journey to the trans-Indus country, concluded by the end of November, Gordon turned towards Delhi, at the opposite extremity of the Punjab, to be present at the great Durbar, appointed for January 1, 1877, at which the Queen was to be proclaimed Empress of India. On this occasion he writes to A. Leslie Melville, Esq. :—

" The sound of the guns which have saluted Queen Victoria as Empress of India have barely died away as I write from my noonday retreat in the middle of this great city. I came here a week ago—not to see the Durbar, as you may suppose, but to proclaim to the multitudes assembled the sovereignty of a 'greater than Solomon,' or our Empress either. The Lord has been pleased to bless my daily preaching to some, I trust, and especially to a Muhamadan Maulvi of learning and influence, who comes daily to read God's Word and pray with me, and whose heart has been turned from the false prophet to look to Christ as his Saviour. That he may have grace to stand firm against the storm of opposition which will be raised against him, and to endure persecution and reproach, is a subject for our most earnest prayers.

" Yesterday I visited one or two of the camps of the native princes, in order to distribute portions of

Scripture and tracts amongst their retainers.   This
is a work which requires a large staff of missionaries,
because the camps are remote, and the constant inter-
change of visits of state and ceremony renders access
difficult and uncertain.   For the last few days the
city has been like Vanity Fair in ' Pilgrim's Progress.'
The crowds of buyers, sellers, sightseers, rajahs on
elephants and in carriages, with all their jewelled and
spangled train, European equipages, incessant firing
of salutes of twenty-one guns each, as every visit of
state is paid or repaid, are quite sufficient to distract
the mind, however bent upon higher objects.   The
Bishop of Madras preached last night to a large congregation, from the text, ' The fashion of this world
passeth away,' and I rejoiced, as I listened to his
godly exhortations, to think that we have, at any
rate, one evangelical and missionary heart and head
of our church in India."

Soon after, we find him once more back in the
Jhílam district, pursuing his usual work.   He was
joined this year by the Rev. and Mrs. C. P. C. Nugent
whom he installed at Pind Dádan Khán.   Here he
built for them a small mission bungalow.

It must now have seemed to Gordon as if one of
his objects in life had been accomplished, and shortly
after this, on April 15, 1877, on visiting the mission,
we find him writing :—

"A boat took us down the river to Pind Dádan
Khán, where we were warmly welcomed by the dear
Nugents, who had just got into their new mission

house. It was pleasant, after five years' wandering among the villages of that district, to see at last the thatched roof of a cottage in the middle of our central town, and a brother and sister occupying it. It seemed like taking possession of that town for Christ, and we all joined in thanksgiving. A little school has been built close by, and a small garden laid out. It is all overlooked by the old Sikh watch-tower, which forms my own mansion."

Owing to the presence of a missionary settled in the Mission, Gordon was able to leave his work in this part of the Punjab for longer intervals, and extend his journeys, as we shall see in the next chapter, even to Kandahar.

CHAPTER XIII.

QUETTA.

IT is unnecessary in these pages to enter into details of the unhappy dispute between the British Government and the Amír of Afghanistan, which led to the miserable war of 1878-80. We seem fated to make mistakes in dealing with the country which separates the Indian and Russian empires. All we have to do, however, from a missionary point of view, is to endeavour out of evil to bring forth good, and to make the best of existing circumstances. This Gordon was ready to do.

While the war department was alive with preparations, and all India and England were looking forward to the coming struggle, thoughts of war, too, were born in Gordon's heart. But it was war of a different kind. He thought that the entry of the Empress's soldiers into Afghanistan might also enable the Soldier of the Cross to go forward and spy out the land, so that another province might be added to the Sceptre of Christ.

He would not have been allowed as a pure and simple missionary to have accompanied the troops. So he proposed to offer his services as an honorary

chaplain for the campaign. His offer was accepted
and his name gazetted. In the autumn of 1878 he
was attached to General Biddulph's force. In the
beginning of October the march was begun.

It was not merely Afghanistan that he had in
view, but it was Bilochistán as well, through which
country the march to Kandahar must necessarily take
him. His journal here, as published in the "C. M.
Intelligencer" of January 1881, is reproduced :—

"The late war with Amír Shere Ali Khan of Kabul
afforded me a long-desired opportunity of visiting
Bilochistán, the Gedronia of the ancients. Bilochistán is the name given to the country west of
Sindh and south of Afghanistan. Its population is
somewhat heterogeneous, comprising many tribes,
amongst whom I was chiefly brought into contact
with Maris, Bugtis, and Brahuis. The country is
mountainous, except in the north-west, and along the
coast. The rivers are insignificant, except after heavy
rains. The inhabitants are more given to pastoral
than to agricultural pursuits.

"Most of the passes leading from India to Bilochistán cross the Sulaiman range. A glance at the
map shows a remarkable pecularity with regard to
this part of the country. Although numerous streams
issue from its heights, and owing to the formation of
the country, take an easterly direction, very few join
the Indus, the greatest number being absorbed by
the soil at the foot of the mountains. Here exists a
more or less narrow margin of horizontal beds of

sandstone and conglomerate. Nothing can be con-
ceived as possessing a more desolate aspect than these
ridges ; scarcely a sign of vegetation breaks the uniform brown of the arid rocks. There are, therefore,
few inducements for a traveller to attempt the Bolan
Pass, if he be in search of the picturesque. Moreover,
the climate is very trying to the European constitution, and even natives have a tradition that nothing
hotter exists than this strip between the River Indus
and the mountains.

"Our starting-point was Rajanpur, which we left
on the 9th October 1878. This little place is situate
on the west bank of the Indus, near Mithankot, where
all the waters of the Punjab unite. The route usually
adopted by caravans through the Bolan is that *viâ*
Sakhur, Shikarpur, and Jacobabad ; but that route,
owing to the inundation of the Indus, was pronounced, at this season, to be impracticable. There
was, therefore, no alternative but to adopt the direct
but more difficult route *viâ* Bugti Dera. Hence the
quiet little station of Rajanpur assumed an unusually
bustling and animated appearance. Numbers of
troops of all descriptions, artillery, cavalry and infantry, were being pushed on to the front, and it was
interesting to observe how the native regiments contained representatives of most of the martial races of
India. The brave little Gurkha from the central
Himalaya marched quite as well as his Pathan *con-
frère* of the north-west, and afforded as marked a
contrast to the Sikh as the latter to the Hindustani.

Moreover, military stores of all sorts were being sent forward in eager haste to Quetta, and demanded all the camels available for their transport. These patient animals were collected from all over Sindh and the neighbouring provinces, and laboured on under their heavy loads. Unacclimatized to the hills of Bilochistán, a very large proportion subsequently succumbed to cold, fatigue, and want of proper food. It is difficult to estimate their loss correctly, but if rough estimates are to be believed, some 50,000 of these patient animals were lost between the declaration of war, and the signing of peace with Yakub Khan.

"*October 9th.* I left Rajanpur with the 2nd Biloch Regiment, commanded by Colonel Nicholets, for Asin, the first halting-place on the road to Quetta. The road lies to the west, the walk across the plain, called the 'thal,' being easy and pleasant. The country is flat and sandy, with low bushes now and then to relieve its monotony. Our march was lengthened by two miles, in order to avoid water and mud, the result of recent rains.

"*October 10th. Lal Gosha,* sixteen miles. There is little variety in the aspect of the country, for the same flat desert spotted here and there with scant herbage met the eye, and there was nothing to mark our track but a furrow on either side, and the carcase of a horse and a camel or two that had died on the march. We found we had two cavalry regiments ahead of us, the 1st and 2nd

Punjab Cavalry, both bound for the same destination as we were. The nearer we approached the mountains the more apparent became the difficulties with regard to the transport. Everyone was eagerly discussing plans upon which the comforts of the soldier depend ; and what is only an ordinary obstacle to the Englishman, to be surmounted with patience and hard work, seems an insuperable difficulty to the native mind. Many camel owners, in consequence, ran away with their charge, rather than face the dreaded Bolan. There is no village at Lal Gosha, only what is called a *chowkee*, a few huts that mark the stage. The rule observed at this season is to march by night, and halt by day. We found the fatigues of the night's march far preferable to the sultry heat of the daily halt. Here also another element was against us, for a dust storm searched every nook of our flimsy tents, which flapped and strained at the tent pegs, while the thermometer registered 104° in the shade.

"*October* 11*th.* *Bandawala*, 16¾ miles. The first part of this march presented no difficulties, except where the road became heavy with sand. As a change from the usually barren appearance of the country, I observed, near Bandawala, some crops of *jawár* and *bájár*. The *jawár* is a kind of millet (*holcus sorgum*), usually cultivated for the *kharif* (autumn) harvest. When used for fodder it is much more thickly sown than when grown as a grain. The *bájár* (*holcus spicatus*) or spiked millet is, like the former, grown for the *kharif.* It is said to be heating, and therefore specially adapted as a food for winter, ground and made up into cakes. There is a fort at Bandawala with an outpost. I received here attention and civilities from Shere Muhamad Khan, who recognised me as the *padré* who had visited his uncle, the Nawab of Rojhan, last year.

"*October* 12*th. Kabudrani,* twenty-one miles. This is one of the longest and most trying marches in the whole route, in consequence of the heavy sand. After a walk of eight hours, we halted for four hours at midnight by a well, where a very limited supply of water is obtained in the bed of a stream. A Biloch guide showed us the way, which would otherwise be very difficult to find, as it lies through a trackless jungle. We reached Kabudrani at eight o'clock in the morning, and found the encampment located in the bed of a *nullah* or watercourse, with good water under a cliff. But beyond this there was absolutely nothing to cheer the weary traveller, not even the sight of a few huts. The only shelter we had was a wretched pilie-tree. This encampment reminded me of the Desert of Sinai. Here my Biloch guide asked leave to stop at sunrise and say his prayers, which he did with the usual prostrations and recitations. Such a custom is somewhat unusual with the Bilochis, as he candidly admitted. 'We used never to say our prayers, but since the Sepoys from Hindustan have come among

us, they have persuaded us to do so.'   So far he
approved of their customs, but to my question
whether, in other respects, they set a good example,
he replied, ' No ; they are a lying, rascally set.'   He
certainly did not much like these foreigners.   As we
sat under a tree he inquired whether the English,
as a nation, had always had the same power and
coherence.   I told him that was not the case ; 'on
the contrary, we were once like you, with your feuds
and forays between the Maris, Bugtis, Brahuis, etc.
We were split up into hostile tribes, Kelts, Saxons,
Angles, etc. ; but after foreign missionaries came to
visit us, and preached to us, we received God's Word,
and became a united nation.'   ' I wish,' he answered,
' that we could do so also.'

"In spite of its general barrenness, the country
abounds in game, and as a proof of this we caught
sight of a few deer this morning.   We had now
reached the confines of the British territory, and the
scene changed into one of peculiar wild picturesque-
ness.

"_October_ 13_th._ _Kajuri_, 14½ miles. This march
was heavy in the extreme, the road being nothing
but a succession of watercourses, the first halt
being stony and sandy, with water in many places,
said to be brackish.   We started at seven in
the evening, as we had a brilliant moon, and
arrived at midnight, with about half-an-hour's halt.
This made thirty miles in one day, and a heavier
thirty miles' march I never had.   Some of the

men had walked thirty-five miles in the twenty-four hours with their rifles and kit. We were so fortunate as to find a pleasant resting-place for a halt half-way, studded with a few trees. On the road I passed a place which was pointed out to me as the scene of a sanguinary encounter in the time of the Sikhs, and my guide showed me the spots, marked by stones, where the warriors fell in the contest. The first few hours after sunset were oppressively hot, especially as a road or track runs through valleys with lofty enclosing rocks. The latter half of the march was somewhat easier. As it was Sunday we had a short service in the mess tent, with the thermometer over 100°. Civilisation seemed to have been left behind ; we had not seen even a village since we left Rajanpur, a distance of eighty miles.

"*October* 14*th*. *Loti*, 6½ miles. After a short ascent a plateau is reached with a small cemetery close by. Here my guide, according to his usual practice, repeated his Fatiha, or confession of faith. He told me that the Bilochis liked having their dead buried close to the road. In a conversation we entered upon, he asked me if it was true that every English child has its pay fixed by Government from the day of its birth. Major G—— said he remembered a field-marshal of eighty years' service who was made a captain at eight, and a major at sixteen years of age. Having reached our destination we encamped on an open piece of ground, with small low trees, of the *farash* or tamarisk kind, giving a scanty shade to little knots of Sepoys. This halt was quite refreshing, especially as the water was good and clear. Evidence of game was likewise procured, as some of our lovers of sport managed to bring in some wild pigeons and sandgrouse. A tent had been erected at Loti for the sick, and I visited this temporary hospital, which was under the care of Dr. A., who attended some thirty or forty invalids, chiefly laid up with fever, most of them being Mussulmans.

"*October* 15*th. Bugti Dera*, sixteen miles. We were now entering a country so far away from the plains that the guides from Bandawala protested and declared they should not know the way, and mine, perhaps designedly, missed the path thrice in three miles, no doubt to impress upon me the impropriety of taking him so far from his home. After some heavy plodding through loose sand it occurred to him that he would like a drink. This desire sharpened his ear to make out voices in the neighbourhood, proceeding from a native encampment, and he went at once and addressed himself to a Bugti family consisting of a grandfather, grandmother, children, and dogs. The old man was quite civil, and gave me a humble saluation in the name of God, 'Bismillah.' He then stirred up a matronly camel, whose calf seconded his appeal for milk. When the calf had sucked, he drew two large bowls of milk, one for me and one for my guide. It was welcome to thirsty people, but had a slightly acid taste, and my dog refused it. Going on we came to another Bugti encampment, with horses, asses, sheep, goats, and cattle. The sheep in this district are excellent eating, superior to those in the Punjab. The shepherds are a fine-looking set of men, with long curling hair. They have no measurement for distance, and can never tell you how far a place is. They gave us a guide who led us on past a conical hill to the entrance of a narrow ravine, whose moonlit cliffs were very striking. After this the road was good the rest of the way, except where it followed a sandy *nullah*. A little owl chattered at us from a tree, and the two Bilochis stopped 'to hear what the bird would say.' They would have stayed long had I not urged them on. They say that when you are walking, and the owl speaks, you are to halt till it speaks again. If you are sitting you are to rise and go on. After marching four hours I spread my plaid on the ground, and lay down, though not to rest, for sleep was difficult, on account of myriads of pertinacious little sand-flies. I rose, therefore, long before sunrise, when I heard the voices of the approaching troops. After prayers I again set out on my march, and went for five miles through a land which had all the appearance of natural fertility about it, and might therefore be cultivated with success. Indeed, here and there I passed through a field where irrigation was carried on by means of small ducts leading from the rivulets. At length I arrived at Bugti Dera, a little village on a broad plain, and saw with pleasure our tent pitched amidst the low shrubs abounding here, with partridges in plenty.

"*October* 16*th.* *Sangsila*, twenty miles. This was a long march of 7½ hours to the west, along a plain flanked with mountains on either side. The land is partially cultivated, though it is difficult to make out anything at night. As soon as the moon made its appearance, at eight p.m., we started again on our journey, but had not got very far when we lost the track, and only recovered it with the help of some camp-followers, who just then came up. At a convenient spot we made a halt for a short time, and watched the *bhishtis* filling their *masaks* with water for the regiment following at a little distance. On the road I observed, half-way, two or three large cemeteries and mounds which seem to indicate the site of an ancient city. The character of country begins to change gradually, for on the right hand the ridges of hills become lower and approach the road, assuming in some places the even outline of a railway embankment. There was a place near this, called Traki, a spot of some historical note, as our troops in former days had there an encounter with the native tribes. After patient plodding I reached the encamping ground at eight a.m., near ancient mounds, but I saw no village anywhere near. The Bilochis came to my tent to take leave. One of them, more observant than the rest, said, 'I perceive you are a fakír, for you say your prayers morning and evening.' As he understood Hindustani I repeated to him the Lord's Prayer,

with explanations, which he translated to the others
in Bilochi. Of course none of these people can read.

"*October 17th. Chigardi*, 8½ miles. The night is
by far the best time for marching, and I consequently
started in the evening with the baggage. It took me,
however, some five hours over this short march, as I had
no guide with whom I could go ahead. The track leads
over very broken ground, now grassy, now sandy, now
stony. At last it descends the steep embankment of
a large river or watercourse, which, like the majority
of these streams, contains water which is barely ankle
deep, but after a few hours of rain becomes a roaring, unfordable torrent. This place invited us to
rest, especially as a smouldering fire showed that the
cavalry regiment had passed before. The water was
good, but the camping-ground as shadeless as usual ;
it was a great relief at mid-day to get a little shadow
under an overhanging rock. All of us began now to
feel that the base of supplies had been left long behind,
and the heat and the diet were beginning to tell upon
some. The food almost exclusively consisted of meat ;
fowls, eggs, and milk were like the vision of a dream,
more to be thought of than tasted. Flour, *ghee* and
dâl for Sepoy, are all that can be got from the solitary
banniah, whose penal task it is to be on the camping-
ground when the regiment arrives. He is always on
the move, a mystery to most, for where he comes from,
or how he gets there, no one knows.

"*October 18th. Gwatch ki drik*, 11½ miles. Nine
days had passed since leaving Rajanpur, and a glance

at the map showed that half the distance to Quetta had not yet been accomplished. But the approach of the Bolan Pass was already becoming more apparent. The road was rough and hilly for nearly the first half of the march, so that we only procceded in single file. As for pushing on the baggage, those alone can speak with full knowledge and feeling, who, time after time, had to exercise all their ingenuity in overcoming the numerous obstacles. How the guns were got over this portion of the road is still a mystery to many. The latter half of the journey lies through a *nullah* called the Sori, which joins the Siaf *nullah* close to the camp, and proceeds in fact for a considerable portion along the bed of this mountain river. The water had therefore to be crossed and recrossed frequently, sometimes up to the knees ; and there is no danger attendant upon such a march provided there has been no rain ; but if a thunderstorm bursts and deluges the country with rain, each tiny rivulet becomes a rushing stream, adding to the fury of the roaring torrent which it joins, and rendering a quiet march like ours an impossibility. At length we reached the camp, pitched on high ground encircled by hills. As there is no village or sign of habitation, it is impossible to say from what source these halting-places derive their sonorous names.

" *October* 19*th.   Dinghán*, 11½ miles. This march was considerably easier that the last one, and the night was actually cold, so that the *khansamah's* fire was a great attraction to us as we rose from our shakedowns

T

at the sound of the bugle. The track towards the resting-place descends again into the ravine, crossing the bed of the river four times, after which it rises into another somewhat rocky ravine. There was good water obtainable half-way ; but it proved quite un-drinkable at the camping-ground, and we had consequently to bring water with us from our last place. I need perhaps scarcely mention that the camp was prefectly shadeless like the last, and void of supplies.

"*October* 20*th.   Lehri*, twenty miles. The road for a time leaves the mountains and enters the plain called Cutchi. There are tracks across the plain, so that the regiment went one way and the baggage another. Starting at night in advance, I felt my way along in the dark, partly by the sensation of a trodden path and partly by the stars, knowing our course to be W. by N. After a nine miles' walk I lay down, but found the road unusually hard, and was constantly awakened by the guard passing with the baggage, who must have thought me either dead or sick. There was no other alternative. I rose from this extemporised bed at four in the morning, and found the halting-place where tea was to be had. The unfortunate regiment had, however, taken another road, and missed their tea altogether. The latter part of the road is through fields of maize, which turn aside the steps of the traveller into tortuous bye-paths. It was a treat to see a village again, however small, where supplies can be obtained. A detachment of the Sindh Horse was on the camping-ground. The headman of the place

is Sorab Khan, who, with his son Mihrab Khan, called
on the colonel, and was very civil.

"_October_ 21st. A halt was made at Lehri for the
day, and I made use of it by calling on Sorab Khan
at his home. He at once sent for his village maulvi,
a learned person who acts as interpreter of the law,
scribe and accountant, and, with the help of Nasirullah,
the maulvi in question, we got on very well. A circle
of Bilochis was soon formed, and we had a long conversation on the Law of Moses, the law of Christ, and
the Law of Muhamad. At last Sorab Khan said,
pointing to his maulvi, 'Take him with you to Quetta
for a month and teach him, and he will come back and
teach us all.' When I expressed my willingness, the
maulvi, who is old, most vigorously shook his head
and declined. He offered, however, to accept the
Bible; so one of his disciples, named Muhamad Yar,
came to my tent, and received the New Testament in
Urdu.

"_October_ 22d. _Mach_, fourteen miles. This march
may be generally characterised as flat and easy. The
crowing of cocks in the dark indicated two little Bilochi
settlements by the way. Hearing there was no water
procurable at Mach, we had to send some men ahead
yesterday to dig suitable holes; but when we arrived,
the water which had collected in them had not had
time to settle down, and was as muddy as ditch-water.
Here we found no shade or vestige of living creatures,
nothing but a baked and cracked plain with hills
around. This general monotony was however re-

lieved in the night by some beautiful meteors shoot-
ing through space. In spite of many drawbacks, the
temper of the officers and men is fully equal to the
occasion. Thus, when yesterday, an officer of the —
regiment mentioned that their mess was devoid of such
necessary articles as chairs and tables, our colonel
quoted a passage from a military handbook, in which
the writer suggests that the officer who wanted such
luxuries ' had better stay at home with his mother.'

" *October* 23*d.* *Mittri,* fourteen miles. As usual,
we started long before the dawn of day, and certainly
felt our way for three dark hours across the same
parched and cracked plain. There was so little to
distract our attention that I distinctly remember how
we passed through a large flock of Brahui sheep.
Their owners are altogether migratory, and move from
one place to another as it suits them. They leave
the cold heights of Quetta about this season, and seek
the more genial climate of the plains.

" *October* 24*th.* *Dadar,* fourteen miles. This distance was got over in about five hours, and afforded, on
the whole, a pleasant march, as there was an easy road
at first for about four miles, after which it winds for
several miles among sand-hills, issuing again upon the
plain, with gradual descent towards the mouth of the
Bolan. Dadar is a much more imposing place than
Mittri or Lehri. The chief man is Sayyid Aurang
Shah, who is well spoken of by English officers, and
in this respect presents a contrast to Faiz Muhamad,
the Khan of Kelat's Naib or Deputy, who paid his re-

spects by calling on our colonel, but did not charm us
by his civility or communicativeness.   Here, with the
guidance of an old Brahui, formerly serving in one of
the cavalry regiments, I visited the site of the British
cantonments of 1839-42.   A number of bér-trees
(*Zizyphus Jujuba*) mark the spot.   The old man also
showed me the remains of two bungalows and a grave
of ' Lubday Sahib ' and another officer.   It is a mound
of mud, without fence, stone, or inscription.   Lieutenant Loveday, Political Agent at Kelat in 1841, was
captured by the Biloch chief, Nasir Khan, and taken
to Dadar in a camel's kujawa in chains, with all the
aggravation of privation, exposure, and torture.   On
the approach of Boscawen's detachment, Nasir Khan
cut off Loveday's head and fled.   The body was found
still warm by our troops.   An account of this barbarous deed was published by M. B. Neill in his ' Four
Years' Service in the East.'   A view of the hills from
here at sunset is very pretty, five ranges, one behind
the other, rising in the distance.   In spring and autumn
this part of the country presents a scene of great ani-
mation ; for then the pass from Darwàzah to Dadar is
filled with countless flocks of sheep, with Brahui families, and all their goods and chattels, moving either to
or from their summer homes.   This patriarchal life of
the Brahuis possesses charms of its own, as they are
always in search of a pleasant climate, and leave a
spot as soon as it becomes uncomfortable.   Thus they
prefer the plains in the cold weather, the hills in the
hot ; and whenever they meet with satisfactory graz-

ing grounds, they pitch their black tents and make themselves a temporary home. As we were passing on our road to Dadar, I observed that the bajra and jawar crops, which were very promising before, had been destroyed by the locusts.

" *Oct. 26th. Kundelani*, eleven miles. This and the next stage are justly considered the *mauvais pas* of the Bolan. ' It is not so much a pass over a lofty range of mountains as a succession of ravines and gorges, commencing near Dadar, and first winding among the subordinate ridges stretching eastward from the Hala chain of mountains, the brow of which it finally cross-cuts, and thus gives access from the vast plains of Hindustan to the elevated and uneven tracts extending from the Hindu Kush to the vicinity of the Indian Ocean. The elevation of its entrance is about 800 feet above the level of the sea, and that of its outlet at the western extremity 5700 feet. There is no descent on the western side, as the road opens on the Dasht-i-Bidaulat, a plain as high as the top of the pass. The total length is about fifty miles.' The first few miles offered no difficulty in walking, and thus the entrance of the pass is reached, consisting of a ravine, with low hills on either side, and a stream winding its way between them. The stony bed of this stream is the road up the pass, which is practicable only when the water is low. We had to cross the water eleven times, and found the sharp-pointed pebbles very trying to the bare feet. We encamped at a high spot with a 'chowkey,' consisting of a

THE BOLAN PASS.

small mud tower for a watchman. About half a mile
further on is a fine large pool, from which a rock
shoots up steep and sharp. Here we bàthed, and I
caught a fish called 'murrel,' and another called a
'mahser,' with a little paste for bait. The latter are
well known to all who ply the rod in the Punjab ;
both are good eating, and easily caught with a fly.

"_Oct._ 27_th._   _Kirta_, twelve miles. We had to cross
the river nine times to-day ; the water sometimes up
to our knees, but generally quite shallow. I found
great advantage in wearing 'chaplis,' or native sandals,
both on account of the ease to the feet in walking
over stones, and the convenience with which they can
be slipped on and off in crossing water. After four
miles' march the light came gradually into the narrow
valleys, shut in by somewhat precipitous rocks which
afford excellent shade long after sunrise. From the
narrow gorge you then emerge into a broader one,
and the path runs parallel with the water, instead of
crossing it. Following the line of telegraph through
another valley, a rapid turn to the left leads over
stony ground, through a broad plain to the camping-
ground, five miles distant. Kirta is a wretched little
village by the water, with a few 'bher' trees, under
which I pitched my tent. Clouds of dust blowing
all day reduced everything to a uniform colour. The
Bolan Pass is disappointing to anyone who looks tor
fine scenery. It cannot compare with either of the
Swiss passes. The river-bed is the only road, and
following this, one ascends almost unconsciously for

sixty miles without a single dip. As the summit of
the Bolan is not more than 7000 feet above the sea,
the ascent is very gradual. Ordinarily there is very
little water in the Bolan River, but after heavy rains
the consequences might be serious to travellers on
the march, or halt, in any of the narrower valleys.
During the former campaign it is said that a squadron
of Skinner's Horse was suddenly overtaken in the
middle of the pass by the rising flood, and that men
and horses were swept away and drowned.

"At Kirta I was attacked by a hornet, whose
sting, superadded to an already troublesome boil,
caused inconvenience for some days.

"*Oct. 28th. Bibinâni*, 8½ miles. An easy march
of three hours. No village or supplies. At this, as
well as at the last halting-place, good fish may be got
from the river.

"*Oct. 29th. Mach*, thirteen miles. A very heavy
and trying march over shingle, like the seashore, in
which the foot sinks at every step. Sometimes a shorter
march of nine miles is made to a place on the road
called Ab-i-Gum; but as we had no supplies for the
regiment, we could not halt. We passed a large company of horse-dealers from Kandahar, on their way to
Jacobabad, with a cafila of horses for sale. Their
camels were laden with fruits, and we found some
water-melons very refreshing. At Mach there is a
telegraph station and store for supplies. The camping-ground is, as usual, in the bed of the river, which
here is much narrower. Here we noticed a perceptible

difference in the atmosphere, and the coolness of the
air was a great relief.

"*Oct.* 30*th.*   *Sir-i-Bolán*, five miles.   A short and
easy march.   The camels suffer much for want of
their accustomed fodder, which cannot be obtained
in the pass.   Nine of them broke down yesterday.
The encampment is close to the source of the Bolan
River, where it gushes out of the rock in a plentiful
cascade.   The elevation here is said to be 4000 feet
above the sea.

"*Oct.* 31*st.*   *Darwázah*, thirteen miles.   A long
march, with more rapid ascent to the top of the
pass by stony and winding ravines, sometimes branch-
ing off to right and left.   It is not difficult to lose
the way, as subsequent experience proved, for the
colonel of a regiment in rear was taken up one of
these ravines by his dooly-bearers, and lost to his
regiment for the rest of the day.   A guide is necessary; but although alone, and considerably in advance of my party, I was guided by the long string
of Brahuis whom I met descending from their villages
with their families, camels, and flocks, to their winter
pastures on the plains below.   Their squalid appearance confirmed the reports of the ravages of fever in
the Quetta Valley amongst natives and Europeans
alike.   Near the head of the pass a short cut to
the right under the telegraph, still leads through a
valley near a steep kotal or ridge, to the Dasht
plain, saving two miles.   Before reaching the kotal
the road seems, by a curious optical illusion, to

descend, while in reality there is a continued ascent.

"The upper Bolan is more picturesque than the lower, and has some fine wild olive-trees, with stems at least 2½ feet in diameter. I observed many part-ridges of three sorts—the red-legged, the grey, and the small variety, called 'susi.' The last ridge com-mands an extensive view of surrounding hill-tops, enclosing a little plain called the Dasht-i-Bidaulat Plain, with a post and telegraph station in the distance. It was, alas! here that a cowardly and murderous attack was made by some ruffians, in 1842, upon the wife of a conductor named Smith, who was travelling alone in the pass. She defended herself bravely, but was killed by her wretched assailants. The plain of the Dasht is covered with tufts of low bad grass, which seems to derive no nourishment, at this season, from the soil. The keen blasts of wind which sweep across the desert in the winter are fatal alike to man and beast.

"*Nov. 1st. Quetta*, twenty-three miles. A tedious march of sixteen miles to Sar-i-Ab, which is lower than the Dasht Plain. The track, which is stony and rough, crosses the undulations of a spur of hills, and then gains the Quetta Plain. Sar-i-Ab is a small village inhabited by Brahuis in the summer, but deserted in the winter. Here I recognised a link with Persia, in the method of irrigation employed by the cultivators. They tap the foot of a hill where water is likely to be near the surface by digging a well. Having found

the water, they turn it on to the plain by an underground channel, often miles in length, with shafts or
air-holes at intervals of about fifty yards. At length
the stream emerges, and is turned into channels over
the fields wherever it is required. The underground
channel, called here *karēz,* and in Persia *kanāt,* has
the great advantage of keeping the water cool in the
hot weather, and preventing its waste by evaporation.
It supersedes also the laborious process of raising the
water from wells, by wheels or levers, as in India.

  " The regiment halted the night at Sar-i-Ab, as the
baggage camels could not do a double march. I
therefore proceeded alone for the remainder of the
journey, seven miles, and reached Quetta by sunset.
The country and scenery bear a striking resemblance
to Persia. The little village, with its fort, lies at the end
of a plain, shut in by hills of from 11,000 to 12,000
feet high. A few small groves of fruit-trees served
to enliven, with their autumn tints, the barrenness of
its surroundings. But everything had a charm after
the fatigues of the Bolan, and Quetta was welcomed
as the terminus to a dreary march on foot of 310
miles in twenty-four days. Bread was a treat after
tough chupatties, charpoys seemed a luxury after the
hard ground, and no midnight bugle broke one's
slumbers. But for the Bolan, Quetta would be de-
cidedly disappointing. There is nothing to see but
a very dirty little bazar, and a mound with a fort.
. . . There is a small cemetery with a wall round
it, and a grave—the grave of Lieutenant Heutson,

R.E., who was murdered by some Pathan fanatics of the Khakar tribe. These men inhabit villages near Quetta, and engage themselves for hire as day labourers, just as other Pathans do in the winter months in the Punjab. They are a wild-looking set, and their habit of concealing a knife in the skirt of their rough coats renders them dangerous neighbours. Several unprovoked attacks have been made by them upon European officials, and now no one goes without a revolver for self-defence. The fanatical impulse to take life at the risk of losing it, seems to be confined to the Muhamadans of the Afghan tribes, and not to exist amongst the Bilochis and Brahuis. The cold at Quetta in November is severe, more especially by contrast with the heat of the plains. There was a large demand for felt coats and ' postines,' or sheep-skins, a demand which far exceeded the supply."

Here there is a break in Gordon's journal during the month he remained in Quetta. But his letters at this time give us an insight into what he was thinking and doing. Thus, in a circular letter written on November 14th, he says :—

" My last letter was written in the course of a long march of three hundred miles over an almost track-less desert and up mountain passes. The novelty of a military camp is pleasant under ordinary circum-stances, but it loses its attraction when you are wakened by the bugle soon after midnight to make a long march of fifteen or twenty miles before break-fast. Long marches on foot, however, are my habit,

and I got on better than those who were mounted.
The breaking up of a large camp is an animated
scene, especially by moonlight. The first sound after
the bugle is the rattling of tent pegs, which suc-
ceeds the striking of the tents. Your bed on the
hard ground is quickly rolled up and tied into a small
bundle. The tent falls, and is soon packed away on
a camel's back. A small fire is lighted, a cup of tea
made and swallowed in ten minutes. The Sepoys
fall into line and the muster roll is called over. The
drums beat, the officers fall into their places and the
'advance' is sounded on the bugle. Then follows
'quick march,' the band plays and the regiment is in
motion. A long line of camels (we had 340) follows,
and the camping-ground has nothing to mark it from
the rest of the desert, except a few smouldering fires.
After a silent march of six or seven miles, a 'halt' is
sounded and the men are allowed to fill their water-
bottles. The water in these regions is so scarce that
bullocks, laden with large skins full of water, have to
be stationed at intervals along the march, for the
native Sepoy is a very thirsty subject, and cannot go
three miles without drinking. It is one good feature
of Muhamadanism, that it is a great total abstinence
association, and no true Muhamadan may touch intoxicating liquors. I wish the same rule applied to
the English army. · · · · · ·

"When we left the plains we had eighty-five miles
of ascent up the Bolan Pass. As we ascended the
air got cooler, which was a great relief, and we had a

good water supply from the river which flows down the pass. The bed of this stream was our road, and a very rough road it was. Sometimes the stream had to be crossed eight or ten times in a single march. There was nothing for it but to pull off boots and socks and wade through over pebbles very trying to the foot. I am fond of mountain climbing, but the Bolan is singularly uninteresting. Day after day there is the same gradual ascent, over heavy shingle like the sea-shore, with bare hills on either side. It reminded me of the rough up-hill plodding of missionary work, and often recalled the text, 'Thou therefore endure hardness as a good soldier of Christ.' Towards the top of the Bolan the mountains are bolder, the ravines narrower and more picturesque, and I was struck with some wild olive trees of unusual size. The absence of animal life in the Bolan is very marked, except at the summit, where partridges of two kinds abound. A species of wild goat also inhabits the ranges, and also bears are met with. The poor camel suffers much in this pass, and it is a common thing to hear of forty or fifty camels in a single regiment being left to die in the Bolan, unable to sustain their loads. After three weeks of toil we were very thankful to reach Quetta. It is a wild, cheerless place, but seemed a paradise to travel-worn frames.

● ● ● ● ● ● ● ● ●

"We are all waiting in suspense the result of the ultimatum to the Amír, but the general opinion is that war is certain, and the troops are ready and

anxious for it. An advance to Kandahar would be
welcomed by all, for the cold is getting intense, and
a campaign in Afghanistan would be much more
congenial to the army than a winter in Quetta. The
elevation here is some 6000 feet above the sea, while
Kandahar is lower and warmer.

. . . .

"I have received great kindness from some of the
officers. They have never had any ministry here, or
seen a clergyman. Some of them have been here two
years. Last Sunday I held service in Major Sandeman's tent and administered the holy communion,
and next Sunday I expect to have a parade service
of the 70th regiment, out of doors.

. . . .

"At this season the population leave their native
villages and go down with their flocks and herds to
the plains, where it is warmer. We met thousands
of Brahuis in the Bolan Pass travelling on foot, while
their rough tents, their wives and families followed
on camels. As I have not yet learned their language
I could not say much to them. They looked as
though they had all suffered from the epidemic of
fever, which has lately prevailed at Quetta amongst
the natives, as well as Europeans.

. . . .

"This is a new country, and one into which the
gospel has never yet entered. Pray for me that 'a
door of entrance' may be granted me amongst the
natives as well as amongst my own countrymen."
And again, in a letter to his aunt, the late Hon. Mrs.

Leslie-Melville, on November 23d, we find him with plenty to occupy his attention and thoughts.

" I have been visiting here every day the poor sick soldiers in hospital. They have few comforts, and are very cold at night, for they have nothing but a flimsy tent to shelter them, and their blankets and clothing are not sufficient. They have left the hot plains only a few weeks ago, where the thermometer was over one hundred degrees, and they are now on the mountains, where it freezes hard, and is no higher than eight degrees, or twenty-four degrees below freezing-point. There was such a hurry in getting them started, and so little preparation for a climate like this, that the result has been worse than a battle. The frost and cold are worse enemies than the Afghans. We are obliged to wear sheepskin coats, with all the wool on to keep us warm, but most of the soldiers and sepoys cannot yet get these comforts, as it is a wild country, with no shops or tailors to supply clothing. There are ten regiments here, with six thousand men, and as many more are expected to come. I had a heavy cold last Sunday, but I held service, and preached on one of our Lord's miracles, the draught of fishes (Luke v.), dwelling on Peter's faith and self-surrender to Christ, and illustrating my remarks by the example of Sir Henry Lawrence.

.   .   .   .

" I trust the campaign will not last long. We are going on to Kandahar, and it is believed that we shall soon take that place, and go to Herat. The Lord grant that good may come out of the present evil."

CHAPTER XIV.

AFTER a month at Quetta, Gordon's journal is resumed, and, once more, it is again given *in extenso*, as the best means of bringing the reader and the missionary chaplain into personal contact.

"*Dec.* 1. *Quetta.* Arrival of 70th Foot on 15th Nov., and E 4 Battery, R.A., 24th Nov. The extraordinary difficulties surmounted in getting the guns through the Bugti Dera hills and up the Bolan will be unknown to future generations when roads are made. The appearance of the bullocks and horses which dragged them told its own sad tale of suffering and hardship. Chopped straw is the only substitute for grass that can be obtained, and camels, horses, and cattle have to eat it or starve. And now the intense cold, with thirty degrees of frost at night, is added to their other trials. It tells also on the men of the 70th, and the battery who have come ' from under the punkahs' at Multān. They had to march at a day's notice, and with such restrictions, that they could not provide themselves with anything warmer than their serge coats. As a natural consequence, they get chest disease, and the coughing at night is distressing to

U

hear.   Some temporary stoves have been erected for
the hospital tents, and a range of mud tents is being
fitted up as a base hospital.   The native dooly-bearers
suffer most.   Having never been inured to cold, they
are defenceless against it, and the mortality among
them is great.

"No church has yet been built at Quetta, although
a site has been proposed.   The civil and military lines
are far apart, and it is difficult to find a central place
for holding service.   On my arrival I found that service had been regularly held in Major Keene's mess-
room, 1st Punjab Infantry.   As regiment after regiment
arrived in Quetta, the hope was encouraged that there
would be a large attendance, and I held a second
service every Sunday afternoon in Major Sandeman's
large durbar tent.   The attendance, however, was very
disappointing.   Almost every one had, or affected to
have, on Sundays as well as week-days, an overwhelm-
ing pressure of business.

"The arrival of General Biddulph and staff was
welcomed at Quetta by all the troops.   The order to
advance was eagerly expected, and every one im-
patiently awaited the Amír's response to the ultimatum.   The Pioneers and Native Cavalry were first
sent on, and reported favourably of the country beyond.   The 26th, 1st, and 19th Punjab Native Infantry
followed, and the Peshawur Mountain Battery.   The
first march was to

"*Dec. 6th.   Kuchlák*, eleven miles.   Encamped by
a large village, where water issues in considerable

volume from the hill, and is very clear, but said by
the natives to be not very good for drinking.

"*Dec. 7th. Saiyid Yaru Karēz,* twelve miles. The
battery started after an early breakfast. After two
or three miles we reached the stream, which divides
the Khan's territory from the Amír's. The ford is
shallow, but the banks are steep, and there was some
delay before the last gun and waggon crossed. The
horses had recovered strength and spirits during their
rest at Quetta, and seemed to enjoy their work. A
number of Seyyids from a neighbouring village ranged
themselves along the bank with their boys handsomely dressed. I inquired whether they had ever
seen artillery before. 'Oh, yes,' they replied, 'we
have been all over India.' It must appear to them
a sign of weakness that we should forego all right to
travel in Afghanistan, while we give them so freely
the *entrée* to India. We passed several villages with
some cultivation, the ground being broken by *nullahs.*
One of these which had water in it I crossed on a
bullock, seated in native fashion behind the driver.
The people seem friendly and confiding, and bring
us their eggs and water-melons for sale. They talk
Pushtu, but understand Persian also, which is the
easier medium of communication. The weather is
perfect, but I was more with the rearguard to-day
than with the advance guard. One's enjoyment of
a day's march depends largely upon physical health.

"*Dec. 8th. Haikalzai,* eleven miles. After three
or four miles there is a steep kotal, from the summit

of which we could see the next encampment. There was some delay in getting the guns up the narrow ascent of the kotal. One or two of the waggons stuck in the middle, and the men of the 70th had to assist at the drag ropes. While this was going on, I walked on ahead for seven miles through the Pishîn Valley. The crops depend upon the rainfall, as there is no irrigation. Passed a ruined and deserted village, and another inhabited one. The unarmed peasants were sitting by the roadside selling melons. One of them knew a little Hindustani, which he had picked up at Karráchi. I offered him a salary if he would teach me Pushtu, but he did not seem to care to go to Kandahar, and excused himself on the plea of a bad hand, which was bound up. Here, a few nights ago, one of the 32nd Pioneers, who had stayed behind on the march, was missing. His body was found next day shot with his own rifle, which was carried off and never recovered. The Pishîn Valley lies lower than Quetta, and is not so cold. At the encampment we rejoined the 70th and sections of other regiments. A sale by auction of some cattle and sheep was going on. It appeared that the baggage of the General and his staff had been looted on a reconnoitring expedition after nightfall. A part only of the baggage was recovered, and it became necessary to read the natives a lesson by seizing some of their cattle to make up the value of the remainder.

"*Dec. 9th. The Lora*, eight miles. The division started early, forming a line of march eight miles long, with the baggage. The latter was not in till after dark. The country flat, but broken by large fissures, through one of which the river Lora runs with a rapid current. The water at the ford is not deep, but intensely cold to the feet. On reaching the further bank, I sat an hour watching the cavalry, infantry, and guns crossing. The camping-ground about half a mile beyond. On arriving I observed one of the 70th, a private, carried to the rear and placed in a dooly with two medical officers in attendance on him· He said that he had been stabbed by a Pathan, who had come into the lines as the soldiers were resting after their march. The wounds, which were in the arm and leg, were severe but not mortal, and the man, who was defenceless, had had a narrow escape. His assailant, who had been knocked down with the butt of a rifle and secured, was an ordinary-looking Pathan (or Khadar), of great strength and forbidding cast of countenance. Upon being questioned as to his motive for the deed, he was not disposed to be communicative, but seemed to consider it a trivial affair, and not one to be regretted.

"_Dec._ 10_th._ _Arambi Karez_, three miles. Completed yesterday's march, which was shortened by a ditch which had to be bridged for the guns. Two villages near, and supplies abundant. A court-martial held on Muhamad Anvár, the prisoner ; found him guilty of death, and sentence was executed in the afternoon. He maintained to the last the same recklessness of life which had nerved him to the deed. He had done his best to kill an enemy and a 'Kafir,' and he was indifferent whether he lived or died. Had he lived, he might renew the attempt, such was the only inducement. He had been to Mecca, and could recite his prayers and parts of the Kuran in Arabic. More of his history did not transpire. He may have been trained to deeds of bloodshed, as many of his tribe are, but his motives, if those of religion and patriotism, are far higher than those of other murderers who take life for revenge or filthy lucre. His only weapon was a curved and worn Afghan knife with a keen point. According to Muhamadan law, 'eye for eye, tooth for tooth, and for wounds retaliation,' etc., his life was not forfeit unless his victim died—so he maintained. But he asked no reprieve, he only deprecated suspense, and the soldiers who saw him shot said ' he died like a man.'

"There are many Pathans in our native regiments, who are now invading the land of their birth and kindred. One of them conversed with me to-day, and told me he had been trained in the Rev. Mr. Sheldon's mission school at Karráchi. He can read and write well, and gave me a little assistance in Pushtu.

"*Dec.* 12*th. Abdullah Khan's village.* Four miles of broken ground leads through low hills to a small plain with the Khojak range in front.

"*Dec.* 13*th.* Joined the headquarters' camp, half-mile on, near the village of Abdullah Khan. Here we stick for the present. The village chief, a man of some importance, came to pay his salaams to

the General. He is said to be in disgrace with
the Amír.

"_Dec._ 15_th_, _Sunday._ Held service in hospital,
and on parade with the 70th Foot, 60th Rifles, and
E 4 Battery, R.A.; also in the evening at General
Biddulph's tent. General Stewart arrived yesterday
and takes command of the column ; General Biddulph
commanding 2nd Division.

"_Dec._ 16_th._ A reconnoitre of the Khojak Pass by
the two Generals, with a large staff of officers and
escort of the 1st Punjab Cavalry and Fane's Horse.
The ascent for five or six miles is gradual. Here for
the first time the barren monotony of the scenery
is diversified by respectable trees called 'khinjak,'
now leafless and tenanted by a number of magpies.
Dead camels all along the road.

"Visited the camp of 32nd Pioneers and 26th
Punjab Native Infantry, who are roadmaking in the
pass. The summit, said to be more than 7000 feet,
is approached by a steeper ascent, and commands an
extensive view. Kandahar is not in sight, nor do
villages appear. A broad barren plain, with rocky
ridges cropping up, is all that presents itself. We
descended to Chaman by a road so steep that every
one dismounted. Here the guns are to be let down
by hand, and there is a zigzag road for the camels.

"_Christmas Day._ Weather very seasonable.
Service at 11 a.m. in Major Sandeman's tent. The
guns have been got over the pass without a mishap.

"_Dec._ 26_th._ Marched with the hospital in charge

of Dr. Manby, V.C. Counted seventy-three dead
camels. They are stripped of their skins by the villagers as soon as they die. There must be a large
trade in camels' skins.

"*Dec. 27th.* The baggage of the 15th Hussars
first went over the pass, then the hospital. The path
is very narrow, so that only one camel can pass at a
time, and much steeper than anything in the Bolan.
The arrangements were admirably carried out. The
sick were first taken over in doolies, and placed at
the foot of the pass. Then the dooly-bearers were
sent back with the poles for the stores. It was a
hard day for dooly-bearers and camels. The latter
took their loads steadily down the steep incline, and
no mishap occurred. Major Tulloch, 26th Punjab
Native Infantry, is the traffic manager, and gives his
orders from the summit. This morning my camel
was returned as 'dead' by the driver, and hidden
away. I suspected a trick, and, after a careful
search, recognised and recovered it. The difficulty
is to see that it is properly clothed and fed at night.
If this were always done, the mortality among the
camels would be greatly checked. Many of the
drivers have an interest in killing or losing camels
which do not belong to them. Some of the officers
have purchased country camels, which are much
hardier than those of the plains. They feed on the
'southernwood' which abounds here, and which the
Punjab camels refuse. The country sheep also thrive
on this coarse dry shrub.

ON THE MARCH TO KANDAHAR.

"*Dec.* 28*th.*   *Chaman.*   We all got comfortably
into camp by sunset yesterday evening, and here again
we stick for the present, while the cavalry brigade,
under General Palliser, reconnoitre in the front.
There is a very marked difference in the temperature
on this side of the Khojak, which is noticeable in the
foliage on the trees.   We have done with the intense
cold, unless snow falls.   The price of marketable
articles is very high, as the villagers are allowed to
make what they can, and the British soldier is reck-
less as to what he pays.   Flour sells at one seer the
rupee, coarse flour at four seers, barley and grain
eight seers, eggs one anna each.   In the Pishîn Valley,
when the troops first arrived, the eggs were twenty-
four to the anna.   The same day they fell to eight per
anna, and so on.   There is a good supply of water
in the Khojak Pass, and also at Chaman.

"*Jan.* 3*rd*, 1879.   *Spin Baldak*, fourteen miles.   The
road descends and passes a low ridge to the right.
All day a dust wind blew, which is the usual precursor
of rain.   A slight shower fell in the evening, and just
wetted our tents, but soon stopped.   This is the first
rain since the August showers in the Punjab.   Clouds
have often gathered and threatened, but all predic-
tions of snow and rain have been falsified.   Hence,
by a merciful Providence, an untold amount of suffering and sickness has been averted.   Water here is
abundant.   There is a small village built in Afghan
fashion, with dome-roofed mud houses like tombs.

"*Kila Fatiullah*, twelve miles.   There is great monotony in the scenery. To-day we passed some rather remarkable black limestone rocks, with mixture of conglomerate and sandstone. The people are well disposed towards us, and whatever their anticipations of our intentions, it is generally true, as the soldiers say, that it takes only one day to make them our friends.

"*Jan. 5th. Mel Manda*, twelve miles. The news met us on our arrival of a cavalry action, which happened yesterday in the front. This being the first encounter with the enemy, created some excitement and impatience to push on.

"*Jan. 6th. Abdul Rahman*, twenty-two miles. We are all ready for an early start by order of our Brigadier-General, Lacy, but on reaching *Saifudden*, eleven miles, an order came from the front to halt. As I was anxious to join the headquarters' camp, I marched on with Mr. C., who was in charge of the postal department. A few miles on we came to a pass between two hills with a small stream of water, and what looked like a cave in the rocks to the right. Following the path we entered a plain beyond, and in a ravine to the right I saw unmistakable signs of the recent action. The corpses of men and horses were lying about on the rough and broken ground, and here and there a hungry villager was prowling about in search of spoil.

" It was a long march to Abdul Rahman, and as daylight waned, we recollected that we had no guards or arms for our own protection and that of the mails.

We could just see some of the mounted forms of
General Biddulph's rearguard on the horizon in front.
Mr. C. therefore rode on and obtained a few Sepoys
from Major Tulloch, who commanded in the rearguard.
There was, however, no information as to where we
were to halt, and it became an anxious matter as to
whether our camels could go much further. The
track as we advanced was well marked by the poor
broken-down camels of the column in front. Some
of them I secured to the tails of our camels, and
brought into camp, but as a feed of straw could not
be got for love or money, they lost their last chance
of surviving. About two hours after sunset we came
to a large village, and heard all the unmistakable
sounds of unloading and tent-pitching. And now
the difficulty was to find one's particular regiment
out of so many. After a vain attempt I pitched my
tent with Mr. C.'s at the headquarters' camp, and
General Stewart kindly invited me to dinner.

"*Jan. 7th. Khushab*, fifteen miles. Everyone
was early astir, and there was a general hope that
we should see something of the enemy. General
Stewart's division took the lead. General Biddulph's
was drawn up in line of march, but the order to
advance was not given. During the suspense all eyes
were directed to the kotal in front, where the flashes
of the heliograph were unusually active. The message was soon interpreted. A rumour ran through
the host, ' It's all over ! Kandahar has surrendered ! '
And many an expression of disgust and disappoint-

ment followed. There were no mutual congratula-
tions upon the successful termination of a bloodless
campaign. It seemed as though the last hope of
distinction had gone. After all the toils of the
Bolan, the sickness of Quetta, and the cold night
duty of December, the troops had not even crossed
swords with the Afghans!

"*January 8th. Kandahar,* ten miles. A very long
day over a short march. The orders were for a parade of troops and march through Kandahar. Some
delay occurred in crossing the River Tarnak, as the
bank was steep, and there was no practicable road
for artillery. The water was fordable, but intensely
cold. A few miles on a small stream turns a water-
mill, and then by a rapid ascent a ridge is attained
which gives a fine view of Kandahar, still five or six
miles off. The city is well situated in a plain, surrounded by sharp, rocky hills. From a distance one
sees gardens and walls, surmounted by the domed
shrine of Ahmad Shah, and the distant view is the
best. To-day, however, there was much to add im-
pressiveness to the scene, in the appearance of the
troops, for a finer army never entered Kandahar.
The Generals and staffs preceded, and were followed
by the cavalry brigade, consisting of 15th Hussars,
and 1st and 2nd Punjab Cavalry. Then came the
Royal Horse Artillery and Royal Artillery batteries,
and the infantry regiments, headed by the 70th.
The absence of brass bands was a felt want. As
we approached the town the road became very

THE FIRST SIGHT OF KANDAHAR.

tortuous, and at length took us over a stream by a solid masonry bridge, which was evidently a relic of the former campaign.   Groups of citizens, with somewhat anxious, but subdued faces, lined the road. These were Muhamadans.   But the Hindus, in red turbans and holiday dress, wore an unmistakable expression of welcome, and fraternised eagerly with their co-religionists amongst our camp-followers. One had asked me about his native place, mentioning a town I knew well near Pind Dádan Khán.   At the gates some fruit-sellers made a tempting display of pomegranates and apples.   As we filed through the bazars there was not much to see, for the shops were all shut.   The explanation was that for four days the town had been in a state of anarchy, and no one considered life or property safe.

"The camp was pitched at some distance outside the city walls, the 25th N. I. only being quartered in the citadel.   The night's rest was none the less welcome for the thought that the long tedious march on foot of 465 miles from the Indus to Kandahar was at length over.   We have had abundant cause to acknowledge the good hand of our God over us in the removal of many difficulties which might have made the expedition a failure instead of a success.

"*January 9th.*   The city of Kandahar is by no means attractive from the inside.   Its unhealthiness is everywhere asserted by bad drainage and bad smells.   Hence the huge cemetery outside the walls. Nor has it any redeeming architectural features.

There is nothing to look at, except the shrine of Ahmad Shah. Two long bazars intersect the city, and are covered, where they cross each other, by arches of brick. They are wider than the bazars of Old Lahore, but cannot compare with those of Ispahan, or even of a second-rate Persian town. In the variety and excellence of their products, they certainly compare favourably with those of the Punjab. Why should the Punjabi merchant allow himself to be passed by the Parsee and Kandahari? The latter will astonish you with his fertility of resources. He will show you Russian samooars and china teacups, skins from Astrakan, and carpets from Herat, mundahs and pastines of first-rate quality made on the spot, fur robes, and Damascene silks and blades, arms and accoutrements, both native and European. But what struck me most was the profusion and variety of English uniforms and ammunition-boots hanging up in the shops. How they came there, and how, except amongst Europeans, they would find a market was a puzzling speculation. Men of the 70th Regiment, the R.A., and the cavalry soldier and Sepoy, each could put on his own particular uniform, and purchase it, if necessary, brand-new at the market price.

" Nor was there any slackness in the various departments of native industry. In the ironmongers' quarter, the goldsmiths', the potters', or the weavers', one might find creditable specimens of native art.

" In several ways the Afghan seems more nearly

allied to us in his tastes than the Punjabi.   Afghan
cookery is very superior.   A good meal may be had at
any time of the day in the streets of Kandahar.   The
baker is always ready with very excellent hot bread.
The confectioner produces a variety of superior sweet-
meats.   The cook has first-rate pillaws, kabobs, and
fresh fried fish from the river.

"Amongst the townspeople two very marked types
of feature were conspicuous by contrast, the handsome
aquiline Jewish type, which one sees so often amongst
the Povindah merchants who cross the Punjab plains,
and the Mongolian type, flat-nosed and almond-eyed,
which belongs especially to the Hazarah tribe.   They
all seemed to understand and speak Persian, but our
Hindustani troops had great difficulty in making
themselves intelligible.

"*Sunday,* 12*th Jan.*—At 11 a.m. held parade ser-
vice with 59th Foot, 15th Hussars, 60th Rifles, R. H.
Artillery, and two field batteries, all belonging to
General Stewart's Division.   Another service in hos-
pital at 3 p.m.   A third at the headquarters, 2nd
Division, at 5 p.m. with 70th Foot E., 4 R.A. Battery,
etc.   General Biddulph and staff attended.   After this
I went into the city and held a fourth service in the
Fort, with Holy Communion, for the benefit of the
officers of the 25th N. Infantry quartered there.

"*Monday,* 13*th Jan.*—Had a very hearty little
prayer-meeting in my tent, attended by four officers
and eight soldiers.   We made room by clearing out
everything, and sitting on the ground, by the light of

a home-made candle, composed of sheep's fat, with a piece of tent-rope for wick. The singing was very good, and we all felt mutually edified.

"*Jan.* 16*th.*—An event of solemn interest occupied us—the funeral of Lieutenant Willis, R.A., who died yesterday morning from a blow dealt by a wild fanatic in the street of Kandahar. His genial and attractive disposition had endeared him to us all on the march, and we mourned for him as for a brother. It was a privilege to attend his last hours, to hear his simple confession of trust in Christ, and to administer to him the Holy Sacrament. The funeral procession, headed by the band of the 70th, left the camp and skirted the city till it reached the fort, when the coffin was lowered from the gun-carriage, and carried by men of the Battery to its final resting-place. The spot selected for a cemetery was a walled garden inside the fort, secluded from all but guarded access. Here General Biddulph and his staff met the procession. The funeral service seemed to be felt as a very solemn one by many officers who attended to pay their last tribute of respect to their departed comrade.

"*Jan.* 31*st.*—Visited the tomb of Ahmad Shah, the founder of the city, and of the Dourani dynasty. The tomb is surmounted by a somewhat high dome, which is seen from a long distance, being the only monument or architectural feature of Kandahar. Under the dome is the last resting-place of the Shah and his three wives. The tomb is covered with

Kashmir shawls, and is considered the most inviolable asylum in the country.

"*Jan.* 31*st.*—The day being Friday, all the Muhamadan shops are shut (as with us on Sunday). At two o'clock, when the prayers in the mosque are over, the Mullahs repair to the principal bazar, and display books relating to the Muhamadan religion for sale. It was at this spot that poor Willis was murdered. Engaging in conversation with a respectable-looking man, named A. K., who proved to be a chief of one of the local tribes, I offered him the New Testament in Arabic, which he gladly accepted. He asked my address, and promised to call on me, which he afterwards did.

"*Feb.* 3*rd.*—Took an early walk to a neighbouring hill, which is ascended by an ancient flight of steps cut out of the limestone rock. At the top of the steps are some old Persian inscriptions, one of which bears the date of the Emperor Baber. On my return, passed a number of boys and men, who were amusing themselves by sliding down a rock in a sitting posture. The rock has been worn smooth by successive generations of sliders."

In February 1879, we find Gordon once more on his way back to the Punjab. He writes to the Church Missionary Society, Feb. 17th, during the journey, as follows :—

"I shall always regard my journey to Kandahar as very important from a missionary point of view; and although the slow and tedious march there, with

X

its long delays, disappointed the hope of an earlier return, yet the time has not been wasted, and I shall henceforth be able to read the Bible to the Afghans in their own language, whenever the opportunity presents itself. It was one of those undertakings in which I felt the leading of God's providence, and when I saw some twenty regiments encamped without a pastor or Scripture-reader, there seemed to me to be an additional inducement to urge me onwards. The generals and officers gladly accepted my services, and I found a missionary sphere in the hospitals and soldiers' tents. If in this venture of faith I have exceeded my duty as a missionary of the C.M.S., the fault is mine, and I hope that your Committee will condone it, and not lose confidence in me for the future. One may be said, in common parlance, to have carried one's life in one's hand every day in Kandahar, for the place was full of fanatics more fatal in their attacks than the enemy in the field ; but my life, thank God, was in better keeping than my own. The language of David and of St. Paul is at such times inexpressibly appropriate : 'I will say of the Lord, He is my Refuge and my Fortress, my God, in Him will I trust.'

"I have received great kindness from many officers during this campaign, and all have been cordially friendly. Some have been more like brothers than friends. The Christian intercourse which I have enjoyed with them has been very refreshing.

"I am thankful to say that the Gospel in Arabic, Persian, and Pushtu was favourably received by some of the learned and influential natives of Kandahar, whose friendship was shown in frequent visits to my tent, and hospitality at their own houses. One of them was the Kazi, or head of the priesthood; another was a 'a doctor of divinity' (Muhamadan), of very inquiring mind, who showed me a copy of the New Testament in Hindustani, which he had not only read, but committed parts of it to memory. I found the same friendliness and cordiality among the leading members of the Hindu community, and I am quite certain that a residence of a few months there would establish an intercourse most favourable to the reception of the Gospel among all classes.

"General Biddulph's Division is now returning to India, and I have taken advantage of the opportunity to return with them. General Stewart's Division remains for the present at Kandahar.

"I now turn in dependence upon God to the work of the Biloch Mission and the Jhílam Itinerancy. May God in His own time raise up an apostle to the Afghans of Kabul and Kandahar! I believe that it is in those cities that one might expect a reception (humanly speaking) for the Gospel, rather than amongst the wild mountain tribes, the Afridis, Waziris Mahmands," etc.

A private letter, dated Derá Ghází Khán, supplies some further interesting particulars :—

"When I last wrote to you, I was leaving Kandahar to resume my missionary duties in the Punjab. The return journey was not an eventful one, as no enemy offered to attack us. The detachment with which I marched consisted of a battery Royal Artillery, part of the 12th Native Infantry, and such of the hospital patients as were able to travel. The first evening after we left Kandahar, the hospital got separated from the battery and lost their way. It was midnight before the last of them got into camp, and yet although they had to pass without escort through two villages, no attempt was made to molest them. A chaplain arrived at Kandahar shortly after I left, so that the services will be carried on regularly, which I was very glad to hear. Yesterday, I received a letter from a Christian officer, commanding one of the regiments there. He writes that some Persian and Afghan Testaments which I left with him for distribution amongst the natives were very eagerly and thankfully received by them, and he asks for another camel-load of Bibles to be sent. He also writes very encouragingly of the weekly Bible-classes for soldiers, which he says are very well attended, and that there seems to be a manifest blessing. I earnestly trust that we may be able to follow up the work commenced at Kandahar amongst the natives, and that at Kabul also, and Herat, there may be openings for Gospel light. Roads are now being made by our Government; forts erected, and depôts formed, so that communication is greatly facilitated. I noticed

this on my return from Quetta. I was able to leave
the troops behind and push on alone, and it took
me only six days to do the 200 or 300 miles, which
last October took us three weeks, by a more toilsome route."

George Maxwell Gordon was elected a F.R.S.G.
in 1879.

CHAPTER XV.

DERÁ GHÁZÍ KHÁN.

GORDON was often likened by his friends to a comet, for it was impossible to say where one would or would not meet him.

The two young colleagues, who were mentioned before as having been sent out by the Church Missionary Society, arrived in the Punjab at the end of 1878. They were under the impression that when they arrived they would forthwith be placed under the fostering care of Gordon, and initiated by him into their missionary work. But, alas! the news which greeted them was that Gordon was hundreds of miles away from the Punjab, at Kandahar.

So they settled down, the one in Peshawar, the other in Amritsar, learning the Urdu language, and waiting for definite news from their future leader. On February 17, 1879, however, Gordon writes :—

"I am now on my way to Derá Ghází to meet Lewis and Jukes, who are to be there with the Bishop and Clark in the beginning of March. General Biddulph's Division is now returning to India, and I have taken advantage of the opportuuity to return with them."

However, the party mentioned above were not destined to meet at Derá Ghází Khán. It so happened that the Bishop of Lahore went to Clarkabad, a Christian agricultural settlement about thirty-five miles west of Lahore, to lay the foundation stone of a new church which was to be built by Mr. Bateman. Mr. Clark accompanied him, and as the two newly-arrived missionaries thought that they had ample time to meet Gordon, they too went to Clarkabad to be present at the ceremony. There, while being entertained in all the sumptuous luxury of Mr. Bateman's mud hut, one morning, looking up they saw a stranger approaching. He was a man about five feet nine inches in height, of middle age, stoutly made, clad in a costume which displayed the calf of a leg of unusual circumference, well befitting one who could walk to Kandahar and back. His tanned face told, too, a tale of travel. His somewhat slow gait, his kindly but solemn glance, the long staff in his hand, all seemed to combine to give one the impression of a prophet of olden time. His constant companion, Dandy, the spaniel, followed too, at a steady pace behind, and added completeness to a scene that will never be forgotten by those who saw it for the first time.

" Who is this? " exclaimed one.

" Why, it's Gordon ! " said Bateman, as he saw the figure approaching.

So it turned out that he had left General Biddulph's force, and had hurried on alone. Thus he had arrived much sooner than he had been expected. On reaching Multan he knew that there would be no one at Derá Ghází Khán awaiting him, so he had come on at once to this place. Of this visit to Clarkabad Gordon writes :—

"I reached Multan on 8th March, and thence proceeded to a village where Mr. Bateman has a colony of Christians, and is building a church. The Bishop of Lahore was to lay the foundation stone, so I went to meet him. It was a very interesting ceremony. Dr. Clark came with the Bishop and also my two young colleagues, Mr. Lewis and Dr. Jukes. Just as the Bishop performed the ceremony there came down a long-prayed-for and much-needed shower of rain, which supplied a fitting illustration of that spiritual outpouring which that house of prayer is intended to draw down. It was pleasant to see the native Christians, men and women, in their working dress, some engaged in the foundation of the church, some at their picks, and others in domestic duties, all earning their own livelihood, and each one brightened up by an encouraging word from their pastor as he moved among them."

On April 5, 1879, the party of three reached Derá Ghází Khán. I make an extract from a report of my own written at this time. "We now began to look round us for some place in which to reside. We were anxious not to reside in cantonments, feeling that missionaries ought to identify themselves in every way with the native, and not with the European population.

"It seemed to be a matter of doubt whether this

place would ultimately prove to be the best position for our mission. Our object being to open work in Bilochistan, we felt that it might be possible to get more thoroughly amongst the Bilochi people. On this account Gordon was unwilling to undertake any building in or near the city, and we quite fell in with his decision, that it would be far better to wait and see what openings might be forthcoming.

"We found a pomegranate garden close to the city walls. It belonged to a Biloch chief. The owner readily gave his consent to our pitching our tent here. Within the garden, too, were the ruins of a native bungalow. In this we found one small room, which still had a roof on it, which, however, was tenanted by a donkey; another room of the same size was partially roofed; but,. generally, the whole place was a scene of _débris_ from fallen masonry, etc. With pickaxe and shovel we set to work to clear the place; we had the roof of the small room repaired, the four-footed tenant was ejected, and then, with our tent, we had ample accommodation. Here Dr. Jukes began his practice amongst the natives, and had plenty of patients every day. Mr. Gordon, as a rule, preached in the bazar each evening, and we accompanied him.

"All this was very invigorating, and we began to feel that we were in the midst of mission-work."

It is strange in India to see how men are constantly meeting where perhaps they least expect it. It so happened that there was a native Assistant Engineer of the Public Works Department stationed in Derá Ghází at this time, whom Gordon had known well in the Jhílam district.

In one of his journals of 1876 Gordon writes :—

" 15*th.*—Had a call from B. P., the Assistant Engineer of the district—a very enlightened native gentleman, who inclines to Brahmoism. He says he cannot find any speciality in the Christian doctrine which the purified Hindu doctrine does not possess. ' If you have martyrs, so have we ; if you have a Mediator, so have we.' On being asked whether Christ's life did not contrast favourably with Krishna's, he admitted it at once as loftier and purer, but said, ' I don't see among you Christians evidence of His teaching and inspiration being better than ours. We have our Sádus and Sants—the Sádu who aims at, the Sant who attains, perfection. Sádus are many, Sants few. So in every religion.'

" 16*th.*—B. P. called again, and opened his heart more — said he had tried everything — Hinduism, Brahmoism — had been to Calcutta to see Keshub Chunder Sen, but was not satisfied—felt that it would be a great gain to him to be a Christian in a religious, though not in a worldly, point of view—had, however, difficulties about inspiration and the divinity of Christ. ' I can believe that He raised Himself by His virtues and austerities to the level of a god, but not that He was God from everlasting.' We then read together passages of Scripture, such as John xx., 1 Cor. xv., Phil. ii. He said, after much thought, and evidently with a struggle, ' Well, my mind takes hold of this ; it is all possible. But this is my difficulty :—When I read other books of other religions, my mind also consents to them, and I don't know which to choose.' Afterwards he came to me again, and again expressed a great desire to learn more. We read and prayed together daily. He expressed a willingness to be baptised, if he could be received on the merits of his present attainments in religious belief. But he has a lingering desire to consult the Hindu fakírs of Lahore, Delhi, and Agra, as well as the Brahmoists, and he would fain, if it were possible, get into the kingdom of heaven 'direct,' instead of 'through a Mediator.'"

The history of this gentleman is an interesting one, and therefore it is given here. It is not merely interesting in itself, but also in its relation to others, as showing the way in which new feelings are spreading, and old systems giving way.

After what is mentioned in this extract from Gordon's diary, it is not surprising that the advice of the latter was that his friend should wait awhile before receiving baptism. But instead of drawing nearer to Christ, the attraction, possibly as involving less sacrifice, seemed to be towards Keshub Chunder Sen.

We find, in a diary of May 11th, 1879, that he is observing the Sunday, and holding religious meetings in his house on each Sabbath evening. Gordon writes:—

"On Sunday evening he invites to his house the leading members of various Hindu creeds for prayer and discussion, conducting the service himself. I was shown to the top of his house, where carpets were

spread, and lights placed in the middle. We all sat
in order, forming four sides of a square, and the greatest decorum was observed.

"The meeting commenced with a short exposition
by an old Pundit, who read and translated from one of
the Hindu Shastras, called the Bhagarat Gita. Then
followed the singing of bhajams or native hymns, to
native musical instruments. After this our friend
conducted extempore prayer in his own language,
commencing with a meditation, 'What are we here
met together for? Not worldly gratification, not vain
discourse. We are come to seek thee, O God.' He
proceeded in a very solemn manner, with confession
of sin, ascription of praise, and invocation. After
prayer he introduced discussion, with a few remarks on
the subject of seeking after God, and alluded to the
Hindu doctrine of three conditions of mind—namely,
(1) the 'wakeful,' (2) the 'dreaming,' (3) the 'heavy
slumberous' condition. Enlarging on the second condition—the dreaming, contemplative habit of mind, as
fitted for revelation of God—he thus illustrated his remarks: 'There is a dark house, and a bird sits in it.
A hawk sits outside and waits for the bird, but will
not enter the darkness. The bird flies out, and is instantly pursued by the hawk until it again seeks refuge
in the house. So with the human spirit; it finds no
rest in the world; care pursues it till it returns to its
ark, and finds rest in the solitude of contemplation.'
These remarks were met by a warm rejoinder from
an old Hindu lawyer, who argued that 'You cannot

find God by merely shutting your eyes and meditat-
ing. There must be successive *steps* from lower to
higher, and these steps are all indicated in the written
word, the Shastras.' He declined all merely speculative discussion.

"The other replied, 'You refer only to the Vedant
Shastras ; you know nothing of the Bhakti Shastras.'
This introduced the old battle-ground of 'faith' and
'works.' The old simile of the 'straight new road'
and the 'old tortuous road' was given, and, as usual,
turned both ways. Neither party would yield the point.

"The company present numbered about twenty-five
persons, most of whom (like my friend) were educated
men in Government employ. Four only took part in
the discussion. The others were listeners, like myself.
One of them told a nice story about an old man and
a Garu or teacher. The former, who was known to
be wealthy, on being questioned about his income,
stated it as only Rs.25. His age, he said, was only
two or three years. On being asked to explain, he
replied, 'I reckon my income as limited to the portion
of it which I have given to God, and my age as only
the time which I have spent in His service.'

"The proceedings concluded with the singing of
another hymn.

"I came away at ten p.m., strongly impressed with
the influence for good which can thus be exerted by
one like my friend, whose views on prayer and worship
are as much at variance with ordinary Hindus as
those of any Christian missionary. He has great dif-

ficulties and prejudices to contend with.   May he be
more and more enlightened by Him who is the light
that lighted every man that cometh into the world!"

Perhaps I may be permitted to say, with regard
to this gentleman, whom I may myself claim as a
friend, that I have met him from time to time since
he left Derá Ghází.   On the last occasion, in another
town, he took me over his house, introduced me to his
family, and showed me a chapel which he was having
built in his house for family prayer.   Surely we may
say of such that they are not far from the Kingdom
of God.   But where is the flower of intellect and
energy of our English Church to come to their aid?

Of the commencement of work in Derá Ghází
Khán, Gordon says:—

"The people listening attentively to bazar preaching, and some of them visit our tent, but the majority
regard us with great suspicion, and seem by no means
confident that their gods and prophet can deliver them
from the dreaded clutches of conviction and the spells
of the Christian preacher.

"Dr. Jukes has already had some patients, one of
these being an old Biloch chief who was formerly
Prime Minister to the Khan of Khelat, and now receives a pension from our Government."

"DERÁ GHÁZÍ KHÁN,
May 18, 1879.

"MY DEAR FRIEND,—I am grieved to hear of
your sad trial, the heaviest that man is called upon to-
bear, and in your case peculiarly so.

"Yet you have been mercifully spared the additional burden of watching through a long illness, and she whom you loved so well has been released from all suffering, to be forever with the Lord.

"May it be your happy experience to have nearer glimpses of that bright home where she has gone, and a closer communion with that Saviour who has prepared a place for you both at His side.

"The lessons of Whitsuntide are full of comfort for mourning hearts, and my subject for preaching to-day is full of it also: that gracious disclosure of *Himself* to His trembling disciples of all ages in their night of trouble. ' It is I, be not afraid.' How many, alas, are brothers with you in affliction! Almost the same post brought me a letter from a dear young friend, son of Sir R. Montgomery, who has just lost a bright, devoted, Christian wife from typhoid fever, and I am daily anticipating the sad news of a beloved aunt's departure, who has been to me like a mother—Mrs Melville. I trust that your son and his wife and children will be a blessing to you in your bereavement, and that you will have strength given you to resume those labours for Christ which are so dear to you. Meantime, your assurance of prayer is very valuable, for every Church needs, as Colosse did, the prayers of an Epiphras.

"My brother, who is at Woolwich, has been asked to collect a few of my journal letters, and I referred him to you, as perhaps able to furnish him with some information. The list has of late, I think, terminated with Mr. Girdlestone, but I do not know his address. If you can recover any of the letters, and read them to my brother, you will much oblige.

"Please give my love to Clifford, and the assurance of my deep sympathy. I shall always feel grateful for dear Mrs. Parker's kindness to me while I grieve at the thought of not meeting her again below."

In June 1879, Gordon left Derá Ghází Khán to pay a visit to the Nugents at Pind Dádan Khán. The two new missionaries then went westward to the Sulaiman Hills to Fort Munro, to make acquaintance with the wandering tribes, and to find out what prospects for work there would be among them.

In July they were again joined by Gordon, who writes to Miss Holmes on the 26th, describing a visit to an encampment of Bilochis :—" I went a few days ago with Dr. Jukes to one of the gipsy camps, an operation was to be performed on a very small baby, we knelt together on the hillside and asked God's blessing in native language. The little baby's foot was crooked, and as it was a *boy* it was a serious matter, had it been a girl they would not have minded. Dr. Jukes made a small incision behind the ankle while I held the little leg, and the mother the infant on her lap. Then the limb was carefully bandaged with a splint, after being straightened. There were a few

NOMAD BILOCHIS OF THE SULAIMÁN HILLS.

cries at first, but before the operation was over, the baby was fast asleep."

Part of Gordon's purpose in coming to Fort Munro at this season, was to pay a visit to the Khetran country, which, it so happened, was accessible at this time. This is a rich valley, lying in the Sulaiman Hills, west of Derá Ghází Khán, and having an elevation of about 3500 feet above the sea level. Although the Khetrans are a people living with Bilochis and Pathans as their neighbours on all sides, they themselves cannot claim near kinship with either. They are, as their language testifies, of the same race as the Jats of the plains living about Derá Ghází Khán. At this time they were an independent people, living under the dual government of two chiefs, like the Spartans of old. But of late, at their own request, their country has been annexed by the British Government, and only one of the two chiefs is now entrusted with authority.

Through this Khetran valley lies one of the most ancient caravan tracks between India and Central Asia, and during the Afghan war the route was used for the passage of troops. A camp was established at Vitakri, five marches from Fort Munro, and this place was the limit of the journey which Gordon now set himself to accomplish. One of his colleagues accompanied him, but Dr. Jukes preferred to remain at Fort Munro, and have no interruption to his studies.

They set out on July 28, and walked stage by stage, varying from ten to fifteen miles each day. It was interesting to notice the character of each village and town. Whereas in India small fortifications are allowed to fall into ruins as being useless, since the powerful arm of the British Government has given its protection to the people, here everything bore witness to the raids that these possessors of a fertile soil might expect from their more warlike and rapacious neighbours. Each village, and almost each hamlet, was carefully walled, while all cattle were brought in before dark, from the fields, within the walls.

The two missionaries almost invariably found shelter in a dark, windowless, dirty, mud guest house, which was usually built just within the gate of each town. And in return for this hospitality, Gordon would give them a message from the Word of Life.

At Vitakri, at this time, were stationed two regiments of Madras infantry, and one of Bengal cavalry, and consequently there was work to be done both among officers and a number of native Christian Madrassis who were in the band. On August 9, Gordon writes to Jukes :—

"Every day the native Christians of the band came to us for instruction, and sometimes we visit them in their tents. Yesterday a young medical officer from Madras spoke very warmly of our visit, and especially the services."

On August 11, the return journey to Fort Munro was commenced, and on the 12th, owing to exposure to the sun, Gordon's companion became seriously unwell. The chief object of recording this journey at

all is, that to Gordon's companion a new side of his
character—that of nurse and amateur medical attendant—was presented. Nothing save the loving hand
of woman could have been more untiring in service
and tender in ministrations. On one occasion, when
his companion was too ill to walk or ride, Gordon
sent off some ten miles to fetch the more powerful of
the two chiefs, Biloch Khan by name. With his aid,
a gang of Khetrans was collected, who carried the
sick man on a charpoy (native bedstead) to the foot
of the hill on which Fort Munro stands.

It might be mentioned that in many ways this
country seemed to promise well for missionary openings. The people were friendly, the country fertile,
well-watered, and, on the whole, probably healthy.
A medical man especially would be well received, as
Dr. Jukes found when he visited the valley some five
or six years later.

It has since become more accessible than it was,
owing to the construction of the Pishîn Road for military purposes, as well as from the fact that it is now
definitely under British control.

In the autumn of this year, a tour was made by
the Bishop of Lahore, Gordon and his two new colleagues, to the south of the Derá Ghází Khán district,
as far as Rojhan, the residence of one of the most
powerful, as he is certainly the most enlightened and
polished, of all the Biloch chiefs. It is the headquarters of the Mazarí tribe, and the chief mentioned
above who governs them is the Nawab Imam Bakhah

Gordon thus writes of this tour :—

"*Nov. 26th.*—Rowed down the Indus in a boat, the Bishop, Jukes, Lewis, and self, on a visit to the Chief of the Mazarís, a tribe of Bilochis. Not forty years ago these men were all at war with us. They are now as peaceful as any of the Queen Empress's Indian lieges. They still cling to the ornamental appendages of sword and shield, but only as emblems, not as instruments of strife. We disembarked on a bank made sandy and barren by the caprice of the shifting, restless tide. This was the nearest point to Rojhan, where the chief or Nawab resides. On hearing of our arrival, he sent camels for our baggage, and his son came to escort us across the pathless jungle. As we neared his village, the Nawab came out to meet us. He is a man of shorter stature than the ordinary, but his fine intelligent face shows a capacity for receiving and imparting enlightened views. There was nothing in his dress to indicate the position he holds, or to distinguish him from his followers. He is true to the tradition of his ancestors for simplicity and hospitality. The Bilochis all dress in plain white, and the only outward distinction of a chief is the superiority of his horse. In this respect they indulge in a little display. They are justly proud of the breed of their horses. Otherwise, rich and poor are alike. ' I dwell among my own people,' was the almost literal response of their chief to a remark upon his position with regard to his retainers.

" He made us his honoured guests as long as we

chose to stay with him. Sheep were killed for us, and piles of rice, sugar, and flour placed before us in embarrassing profusion.

This tour, and the year 1879, came to a close, full of hope that there were openings more effectual than had been expected amongst the Bilochis. Little could anyone have foreseen the trial that the new year was to bring upon the infant Mission.

CHAPTER XVI.

FOR some time past Gordon's health had not been
so good as could have been wished. He felt that
some complete change was necessary to set him up.
He began to think of home, but he resolved, if
possible, not to indulge himself thus, until he should
have completed his ten years of service since last
leaving England. The renewal of the Afghan war,
consequent upon the massacre of Sir Louis Cavagnari
and his staff, seemed to open the way for a partial
change meanwhile. There was, as was seen on his first
visit to Kandahar, plenty of work to be done in one
way or another. Without this condition Gordon could
not have been happy, and it was supposed then, whatever subsequent experience may have taught, that the
high level of Quetta or Kandahar would prove neither
unhealthy nor disagreeable for the summer months.

Accordingly, when the Bishop of Lahore invited
Gordon to accompany him on his journey into Afghanistan, and proposed that he should spend the summer
there, he readily acquiesced.

In January 1880, Gordon started on his last journey, and long after his arrival in Kandahar the subject

came before the Committee of the Church Missionary
Society in Salisbury Square. In the *C. M. Intelligencer*
of May of this year we read :—

"A letter was read from the Rev. G. M. Gordon,
dated Jan. 24, 1880, referring to his acceptance of
an invitation which Bishop French had given him to
accompany him on a journey to Quetta and Kandahar,
and asking the wishes of the Committee as to the
advisableness of his spending the hot weather, for the
sake of health, on the high plateaus of Afghanistan.
The Committee cordially acquiesced in Mr. Gordon
taking some suitable change in the hot weather, if
his health should need it, but directed that he be earnestly urged to use great caution as to exposing himself in unsettled parts of Afghanistan, both for his
own sake and on account of political complications
that might ensue."

This passage is quoted here for the sake of the
concluding sentences, which seem to show that the
Society at home, as well as a great many of Gordon's
friends in India, knew how totally devoid he was of
fear for himself, so long as he thought that he could
do Christ service.

On many occasions officers who were engaged
through the Afghan campaign, and intimate with
Gordon, have borne testimony on this. He would
appear at mess in the evening, and to the question,
"Well, Gordon, what have you been doing to-day?"
he would quietly answer that he had been in the city
visiting some of the leading Maulvis, and holding

religious discussions with them.   And this was at a
time when no man, venturing alone and unarmed
amongst the native population, could be safe for a
moment from the assassin's knife.

At times the orders were very strict, that no one
should go away from camp without being armed with
a revolver.   It came to the commanding officer's ears
that Gordon disregarded this order, and at the same
time went alone into places of very great danger.
The culprit was then informed, that if he did not
submit to discipline and orders, he would forthwith
be sent back to India.

The following letter, of which the date has dis-
appeared, may be identified with one which Gordon
is known to have written on February 13, 1880 :—

"1880.

"There seems to be a great deal of interest at home
with regard to Afghanistan, and as I am again, after
a year's interval, on the road to Kandahar, I venture
to think you will be glad to hear something of the
present aspect of affairs in these parts.   The Bishop
of Lahore had a great wish to visit the military cantonments at Quetta and Kandahar, cut off as they
are from intercourse with India.   He asked me to go
with him, and we started from Multan on the 23rd of
January.   It had been a much easier journey than it was
in 1878, when we toiled on foot across barren plains
and up the shingly bed of mountain torrents.   The
recent extension of the railway from Jacobabad to
Sibi has brought us 100 miles nearer to Kandahar,

and the difficulties of the Bolan Pass have been greatly
lessened by a good road which General Phayre has
made to Quetta. Notwithstanding these facilities,
and the improved state of the transport and commis-
sariat, there is, I am sorry to say, a great deal of
suffering among the men (natives) and cattle employed
in carrying stores and provisions from the base of
operations to the front. This is mainly entailed by
the renewal of the war consequent upon the menacing
attitude of Russia. The army at Kandahar has been
ordered to move to Ghazni, to co-operate with General
Robert's army at Kabul, and another army from Bombay, under General Phayre, is ordered up to Kandahar.
These operations are putting a strain upon every
department, and the intense cold of these mountainous
and wintry regions is proving fatal to men and to
cattle. Camels are not much used now that cartroads
are made, and one is no longer shocked by the daily
spectacle of hundreds of those patient animals dying
and dead along the line of march. But as we ascended
the Bolan, and the cold increased, we were horrified
by seeing the bodies of several bullock drivers who had
perished the previous night, and of a dozen or more
bullocks which had shared their fate. The violence
of the wind, as it swept down the narrow ravines,
and carried dust and grit into our faces, was almost
irresistible by man and beast. It took me three hours
to walk four miles against it one evening after sunset,
and some natives who accompanied me gave in, and
sat shivering under the rocks, and were not brought in

till after midnight. We spent four days at Quetta, where the Bishop held services for the soldiers and the officers now stationed there. There is no church nor room large enough to hold fifty men, so we borrowed a large tent, and they extemporised sittings by means of sundry boxes and planks placed across them. The troops consisted only of a battery of R.A., whom I had formerly known at Kandahar, their excellent commander, Major Collingwood, being now at Woolwich on sick leave. Some of the officers of native regiments and of various departments attended the service, and seemed very glad of the opportunity afforded them, for they have no public service at Quetta, nor any chaplain to administer the sacraments. We are now delayed by a heavy fall of snow in the Pishîn Valley. The ground is covered by a white sheet at least half a foot thick, and the Thajah range in front, which has to be crossed, is for the time impassable. We are fortunate in having a hut to shelter us, and an old Punjabi friend as our host. On our former visit here in '78, we had only thin tents to cover us, and General Biddulph's army was delayed here a fortnight in the cold of December, waiting for General Stewart to come up. The inhabitants of the valley are friendly, and apparently very glad of the English occupation, for Shere Ali's rule was very unpopular. The resources of the valley are yet to be developed. The soil is good, and so is the water, but cultivation scant. No doubt, when the railway comes here, there will be a great improvement. The last time I camped here on my way from Kandahar, we were not certain of the friendliness of the natives. A shot fired after dark was taken for the signal of an attack upon the camp. A company was ordered to be under arms at once, and guns were to be pointed at the neighbouring village. It was afterwards ascertained that the shot was an accidental discharge of an unoffending Parsee merchant's pistol in camp, and the panic was soon allayed.

" Those who are conversant with the facts of these countries, and the great boon which good government brings to these warlike races, to say nothing of the blessings of the Gospel, are apt to read with some astonishment the utterances of certain orators of the Gladstone School, who might learn much by coming here."

Gordon again writes :—

" KANDAHAR, _March_ 22, 1880.

" As I sent you last time some extracts from my journal, of a journey with the Bishop to Kandahar, I think you will be interested to hear more about the Bishop's visit.

" On _Feb._ 24, we went to see the ruins of old Kandahar, about three or four miles off. They consist principally of earthworks, surrounded by a moat, and surmounted by the mud walls and bastions of an old fort. Although they have nothing of the solidity of many of the old Roman ruins of far greater anti-quity, yet they are very picturesque, and the position is one of great strength. It was taken by Nadir Shah, King of Persia, who carried his conquests to Delhi. Having destroyed the place, he built another Kandahar, and the present town, built by Ahmed Shah, is the third city. Should we, as seems probable, build a cantonment in one of these valleys, we shall certainly see a fourth city spring up. And it is high time that another were built, for the present one cannot be healthy, on account of the enormous cemetery which surrounds it. One of the most interesting relics of old Kandahar, is a huge bowl of blue limestone, covered with Old Arabic inscriptions. They say that there were formerly two, and that one found its way to England. I fancy you will see this one some day in the British Museum.

"On *Feb.* 25, the Bishop addressed a large gathering of soldiers on total abstinence. He told them that he had signed the pledge to encourage others to do so, and exhorted them not to regard temperance as everything, but as a link in a chain. 'Add to your faith, virtue,' etc. etc. I afterwards signed the pledge with one or two soldiers, for I thought that having been for eight years a total abstainer, it might add to my usefulness to become a pledged one.

"On *Feb.* 26, we visited the English cemetery. It was the same that was used during our former occupation, 1839 to 1842. For some time no clue as to its position could be found. Afterwards an old resident pointed out the spot. Nearly 100 graves were traced, all lying east and west, instead of north

and south, like the Muhamadan graves which surround them. On opening one of the graves, all doubt
was removed. Orders, therefore, were given, and the
cemetery was carefully restored, and enclosed by a
wall and gate. Here the chaplain pointed out to us
many new graves of soldiers and officers who died
last year of cholera. We afterwards went to see the
tomb of Ahmed Shah, the builder of the present city,
and founder of the Dourani dynasty. A handsome
domed building has been erected over it, the only
architectural ornament at Kandahar. It is very
elaborate inside, and is held in great veneration
by the Muhamadans. Near it is a smaller building
in which they preserve an old shirt, said to be that of
Muhamad himself. The Bishop addressed a nice
little meeting of Christian officers in the evening.

"On *Feb.* 28, I went to the city to breakfast with
a Persian gentleman, who holds a post here, as assistant to the political officer attached to the force. I
recognised in him an old friend, for, in 1872, I was
his guest at Shiraz, in the very same house where
Henry Martyn had stayed in his father's time. I
was glad to renew acquaintance and hear about
Shiraz. He told me that the orphanage, which I
then started on the interest of the famine fund sent
out from London, is still going on, and that the roads
and sanitary condition of the town had been improved
by the relief works. The Bishop called in the afternoon on Shere Ali Khan, the governor of the city.
The chief mullah was also present, and the Bishop

did not lose the opportunity of saying something on
the subject of religion, which was well received. In
the evening he addressed a large number of soldiers
who had been invited to hear him by Col. ——, and
there was a great tea-drinking.

"On *Sunday*, 29*th February*, the Bishop addressed
the soldiers on parade, taking for his text Israel's
marching song, 'Arise, O Lord, let thine enemies be
scattered.' There were two regiments on parade, the
60th Rifles, the 59th Foot, and a battery of Artillery.
The band played and sang a hymn very nicely.

"On *Monday*, *March* 1, the Bishop started on his
return journey, and I am happy to say that I have
to-day heard of his safe arrival at Multan, and start
by train for Lahore, where he would arrive March
20. He is said to be looking none the worse for his
adventurous journey, and I feel very thankful for the
good he has done, and for his safe return. I have
endeavoured since his departure to carry on the
prayer meeting for the soldiers, in conjunction with
Col. ——.

"General Stewart's forces are about to start for
Ghazni, and I shall lose most of my friends among
the officers and men. But there will be another
sphere of work amongst the Bombay forces, who are
arriving daily to occupy Kandahar, and I am daily
reminding myself, in various ways, that I am here first
and foremost as a missionary. I am reading the Bible
and Pilgrim's Progress daily in Persian and Afghan
with a munshi of the town, and making occasional

calls upon respectable natives, who are willing to cultivate friendly relations ; and I hold weekly services in Hindustani for some native Christians attached to the regiments.

" One great barrier to missionary work and friendly intercourse with the people, is the fanaticism of a class of Afghans who call themselves Ghazis. They are a set of poor ignorant men of the ascetic type, who are inflamed by the Muhamadan priest to sacrifice their own lives in the endeavour to take the life of a Christian or a Hindu. It is evident the movement, is directed against us, and those that serve us, and is therefore to a certain extent a patriotic movement, because they do not attack the Hindus who are established as traders in the country, only those who are attached to our camps. One cannot help pitying these misguided men, who firmly believe they are doing service to God and their country, and are therefore much better than the shooters of landlords in Ireland. One of them was caught and hung the day before yesterday, before he could effect his purpose. When questioned, he avowed his intention without the slightest reserve. He was greatly disappointed at having failed to kill one of us, but had no other objection to be hung. Last Saturday a poor soldier of the 59th was found murdered by another Ghazi just outside his barracks, and the murderer was instantly despatched by his comrade. Since I have been here, these attempts to assassinate have been of constant occurrence. One officer was shot at, and hit in the shoulder, but is now recovering. Another was stabbed by a mere boy of twelve, but he happily recovered. This boy, and another of the same age, have been transported to the Andaman Islands. They are nice-looking boys, and I hope the day may come when we shall be able to have a mission school in Kandahar, and teach them the lessons of the Sermon on the Mount.

"There is a large class of Afghan boys who are receiving no instruction in anything good. Some of them are glad to engage themselves as servants to the officers and soldiers, and they are wonderfully quick at picking up Hindustani and English. They can, most of them, speak Persian as well as their native tongue. General —— suggested to me that a secular school might be desirable; but I discussed the matter with the Bishop and General Phayre, and they both regard secular schools as conducive to no good, if not to positive harm. And certainly our experience of secular education among the natives of India is anything but favourable. General Phayre is so good a man, and so devoted a servant of Christ, and has had so long an experience, that, next to the Bishop, I attach great weight to his advice. I regret very much that he is not to succeed General Stewart in the command here, but is to be in command of the communications between Kandahar and Quetta. Meanwhile, I am expecting a large consignment of Persian and Pushtu Bibles and Testaments, which have been ordered from Lahore by Colonel —— for distribution in Kandahar.

" There was an interesting instance the other day
of how an officer may assist the missionary cause.   A
friend of mine, Major ——, of the —— Punjab Cavalry,
was out on duty in one of the villages, amongst the
tribe called Achahzais, who inhabit the country of the
Khojak.   He made friends with the Chief Mullah, or
High Priest of the tribe.   This man asked him various questions respecting the Christian religion, such
as, ' Do you ever pray ? '   To which, I am glad to
say, the Major was able to answer, both for himself
and for many of us, in the affirmative.   ' Is it part of
your religion to destroy Muhamadan mosques as the
Russians do ? '   ' No,' said Major ——.   This was
highly satisfactory to the old man, who proceeded to
ask, ' Why is our country getting worse and worse, and
your Hindustan better and better ? '   ' Because,' said
Major ——, ' you allow bribery and corruption, and
we don't.'   The old man then asked for a Persian
Bible.   Major —— said, ' But if you read it you may
find things you don't approve.'   The old man would
take no refusal ; he must have the Bible, and he insisted on Major —— sending for one, which he did.
I hope I may meet this old man some day, and have
a good long talk with him over his Bible, as Major
—— is ordered to Ghazni.

" I hope it may not be long before a medical missionary is sent to Kandahar.   The people would give
no one so hearty a welcome.   There is not even a
Government free dispensary here, as at Kabul, where
Dr. Owen has won the gratitude of thousands of native

patients.   A curious disclosure was recently made
here, through one of the medical officers attached to
the force.   He had been urgently requested to attend
a native lady, who was one of the late Amír's State
prisoners, and whose history was a secret to our political officers.   He attended her, and performed successfully a difficult operation.   She was very grateful
for his skilful advice, and told him she was no less a
personage than the favourite wife of Abdul Rahman,
the chief on whom so much depends, and who is
supposed to be hesitating between a Russian and an
English alliance.   He is more influential at Kabul
than anyone else.   His wife said she would be glad
to let her husband know what benefit she had derived, and bring him over to our side.   This is only
one instance out of many to show how greatly they
appreciate that medical treatment which only an
English doctor can give."

Though Gordon was so far away from his colleagues,
he continued always to take the keenest interest in
his Punjab missions.   He was not satisfied unless the
mail brought him letters continually posting him up in
the latest intelligence, and telling him of the advance
of the Kingdom of Christ in the hearts of men.   But
if he expected much in this way, he was always ready
to give as much.   He was a most faithful correspondent, almost always asking in his letters for the support of the prayers of those to whom they were sent.

Writing to Dr. Jukes, on April 9, 1880, from Kandahar, he says,—" I have now received my instruc-

tions from the Corresponding Committee at Lahore.
They wish me to remain here, or at some cooler place,
during the hot weather.   At present the climate here
is very cool ; when it gets hot (in June) perhaps it
may be desirable to go up to Khilat i Gilzai or
Ghazni.

"The Afghans in different parts are still unsettled
and warlike.   Poor Showers, who was killed near
Quetta, was with G— at Derá Ghází Khán this time
last year.

"Yesterday we were told of seventy armed men
prowling about outside the city, and the English
soldiers were confined to barracks anticipating an
attack, but nothing came of it.   Letters from General
Stewart's force say they expect resistance towards
Ghazni, and I am afraid they will have difficulties
about transport and supplies.

" We started a soldiers' prayer meeting in cantonment yesterday, General Phayre taking the lead.
Unfortunately, we shall lose him, as he goes to Quetta,
but I hope to keep up the meetings.   It is always difficult to begin again when a prayer meeting is broken
up, and others come.

" I have had less fever lately, but indigestion
troubles me as usual.

" A chaplain has come up and taken the services
in cantonments, while I take them in the fort.   Last
Sunday, as I was going to service, I passed a tent
where two poor natives of the transport had been
fired into during the night by some miscreants.   One

was lying dead, the other wounded, but likely to recover. As usual there is no clue to the marauders.

"I hope, if you can get a riding camel for me, you will do so, and let me know the cost, as I fully intend to keep one, and you and Lewis are welcome to the use of it."

This last sentence shows that he was at this time thinking as much as ever of those who were associated with him in his work, and wishing to help them with his advice and means, if not by his presence. In another letter, about the same time, sent to myself, he expresses his readiness, under certain conditions, to put down at once Rs.3000 or Rs.4000 for the building of a hospital for the Bilochis.

"KANDAHAR, *April* 25, 1880.

"I have had the fever for more than a week, and from the little cell in the fort, my thoughts have gone out much towards the sick and afflicted in all parts of the world. I daresay this fort has held many a sorrowful captive in the hard days of Mussulman rule, and, maybe, witnessed many a deed of horror. Our men found the other day, while they were excavating, the skeleton of a poor wretch who had evidently been buried alive, as he was in a crouching position, which is never the case in ordinary burial among Muhamadans. This is the most peaceful province of Afghanistan, but yet here, of late, we have been having disturbances. Twice it has been given out that an attack would be made upon us in the fort on a particular day, but the day has passed without in-

cident. I often think of Colonel Lumsden's mission
here with Dr. Bellew in 1857. They were lodging
close to my present quarters. But instead of moving
about freely, as we do, they were in a kind of confine-
ment for several months, in constant apprehension for
their lives. On one occasion the whole city rose
and besieged the fort, and but for the fidelity of some
of the native troopers of Colonel Lumsden's escort,
they would all have been murdered in the same way
as poor Sir Louis Cavagnari and his suite.

"I have had some nice letters from my friends
among the officers and men of General Stewart's force,
on their march to Ghazni. Our latest news is that,
on the 19th, they encountered a large body of the
enemy, who fought for an hour and then fled, leaving
a thousand dead bodies in the field. The loss on our
side was 15 killed and 115 wounded, including several
officers. The following day General Stewart's advance-
guard entered Ghazni unopposed.

"The country between here and Quetta, which I
have three times traversed in perfect security, is now
anything but safe. Armed bands of tribesmen are
going about cutting the telegraph wires, stopping the
postal communication, and attacking our outposts.
First, we heard that a political officer, whom many of
us knew and admired, named Captain Showers, had
been attacked and killed near Quetta. Then there
came rumours of threatened attacks upon other places
which were quite defenceless. Officers (like my friend
Major ——, of the 2d Punjab Cavalry) who had been

on the frontier all their lives, knew the language and the people, and were most fitly entrusted with the charge of the roads, were withdrawn when General Stewart's force left, and their places supplied by men from Bombay, who could not speak the language, and were utter strangers to the country.   The consequence has been the sacrifice of another valuable life.   Majoi Waudby, who succeeded Major —— as road commandant, was a good officer and popular man, but he had everything to learn as to these parts.   Last week, in the course of his duties, he halted for the night at a place fifty miles from here, which used to be considered perfectly safe.   The Bishop and I passed a quiet night there two months ago, with only four Sowars for escort. But latterly the man in charge of Government stores there urgently represented that there was danger, and requested to be removed.   His appeal was not attended to, and on the night of the 16th some hundreds of the enemy attacked the place.   Major Waudby had only two Sepoys with him and three Sowars of the Scind Horse, who behaved badly, and sought how to escape.   Two days after, an officer, on his way here with troops, came to the place, and found the body of Major Waudby and his two faithful Sepoys fearfully mangled, and a heap of the enemy whom they had killed.   The sole survivor was the Major's faithful dog, who stood there to identify his master's body.   It is to be hoped that the faithful creature will recover, but as he had received two sword cuts, and was half starved, it is very doubtful.   They are now sending

out troops in all directions to punish the offenders and
check these outrages, and orders have been given to
fortify all the posts along the road to Quetta. It is
to be hoped that we shall learn a lesson not to be
careless and over-confident. The Afghans know well
our weak points, and are exceedingly clever in watching their opportunity and striking a blow when we
least expect it. It is fully expected that clouds will
gather from the Herat side before long. Meanwhile,
every one looks towards Kabul, and wonders what
Abdul Rahman is going to do. If fighting is his intention, he will not have much chance, humanly speaking, between General Roberts and General Stewart.
But it is a great cause of confidence, that 'the Lord
reigneth, be the earth never so unquiet.'

"Yesterday I had a visit from some of my Afghan
friends in the city. They have got the Bible, but they
say that others want it also, and we had a long talk
over it, and I promised to get some more Bibles from
Lahore, but they take a long time coming. Letters
travel in a week, but books take months to arrive. I
was talking to my Munshi about preaching a 'Jehad,'
as they call it (or religious war), and he agreed with
me it is better to make a 'Jehad' against Satan and
our besetting sins, than for a deluded rabble of fanatics
to rush on British bayonets and leave a thousand of
their slain upon the ground. I have got a young
Afghan as a servant, and I am going to make a commencement with him in the elements of a moral
training and education, hoping that others may follow.

My Bible class with the soldiers in the fort has begun well. Some who had grown cold through want of the means of grace are reviving, and it is touching to see how the word of God and the singing of hymns wake responsive chords of love, and rally them to their old allegiance. I grieve to say we have our Sanballats and Tobiahs in camps, and they have shut up and dismantled the prayer-rooms in cantonments which Colonel —— used for a year with such a blessing, and which General —— recently rebuilt at his own expense and re-opened. Colonel ——'s successor in the barracks, being a man with no sympathy with religious things, claimed and obtained from the General who now commands the possession of the prayer-room, although built by private friends, and then, without a word of reference to the chaplain or myself, who were holding meetings there, turned it into a barrack-room. Apart from all considerations of courtesy, it is an act of great injustice towards the soldiers, and especially the Presbyterian soldiers, who have no other place for their meetings and services except this prayer-room. I do not believe that any commanding officer in General Stewart's army would have done such a thing. Unfortunately we have no appeal, and the only thing to be done, if the chaplain agrees, is to build another prayer-room somewhere else."

Again, in a letter to Miss Holmes, Gordon speaks of the cause of his remaining in Afghanistan, and gives some idea of his work in Kandahar :—

" *Kandahar, June* 1, 1880.—The Committee wish me to stay here till October, on account of my health. I have had frequent recurrence of fever the last two months, but the climate is much cooler than that of India, and though I may have to go home next year, yet I hope (*D. V.*), by remaining here, to recruit for a cold weather campaign among the Bilochis. I am reading the Bible and Pilgrim's Progress in the Afghan language with such of the Mullahs as visit me, and I have also plenty of work among the English soldiers. I believe Kandahar is the most favourable place for a missionary in Afghanistan, but one is here at the risk of one's life, and at the risk, also, of being turned out by the politicals at any time."

During this time the missionaries in Derá Ghází Khán had been somewhat tried by the shifting conduct of the chief of the most powerful Biloch tribe on the frontier. After he had derived a vast amount of relief and care from the treatment of Dr. Jukes, it struck him that it would be a good thing to have a European doctor near him in his own town, about twenty-four miles from Derá Ghází. He accordingly had made proposals some time before Gordon started for Kandahar, offering to build a hospital, and give a grant of land, if the Mission would fix its headquarters with him. This the missionaries were all eager to do. Negotiations were entered into, the chief somewhat moderated his eagerness, pressure was probably brought to bear upon him against the mission by energetic Muhamadan Maulvis. It seemed at last as if the chief wished for the doctor, but no preaching ; then he was unwilling to alienate any land, and one difficulty after another turned up until, finally, the plan had to be abandoned.

Most of Gordon's letters at this time show a keen interest in the question. The following is a sample of the way in which he would encourage his friends :—

" Many thanks for yours of 3rd, just received, which explains your negotiations with the Nawab.

" Yes, I think it is as well to wait a little. We are taught in mission work the necessity of the old rule, '*Festina lente.*' You have not yet had as many disappointments and checks as have fallen to my share in the Pind Dádan Khán Mission. You naturally wish, as I do, for a base hospital. But in so important a matter, all we can do is to seek God's guidance, and He has not yet made it clear where we should fix our headquarters.

" For six years I tried to centralise myself at Pind Dádan Khán, which I thought could be done by building a house and school. But land could not be got, and again and again I was driven out to preach the Word in the villages. *That* was God's way of working, although it did not seem to me the right way at the time.

" What I am very anxious for is, that you should be free to work in the way that you feel to be right. And yet God's way may be otherwise. The ' common-sense way,' the ' way of experience,' as men say, is by no means always God's way."

" We have had no great event here since I wrote
last, unless the installation of the Governor, Shere
Ali Khan, can be called an event. The ceremony
was rather of a private character than public. The
presents given to Shere Ali Khan seemed suggestive
of what would happen on the withdrawal of our troops
from Afghanistan. One of them was a sword, to
show that he would certainly have to fight for his
life, and another a clock, to show that his days were
numbered. He was then told he might call himself
a Wali or Governor, and a salute of twenty-one guns
was fired from the fort. A few days after, he returned the General's visit at the cantonment (one
and a half mile from the city). He was dressed in
a gold embroidered coat, with an Astrachan cap, in
shape like a teapot cosy. They lined his road with
soldiers, and fired all the guns in the station. He
has now gone out with his troops and a battery of
six guns, which we have given him, to the Halmand
river, on the way to Herat. There is a district there
called Zamindawar, which does not acknowledge his
authority, and some think the warlike inhabitants
will rise and take away his guns, in which case we
shall have to send a force to get them back again.
There is also apprehension of an army from Herat
coming to attack us. On the Queen's Birthday there
was a parade of all the troops, and a royal salute
fired. It was curious to observe how indifferent the
townspeople were to the demonstration. With the

exception of the Governor and suite, who were officially present, there seemed to be absolutely no representation of the Afghan population. They are 'a fortuitous concourse of atoms,' with no cohesion, accustomed from long misgovernment each to look out for himself, and to hate every one else.

"Last week I called on a wealthy landed proprietor, who lives out in the country. He was away in the wars; but his friend and kinsman did the honours, and was very civil to me and my companions. He ordered tea and sweets, which were brought out and served in an orchard. The tea, which was green, was made as usual without milk, and poured from a Russian china teapot into little cups. An attendant then brought a lot of fruit, which he had shaken down from the trees near where we sat. The absent landlord's youngest child was then brought and introduced to us. He was about two years old, and could trot about by himself. He was very smartly frocked in silk, and covered with charms—verses of the Kuran written on paper, and sewn up in leather, after blessed by some priest of fame and sanctity. Colonel T—— gave the little fellow some sweets, which he would not eat, but gravely handed on to some member of the company. This he did to one by one in succession, till all were supplied. We were told that his mother is a daughter of the celebrated Dost Muhamad Khan, about whom all the fighting and disasters of 1846 took place; but we were not introduced to the lady. We had a long conversation

with our host in Persian, and when I drew his attention to some point of contrast between the Kuran and
the Bible, he seemed by no means averse from religious discussion.　We asked him among many other
things if he could account for the absence of rain at
the present season.　He replied that, 'Whenever
Shere Ali Khan is Governor of Kandahar there is
no rain.'　This meant, of course, that he had a very
low opinion of Shere Ali Khan.　But when I suggested that God only can send or withhold the rain,.
he agreed that we must leave the matter in his hands.
We returned by a very pretty ride along the banks
of the Argandab river, the water of which is skilfully
turned by the villagers into numerous channels, which
irrigate their fields and orchards.　The authorities
here have taken advantage of the mulberry groves
on the bank of the river for the purpose of a sani-
tarium, and have sent out some of the invalids and
convalescents to live in tents under the shade.　Many
of the officers and men are suffering from fever, and
many more from home sickness.　I had a nice tea
meeting in the garden of the Fort last week.　My
guests were fifteen soldiers, who attend the Bible-
class, and form the church choir.　Several of the
officers were present, and after tea we had sacred
songs and hymns, and concluded with prayers.　They
all enjoyed it very much.　Here everything is done
in camp fashion, and when anyone is invited out, it
is always understood that he brings his own plate,
cup, knife, and chair.　The weather is hot, but not

nearly so hot as in India. I go out to my work morning and evening, and spend the middle of the day in study. I was able to bring very few books up here, but I have books in ten different languages on my shelf. I read the Bible and 'Pilgrim's Progress' daily in the Afghan language with a Mullah from the city. He is greatly captivated with the latter, and often says we have no such book among us. He remarked one day, 'You English have a great deal of love, we have very little,' and he gave a proof of it when he added, 'No Jew could live in Kandahar; we would kill him at once.' I argued that there are lots of Hindus living in Kandahar, and you don't kill them, though they are idolators. Why should you kill a Jew who is a worshipper of the true God?' He said, 'The Jew is a worse infidel than the Hindu, because he professes to believe, and the Hindu doesn't.' I replied, 'That's not the reason you spare the Hindu. The reason is simply because they are your bankers and shopkeepers, and you can't do without them.' He smiled, and agreed that I was right. It is very curious how ubiquitous the Hindu is, and how he can live and thrive in the most fanatical cities of Central Asia. I sometimes visit them in their temples in the city, and have a chat over the Gospel with grey-bearded men, who have talked with Russians in Bokhara.

"On Sunday morning, after church, I walked through the town, and shortly afterwards heard of an attack made by a small native boy upon a Hindu in the same street. The boy was caught, after stabbing the man with a pocket-knife, and questioned. At first they could get no information, but on receiving an electric shock, the little ruffian confessed that he had been prompted to the fanatical deed by a bigger boy, who said he was going to do the same himself. Accordingly, yesterday, a soldier of the 66th was attacked, and stabbed in the same street by a bigger boy, supposed to be the one indicated. I visited the soldier in hospital, and found that the wound is not deep. Happily for him he had a comrade with him, who stopped the assailant, and transfixed him with his bayonet. The two boys were probably set on by some fanatical Mullah. We never can go out without the risk of encountering some murderer, who has taken the pledge. There is little wonder that the country, accustomed to deeds of violence, has come to grief. Afghanistan is like Canaan was in the days of the Judges, as we read in our lesson for last Sunday (Judges v. 6, 7), 'The highways were unoccupied, and the travellers walked through byways. The inhabitants of the villages ceased.' This is literally true in parts we have passed through, where you see the ruins of old villages on the highways, and other villages built at a distance, so as to be out of reach of the exactions of the rapacious soldiery. I received encouraging letters from Mr. Lewis and Dr. Jukes at Derá Ghází Khán, and I hope to join them in October. Mr. and Mrs. Nugent have had to go home, but Charles Matthews is at Pind Dádan Khán, and he

writes hopefully of some of the boys in the school.
The report of the anniversary C.M.S. in the *Record* is
cheering to read.   And one is thankful for news from
home, such as the appointment of Bishop Ryle.   But
I fear such appointments are over for some time to
come.   And certainly we cannot hope for religious
progress of the right sort under a Roman Catholic
Viceroy.   I see that my last journal letter was dated
April 25th ; I hope it arrived safely, for another letter
that I sent in April with a cheque was not received,
and the explanation was, that about that time various letters with money were abstracted by someone
in the Kandahar postal department."

In a private letter, dated Kandahar, June 8, 1880,
he writes that he hopes, "if spared, I may have the
pleasure of seeing you all next year.   For I cannot
help dwelling by anticipation upon what at times
seems necessary to maintain and animate me in my
work, namely, the hope of a return home.   At other
times, when not out of health, I feel as though I
could do without going home, in order to take the
post of someone else who requires a change."

Mr Parker writes as follows to the *Record* newspaper :—

"Sir,—In unwarehousing some of my furniture, I
have come across the last letter written to me by the
Rev. George Maxwell Gordon, whose work I shared
in London, and whose loving friendship I retained
until he fell in a sortie in the act of ministering to
the wounded on August 16, 1880.   The quinine

'never' reached him, but was wisely used for others not beyond the reach of temporal aid. His biographer, the Rev. A. Lewis, and other Punjab missionaries and officers, may be interested in Mr. Gordon's last words to a former fellow-labourer.—J. C. P."

"_June_ 16.

"'KANDAHAR, _June_ 14, 1880.

"'MY DEAR PARKER,—Will you kindly send me by letter post one ounce of Quinine done up in paper or waxcloth, unless the chemist says it will spoil. If it travels in a bottle it has to be packed in a box, and then it will never reach me. Parcels take many months to reach Kandahar, and I shall be gone elsewhere. That's why I ask for it in a letter. Please let me know what it costs. I am a great consumer of quinine. Here they would probably ask £2 for one ounce, if it is to be had at all. I write to catch post. I hope you have got all my circular letters, dated February 13, March 12, April 25, June 8.— Yours affectionately,   G. M. GORDON.'"

There is one more short letter from Gordon on June 29, and then comes a silence, which is only broken at last by the sounds of disaster and defeat.

Many will remember the course of events of that miserable and inglorious Afghan campaign. Ayúb Khan marched on in the direction of Kandahar with a large force. He was met by the British with vastly inferior numbers about forty miles from the city, and the battle of Maiwand was fought, which added

one more to the list of black letter days in our historical connection with Afghanistan. After a humi-
liating defeat, the remnants of the shattered army
reached Kandahar, and, with the garrison, were shut
up and beseiged until General Roberts retrieved the
honour of the British name by one of the most glori-
ous marches that history can record, at length gaining
a brilliant victory with his travel-worn men, captur-
ing all the enemy's guns, and setting free the besieged.
But, alas! too late as far as the subject of these pages
was concerned.

It seems that, on the morning of August 16, it was
determined to make a sortie to the neighbouring
village of Dehi Khwaja. The enemy had planted some
guns here, which caused a great deal of annoyance
to the beleaguered garrison, and it was felt that they
must be silenced. Gordon did not go out with the
party, but was in the hospital within the walls, receiving the wounded as they were brought in off the field.
After a time he went to the Kabul gate in the per-
formance of the same duty. Whilst there he heard
that there were some wounded men lying in a ziyarat
or shrine, some two hundred or three hundred yards
outside the gate. He got a dooly and bearers, and
went out to this spot for the purpose of bringing them
in. This he did under heavy fire. On arrival at this
ziyarat he found that there were no wounded there,
but that they were lying at a second ziyarat about
thirty yards further on. An officer was with him, and
he told Gordon that it was quite impossible to go on

THE CITADEL OF KANDAHAR.

as the fire was too hot. He was not, however, to be
dissuaded from his purpose. He was about to set
out when he was struck by a bullet, which passed
through his wrist, and entered his side. The dooly
which he took out for others brought him in. This
was about seven a.m.

The Rev. A. G. Cane, at that time Chaplain at
Kandahar, writes:—

"I soon saw his case was hopeless. At first he
said, 'I am not so badly wounded as some, and they
have not the consolation that I have.' A little later
he knew that he could not recover; but he was perfectly resigned and contented. I several times asked
him if he had any messages, but he said nothing,
beyond a few instructions to his servants. He lived
such a God-fearing life that he was quite prepared to
meet death. He passed away quietly the same afternoon about 3.30, and we buried him in the evening
with the other officers. On that sad day we lost
many officers; but there was not one so universally
regretted as poor Gordon. When the siege began
he once said to a wounded colonel, 'How fortunate
I am to be here, where I can be of some use.' And
all felt that he was giving up his life in the per-
formance of a voluntary duty. He and I had become firm friends, and his loss I now feel keenly—
and I am afraid not only I, but the wounded too,
miss him."

And so, like Elijah of old, he was, as it were, taken
up to heaven in a chariot of fire. May the simile be

carried out to the full, and many an Elisha be raised up to be the possessor of his mantle.   And may the waters of satanic pride and power be scattered hither and thither in Afghanistan, and a path for the messengers of the Lord be prepared through the midst of them. " My ways are not thy ways, saith the Lord."   It was inscrutable that he, of all men, in the vigour of manhood, with so much work in the vineyard apparently depending on him, should be taken away thus. It may be that the Lord had need of him for even higher work, and thus taught his friends and colleagues to look up through tears of bereavement, and to trust henceforth not in the servant, but in the servant's Lord, the master of the vineyard.   " If it die, it bringeth forth much fruit," wrote the Bishop of Lahore at this time, seems the one thought at present which comforts and *partially* upholds me.

Deep and sincere was the sorrow with which the intelligence was received in England.   Three extracts from the obituary notices it elicited, recording characteristic anecdotes of Gordon's Christlike, self-denying life, and the impression produced by it on his fellow-workers, may not unfitly be here preserved, even at the risk of some slight repetition, *in memoriam* of the feeling awakened when the news was fresh,—a feeling which survives the lapse of the rushing years which have since succeeded.

The first extract is contributed by the brother of Dr. Jukes, from the *Sussex Daily News*, to which a correspondent wrote as follows :—

"THE LATE REV. GEORGE M. GORDON.

"Mr G. W. VYSE, who can boast that he was the only civilian engaged in the field against the Afghans, sends some interesting particulars, in addition to those which have appeared about George Maxwell Gordon, the missionary, killed while attending to the sick and wounded during the sortie from Kandahar.

"'Maxwell Gordon, an M.A. of Cambridge, was noted at college for his muscular strength and endurance. In India, he gave himself so wholly up to the natives, that his services could be commanded at any hour. For his labours he took no pay, whether as acting chaplain, or as a missionary. Whatever money he received, he gave to the Mission fund, or to the poor. "I never," says Mr Vyse, "met with so unselfish a man. I have known him walk from early morn to late at night through a burning sun on the Derá-Ismail-Khán road, in order that a poor, tired, sick native should ride his pony. The cold weather is very keen on the frontier, and three winters ago, I accidentally came across Mr. Gordon, many miles from the station, without overcoat or vest ; he had actually taken them off to give to a sick native and his child, who were both lightly clad, and suffering from the cold. When I spoke to him about it, he was distressed at my having found it out, and said, " I am strong, and can rough it a bit sometimes." I never knew him sleep on the commonest of *charpoys* (native beds), "the ground was good enough, he would say," and add, "with straw or date palm leaves for a bed, I can sleep very soundly." He never drank but water, or water and milk, and his food was plain *chuppaties*, or unleavened bread, fruit and vegetables; but, if purposely prepared for him, occasionally a little meat. He was no bigot. I never knew him say anything harsh or severe. Last year I had a very clever fellow as *sowar* (trooper), who was great at Bilochi and frontier languages. Mr. Gordon was anxious to engage him as *Moonshee* (or teacher of languages), and offered him 70 rupees a month, or double what the Government was giving him; moreover, that he should receive substantial compensation in lieu of his far-off pension. "Sahib, I dare not," said the *sowar*. "I should be made a Christian." Mr. Gordon promised not to mention the subject of religion. But the *sowar* replied, "It is too tempting. I love Gordon Sahib, and in spite of myself, I am sure I could not help accepting his religion." There is a grand field for missionary enterprise on the north-west frontier of India, but you want men of the stamp of Mr. Gordon, who has now met his death as a volunteer chaplain, where he thought he was most wanted.'"

A second "In Memoriam" notice is by GENERAL MACLAGAN, and begins with a reference to the almost coincident removal of the Hon. Secretary of the Church Missionary Society, George Maxwell Gordon's relative by marriage.

" Very brief was the space of time that had passed
after the news of the sudden removal from among
us, of a devoted labourer in the home service of the
Church Missionary Society, when we were called on
to mourn the loss of another ardent worker, taken
off by a stroke as rapid, in a far distant field, amid
very different scenes and surroundings. Beneath the
calm waters of a peaceful lake of our own mountain land, Henry Wright passed away, when he was
enjoying, in the midst of family and friends, the quiet
retirement of a well-earned summer holiday. Far
from home and country, and amid the noise of
battle, fell George Maxwell Gordon, the faithful messenger of the gospel of peace, sharing an enterprise
of peril with those among whom he was ministering,
and sharing, with those who fell around him in the
strife, a soldier's grave.

"How came the missionary to be at Kandahar,
when that small British garrison was straitly shut up
and hard pressed by a numerous enemy, elated and
emboldened by a little temporary triumph ? A double
object had drawn him there, and a felt duty had kept
him. When engaged on the Punjab frontier in de-
vising and organising a mission to the Bilochis of
our border districts, he resolved to take advantage of
the presence of a British force in Quetta, and of a
British representative in Kelat, to proceed into Bilochistán, and see whether the time had come for extension of the Mission to the territory beyond our border.*

* See Mr. Gordon's "Plea for Bilochistán" in the *C.M.S. Intelli-*

Then from Quetta he advanced with the force proceeding to Kandahar. He seized that opportunity of making some acquaintance with Southern Afghanistan and its people, and of forming a judgment with regard to missionary action at some future in that country, seeing that he might also at once be of service in ministering to the British troops on the line of march. And with them he remained in Kandahar, performing the duties of chaplain, to the great satisfaction of officers and men. The position in which he was now placed, and the work it enabled him to do, confirmed and satisfied his own sense of the importance of the step he had taken, and of the usefulness of his offered and accepted service.

" Mr. Gordon was a missionary at his own charges, his private means not only maintaining his mission work without cost to the Church Missionary Society, but being ever liberally bestowed on useful objects conducive to the temporal or spiritual well-being of people whom he could help. Such a man, with felt capacity for a certain line of action, with opportunities presented to him of which he perceives the value, is guided by an impulse which is true for him, however differently others might be affected by it. He was urged, as his letters at the time quietly but unmistakably showed, by a pressure which he felt was not to be resisted. He at once accepted the leading which was indicated to his

gencer of February 1879, and his letter respecting Kandahar in the May number of that year.—[ED.]

willing mind, not without something of that adventurous spirit which animates every man who is in earnest, which has stirred the heart and quickened the steps of many a noble missionary in days past and present, and will in all time to come. It was the same spirit, with the same views, which took him back from England to India on the last occasion through Persia, and which enabled him there, with his wonted devotion, to be the means of so great usefulness, in co-operation with another active missionary of the C.M.S., at a time of grievous famine and distress.

"When we hear of the missionary killed in a sortie from a besieged fortress—a difficult and perilous operation, undertaken to check the harassing fire from a strongly-occupied and well-armed place of cover—let us think of him as the minister, for the time being, of the British soldiers employed on this duty. He was their friend, who sought to be their helper wherever he could, not only in the tent but in the field, in the time of danger, and in the hour of death. Not altogether profitless, we may well believe, was this last service, though it was the hour of death also for himself.

"Thus was he taken away, at an age little over forty, in the full vigour of earnest usefulness, like Henry Wright, with whom he was not distantly connected.

"After having been for some time attached to the Divinity School at Lahore, Mr. Gordon went

out as an itinerant missionary into a central part
of the Punjab, which had not before been syste-
matically visited in this way, and which was not
included within the limits of any of the established
local missions. The tract of country is that between
the Indus and Jhílam rivers, known by the general
name of the Salt Range. It is occupied by a mass
of hills containing inexhaustible stores of rock-salt,
which has been excavated in large quantities for
many centuries, and at the present day supplies the
wants of a great part of the Punjab and neighbouring territories. The chief town of this region is
Pind Dádan Khán, on the river Jhílam. This place
Mr. Gordon made his head-quarters—if any place
could rightly be so called by one whose home was
anywhere. His work was to see and know the
country and the people, to give them his message
and his help; and he made himself thoroughly
independent of any local habitation. It was this
freedom from the cares belonging to a fixed abode
or personal requirements that fitted him to do what
he did. That he might move about with the greater
facility, he accustomed himself to such fare as even
the lower classes of natives of the country could
ordinarily command. He used, likewise, like some
other missionaries, to adopt the local native dress
when this seemed desirable. He thus had occasion
to carry little about with him, and he made small
and few demands on the resources of the people
and of the places he visited.

"Wherever he stayed, and whatever his habits for the time, he gained the respect and esteem of natives and English alike, even of those who did not quite admire his simple mode of life. But it had its uses, specially when they who saw it knew that he had means which could have procured him all he could desire. Possessed of private wealth, he used it for others, and denied himself. The manner of his life varied according to the needs of the occasion, but this was its principle at all time— self-denial, and labour for the good of others. His influence and his example impressed those among whom he worked, for this principle ruled his action.

"But only such a constitution as his could stand what he did. That his mission journeyings were on foot, and that he walked to Quetta and to Kandahar, was nothing more than many other missionaries are accustomed to, even in such a climate. Mr. Gordon's strength, however, submitted to privations which are not often consistent with demands for personal exertion and exposure. It was little to say that his English friends thought he over-did his self-denial in this respect, and that even he would have been better if he had not carried it so far. But it was something more when his native assistants found it a struggle to follow his example, and plainly showed that they could not manage to rough it like Padre Gordon. It is rightly considered in India that, in such a climate, imperfect protection from the weather, with defective food, is not suitable for any ordinary Englishman.

But Mr. Gordon was not an ordinary Englishman. And there are not many who could wisely or safely do as he did, or who could attempt it with any propriety, having regard to the services expected of them in the great work they have undertaken, and their obligation to preserve their bodily health unimpaired, so far as this is in their power.

"It was no fanciful experiment on himself, or neglect of duty with respect to his health, that induced him to adopt his simple mode of life among the people of the country for whom he laboured, subsisting as they did, and inured to native ways. It was a conviction that, for the work he had in hand, and the position in which he was placed, this method best answered his purpose, and that he was able to carry it out. His simple habits did not make him appreciate less the ordinary social requirements of English life in India. He had equal aptitude for quiet companionship and general society, much readiness in conversation, and enjoyment of music. In camp he was a welcome and valued addition to the mess of the 32nd Pioneers, of which he was an honorary member on the line of march, and at Quetta.

"Like other missionaries who live much among the natives of the country, he learned a good deal about their condition, their thoughts, and their wants, and he gained their goodwill by his free intercourse with them, and his ready sympathy which could be expressed in action. At a place near Pind Dádan Khán, which he had occasion to pass frequently, he found that a well was much wanted, and would be of great use, not only for the cultivation, but for travellers also, and for cattle; and, after due inquiry and consultation with the local civil officer, he made the necessary arrangements, and had a good well constructed.

"Having prepared the way for a permanent mission in the Salt Range district, and having started a new missionary on the work, Mr. Gordon proceeded to the Deraját districts, west of the Indus. For the special mission to the Bilochis he obtained the services of two more men, one of them a medical missionary, who commenced the work under his guidance, and have since carried it on. It was while thus engaged that he saw and took the opportunity of going into Bilochistán as a missionary pioneer. And thence, as the minister and comrade of the British soldier, to Kandahar.

"His missionary life was directed by singleness of purpose with a zeal guided by knowledge. His eye was ever attracted to openings for the preaching of the Gospel, which he longed to see occupied, while his wisdom taught him how to watch and wait. His every step was taken with fullest trust in the leading of God, to whom he committed his ways. A life such as his could not fail to make its mark on the minds of men with whom he came in contact. If we lament, as we must, its too early close, we rest satisfied, as we look at his character and his work, that his labour has not been in vain."

The Rev. C. P. C. NUGENT, who worked under
Gordon in the Jhílam Mission, thus wrote :—" This
notice of a dear and honoured friend and leader in
the Lord's army cannot have a better preface than
the following words from a letter of his to a relative :—
' I like the Latin motto, *Bene vinit, qui bene latuit*,
He hath lived best, who has concealed himself best.'
In every great work much retirement is necessary,
and especially in missionary work.   But it is no easy
thing to hold the balance between one's duty to the
outer world, and one's duty to God and the special
charge which He has committed to one—to be, as St.
Paul says, ' as unknown and yet well known.'   By
grace he was enabled to hold that balance ; and into
whatever society he entered, he seemed to carry about
quiet Christian dignity, and charmed and won the
lasting love and respect of not a few.

"Although one of the very greatest labourers for
Christ, his life was indeed a quiet one—one, we
always felt sure, ' hid with Christ in God.'   He
always set the Lord before him ; and this was the
secret of his unwearying labour for Christ.   I believe
I do not exaggerate in saying, that for almost six
years in which he served Christ's Church as an
evangelist he never knew what rest was, save when
he lay down at night.   And here I do not speak of
his work in Madras.   He could not rest with the
burning thought ever before him that there were souls
for whom Christ died, all around, who had never
heard the message of God's love.   The words we

extract from a letter he wrote from Kandahar at the
beginning of this year, express the great fact ever
before him, 'Life is so short, and the field so vast
that if we don't preach, the precious seed is un-
sown;' therefore he felt bound 'to extend the
preaching of the Lord as far as possible.' One
could not know him for a week without feeling his
sympathy with St. Paul's expression, 'Necessity is
laid upon me ; yea, woe is unto me if I preach not
the Gospel.'

   " He laboured as an evangelist for six years in
the Punjab and Afghanistan. We mention the latter
place, because there may be some who imagine that
his entry into that country was only for the purpose
of ministering to his fellow-countrymen in the army.
But, in truth, the idea still uppermost in his mind
throughout his two visits to Kandahar was to carry
the Gospel to the natives.

   " Prior to his going to Kandahar he had an immense stretch of country committed to his prayerful
oversight and labours—Multan Jhang, Derá Ghází
Khán ; each of these places, far distant from one
another, claimed him as a 'chief.'

   "Let me extract from one of his letters an
account of not the longest journey undertaken by
this devoted, self-denying soldier of Christ, simply
for the purpose of comforting and cheering a brother
missionary :—'I started off as soon as I could to
pay them a visit of consolation. I had five rivers
to cross, two of them without bridges. At this time

of the year (June) the river Indus gets swollen by the melting snows of the Himalayas, and is several miles wide. However, the wind was favourable, and took my ferry-boat across with a sail very quickly. Then I took a horse and rode all night, till I came to another river, the Chenab. This I crossed more easily in another ferry-boat; and then I got to Multan, and went 200 miles by rail in the night to Lahore, and from thence by rail 100 miles to Jhílam. And at Jhílam, which is a little town on the Jhílam river, I took a boat, and rowed down 50 miles to Pind.' He never spoke of the weakness, and subsequent illness, which accrued from this trying journey, the second of the same length he had made during that year.

"To those who had the happy privilege of being his fellow-labourers in the Salt Range, and in some of his missionary tours, he ever endeared himself by his loving unselfishness, and solicitude for their comfort and happiness. Although believing strongly, as he did, that missionaries in contact with Muhamadans and Hindus obtained a much greater degree of influence over them by a life of the strictest self-denial, and even asceticism, he never attempted to force his views on others. His life spoke them. Many a weary hour has been made happy by his cheerfulness and courage under very depressing circumstances. Hunger, inhospitality on the part of natives, weariness, have been quite forgotten when one listened to his quiet dry humour,

or perhaps was struck by his great forgetfulness
of self in cheering up those still but new to such
a life.

"The question will be asked, What are the results
of such a life? If a number of converts gathered in,
and little bodies of believers walking in the fear of
the Lord, only be results, then our dear brother's
work was unsuccessful. But if our blessed Lord's
words in St. John iv. 36 be true for all time, and if
the joy be the same for sowers as for reapers, then I
do not hesitate to say it was eminently successful.
I do not think he ever felt stumbled at the possibility
of never reaping; it was quite joy enough to sow.
Writing to a relative at the commencement of his
work in the Salt Range, after speaking of the great
difficulties in the way, and of his loneliness (in all
this immense district he had no helper save one
native catechist) he says: 'I often think of that
text, "Show Thy *work* unto Thy servants, and Thy
glory unto their children." We should be thankful if the *work* only is our's, so that God's glory
is manifest to the next generation.' Those who
believe that the work of sowing is indeed a special
work for God, and the faithful discharge of which
earns a no less gracious word of welcome from the
Lord of the harvest than that of the reaper, can
sympathise with our earnest conviction that at last
many will rise up and call George Maxwell Gordon
blessed, who had heard the story of the Cross from his
lips in the villages on the banks of the Jhílam, in the

Salt Range, in the Derá Ghází Khán district, about Multan, and in Kandahar itself.

"All the time we knew him he seemed to have been particularly free from moving in what may be termed one 'groove' only. He had large sympathies, which made many who had little interest in mission work (perhaps because not understanding it rightly) esteem him highly. To officers and soldiers in our army, with whom he very frequently came in contact, he endeared himself greatly, and proved no little help to many of those who were searching after truth. He won their esteem too by the continual exercise of that great qualification for a good soldier, the patient endurance of hardship. His letters from Quetta and Kandahar, written when he, in common with the troops, was suffering many privations, never breathe the least spirit of discontent. He was happy wherever he was, and was ready to do anything that came to his hand well and thoroughly. His supervision of necessary works connected with the erection of mission premises, and efforts for the comfort of natives travelling along the hot and dusty roads of the Salt Range, all proved how much he realised that a good missionary ought to be ready for anything.

"He read much. He used to read books recently published and sent out from England as he marched along from place to place. It was thus that we saw him reading the life of Canon Kingsley. Thus he kept his mind fresh and acquainted with the doings of

the world from which he was so much shut off, and
in this way he never lost the influence obtained over
many who loved his thoughtful and really charming
conversation.

" But undoubtedly the two most striking features
of his life were his self-denial and his prayerfulness.   His was no gloomy, morbid form of self-
denial which would repulse people, but one so
impregnated with the principle 'For Christ's sake,
and the souls of men,' that he was never unhappy
in it.   Grieved and wearied in soul he often was—
as who would not be that fully realised all Christ's
love and all the ingratitude of man?   Often and
tenderly as he longed for the joy of seeing home
and friends again, keenly as he appreciated the
many delicacies and refinements of European life,
he never, I believe, regretted the step he took,
when in 1874 he left Lahore for a life of voluntary
poverty among the people to whom God sent him.
The uppermost wish of his heart in re-visiting home,
which he had purposed doing in 1881, was to beat
up recruits for the Salt Range.

" In May 1878, he wrote from Pind Dádan
Khán: 'To many people India is full of variety
and amusement.   If it has a hot season they avoid
it by going to the hills, or if they are obliged to
stay on the plains they can surround themselves
with comforts and luxuries ; and as for the cool
season, it is far pleasanter than an English winter.
But to a missionary who is intent on knowing the

natives and being as one of themselves, these comforts are quite foreign, and by degrees he finds
that they are by no means necessary to existence.
And in order to get the confidence of the people,
and do them any good, one has to make up one's
mind to devote one's life to it, and all one's dreams
about ending one's days in a cottage near a wood
in some pleasant English nook give place to the
prospect of a mud hut in an Indian village, and
the enviable distinction of a rough tombstone rever-
enced alike by Christians and Heathens.'   And
these words are simply the expression of his every-
day life. I have known him even in Amritsar go
to the Seria (a native inn) and lodge there for the
purpose of being among the people whom he loved
for Christ's sake.

"It is a mistake to suppose that he was rash in his
self-denial. He believed, indeed, that it was only
given him to work while it 'was called to-day ;' and,
therefore, he was never idle, but rather most abundant
in labours. But, whilst ruling his body, as St. Paul
teaches the true Christian to do, he never forgot
that he had to take care of his body for the Lord's
sake, Whose it was. He was most cautious about
himself, and this those who were most with him can
testify.

"His constant prayerfulness struck one at once.
The little time of prayer preceding each visit to the
bazar or village was a very blessed time, and one very
full of reality to him. Very often have we noticed,

and felt justly rebuked by, his solemn and reverent demeanour during the walk to the daily preaching, and the short replies to any thoughtless or irrelevant remarks, and subsequent silence taught us not a little the awful solemnity of our mission, and of the frame of mind with which one should leave the King's presence to execute His command.

"He wrote the following, after a year's labour in the Salt Range : 'I cannot call my room a lofty one '—he had been speaking of the usual height of Indian rooms, —'there is nothing attractive in it, except a motto on the wall (a scroll which I have had framed) *Ora et labora*, Pray and work. Whenever I come in from a long preaching tour this scroll animates me to go out again and alternate labour with prayer.' Thus believing in the power of faithful prayer, his great energy never flagged until the day when God called His faithful servant home.

"His best memorials will be the Salt Range and Biloch Missions, and the proposed College Chapel at Lahore. The work connected with each of these places was very dear to him, and indeed the first two missions were practically founded, and the premises given, by his Christian love and generosity. May it please God to raise up faithful followers of so true a pattern of a missionary. He was but one of the blessed company 'who loved not their own lives unto the end,' but it is helpful to study the great features of the life of each of these as they are set before us. Self-denial, prayer, and hard work, were those of this true servant of God, eminently scriptural graces well worthy our imitation.

"As we think of him now, we can find no words more suitable with which to conclude than those in the Collect for the Twentieth Sunday after Trinity, 'That we being ready, both in body and soul, may cheerfully accomplish those things which Thou wouldest have done, through Jesus Christ our Lord. Amen.'"

Gordon's services to the missionary cause did not finish with his life, for it was found that half his property was left to the Church Missionary Society for the support of those missions which he had himself founded. These are his memorials, more abiding than brass. No costly monument marks his last resting-place on earth. But his name is written in the Book of Life. May there be many following in his footsteps, of whom the Gospel words are true, quoted on the tablet in Hadlow Churchyard, after the inscriptions commemorating the other members of Captain James Edward Gordon's family, "In memory also of his youngest son, the Rev. George Maxwell Gordon, M.A., of the Church Missionary Society, who was killed at Kandahar when ministering to the wounded in a sortie, as Acting Chaplain to the Forces, 16th August, 1880. Aged 41 years."

"And he left all, rose up, and followed Him.'— S. Luke v. 28.

"For My sake, and the Gospel's."—S. Mark x. 29.

APPENDIX.

THE following account of the Travancore and Cochin Mission of the Church Missionary Society is kindly furnished by the Rev. J. H. Bishop :—

"Since the Rev. G. M. Gordon's visit to the Native States of Travancore and Cochin in 1870, very considerable progress has been made all along the line of missionary work—pastoral, evangelistic, and educational—in this interesting corner of the mission field. There are not wanting signs of remarkable spiritual vitality and expansion in the Native Church. This is the more noticeable, because there have been many changes and deaths during the last twenty years in the European staff, which has always been weak, and is now reduced to its minimum of weakness, there being only four European missionaries in the whole of the C.M.S. Travancore and Cochin Mission field. Three of these much need a furlough home, and the remaining one has only recently joined the Mission. But the Rev. F. Bower and Mrs. Bower are on their way back to Travancore for the third time.

"Most of the various congregations of native Christians, scattered all over the country, have been grouped into two district church councils, which manage their own financial matters, each pastorate sending lay delegates with the native pastor to the periodical meetings of its district council. There is also a provincial council for consultation on general matters of missionary interest, consisting chiefly of the members of the two Native Church councils. The C.M.S. give an annual pecuniary grant on a gradually diminishing scale to each district council.

"In 1879 the Right Rev. J. M. Speechly, D.D., formerly Principal of the C.N.I. Cottayam, was consecrated Bishop of the newly-formed diocese. He has under his jurisdiction, besides the European missionary clergy, one native archdeacon, and seventeen native pastors. The total number of native Christians, including catechumens in connection with the C.M.S. in the diocese, reaches very nearly 20,000.

"At Cottayam, the headquarters of the Mission, where Mr. Gordon spent some days—though the missionary staff has since then undergone a complete change—real progress has been made. The Rev. H. Baker (Mr. Gordon's host), founder of the Hill Arrian Mission, died in 1880, and his mother, the veteran Mrs. Baker, who superintended a Girls' Boarding and Day School for nearly seventy years, has just been called to her rest and reward (1888).

"Miss Baker, the daughter of the late Rev. H. Baker, carries on a large Girls' Boarding School, and has been much helped by the Rev. H. B. Macartney, and other friends in Melbourne, in response to an appeal made by Mr. Gordon after his visit to Cottayam (see p. 46). Caste Girls' Schools have also been opened in and around Cottayam. The Dewan Peschcar of Cottayam, a Brahman gentleman, on being lately promoted to the office of Dewan (Prime Minister) at Trevandrum, handed over Rs.500 (£50) to the Bishop, as a private contribution to one of these Caste Girls' Schools, superintended by Mrs. Neve. Archdeacon Koshi, the senior native clergyman, is the pastor of the Cottayam congregation, and, with the generous co-operation of the Rev. W. J. Richards, has lately restored the large mission church there. A beautiful stained glass window has been put in the east end of the church, in memory of the Rev. H. Baker, by his widow. The Cottayam College has greatly improved in numbers and efficiency. There have been within recent years some deeply interesting cases of conversion in and around Cottayam from the Hindus.

" Mr. Gordon appears to have been much interested in the Hill Arrian Mission. Its wild, romantic character possessed a peculiar charm for him. After his monotonous tent life in the arid plains around Madras, he revelled in the grand mountain scenery of the Western Ghauts, and in the uncleared jungle, where he heard the chattering of monkeys, and at night the trumpeting of wild elephants, and saw the footprints of the tiger. Then, too, the rude simplicity, uncouth manners, but withal the honesty and truthfulness, of the Hill people greatly pleased him.

" The work among the Hill Arrian and other jungle tribes is still being vigorously prosecuted, though under

great difficulties, not so much from wild animals as
from the unhealthiness of the climate (especially at
certain seasons), and the inaccessibility of the inhabitants, the opposition and jealousies of petty rajahs and
others, and the introduction and sale of intoxicating
drinks by native traders from the plains.   Melkâwa is
one of the chief centres of the Arrian Mission, where
there is a flourishing congregation of native Christians,
all Arrian converts, under a native pastor, numbering
1100.   It is one of the most satisfactory of all the
native pastorates in the Mission, and for the year 1886
raised nearly £46 (reckoning 2s. to the rupee) for
church expenses and endowment.   The Rev. A. F.
Painter, who took charge of the Arrian Mission in
1882, has given a great impulse to aggressive work
amongst the heathen.   He has opened several new
stations, and baptised many converts from the Arrian
and other jungle tribes.

   "Mr. Gordon mentions the Metran or Syrian Bishop,
' Mar Athanasius,' as being favourably inclined towards
reformation in the Syrian Church.   The arrival of the
Patriarch of Antioch in 1876, who was greatly opposed
to Mar Athanasius and the reforming party, and
favoured the rival Metran, ' Mar Dionysius,' led to a
reactionary movement.   Before the Patriarch left Travancore, he consecrated six metrans, confirming Mar
Dionysius as the Metropolitan of Malabar.   But Mar
Athanasius, before his death in 1877, appointed his
nephew, Mar Thoma Athanasius, as his successor.
There has consequently been a great deal of confusion

in the Syrian Church, and continuous litigation in the heathen courts. Matters are not yet settled.

"When Dr. Milman, Metropolitan of India, visited Travancore in the year 1871, he urged the formation of a National Synod of the Syrian Church in Malabar, which should frame rules for the election of a metran, the education and support of the clergy, and should manage its own ecclesiastical affairs, independently of Antioch. The connection with that ancient See has not tended to promote unity and prosperity in the Syrian Church of Malabar, but has been fruitful in producing party strife and dissensions.

"In Trichur, the first C.M.S. station which a visitor from Madras to the Travancore and Cochin Mission would arrive at, there has been a marked improvement and growth since Mr. Gordon's visit. There have not yet been many conversions from the high castes in this stronghold of Brahmanism; the progress has been intensive rather than extensive, in the increased vitality rather than the numerical strength of the native congregations.

"Parochial missions have been very helpful in stimulating the spiritual life of the native Christians. In 1885 and 1886 there was quite an outpouring of God's Holy Spirit; many were led to decision for Christ. On these two occasions the Rev. Isaac F. Row, of the Anglo-Indian Evangelisation Society, was the chief missioner. He preached the word with remarkable power and simplicity through a native interpreter. Thus the way was prepared for the labours

of the Rev. Gilbert Karney and the Rev. B. Baring-
Gould, of the C.M.S. Winter Mission to India and
Ceylon, who commenced their missions to Travancore and Tinnevelly at Trichur on November 30th,
1887.

"This Winter Mission has been a very great blessing indeed to the native churches. Missionaries, too,
and their native fellow-workers have been much stirred
up. Educated Hindus have openly confessed Christ
as their Saviour, and have been baptised. European
Christians in India have been led to see their privileges
and great responsibilities.

"The Church of England Zenana Missionary Society has now a flourishing mission in Trichur, and
there have already been several converts from the
Nair women and others. A C.M.S. Middle School
for high caste youths has been opened in the centre
of the town, which may probably soon be further
developed into a high school. Village itinerating work
is being vigorously carried on. There is a native
Christian Total Abstinence Association in Trichur,
and a branch in Kunnankulam, which together number about 100 members. A Young Men's Christian
Association has also been formed by the native Christian young men themselves, with a view to voluntary
work among their fellow-Christians, and the heathen
around them.

"The large Roman Catholic population have se-
ceded from Rome, and elected Bishop Mellus, a Syro-
Chaldaic Bishop, as their head. They still retain the

Roman ritual, but are much less prejudiced against hearing and reading the Word of God than they formerly were. Altogether the prospects of the furtherance of the kingdom of Christ in the Native States of Travancore and Cochin are very much brighter than they were nearly twenty years ago, when the Rev. G. M. Gordon visited them and wrote in his journal and private letters so graphic and interesting an account of what he then saw and experienced."

COLSTON AND COMPANY, PRINTERS, EDINBURGH.

THE PUNJAB, SIND AND THE AFGHAN FRONTIER

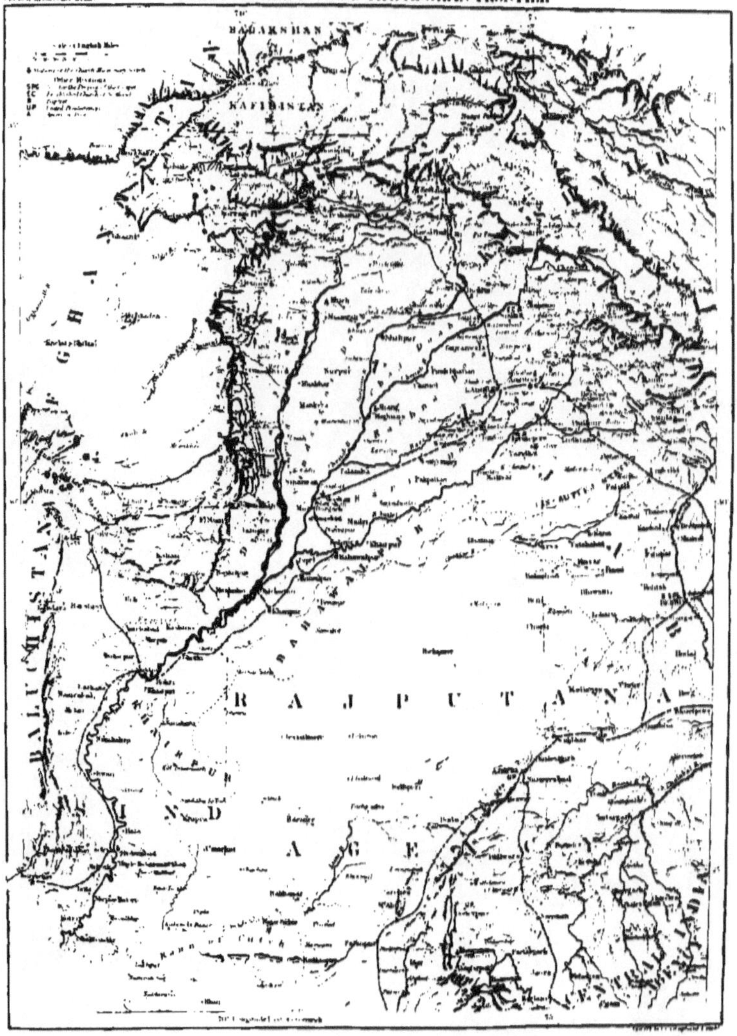

www.ingramcontent.com/pod-product-compliance
Lightning Source LLC
Chambersburg PA
CBHW030955110726
47900CB00004B/1283